P9-ECP-888

DATE DUE

MY 4 7		
MY 25 7		
FE 14 7		

RIVERSIDE CITY COLLEGE
LIBRARY
Riverside, California

DEMCO

Books by Peter Ustinov

NOVELS

The Loser

Krumnagel

SHORT STORIES

Add a Dash of Pity

The Frontiers of the Sea

COLLECTIONS

Five Plays

PLAYS

The Love of Four Colonels

Romanoff and Juliet

Photo Finish

House of Regrets

Beyond

The Banbury Nose

Plays About People

The Moment of Truth

No Sign of the Dove

The Man in the Raincoat

The Indifferent Shepherd

The Unknown Soldier and His Wife

CARICATURES

We Were Only Human

Ustinov's Diplomats

KRUMNAGEL

Peter Ustinov

KRUMNAGEL

An Atlantic Monthly Press Book
Little, Brown and Company – Boston – Toronto

Riverside Community College
Library
4800 Magnolia Avenue
Riverside, CA 92506

PR6041.U73 K7 1971
Ustinov, Peter.
Krumnagel.

COPYRIGHT © 1971 BY PAVOR, S.A.

ALL RIGHTS RESERVED. NO PART OF THIS BOOK MAY BE REPRO-
DUCED IN ANY FORM OR BY ANY ELECTRONIC OR MECHANICAL
MEANS INCLUDING INFORMATION STORAGE AND RETRIEVAL SYS-
TEMS WITHOUT PERMISSION IN WRITING FROM THE PUBLISHER,
EXCEPT BY A REVIEWER WHO MAY QUOTE BRIEF PASSAGES IN A
REVIEW.

LIBRARY OF CONGRESS CATALOG CARD NO. 77-160695

THIRD PRINTING

T10/71

ATLANTIC–LITTLE, BROWN BOOKS
ARE PUBLISHED BY
LITTLE, BROWN AND COMPANY
IN ASSOCIATION WITH
THE ATLANTIC MONTHLY PRESS

Published simultaneously in Canada
by Little, Brown & Company (Canada) Limited

PRINTED IN THE UNITED STATES OF AMERICA

KRUMNAGEL

1

The City stood, a set of mislaid dentures, somewhere near the middle of nothing. There was no discernible reason why it should have been built there rather than anywhere else, no great river, no range of protective mountains, not so much as an inflection in the ground. Some pioneer or other must have dropped his knapsack there out of weariness, or else a horse had died, and the City had grown from this negligible seed like a tree, or a disease.

It was impossible to say whether it had grown too fast to acquire suburbs, or whether it was composed of nothing but suburbs; it came to the same. There were, as is usual in such places which freckle the great flat face of the Middle West, rather more secondhand vehicles for sale than potential purchasers, and puritanism notwithstanding, come nightfall, the neon signs blinked, twinkled and insinuated like prostitutes muttering to the passing trade. Then the sky would be red with hellfire, a sign as clear as the star which summoned the wise men to Bethlehem that the electric oasis in the desert of oil and wheat was bubbling with the murky spring of life, and loneliness need not be.

During the day it was different. There were touching attempts at style, as though history had been speeded up like a tape recorder, and all evolution had been squeezed into the paltry half century of the City's existence. The state legislature — for the City was also the capital of the state, although not the largest agglomeration — was housed in a passable imitation of the Parthenon, whereas the local armory was conceived in the manner of a medieval fort, revised by a toy manufacturer. Some of the more venerable skyscrapers were evidently inspired by organ pipes, and their perilous heights were peppered with gargoyles, while Pre-Raphaelite mosaics with satanic undertones and morally elevated overtones abounded at a lower level. It was, in short, a City indistinguishable from many others, whose inhabitants, seeing poetry and enlightenment in places where strangers saw but monotony and grayness, considered it was a great place to live and rear children in, despite marijuana, race riots, university upheavals, a relatively high murder rate, and worse — to the morally inclined — a relatively high rape rate.

The man whose duty, whose mission it was to oppose these evils on behalf of the citizenry was called Krumnagel. He had many friends, and many enemies, and naturally enough they were often the same people, for Krumnagel was the chief of police. He was a big man, both tall and corpulent, with an eye wide and furtive enough to be characterized as intelligent in a dog, although in a man this particular form of aggressive vigilance is less reassuring, even to the innocent. The restlessness of the eye was mitigated, however, by the determination of the man to be approachable, human, liked, loved. He encouraged criticism, yet never forgave it. He had an immensurable faith in the guy in the street, and yet a low opinion of him. He was an American, and the way of life was in his bones as the furled flag was ever behind him, in the corner of the room, in the back of his mind.

"Great day, Chief," called Mr. Polowsky, the custom tailor, standing in the doorway of his store. Mr. Polowsky was a first-generation citizen, and found reassurance in human contact — the more trivial, the less open to discussion, the better.

"Isn't it, though?" called Krumnagel, as he walked down the sidewalk.

"For you, 'specially." Mr. Polowsky nodded hopefully, his glasses glinting in the surprising sunlight.

Krumnagel may have heard, but he failed to react. Mr. Polowsky returned indoors, prepared to attach importance to the anecdote in the retelling.

Indeed, today of all days, Krumnagel could have driven in his black police car, with its golden star, either at the wheel himself, his torso half against the back of the seat, half against the door, his elbow on the sill, his fingers drumming on the roof, or else sitting beside the official driver like any good democrat playing down his wealth or his position, and yet he chose to walk.

"He's a wonderful man in many ways," said Mr. Polowsky to his assistant. "Unpleasant yet, but wonderful — imagine, walking — and then who says a police chief should be pleasant?" The assistant was not born in Poland, so he neither knew nor answered.

"Great day for September, eh Bart?" Mr. Massoulian called from the entrance to his cut-price, drastic-reductions, must-sell-out, lease-expired, going-out-of-business kind of profitable enterprise, with its mountain of odious knickknacks described as novelties, representing a cross section of all that is tawdry east of Suez.

"Isn't it though?" replied Krumnagel, chewing on his gum.

[5]

"Sure is," declared Massoulian, taking the remains of his cigar out of his mouth as though he had been contradicted. Massoulian's everlasting fear was not to have the last word. It gave him a sense of security to terminate a conversation on his own terms, even if the other fellow was out of earshot.

"Sure is," he repeated long after Krumnagel had gone his way.

As Krumnagel neared the Gateway-Sheraton Hotel, the newest jewel in the crown of civic hospitality, he tried to catch sight of himself in shopwindows as a final reassurance.

"How about it, Chief?"

"Yep."

"Hey, I got some new ones, Chief — are we in trouble again?"

Mr. Boone, the owner of the semi-serious bookstore, in which the complete Aeschylus, Isaac Newton and Hermann Hesse rubbed jackets with a three-volume history of masturbation through the ages, held up a magazine on the cover of which a recumbent nude lay with her legs wide apart, as sexy as the entrance to the Lincoln Tunnel.

"I'm not on duty today, Byron — you ought to know that."

"Anytime you want anything, Chief — anytime — day or night."

"See you."

The doorman saluted him. He saluted back. Their eyes met for a moment with affection and mistrust. Once in the hall, Krumnagel looked around anxiously, towards the newsstand, the coffee shop, the Pioneer Gift Shop, the auto-rental counter, among the guests.

"Help you, Chief? It's in the Buffalo Room —"

"I know where it is. I'm looking for Mrs. Krumnagel."

"Oh."

Edie walked in just then through the automatic doors. She had the kind of looks which would have gone far in the days of

[6]

the silent screen, button nose, eyes with a tendency to water, pouting mouth, a look of innocence pleasantly perverted.

"Hi."

"Hi — you're late, Edie."

"You're early, Buster. I'm never late. I'm a policeman's wife, remember."

Krumnagel remembered it indeed, and with some misgiving, since Edie had been married three times, always to policemen.

The medieval-type electronic glockenspiel on the Beechnut Building sounded twelve.

"See," said Edie, indenting the tip of his nose with her silver nail in playful fashion.

"So you're right," Krumnagel sighed. "It can happen. O.K., let's go."

The Buffalo Room was the banqueting hall of the Gateway-Sheraton, modern in style, and yet with authentic covered wagons, stagecoaches and stuffed bison hindering the movements of the waiters. The view was panoramic. On a good day one could not only see the confines of the City, but the prairie beyond. As the Krumnagels entered, spontaneous clapping broke out. One man especially surged forward as though to make his peace.

"We've been enemies for a long time now, Bart — no offense, Edie — but I want to be the first to tell you that I am deeply personally honored to be here today, and that I canceled a major consultation to make it. The City wouldn't be the same without you, Bart . . . Edie . . . and that's what we all love and work for, isn't that right . . . the City?"

"Arnie," said Krumnagel, "I couldn't have put it better myself if I tried." There was appreciative laughter at this bonhomie. "No, but seriously," Krumnagel went on, "we've had our differences, O.K., who hasn't? Edie and I, we had difficulties, nothing but." (Laughter.) "That don't mean I don't love her, does it?" (He clutched her to him until she was ready to scream

[7]

with pain. Instead she smiled agonizingly at the women present, who envied her moment.) "I'm not going to say I love you, Arnie." (Laughter.) "I guess I'm one of those rare guys who believe men should be men and gals gals." (More laughter, overflowing into applause as the profundity of the statement began to sink in.) "— but I appreciate you, Arnie — always have, always will — and who knows? One day I may need some headshrinking work done — I'll sure know where to come."

Arnie Brugger, the state's most respected psychiatrist, extended his hand, and a few cameras flashed. This was a great reconciliation indeed.

The banging of a gavel told the dignitaries it was time for lunch. The banquet began.

As the plates flew from waiter to waiter, the room seemed a little like a football field during a practice session. The maître d' stood near the doorway to the kitchen like a trainer, making mental notes, chiding those who left the field with empty dishes, encouraging those who emerged with fresh supplies. Krumnagel hardly tasted his food. He would have to make a speech, and he hated that. Like most of those who see themselves as men of action he was lazy, enjoying nothing better than to be coiled up in an armchair watching a whodunit on television, and identifying with the detective.

This was perhaps understandable, since he had the misfortune to be chief of police at a time in American history when the only solvable crimes were the fictional ones on the video screen. And they had the additional virtue of being solved within the space of twenty-seven minutes, owing to the rigors of a commercialism that left three minutes for the sponsors. He sighed. It had been a difficult year. The press kept badgering him. The press always bothers the man in office in a free democratic society, especially if all its organs are owned by the same family. Was it really his fault if the Rabnick slaying, the mysterious death of the six Penapoli brothers (including the notorious Mafioso "Joe Pineapples"), the discovery of the mutilated body of a sticking-plaster heiress in an abandoned mailbag, the case of the war veteran bludgeoned to death by his own false leg, the blowing up of a civil airliner by a berserk Green Beret, still at large (which made the national press) — was it really his fault if no arrest had yet been made in any of these cases? And then, what was the use of making an arrest in this age of the incomprehensible specialist? The one cast-iron case he had recently was that against a kidnapper trapped at the very moment of attempting to collect his ransom. And then what had happened? Arnie Brugger turned up at the courthouse to represent the criminal and got the local judge all confused with his psychoanalytic filibuster — three days of solid Freud, Jung and Theodor Reik — and by the end of that time, the poor God-fearing judge and the exhausted jury relegated the criminal to a short period of observation, after which he was freed. Admittedly, since the kidnapper had asked for the money to be dropped at the bottom of a swimming pool in a metal box, only to be arrested as he surfaced after having fetched it, it was not very difficult for Brugger to prove that he was momentarily crazy, but this was merely one case in hundreds in which Brugger had cheated justice if not the law, with a mixture of Olympian gall, bombastic eloquence about America (that massive and endlessly pliable abstraction), and appeals to simple, homely virtues, to say nothing of a fathomless supply of natural gas which enabled him to talk for hours on end about nothing in particular with unmistakable sincerity and deep involvement.

As he thought these thoughts, Krumnagel caught Brugger's eye, and smiled guiltily. Brugger not only smiled back with alacrity, but went as far as to wink, which made Krumnagel wonder what kind of thoughts that bastard had been entertaining about him.

They were all there, the big shots of his world. The governor of the state, Darwood McAlpin, a man of measure and design, who retained his physical equilibrium even in a high wind. His mother, Alice Hokomer Darwood, had inherited two large fortunes, that of her mother, Niobe Hokomer, of the Beer (with a picture of Rip Van Winkle on every bottle, the slogan being "Hokomer — worth waking up for!"), and that of her father, Lincoln Darwood, who had patented the first crenelated rubber heel for gentlemen's shoes ("Be proud — there'll be no fall with a Darwood Doublegrip"). From his father the governor had inherited his disdainful, athletic, ageless look and a few more fortunes. He had accepted his position in society without a murmur of either dissent or surprise from his earliest youth, and now, at the beginning of the long autumn of his life, he seemed neither satisfied nor dissatisfied with his lot, since he had been born with it and it was as much part of him as his skin. He believed utterly in a democracy in which even the poorest and darkest had the vote, but in which only the richest and the whitest could be voted for. He believed in it because he had neither the capacity nor the inclination to entertain any other beliefs. All he was able to entertain were guests, which he did without respite and apparently without fatigue.

Talking to the governor at the moment was the mayor, Otis Calogero, a man of Greek origin, who was neither liberal enough to please liberals nor conservative enough to please conservatives; neither corrupt enough to please the rackets nor narrow-minded enough to please the bigots. In other words, he was the archetype of that new phenomenon, the man who wins the elections because nobody is as much against him as they are against the others. He was not the best of men, merely the least of evils.

It was at functions of this kind, Krumnagel reflected possessively, that people of importance take the opportunity of talking to other important people about things of common interest. But for a man in the limelight, he was suddenly and inexplicably bad-tempered. His wife was speaking intensely to Al Carbide, his deputy, and it seemed to him that she stared at his lips as she listened, as though lipreading. Why couldn't she look him in the eye like anybody else? Sensing she was being observed, she suddenly swung round, bounced delightedly in her chair, and blew her husband a few rapid kisses. He forced a grin to his face, while Al Carbide winked, as did Arnie Brugger. It was his day after all, and there was a hell of a lot of friendship in the world, even in the black hearts of deputies and psychiatrists. A gavel sounded again. The mayor called on Monsignor Francis Xavier O'Hanrahanty, president of Crown of Thorns University, to say grace.

"O God," said the monsignor, as though correcting an exam paper in which God had made the same mistake yet again, "O God, we marvel at the fullness of thy wisdom, at the extent of thy presence and the utter bleakness of thy absence, at the loveliness and wonder and industrial power of this great land of ours, in which thy sons and daughters are able, under the Constitution, to worship thee according to their lights and beliefs. A handful of such sons and daughters do now thank thee for the bounty of this board, and ask thee to bless this wonderful state and our City, with special reference to its police department . . ."

All eyes glanced at Krumnagel, and he felt he had been touched on the head with a nightstick of grace, and blushed.

"Our police department, under its Chief Bartram C. Krumnagel, has always sought to walk in the path of righteousness, and to make this City a better place to live in, O God. Help it in its vital, yea, in its overwhelming task. Sanctify the unit of the family, remind fathers of their authority, mothers of their maternal love, and teach our children to worship thee through the inviolable fortress of the American home!"

The mayor glanced at his watch. They all had offices to get back to. The monsignor noticed the gesture and nodded reassuringly. After all, he had an office to get back to, same as everyone else.

"Let thy scourge and thy ointment both be the city police

[11]

department — thy scourge to punish the malefactor, thy ointment as a balm for the incidental wounds of modern life. Let its vengeance be tempered with mercy, its charity alloyed with steel. Amen."

Some foolish people laughed at this point because a waiter dropped a huge pile of plates, but most of them kept their heads admirably by thinking hard of God. The mayor rose.

"Thank you, Monsignor," he said. "Certainly that was a wonderful grace, and if there's no response to that on high, well, something's wrong with our communications satellite." There was warm appreciation of this, for although reverence was a cornerstone of almost everyone's behavior, there was still a feeling that the Almighty, for his own good, must move with the times. Monsignor O'Hanrahanty was probably more infected with this spirit than anybody else, since he was the "local ad agency with heaven's account," as he himself used to say frequently. As an additional selling point he had a wealth of comic stories about sinners and children, which successfully reduced faith to the level of a dose of laxative salts.

"Now, we're all busy people," the mayor went on briskly, "and we all know why we're here. We're here today to honor a great policeman, a great citizen, and a great American." (Applause, while Krumnagel stabbed the table nervously, feeling that such praise, while perhaps deserved, was excessive. The mayor nodded insistently, and fiddled with his silver fish-scale tie.) "I don't have to tell you who I'm talking about." (Laughter. All eyes switched to Krumnagel. Edie bounced up and down in ecstasy.) "Bartram C. Krumnagel." (Applause. The mayor's tone changed to one of appalling sentimentality, as though Christmas were suddenly upon them and the glue of good-fellowship were oozing into the room like lava.) "Bart, you and I have known each other a good many years . . . I won't mention how many years, or we'll both be out of a job." (Laughter, turning to applause. There was nothing they all liked better than a man who could see himself as others saw him, lightheartedly. Inwardly Krumnagel was raging. The mayor was a year older than he, and knew it. He had no right to start making insinuations. Outwardly Krumnagel forced a grim smile to his lips, and saluted in the air.) "During that period, you've certainly labored as maybe only I know how, to make our police department the finest in the state." (Clapping, but what kind of faint praise is that, for Christ's sake?) "Although I notice crime was down a bit during the incumbency of my Democratic predecessor, Seymour Fensey. But then, maybe his was such a dull tenure that organized crime kept away out of sheer boredom." (Laughter from Democrats.)

"Crime was down on account of the population was down, that's why," Krumnagel called out.

The governor was startled. Could it be that every ironical allusion was lost on this bonehead?

"I am aware of the reasons, Bart," the mayor cried, and smiled. "Now, I am sure it is not generally known that Bart Krumnagel was at the recruiting center twenty minutes after the news of Pearl Harbor came through . . ." (Oh shit, he's going to tell that one.) ". . . volunteering to start at the bottom of the ladder once again, in order to serve his country." (Great approval, but before the mayor could go on, a cry came out from one Red Leifson, a self-appointed one-man watch committee, with several radio and television outlets, and a newspaper column, who sat beaming in his wheelchair.)

"What happened? Why didn't he go?"

The mayor and Krumnagel exchanged an almost imperceptible look.

"Surely it is the gesture which counts, Red — what happened subsequently is hardly relevant," the mayor pleaded sternly.

"Don't I have a right to know?" asked Red, placing the emphasis heavily on the I.

The creep. He had lost both legs in the war. It was subsequently generally assumed, an assumption which Red himself did nothing to allay and a great deal to encourage, that he had lost them in a particularly hazardous and heroic parachute jump on some hopeless mission very far behind the lines. He was careful never to specify which lines, which was perhaps just as well.

"Bart was turned down by the military authorities —"

"On health grounds?"

"Not only that," the mayor continued. "One of my predecessors, Mayor Kassback" (Notice that the mayor chose a dead predecessor.) ". . . Phil Kassback, told me he had made special application to the military to have Bart retained in his job as being of vital importance to the war effort."

"But he wasn't police chief then."

"No, sir, but he was obviously going to be one day."

Red smiled good-naturedly. There was no comment or reaction to his intervention. He was feared in the City because he made his own rules and abided by them when it suited him.

Krumnagel was fuming. Why in the hell did that goddam mayor have to bring up the past? Whose business was it if he had gone and volunteered? The next thing they'd be revealing was that he got turned down for hemorrhoids, and attractive copy that'd make. It was hard to deny it. It was part of the record, someplace. Frig the record.

"What happened since those early days of promise is part of the record," the mayor went on. (There we go again, friggin' record.) "An uphill struggle against growing crime and delinquency which Bart conducted untiringly — and if the murder rate went up — seventy-six the year before last, ninety-one last year, fifty-four in the first six months of this year — so also did the number of arrests. We all know the problems — if anyone knows the solutions, Bart is closer to them than the rest of us. With the cleaning up of Chicago, many of the rackets sought refuge elsewhere — we got the Perilli outfit, the Penapoli brothers — this is something that has too rarely been said — Chicago was cleaned up *at the expense* of other cities. It was no great patriotic cleanup job they did out there. All they did

[14]

was to shake the carpet of corruption out the window, and who cares where the germs go?" (There was clapping, and few were there who noticed that the mayor made no mention of existing rackets, but merely cited the Perilli and Penapoli gangs, who had materially helped the police by virtually exterminating each other.) "It was Bart Krumnagel who first instituted what he likes to call the Q-ship police officer." (Krumnagel nodded sagely.) "Police officers disguised as women, as drug addicts, as hippies, as perverts, infiltrating crime, moving freely in the underworld, spreading suspicion and fear among the lawbreakers. It was Bart Krumnagel who first got the idea of encouraging our schoolchildren traffic wardens to take down the numbers of suspect cars infringing the highway code — 'A policeman is born in the playpen' is a favorite catchphrase of his — and we bless him for his farsightedness, his civic pride, his superior sense of reponsibility, his patriotism." (Applause.) "I now call on the governor of this great state, my old friend, a wonderful human being as well as a heck of a politician, and take my word, that takes some doing" (Laughter and applause.) ". . . Darwood H. McAlpin."

The governor rose and stared at the ceiling for a while, as though amused by some vague recollection. Then he spoke in his attractive rasping voice, so elegant and measured, and yet with the jagged edge of superior parchment, a roughness born mostly of martini.

"Mr. Mayor," he said, "Otis. It's been a wonderful occasion this, for a guy who has to keep up with the overall picture of the way our great state functions, and who has all too little time for the details. The banquet has been just about as sumptuous and magnificent as any I have ever attended, and I certainly want to thank the wonderful executives and hosts of Gateway-Sheraton International for their courtesy and their efficiency." (Applause.) "I want to thank the monsignor here for a thoroughly delightful grace, which was both reverent and wonderfully thoughtful — and politically sound." (Laughter,

[15]

led by the florid monsignor.) "Naturally, I don't have to embroider on all the heartwarming and wonderful times I have spent in your company, Mr. Mayor, even on those occasions when certain differences of opinion have tempered our harmony with . . . well, if not acid, at least, let us say charcoal-filtered sippin' whiskey." (This folkloric reference, spoken in the slurred accents of an old-timer, occasioned a few shouts of "Yippee" and "Yahoo," and two or three souls, elevated by the sweet hock, began singing the state song, "Where the stickleback swims and the hollyhocks bloom, that's the place for me." The governor held up a calming hand.) "But we are here today chiefly to honor Chief Krumnagel. I have neither the qualifications nor the ability to add to the eloquent homage paid to this fine police officer, but I do wish to say this. In these days of campus disturbances, of dropouts, of a general decline in parental authority and a widespread desecration of those standards of personal decency which we were taught as part of the Christian ethics of our forefathers, why, we need nothing so badly, so desperately, yea, so urgently, as good, tough police officers." (The applause grew to monumental proportions as all the domestic frustrations of the City fathers and mothers found expression in approval of a no-nonsense attitude.) "Chief Krumnagel, you are the symbol of the kind of officer we need more of . . . born of humble parents, the street was your playground, Locust and Pontiac Streets were your horizons . . . you could have turned to crime like some of your playmates, and yet, with no incentive but that small still flame in your heart which was fed by the spirit of service, you opted for the public good, the people, for light and right, for heaven. You were right then as a small American kid. You are right now as a mature American adult."

During the thunder of approval, Krumnagel was led by friendly hands to the governor's side.

"I have here a testimonial scroll," the governor said, "which states better than I have what we owe this man. It is with in-

[16]

tense personal pride that I present you with this . . . this handsome document. Long may it remind you of this day."

Krumnagel took the governor's hand and was shaken by the sheer masculinity of its grasp. It was practically a technical knockout. Krumnagel glanced at the scroll. "Be it known that, by these presents —" it began, in its jaunty neo-medieval way. The first letter was illuminated, and there were garlands of laurel leaves and handcuffs, of nightsticks and cartridges, and a bright sunburst over a skyline of the City within which the word "Service" stood out like a caption of an old political cartoon. He could hardly read, or indeed see. The clapping began to sound like some electronic instrument in his mind, a heartbeat with an echo, a nightmare effect.

"Mr. Governor . . . sir," he began, out of sheer instinct.

"Just a moment."

"What was that?"

"Just a moment." It was someone quite different who was talking, someone new, from the governor's entourage no doubt. His cigar was too green. Its smoke made Krumnagel swallow, and his breath was foul, stale boardroom smoke.

"The governor isn't through yet."

"What was that?"

The mouth with the cold cigar breath approached his ear.

"The governor hasn't finished."

"Oh."

Krumnagel, the groggy boxer, couldn't recognize his corner anymore.

"I would like to add to the scroll," the governor continued, "this token of esteem which was passed to me just a minute ago — a token of esteem from the whole police department, a vote of thanks from your peers. First class tickets for a trip around the world for you and your lovely bride!"

There was a roar of mingled emotions, a roar that might greet a Rockefeller who had won a Cadillac at a charity tombola. Lucidity came back to Krumnagel in a flash. The adrenaline was coursing through his veins, and he noticed Al Carbide creeping back to his place, clapping the while. It must have been he who had slipped the governor the tickets. Unreasoning hatred took hold of Krumnagel, in direct opposition to the sea of smiling faces that waited expectantly for his reply.

"Mr. Governor . . . Mr. Mayor . . . oh, Monsignor, beg pardon." In spite of his anger, his voice was mild, humble, searching. It was sheer savoir-faire that was keeping him in check. The boxer heard the bell and came out facing the right direction and pawing the air. The enemy mustn't know that he was wounded.

"I want to thank everyone associated with the police department, directly and indirectly, who made whatever I may have been able to do possible . . . it's certainly . . . certainly a wonderful . . . a wonderful feeling . . . to be appreciated . . . that goes for everyone . . . there's no good work done in God's green earth unless it's appreciated . . . I don't care what anyone says." (The monsignor nodded in a kind of bleak surprise at the truth of this observation, and people liked its ingenuous forthrightness.) "Another thing, of course. The guy hasn't been born who can do everything alone . . . the guy, what I mean, the guy hasn't been born who can live without help . . . and you can't be helped, see, unless you're able to help . . . I don't know if I'm making myself understood, but . . . but I got a lot of help from my mother, my mom . . . " (The very mention of the word set off a reflective stillness and brought agonized little smiles to many lips, even those folded around cigars.) ". . . I guess there's nothing new in what I'm saying, but I'd rather be old and true than false and new . . . my mom, well, I guess I only knew later the sacrifices she was making to keep us all . . . there was three of us kids . . . fed and clothed and God-fearin' . . . and if I am what I am, well —" (His incoherence was eloquent.) "Dad . . ." (He smiled with a kind of tortured delight, and everyone relaxed slightly now that the more sainted subject was dwindling into the lavender background.) "Dad . . . he had a kind of attitude which was rough, but by golly it was fair. If he caught any of us fibbin' or telling what I might call untruths, his belt slid right off the top of his pants like an old rattlesnake, and we'd start walking down to the woodshed without no second bidding. Yep, he was rough, but he taught us to tell black from white." (The ambiguity of this allusion cast a shadow over the general pleasurable masochism, and there was coughing which Krumnagel didn't understand.) "And then I got to say a word about my wonderful wife, Mrs. Krumnagel . . . stand up, Edie, and take a bow . . ." (Edie did so, on the verge of tears.) "I don't think there's anyone in the whole wide world as lucky as I am. When I found her, it was just after her husband — yes, I'll mention his name . . . he was my friend, my buddy, and he lost his life in the line of duty . . . sorry about this, Edie, but I got to say it . . . Chet Koslowsky was a great cop, one of the all-time greats, and Chet, wherever you are now, I want you to know they don't come like you no more. In spite of her great personal loss, Edie saw fit to . . . well, even if I could never be a substitute for Chet . . . she consented to become Mrs. Krumnagel . . . God bless you, Edie." (She was crying so copiously by now that she was in no condition to respond.) "Now, as far as the police department goes, I just want you people to know that as long as there's a breath o' life . . . I'd like to repeat that . . . a breath o' life in my body, I'm going to damn well see to it that we have the smartest, most efficient police force in the state . . . I'd like to go further'n 'nat . . . in the goddam world." (That was telling them! Applause, naturally. He changed his tone to one more conciliatory, as most orators do for purely musical reasons when the intensity of the approbation warrants it.) "I know there have been criticisms leveled at us." (He glanced at that lousy creep Red Leifson, grinning in his wheelchair, and met his grin with another.) "There was the case of young Tad Morasaki, the Japanese-American boy handicapped by a speech defect, who answered the description and identikit picture of a Filipino boy wanted on a federal warrant for drug pushing. He stopped a patrol car to ask for some information — you may all remember the case — and the officer figured he recognized him, and asked him for proof of identity, see . . . well, the young fellow reached in his pocket to get his driving license, and the officer figured he was going for his gun, so he got there first, and shot the guy . . . you may remember the funeral . . . I personally sent a wreath, and the police department sent a guard of honor . . . we got a letter of thanks from the parents of the kid which is just a wonderful human document. Now, lookit, I'm not defending that action of that officer. He got a reprimand and a transfer from Homicide to Morality. That's how strongly I felt about it — and yet, let me tell you something — when a guy reaches in his coat and you got every reason to believe he's got a gun in there, well it's no time for fancy speeches. It's you or him, and we'll ask the questions later at headquarters."

"Or in the morgue," Red Leifson said pleasantly.

"Another case," Krumnagel went on, overriding him. "Young Cass Chalkburner, a fine, upstanding young American with a great record in the U.S. Army — he was going to get married, see — went into Zigler's at Monmouth and Seventh to buy the ring. He paid for it, see — this was way back in the forties — when he saw the uptown bus pulling to a stop — in those days the uptown bus still went by way of Seventh Street, see — that was before it become a one-way street. Well, he put the money down, took the ring, and ran out of the shop. An officer on patrol saw him running out of a jeweler's shop, and shot him dead. That officer, ladies and gentlemen, was me — and I got into trouble over that one, I can tell you. I was sorry, sure I was, but what are you going to do? You see a young guy run out of a jeweler's — he may have killed the owner — you got no time to figure he's going for a bus — in any case, if a guy's got the dough to go to a jeweler's, it don't spring to mind he's running for a bus, does it? And if he had been a felon, the owner could have run to the door — and if the owner saw an officer doing no more than call out to the guy to come back and answer a few questions, then where would that officer be?"

"I thought you said the owner was killed," Red said.

"In the doghouse, I can tell you," Krumnagel went on, "so when you criticize an officer on duty for making a mistake, remember he's making that mistake in one-thousandth of a second, and in that time the benefit of the doubt don't mean much. And think how many lives has been saved, how many felons caught or shot dead because the officer made the right choice!" (His face hardened.) "A felon is an outlaw who respects nothing but his own ability, fears nothing but his own nerves, loves nothing but his own success." (He was talking to recruits, and after all these years he had his formulas.) "I don't care how or by what means or whatever we win this war, but we're going out to win it, and by golly, Lord love us, that's what we're going the hell . . . pardon me, heck . . . to do." (Applause.) "I don't care if I kill or maim a vicious homosexual, I don't care if I shorten the career of a dope pusher or transie, so long as I protect the innocent kids and make the streets a place fit to live in. And that's why I am personally so wonderfully gratified by this fine, artistic testimonial scroll, with the great things it tries to say, and the fine and wonderful artwork. It'll certainly hang in a place of honor in my humble home." (He frowned.) "Sure, I'm grateful for the 'round-the-world tickets too, but I feel there's so much work still to do . . . the world's not going to run away . . . and I really feel I shouldn't chicken out now that we've gotten the other guy on the run." (People tended to look at one another. Was this a conspiracy to retire him, then? There were sudden spontaneous cries of solidarity and affection.) "If it wasn't for Edie . . . well, I tell you what, fellows — I'll go, if I have the mayor's word that my job's open for me when I return."

The mayor was on his feet at once.

"This is a testimonial luncheon, Bart. There was never any thought in anyone's mind of you retiring." (There was now, by God.)

"You was saying how old we both was —"

"Jokes, jokes, Bart. Come on! Never heard jokes before?"

"Yeah, I heard jokes. I heard jokes and jokes."

"Well? Surely we've known each other long enough —"

Krumnagel looked across at his deputy. "This is no reflection on you, you understand Al."

Al Carbide's face hardened. It had only just occurred to him that it could be a reflection on himself.

"O.K., O.K., if it'll make everyone happy, I'll go . . . I'll go . . . but not for long."

The governor rose.

"I just want to say that what I will take back with me to the State House from this memorable occasion is how wonderfully and vibrantly alive the spirit of service is in this man. It's certainly an inspiration to find it in this day and age of faint hearts and doubting Thomases, and I want to thank you once again, Bart. The old lesson is not forgotten, sir."

They all arose amid sporadic clapping, their minds already on other things.

2

By the time Krumnagel entered his den, carrying a kitchen stool and a hammer in order to nail his testimonial scroll to the wall, he had already drunk too much. It was probably for that reason that he drove the nail into his finger, and yelled obscenities at the top of his voice until his wife reminded him that he was an adult policeman, and an example to others. After the luncheon, he had walked back to police headquarters, reconstructing the event, and wondering, through the opaque veil of inhabitual wine, whether he had pulled off his hour of triumph or not. It had seemed to him that the people in the street were less friendly than they had been on the way to the banquet, but that might just have been the persecution mania which lies dormant in all men. Back at the office, he had pretended to work, but had fallen asleep once or twice at his desk, once waking himself up with his own snores, only to find Al Carbide looking down at him with a smile — could it have been satisfaction? You're getting old, Father Bartram, the young man said. I'll show 'em, and then another moment of oblivion. Can't be age, must be that friggin' California Burgundy-type table hock.

He had left the office early, early for a man who habitually worked late. The corridors were full of policemen dressed as women, putting the finishing touches to their makeup before hitting the pavement with their provocative, mincing heels and the secrets of karate only half-hidden up their mini-skirts. Others were joking in tough, masculine terms as they adjusted their hippie wigs over their cornfield heads and let the ringlets hang down over their blue jowls. As Krumnagel approached the main exit, there was a sudden surge of orthodox Jews, white as yogurt, a snowfall of dust and dandruff on their velvet collars, big black hats and spiraling curls framing faces of sickly innocence.

"Who the friggin' hell are you?" Krumnagel had asked.

"Sergeant Wolinski."

"Patrolman Jaeger."

"Lieutenant Siverts."

"Siverts?" Krumnagel had roared. "What is this? Some fockin' office party?"

"A.S.P., Cap'n."

"A.S.P.?" Krumnagel cried. "Christ, forgot all about it. Hey, you know something? You look great. Christ, isn't that something, though? Christ, what am I mentioning Christ for?"

A.S.P. stood for Anti-Semite Patrols, a new artifice thought up by Krumnagel (or was it in fact Al Carbide?) as a consequence of an urgent appeal from the leaders of the city's Jewish community. Groups of youths with inflamed imaginations had been riding through the streets like uncertain Valkyries on oversize motorcycles, dressed in black leather with insignia from the 1914 war, and coshing rabbis near the Hebrew Theo-

[24]

logical Seminary. The brusque confrontation with a more playful kind of holy man was calculated to strike confusion in their
ranks. Cackling with opulent pleasure, Krumnagel had tum-
bled into the street and allowed himself to be driven home in a
patrol car. All that wine, then a couple of beers in his office,
and a bourbon with Al Carbide to show there was no ill feeling, and three or four more with Lieutenants Armstrong, Kulick,
and Perry, to create a little ill-feeling against Al Carbide — all
that alcohol and politics had taken their toll, and Krumnagel
had to be awakened again when the car pulled up before his
residence.

Now he was in pajamas, joke pajamas given him by Edie,
with prisoner's stripes and a number and the legend, "I'm
wanted — in bed" written on the back. His finger was copiously bandaged, and he was eating his third TV dinner running, while watching the summary of the news on one of seven
channels. He had already seen himself on three channels, and
he was disgruntled. They had lingered on his hesitations and
cut out his more militant passages. In any case it was so dark
that the governor's teeth sparkled like the headlamps of an approaching stream of traffic as he handed over the scroll. The
camera showed the smiling faces of people who didn't matter
and whose presence needed no explanation. The commentaries
were noncommittal and bereft of praise.

The fourth channel was that on which Red Leifson read his
version of the latest news. While according to the ratings his
program was not a major news outlet, it was the only one
which absolutely everyone watched. Krumnagel awaited it
with misgiving and the steam of resentment began building up
long in advance. By the time Red appeared, grinning like an
evil piece of garden sculpture in his invalid carriage, seated
before a tiny globe psychedelically shivering in a shower of
celestial dust (presumably his world), Krumnagel was already
furious.

Red Leifson admonished the Chinese hierarchy as though his

[25]

views carried weight in Peking; he implied that the Russians were five years ahead of the United States in space. Nobody knew or cared where he got his information or indeed if he got his information; the fact that he said it got almost as much attention locally as if it had been said by a U.S. senator on an equally slender pretext. He dwelt truculently on the almost daily tidbits of corruption — Supreme Court judges who had negligently accepted huge gifts in exchange for unidentifiable favors, generals who had large financial interests in troop entertainments, right up or down to a low-church missionary who was discovered to be the business manager of a ring of syphilitic call girls in Saigon. Every item was dealt with in a mood of chastising, this-hurts-me-more-than-it-does-you benevolence, and if it had been suggested to Red Leifson that the manipulation of news was a form of corruption like any other, he would have snarled a reply implying that the freedom of the press was under attack, presumably from Communist or Crypto-Communist or New Left elements, whatever that might mean.

His coverage of sports was less controversial in that the results were verifiable, but he was free in his advice to the players to retire if they were having a bad season. Their recent careers would be analyzed with a series of stills of them in action, carefully selected to make them look inept, and once again, wearing his avuncular aura like a dressing gown, he would ask, "Is it curtain time at Crown of Thorns U. for Holly Smetecek? It's not always pleasant to ring down the curtain, Holly, but your audience is starting to leave in droves. Isn't it better, old-timer, to ring it down now and eke at least a smattering of applause while it's still there for the begging?"

Current events, sports, and still no mention of the banquet. Local events. Another mugged rabbi in a pool of blood gallantly murmuring some platitudes about the need to forgive; a half-drugged Negro being pushed and pulled by policemen after having killed his brother because they couldn't decide where to sit in a snack bar — his mother, her eyes rolling, darting in and out of sight so quickly the camera couldn't keep up with her; a mobster newly acquitted from a charge of swindling the City, saying with metronomic regularity that he had nothing to add to what the judge had said, his delighted lawyer adding that he would be taking a complete rest in the Bahamas; a montage of hippies being carried off a campus, bleeding, lolling, rolling with the punch; the raucous voices of those in command, the raised hands of those unable to face the disgrace of being seen, the odd frame of eloquence, the cocked ear and quizzical eye of the obedient dog, man's best friend about to spring at man, the noise, the lack of design, the hopeless incoherence of it all, an afternoon of local events, death as unexplained as life, a screenful of nervous tics.

"There he goes, the son of a bitch," cried Krumnagel.

"While we're on the subject of the police department, it would be unfair not to mention one of those fine social events which still give us an echo of a bygone age," Red Leifson purred. "The wine was California hock or was it Moselle, the food was steak, or was it veal, and the hero was Bart Krumnagel — or was it the holes in the structure of the police department, of which there are as many as in a target after F.B.I. small-arms practice."

"Bastard."

"Let's be fair. We heard many interesting things. Chief Krumnagel volunteered for the marines half an hour after Pearl Harbor. The army sure lost a good man when they turned him down for reasons which my researchers have . . ." (He laughed as he read the paper before him.) ". . . but which are strictly, but strictly, censorable. I wish the police department had been left with us good a man as the army lost. Let's face it, Bart, we're not arresting many hoodlums these days. It don't seem to be the fashion anymore. And how many rapists has the City's proud squadron of transvestite cops arrested? It sure is picturesque to have a group of officers doing a thing a normal guy'd get arrested for — I'm not saying it's the greatest public relations, but as I say, it sure is picturesque — and there's a rumor around that some of your officers are getting a real kick out of this work — but where are the arrests? And how's the latest brainstorm — your patrol of rabbinical students, how's that going? How many potential gauleiters and red barons have they low-tackled on Sixteenth Avenue and Chippagunk Drive? How many?" (He whistled.) "You don't say. These ideas of yours must sound just great in the office, Bart. They probably retain some of their glamour in the briefing room. What the heck happens to make them fall flat on their faces in reality? No, don't tell me, Bart. Tell the City."

"Shit! Shit! Lowdown friggin' shit!" yelled Krumnagel, switching off the set. He picked up the phone and called police headquarters. Lieutenant Armstrong was on duty. Krumnagel, his eyes twitching convulsively, told him to have Red Leifson's car followed wherever it went. "I want that thing so covered with tickets it looks like a Christmas tree . . . any kind of offense, technical or otherwise . . . throw the book at him . . . both books . . . all the books . . . and if he really does something wrong, so much the better . . . I know he don't drive himself, what's the difference . . . yeah, and Marvin, while we're on the subject, I want you to find out from the record how that small-time Judas lost his legs . . . that's what he says, I'll bet he got them caught in an elevator, or else had a pileup with a dumbwaiter in a hotel corridor while he was bending down all unsuspecting with his eye to a keyhole . . ." (He roared.) "I don't care if you have to go to Fort Knox to get it. I want that information on my desk." He hung up. Since he was now calmer and more receptive, he switched on the television again, taking care to change the channel so there'd be no risk of another encounter with Mr. Leifson.

"We was friends, remember, Sidney? Remember how we used to go fishin' together, Sid, just you and me . . . fishin' for fish . . ."

The gun rang out. There was the noise of a slumping body.

Krumnagel settled into his rocking chair, reaching for his can of beer like a blind man, already deeply involved in this new situation, Leifson forgotten.

It was towards the end of the program that Edie appeared at the door. The mixture of drinks had not left her insensitive. Now she had brushed her hair into a wild bush, some of it falling over her eyes. She wore a black transparent negligee over black transparent pajama-trousers, with fringes of plastic fur at the wrists and ankles. On her chest, vaguely visible through the twilight transparency, she wore a spangled bra which cupped her breasts, while leaving the nipples ludicrously exposed. She was smoking a cigarette through an ivory holder.

"Hi, lover man," she said, gruffly.

"Ssh! He's just made one hell of a mistake. Christ!"

"Who?"

"Lem Craddocks."

"Who in the hell's that?"

"Private eye. Tipped off the Chinaman, see, without letting the old guy know, see, and —" He glanced at her for a second, and whistled.

"Sex, anyone?" she inquired.

"You look so good I could eat you," he said, looking back at the screen.

She was used to him and his ways. Marriage to three police-men had given her the lowdown. She went to the turntable and put on a record. Mood music. Music to unzip by. She lit a stick of incense, and a coil of intense blue smoke rose into the air like an anemic cobra. She dimmed the lights. He stared at the tele-vision, hoping Craddocks would effect his arrest before he was expected to do his duty. Craddocks lingered. Krumnagel was of two minds. He glanced at his watch, and the screen was oblit-erated by Edie's heaving, bony little chest, and then her lips facing his, as wet as a street on a rainy night, her eyes closed in the expectation of ecstasy. There was a little lipstick on a front tooth and the breath smelled of alcohol.

[29]

"Come on, come on, come on," she hissed.

There was nothing for it but compliance, although abject surrender was not in Krumnagel's mind. He attacked the half-open lips with such ferocity that the head fell into the cradle of his arms, thereby leaving the screen unobliterated. Craddocks was climbing into a building through a skylight. Hell, he had missed a vital moment. Why would he be climbing in through a skylight when there were perfectly good doors to the building? Oh, wait a minute . . . could it be that the Chinaman . . . ? An onyx sheen appeared in the crack between Edie's eyelids. Guiltily he shut his eyes, and let his left hand wander to her exposed nipple.

"All right McMichael," said Craddocks in a tough and muffled voice, "if that's the way you want to play it." There were the sounds of a scuffle, but Krumnagel did not have the courage to open an eye. He wished he could turn the sound up.

"Ow," cried Edie annoyed. "What the hell you doing, for Christ's sake?"

"What am I doing?" asked Krumnagel, genuinely surprised.

"Twisting my goddam nipple. You crazy or something?"

"Sorry."

Edie took his lower lip between her teeth and bit.

"Shit," he cried, "that hurt!"

"Come on, caveman, get active."

He brought his cupped hand down on her left buttock with a ringing report. She drew in her breath sharply, and dug her nails into his scalp, dragging herself up to him like a desperate mountaineer.

Krumnagel could be violent, but his temperament was much more that of a large dog, who could be goaded and teased up to an extreme point, after which he abruptly lost what sense of humor he had. He had a pretty scanty concept of the possibilities of human encounter, either mental or physical. That is to say, he knew the facts of life. If the police department were ever to institute a license for sexual intercourse, he would be able to pass at least the written test, but when it came to the temperamental needs of a girl like Edie, with her restlessness and fidgeting, that was just plain silly to him. Now she was scratching his back with her long nails. She no doubt figured this was the height of sensuality, but he saw absolutely nothing constructive in it. Slowly her fingers found their way under his shirt. Now what? They strayed up to his shoulders where two tufts of yellow hair grew, and they began to twist first one and then the other of these tufts into spirals, and tug at them, and smooth them out, and then coil them again. It was time to counterattack. Clumsily he tried to unhitch her bra. She bit him again, on the cheek.

"Quit biting me, will you?" he roared.

She bit the end of his nose, and tried to force her tongue up his nostrils.

He reared like a horse.

"How would you like it if I did that to you?" he cried, putting her nose on his mouth.

She recoiled.

"Don't like it, huh?"

"I don't like beer," she screamed, closing her mouth on his ear, and boring her way into his navel with her forefinger. Her concentration on her own concept of sexual loveplay was so intense, and her pursuit of it so dictatorial, that an active partner in these delights was really superfluous. Krumnagel felt nothing but profound irritation at having a sharp instrument worrying his stomach, and he withdrew her finger forcibly, even threatening, by gesture, to break the damn thing. She hissed again, and bit into his earlobe. He was fed up. He laid a rough hand on Edie.

"Not yet, not yet," she pleaded, very feminine all of a sudden. He was confused; once more he did nothing while she bored her knuckle into the flesh above his hip while running the bottom of her tongue gently up his profile. He burst out laughing.

[31]

"Don't laugh," she pleaded.

"Tickles," he replied reasonably.

Her hand wandered lightly over his lower stomach, while her tongue ran against the grain of his eyebrows. One sensation was pleasant and full of promise, while the other was frankly irritating. Why couldn't she stick to one thing at a time? He suddenly became conscious of a commercial on the television, a female chorus with a glacial echo, extolling the virtues of a mentholated deodorant amid splashes, drips, and the crunch of dislodging ice floes. Now he'd never know who did it. Shit.

He woke up around four thirty in the morning. He still had his pajama jacket on, but his pants were down around his ankles, while Edie lay across him like a murdered person, her mouth wide open. Curiously enough she was stripped to the waist, but she still wore her macabre pair of black neo-Victorian panties. There were one or two glasses around, the early light was trying to tease its way into the room, and the television was ticking, a series of white lines parting and rejoining each other. Krumnagel had no very clear recollection of what had happened except that his splitting headache suggested that there had been some more drinking, probably after an over-delayed assault on his senses. It had often happened that way between them. The idea of sex, which usually came to Edie first, was invariably inspired by alcohol, which ironically took a premature toll of the very stamina it so pressingly mobilized. Then the night would drag on in a series of noisy snoozes, interspersed by moments of drugged eroticism, enacted with all the urgency and passion of an underwater ballet. Dawn was the bell that saved them. Krumnagel blinked, and tried to get out from under Edie, who turned in her sleep and clung to him as though he were a life buoy. She muttered something, a long and complicated sentence, culminating in an obscenity.

"What was that?" asked Krumnagel, hoping to wake her.

She made herself comfortable, and half opened her lips as though searching for something to bite. He kept clear of the

[32]

greedy teeth, and carefully unwound her arms from around him. He got up, and began waddling across the room, leaving his pants on the floor.

"Where are you going, lover man?"

"Going to take me a piss."

"You just are about the most romantic goddam guy in the world." She was wide awake and angry.

"What I say?"

"Get out of here and don't come back."

She threw a pillow at him.

He came back as though to cover her, changed his mind, and turned the television to another channel, a show called All-Nite Showcase, on which a TV personality gossiped all night long with a weary chimpanzee, and tried to sell the products of manufacturers who couldn't afford the prime time.

"Turn it off," she murmured, half-asleep again.

He left it on and went to the bathroom.

Three hours later they sat drinking the coffee he had made in silence.

"What's the matter, hon?" he asked.

She began to cry. He added a little milk to his coffee.

"Oh, I know," he consoled her. "It wasn't too good last night, but it'll all be different when we hit Asia . . . maybe they're right, I've been working too hard, ought to take it easy . . . it's not fair on you . . . although, God knows —"

"What does God know?" she asked flatly, drying her eyes with a napkin.

"God knows, you've been married to policemen before — you ought to know what it's like."

"Chet Koslowsky, wherever you are, I want you to know, they don't come like you no more." Her imitation of him was outrageous and cruel. She relapsed into her own bitter tones. "Chet Koslowsky was a fag."

"Don't say that!" He rose from the table.

"It's just the goddam truth, that's all," Edie said.

[33]

"Don't say that! He was a pal of mine!" Krumnagel howled.

"Oh? Didn't he ever make a pass at you?"

"He was a fine, upstanding —"

"He was a fag. Couldn't make it with a woman. Are you going to pretend you know more about that than me?"

Krumnagel sat heavily. Perhaps Koslowsky had been no better able to maintain his passion against the rising tide of pinches, scratches, bites and abrasions than other men, and from there on it doesn't require imagination for the woman to believe a guy is impotent if she wishes to be hurtful, or a fag if she wishes to be more hurtful.

The atmosphere was now so heavy that, in spite of his annoyance, Krumnagel felt it incumbent upon himself to lighten it.

"Yeah," he said. "I see a picture of the Taj Mahal once in a book. Like fairyland. Marvelous workmanship."

"We don't go to the Taj Mahal," Edie replied bleakly.

That was that. Krumnagel placed his huge hand on hers after a moment.

"There are other places," he said courageously. "It don't have to be the friggin' Taj Mahal." Since there was no reaction to this, he asked, "Where do we go?"

"I got it all written down."

"Great."

There was another endless pause.

"What's great?"

"You got it all written down. That way we get to know where we're going to go, see. So there aren't no surprises. I'm really looking forward to it."

"I thought you said —"

"Never mind what I said. Greece? Do we get to see that? The cradle of civilization as we know it — yes, sir — the acorn from which our Constitution grew. And Italy, huh? The glory that was Rome. Remember that movie, *The Robe?* It was all in there. Israel too. And Arabia."

He ran out of countries. After a moment of mature reflection, he could find no more, so he rose.

"Where are you going?"

"Shower."

Once in the bathroom, he examined his body. There were thin scratches on his back, two parallel lines of four marks each on his right cheek, traces of blood on his ear, and a huge plum-colored bruise on his hip.

"Brother," he said aloud, "she should have married Bela Lugosi."

3

Before the start of their great adventure, Krumnagel took care to pay a series of visits, in order, as he put it, to "straighten the record" before he left. He took Al Carbide to lunch in an inexpensive steakhouse. Much as he desired to hide his antagonism towards his deputy, the sight of that thin gray face, with its latticework of veins at the temples and the deep lines in the cheeks, snapping and sniffing at the chives and sour cream like some hysterical tropical fish, was enough to fill him with a purely animal aversion. It was all wrong that a man should be able and inclined to eat mountains of food with the application of a glutton and the concentration of a voluptuary, and yet remain as spare and sinewy as a coil of hawser.

"Well, how would you run the police department?" asked

Krumnagel, exasperated by the turn the conversation had taken.

Al smiled, and replied quietly. "It's hardly my place to say how I'd do your job, Bart."

"How come?"

"On account of I don't have your job."

"You may one day."

"There's a great difference between may and will."

Krumnagel paused.

"What if I make it an order?" he inquired.

Al only smiled the more, showing more teeth than most people would.

"Are you making it an order, Bart? I'm off duty."

"I just care to know what you think I'm doing wrong."

"Why should I think you're doing anything wrong, Bart?"

"It's not human not to think I'm doing something wrong, Al, that's why!" Krumnagel cried.

Al Carbide thought for a moment. Then he spoke reasonably.

"O.K., I'll tell you, Chief. I think you're asking too much of the men."

"Think I work 'em too hard?" It was a reputation Krumnagel had no objection to.

"No, I don't think you can expect them to play the parts of hippies, transvestites, whores, rabbis, and all that. They're not actors, they're policemen. They do a lousy job simply because too much is asked of them."

"What do you suggest?"

"Put them in the clothes they look best in. The kind of clothes they'd put on themselves when they're off duty. Don't just pick a guy out of the force to play rabbi because it's his turn for rabbi duty, or expect some football halfback to be a convincing transvestite. Why, only last Tuesday, I had to get Sergeant Lambert off A.S.P. when he'd already left on the

A.S.P. patrol. There was no one willing to take the responsibility because you'd signed the order, Bart. It's things like that make the department look ridiculous."

Krumnagel was annoyed. Annoyed enough to attack.

"Why shouldn't Lambert go on patrol like any other officer?" he asked. "And what's he got against A.S.P.? He a Jew hater or something? Why don't he care to be a rabbi?"

"Sergeant Lambert is black," Al said gently.

Krumnagel lost himself in his beer for a moment.

"Well, you may be right," he sighed. "Maybe we ought to try something else, but these Q-ship patrols are my baby, Al. Give them a little more time. They may work yet. Let's have a little faith, for Christ's sake. Faith, isn't that what life's all about, Al?"

"Sure, sure. I'm only telling you what's on my mind because you just forced it out of me. I know it's your baby, Bart. I want no part of it. I mean, I want none of the credit, not only because I don't deserve it, but because we're not making any arrests with it. I don't have any faith in it."

"Is that all?" Krumnagel rasped. He didn't care for insubordination.

It was Al Carbide's turn to be irritated. His eye grew colder and bluer.

"No, it's not all," he said, very quietly. "What exactly are we after in this police department? Are we after organized crime, or are we just doing a balancing act?"

"What was that?" Krumnagel snapped.

"Just a question, Bart, just a question. You encourage questions. What are we after, the odd transvestite, the fag whose loneliness is bursting at the seams, the stupid rotten leather-jacket wild one with his swastikas and pimples, or are we out to get the rackets, the big-time gangsters, the guys who greet you and me when we go to the classy places, who send us Christmas cards —"

[38]

"Now lookit!" Krumnagel cried, furious, and then, before continuing his diatribe, looked around searchingly and lowered his voice. "I heard that kind of talk, Al . . . I heard it all my life and all the way up to the top of the tree . . . you got to be young to talk that way, and you got to be young to listen to it without blowing your top."

"You're not as old as all that, Bart, are you?" Al asked, so that it hurt.

"I'm old enough and young enough to hold my job — and it's not age counts, Al — it's just that I'm the best goddam police officer around!"

No comment.

"Ideals," Krumnagel grunted. "We live in a world we didn't help to make, Al. I don't like the rackets any more than you do — listen, I like them less — but they're a fact of life — it's like my office at police headquarters — one day they give me my room, see — I didn't furnish it — shit, I may not care for the furniture, but it's furniture I got to live with."

"As police chief you got the authority to change the furniture if you don't like it, Bart."

"It so happens I like the furniture," Krumnagel said decisively.

"And so you like the rackets?"

"And so I chose a bad example. That's all. I chose a bad example. Can happen to anyone." He suddenly spoke very quietly, and with great intensity. "I got my eye on the rackets," he said, "and when the time comes, when I got the evidence I need, I'll crack down on them like they won't know what hit them."

Al frowned. "You may have your eye on the rackets, Bart — I can't tell —"

"If I say I got my eye on the rackets," Krumnagel exploded, "you can take it I got my eye on the rackets."

"They don't seem to bother to have their eye on you, that's

[39]

what gets me down. They go on like there was no police force."

Krumnagel dropped his voice to a conspiratorial level, sly and pleasantly self-satisfied.

"That's the way I want it. I don't want them looking for trouble. I'm ready to wait till every window box in town is growing marijuana and there's fockin' cannabis in every backyard, and then I'll move, not before. I'll get them when they think they're safe."

"That may be too late, Bart. Take a trip to some of the other cities in the state. People out there all think our police force is corrupt, and there's nothing about the figures of crime and dope addiction which does us any credit — you can't quote statistics in our defense."

"Let them think that . . . let it get around . . . it all helps the final crackdown."

Al shrugged, and was silent for a moment, but he smiled no longer.

"You got all the answers, Bart."

"Put it down to experience, Al."

"Let me just ask you this, Chief. Is our police force corrupt?"

Krumnagel hit the table with his fist, and controlling his fury visibly, said in a voice full of menace and hostility, "You ought to know better than ask me that."

Al Carbide did not flinch. He gazed at Krumnagel with his pale blue eyes.

"I only asked because I need to know, Chief. When we talk of the rackets, are we talking about the same guys?"

"We're talking about the syndicate," Krumnagel replied thickly.

"Names, Bart, names."

"You know them as well as I do."

"Jo Tortoni . . . Milt Rotterdam . . . Boots Shilliger . . ."

"Yes," Krumnagel conceded nervously.

"Judge Weyerback . . . His Honor, the Mayor . . ." Al suggested.

[40]

Krumnagel flushed. "You must be out of your cotton-picking mind," he said.

He paid the check and the two men left in silence.

In his brief interview with the mayor, Krumnagel took care to explain his sensitivity about his age, without for a moment stooping to an apology. The mayor made light of the incident.

"None of us is perfect, Bart, as my old Greek mother used to say to me."

Krumnagel thought the remark gratuitous, for though he did not have the sheer gall to consider himself perfect, he never for a moment entertained the idea that he might be in any way imperfect. It was strange the way this lousy mayor had a gift for rubbing him up the wrong way.

"What kind of arrangements did you have in mind during my absence?" he inquired.

"There's no problem about that, surely," the mayor replied. "There's a legal provision for the eventuality of your absence, sickness, incapacity, excetera, excetera" (In the mayor's mouth, these sounded like a couple of ceteras in retirement.) "— and that provision provides that your place be taken — temporarily, of course — by your deputy chief, in this case Al Carbide."

"I had lunch with Al only yesterday, Mr. Mayor."

"That was nice."

"Yes. He don't think we're doing enough to smash the rackets."

"What rackets?" The mayor looked amazed.

"That's what I asked him," Krumnagel said eagerly.

"The Perilli outfit? The Penapoli Brothers? That's all ancient history. What rackets do we have here now?"

"Well . . . I couldn't answer that, so I challenged Al . . . I said, same as you did Mr. Mayor, I said, name them, I said."

"So?"

"So he named them," Krumnagel said carefully.

The mayor lit a cigar. He looked at Krumnagel through the smoke.

"Ought I to know his opinion of who they are?" he asked guardedly.

"Well . . . maybe I'm telling tales out of school."

"You're police chief, Bart. I'm mayor. Without tales out of school neither of us would be able to run our departments."

"O.K. . . . so Joe Tortoni was one name he mentioned." The mayor smiled. "Who else?"

"Boots Shilliger."

The mayor smiled a little less.

"Milt Rotterdam."

The mayor smiled hardly at all.

"Judge Weyerback."

The mayor winced, then laughed.

"In such company, I'm surprised he didn't include me," he quipped.

Krumnagel laughed too. "He's not that out of line, Mr. Mayor."

Just then the buzzer on the desk sounded.

The mayor flicked up the switch with a peremptory "Yes?"

The canned voice of his secretary reverberated in the machine.

"Mr. Rotterdam to see you, sir."

"Tell him to wait a moment."

The mayor flicked the switch down again.

"Well, Bart, if you'll forgive me. Have a wonderful time, and my fondest personal regards to Mrs. Krumnagel."

They shook hands and Krumnagel left.

No sooner was he out of the door than the mayor flicked the switch up again.

"Is Mr. Rotterdam alone?"

"No sir, he has Mr. Tortoni with him."

"Bring them up through Comptroller Harker's office, will you? I don't want them to run into Chief Krumnagel."

"O.K., sir."

[42]

The mayor wandered to the window, half closing his eyes as he drew deeply on his cigar, and reflected that Al Carbide was a man of substance and resource, and that it was safer to have such a man as an ally rather than as an enemy.

Meanwhile Krumnagel left the building, aglow at having so nefariously, so cunningly cooked Al Carbide's goose. At the same time, he was amazed at his good fortune. He had actually been a witness when the mayor was told that Milt Rotterdam was waiting to be shown up to his office. This could be damaging testimony if events took a certain turn. He was glad for the ammunition. The way things are, you never know.

Back in his office, he sought out Al Carbide, but asked no more of him than to watch Rotterdam.

"Do you have any proof?" Al asked.

"Just a hunch — and another thing, find out the name and background of the mayor's receptionist, the petite one, red-head, about twenty-five years old."

"Marilyn Shopenhower."

Krumnagel stared at Al coldly.

"Find it out," he repeated, as though he hadn't heard, and left the office.

He was pleased with his own astuteness at having set that shit-heel wiseguy Al Carbide on a dangerous course, a course which he guessed would be his ultimate undoing. The nearer the ambitious Al got to the truth, the more liable the mayor and the rackets would be to panic, and in an open war between the law and the mayor, Krumnagel knew which one his money was on.

He was, of course, judging others by his own potential reactions to things, and few are the men capable of doing more than that. Enmities were clear-cut in Krumnagel's mind, and it was in a way the measure of his integrity that he was incapable of conceiving a compromise between enemies of equal strength, who see nothing but loss in war, and profit in peace.

Who are, in other words, not only enemies, but intelligent as well. At least, that's how he saw conflicts in which he was not involved personally.

His third and final visit was undoubtedly the most difficult. It had, in fact, been arranged before Krumnagel knew of his journey, and he was in no mood to cancel it now that he needed reassurance, an extension of that cordial public handshake. He called on Arnie Brugger. Although Arnie had confirmed the appointment, he was not alone. Sitting comfortably in a leather chair was Mervyn Spindelman, a lawyer and close collaborator of Arnie's who was beginning to be known nationally for his extravagant courtroom antics, and who spent more and more of his time away from the City as a consequence, clouding issues he was purporting to clarify with a style as ebullient as it was pedantic. He seemed to regard each trial as a sporting fixture, with the judge as a deceivable referee, himself as champion, and client as ball.

The third volume of his autobiography had just appeared, modestly entitled *A Habit of Winning*, and now he inscribed a copy to Krumnagel. "To Chief Krumnagel, sometime opponent, never enemy." Krumnagel thanked him.

"We all love you," Spindelman said negligently, tapping him lightly on the arm. "I only stayed behind so I could give it to you personally." Still, he gave no sign of going.

Krumnagel frowned. He had acquired the habit a long time ago, at school, in order to indicate to the teachers that he was working a problem out. Even now, when he felt lost for a word or a course of action, his energy would go into frowning. Arnie grinned, and agitated his highball so that the ice crackled.

"To what do we owe the honor of this visit — quite apart from the fact that we're just delighted to see you?"

Krumnagel looked him straight in the eye with a sudden and disarming intensity.

"Give me a break, Arnie," he said.

"A break?" Arnie was frankly surprised.

[44]

"You think law enforcement is easy?"

"Just a minute," Spindelman interrupted. "If the trend of the conversation is going the way I think it is, I want to place it all strictly off the record."

The lawyer was at work.

"Of course," Krumnagel replied. "D'you think I want it known that I've come begging?"

"Begging? You don't come here begging," Spindelman cried. "You come just like any self-respecting policeman, asking as a friend for a couple more convictions here and there to make you look good."

"Not to make me look good," Krumnagel replied hotly. "It's for the police department, Spindelman — it's for the cause of law enforcement, not only here but throughout the goddam state, throughout the goddam country, come to that. Can't you see what's happening, man? Every time we make an arrest other than drunk driving charges or some such peanuts, one of you, or both, turns up in court the next morning and starts confusing the issue. This homicidal maniac had an unhappy childhood, that child raper has a tough time with his erections owing to shell shock. You got it all down pat. The local judges, they're not too bright — you just wear them down with all that fancy talk of yours — so what happens? The maniac and the child raper go to a psychiatric hospital for observation, and after a while they're at large again, cured. Cured until the next crime, that is."

Arnie Brugger spoke very softly, even mysteriously, after indicating to Spindelman by a gesture that he wished to take over the argument.

"Bart," he purred, "do any of us really understand the world we live in now? Does any generation ever understand the world it lives in?"

"What that got to do with it?"

"A hundred and fifty years ago, sailors were keelhauled for minor offenses and men were hanged for sheep stealing."

[45]

"Where the hell would anyone go looking for a sheep to steal today?"

"Do me the courtesy, will you Bart? I'm trying to say something meaningful. What I'm trying to say is that values change. Before, it was death for everything. The prisons were full. It was a solution of expediency. Gradually, with a growing respect for life, we began restricting the death penalty to offenses that seemed to merit it. Murder, kidnapping. But have we gone far enough — fast enough? Is *any* crime deserving of punishment if the condition of aberration is only a temporary one, and if it is curable? A murderer is only capable of murder at certain moments — at other times he may be an utterly charming fellow. The question arises, do we judge him by his moment of aberration or by the sum total of his acts? And if we can get to the roots of his trouble, and turn him into a reliable citizen, whatever that may mean, are we justified in punishing him for what amounts to an illness? Would you send a guy to prison for having a common cold — or worse, for having *had* a common cold?"

"There you are, doing it to me now, what you do to the judges!"

"Do you follow me?"

"No."

Arnie smiled.

"No," he echoed, "because you and the judges have your terms of reference which are rigid. I suppose you couldn't function without your rule book. You've just got to think and act as though the world were static, as though time stood still. It doesn't, you know, Bart."

There was a strange little tinkling noise from the street. Arnie walked to the window, and pulling apart the curtains, looked down into the street.

"What d'you make of that?" he asked.

"Nut cases," Krumnagel replied.

A little group of youthful Buddhists in long yellow robes were crossing the road. Both men and women were entirely bald, and they chanted as they sounded their tocsins, moving with reflective slowness, entirely oblivious to the impatient hooting of the evening traffic. Arnie and Krumnagel watched them until they had reached the sidewalk, and settled in a half-empty parking lot for a prayer meeting.

"I suppose you think of them as a traffic obstruction?" Arnie asked.

"Sure do. They got no business in that lot either. It's owned by the Leverett Corporation."

"That's what you see in the situation. Their possible glimpse of heaven leaves you cold."

"Hey, you sound as though you take that shit seriously," Krumnagel said. It had never occurred to him that Arnie Brugger's motives were other than purely antagonistic and selfish.

"I take everything seriously that has any mystery attached to it. That includes everything, Bart. Even, under exceptional circumstances, the police department and the judiciary. Man. Man, Bart, the greatest mystery of all. I take him seriously."

"I hope you make a difference between law-abiding citizens and lawbreakers."

"None, none whatever."

"Are you crazy?"

"Remember the Bostrom case? The dropout who committed all those arbitrary murders a year or two back?"

"Sure I remember it. Are you trying to tell me you were right in saving Hallam Bostrom from the gas chamber?"

"Were you right in not prosecuting his dad?"

"His dad?" Krumnagel asked, bewildered.

"His dad. Remember the details? I traced Bostrom's family history. How he was the son of a hooker in Peoria, Illinois? How his dad was a colonel in the U.S. Army?"

"Any hooker can say that."

"And what if it's true?"

"Are you going to blame a colonel for hitting the sack with a hooker, 'specially in Peoria, Illinois? Might as well lock up the entire army."

"And what if the result of that light-hearted negligence is a little monster like Hallam Bostrom? The colonel in question is probably an upright, God-fearing citizen and father — the kind you eulogized in your speech, Bart — when he's at home, held in place by his wife, the preacher, and the uniform. But when he's in Peoria, Illinois, on official business, it's a different story with different consequences. Is that fair?"

"I'm not saying anything's fair, Arnie. I'm saying that it's the best possible system — but I'm not ruling out luck. After all, we're only human."

"Now you tell us!" Spindelman declared. "And that's why you come here asking for a head or two, in the parlance of the French Revolution, to make the police department look good. Because we're only human."

"You're twisting my words."

"Untwist them."

"You know damn well what I want, Spindelman, and you too, Arnie — I want a break for the police department."

"You want a conviction or two without the kind of opposition you meet from us," Spindelman said.

"If you want to put it that way —"

"Are any specific cases more deserving of this treatment than others?"

There was a pause.

"I just wish you'd go to some other town, both of you — let us get on with our own business our own way."

Spindelman laughed; Arnie smiled at Krumnagel's abject misery.

"Bart." Arnie was back in his hushed, mysterious mood. He spoke with understanding and compassion. "Have you the merest inkling of the black night through which the human race is at the present passing — and more especially these United States of ours, because we are the wealthiest, the most affluent, the most guilt-ridden, the most vulnerable?

"In the last fifty years, there have been more changes in our way of life than in the preceding fifty thousand. Space has dwindled, sometimes it's disappeared altogether. We can talk intimately to people thousands of miles away, and see them too. All complicated mental problems are done for us. There is nothing left to do but enjoy. And that leads to idleness of the soul, Bart. Natural or not, it's all happened too fast. Today's child no longer has time to get to grips with fundamentals — he never need think what life was like without the streamlining. In fact, he is incapable of conceiving an existence without today's devices. What's more, history bores him. He is permanently forward-looking if he stays in society — forward-looking to Spaceman, Batman, and other Nietzschean heroes who single-handedly win wars between planets in the comic strips. And even if he drops out of society — he still couldn't care less about history. It's prehistory which captures his imagination: screwing the available females in communal clusters, stealing to eat, and dispensing with responsibility as though it were stale breath. And out of this turmoil, this interference with evolution, this affront to the architecture of existence, there come reactions from nature herself, explosions, cataclysms, disasters, a wild and heartless cacophony; actions which defy explanation; murder committed for insane and trivial reasons; procreation as part of a diabolical keep-fit program, with scant attention to the consequences; weird attachments and obsessions, as though nakedness were the ultimate honesty and the existence of genitalia had only just come to light; and all of this new cymbalum mundi bathed in the flickering, stereotyped and monotonous light of the psychedelic imagination."

He paused. Then added slowly, "I hate it, Bart. Because I

don't understand it. I hate what I don't understand if I feel I ought to. That's maybe the difference between us. You think you understand. I know I don't. I try. You don't have to."

"Christ, if I allowed myself to think the way you do — I'd never arrest anyone," Krumnagel said. "Apart from which I'd go crazy."

Arnie smiled sadly. "That's probably why you're a police officer and why I'm a psychiatrist."

Krumnagel was in no mood for compromise.

"If I didn't know you was a psychiatrist," he said, "I'd say you were nuttier even than those wild Boodists illegally parked in the Leverett Corporation's lot."

"Our opinions are always formed by our capabilities and our temperament, Bart. You're a wholesaler. If there are five hundred arrests in January, you want to improve on that figure for February."

"That's natural, isn't it?"

"I guess so. For you. If I understand a single motive or complex in January, I hardly dare hope I'll have the same luck in February."

"You're just a friggin' pessimist, that's what's the matter with you Arnie."

Arnie didn't smile. He seemed to be struggling with some inner conflict. At length he spoke.

"I got a son, Bart."

Spindelman started, but Arnie reassured him with a quick gesture.

"I didn't know that," Krumnagel said, sensing that some tragic circumstance had been invoked.

"Once we're off the record — and I see no reason why you should remember this later on —"

"I'll forget it," Krumnagel promised softly.

"Before I go into all that, Bart. What, in your experience, causes most of the juvenile delinquency we got?"

"Broken homes, I'd say. Lack of parental control."

"Yes, the usual. It's the clichés, isn't it. The conditioned re-flex. Broken homes are responsible for everything."

"There are exceptions, I guess."

"Sure there are. My son, Bernard, his mother, and I had a just wonderful family relationship. Just ideal. There was every-thing. Love, affection, humor, mutual respect, you name it. If ever a marriage can be said to have been blessed with issue, this was it. He played football like a young god, six foot three and a half, engaged to a fine girl, he had everything . . . to look forward to, everything going for him. And then . . ." Arnie hesitated.

"Then . . . maybe a too-stable upbringing has its dangers too . . . a young man feels square and out of things, as though dissension and misery have their therapeutic values in today's society. I don't know. Anyhow, one day he just took off. That's all there is to the story. Don't ask me any more. I don't know any more."

"Where is he now?" Krumnagel asked, frustrated by the abrupt end of the narrative.

"I don't know."

"Is he alive?"

"Who knows?"

"That's ridiculous. You got to be able to find a guy. Was there a police search?"

"Oh, sure. All this was some years back. Before we came to live in the City. This was in Omaha, Nebraska, when I was attached to the hospital there."

"You mean he just vanished into thin air?"

Arnie nodded.

"By now," he said quietly, "I'd rather not know whether he's alive or dead. If he wants to come back, let him do so of his own free will, if he's able. I'm forced to assume that he's dropped out. But I will say this, Bart, all I do in my life is a kind of silent appeal to him to . . . to come back . . . to understand . . . that I'm not a square . . . that I do make the

[51]

effort to comprehend the world I so gratuitously gave him . . .
and that if there's still a fatted calf around, it's his for the
asking . . . but that if, as is probable, he insists on the calf
staying alive . . . that's O.K. with me, too."

And after a moment, Arnie added rather painfully, "So you
see, if you want me to help you, you've come to the wrong
guy."

"I don't see that —" Krumnagel began.

"If ever you drop out, then I'll help you."

Krumnagel shook his head.

To lighten the atmosphere, Spindelman sailed into the conversation in bombastic style.

"You see, Bart, there's irony for you, irony and paradox ga-
lore. I'm a lousy father, always have been. I don't understand
children; don't care to understand them. They lack maturity to
a depressing degree. They talk nonsense, and they bring out
the worst in women. I can safely say I hate them. And yet I
have four of them owing to some oversight. Since they are all in
their twenties, they are on the verge of becoming tolerable. Yet
I never gave them an unnecessary moment of my valuable
time. All I had to offer was my example. Apparently that was
sufficient. Howard is just leaving law school, Ernest is in his
second year in law school, Luther is going into law school,
while Sylvia . . . well, Sylvia's a girl. She's engaged to Lionel
Weinflasch, one of the brightest young men at Levins, Connor,
Jakobovits and Lehmann. You see, Bart, it's fatal to complicate
the issue with love, affection, care, all that personal stuff. That's
strictly reserved for intimate relations with your woman of the
moment. Spread the precious commodity around you like but-
ter on a sandwich, you're asking for trouble, and what's more
you deserve it. Half the things that go wrong in human affairs
are due to the fact that people don't ration themselves. They
believe their founts of goodness, of patience, are endless. They
are wrong. They believe it is incumbent on them as people to

care deeply about 'most everything. It isn't. Worst of all, they believe they themselves are creatures of infinite depth and value. What a delusion. Most people are worth no more than the chemicals in their skin and bones. Look at you, Bart, the zealous policeman. Why bother to make the police department look good? What the hell has the police department done to deserve such sympathetic treatment from you? Given you headaches and disappointments all along the line, and most probably ulcers on the side —"

"There is such a thing as duty —" Krumnagel began to remonstrate.

"Fiddlesticks!" cried Spindelman with a fluid flourish. "Hark at the phonograph record! Duty? You think you're getting the best mileage out of yourself worrying about the image of our beloved law enforcement agency? It's about the same relationship you have with the goddam outfit as an unenlightened Cherokee has for his totem pole. Get wise to yourself, Bart, and to your possibilities. You do more good taking it easy than ever you do straining to get results. Roll with the punch, Bart, and outlive the opposition. That's the way to survive. You make more friends helping an old lady across Main Street than you do shooting down a petty thief in cold blood in the ghetto."

"What about you?" Krumnagel asked hotly. "Are you trying to tell me that you don't care whether you win cases or not — that you don't give a damn if you look good or not?"

"I'm different," Spindelman replied charmingly, "because I really am an exceptionally intelligent individual — a brilliant legal brain — that's not your servant talking, it's the book critic of the Toledo *Blade* and I'm merely forced to agree. I know that reputations are made on impossible cases, even if money is made on the others. The greater my reputation, the greater the eventual inflow of cold cash. Consequently, my defense of the psychopathic killer, while not actually remunerative, is by way of being a deferment of vast eventual sums. You see, Bart, I

[53]

don't have to roll with the punch, because I do the punching. And with all I've told you, we're back on the record again. I have nothing to hide. Not even success."

Krumnagel drained the iced water at the bottom of the glass. He understood the interview to be over and wished he had never come.

"Remember what I said," Arnie said mournfully, "not about the boy — about you."

"That'll be the day," Krumnagel replied.

"When d'you leave?" Spindelman asked jovially, hitting Krumnagel hard on the arm.

"Was going to leave tomorrow. Got all my shots for Europe. We're told the water's none too safe. Put off our departure till Tuesday."

"How come?"

"Tomorrow's the thirteenth. I'll never do anything the thirteenth. All my life it's been that way."

"A case of chronic triakaidekaphobia," Arnie said gravely.

"What in the hell's that?" Krumnagel asked.

"An irrational terror of the number thirteen."

Krumnagel gulped. "That exists?"

Arnie nodded slowly.

4

As the gigantic plane rose over the City, Krumnagel gave in to a feeling of well-being. Light music was still playing on the intercom, and the nerves of modern man understood the signal like a circus dog. He knew he was intended to feel relaxed, rich, cradled in a spiritual hammock of sterilized luxury, and he obeyed, testing the angle of his seat and its resilience, meeting the public-relations smile of the hostess with a public-relations smile of his own. Having helped Edie identify various public buildings from the air, and even noticed with passing annoyance a traffic snarl-up on one of the freeways leading into the City — (What the hell's Al doing about it? Where's the goddam chopper?) — he quickly settled back, drank a preprandial martini now that lunch was only three hours away, and dozed while Edie read *The Snow Goose* in order to better understand the British.

The flight was uneventful, but endless. In his dream, Krumnagel took fitful and surreal stock of his situation. He seemed to be speaking soundlessly at a massive banquet at which no one was listening. They stood in groups, cigars burning like forest fires, waiters struggling through the mass of smoking humanity, their trays held high. Groups of Buddhist monks began walking down the banqueting tables as though treading clouds, carrying a palanquin, on the roof of which a bald Edie, her nipples sparkling like sunbursts, made gestures of seduction with indecent energy. Krumnagel suddenly noticed that he was naked, and his precipitate discovery of his condition seemed to occasion hysterical applause in his audience. His nostrils twitched with a slight awareness of spearmint, and he woke up to find the stewardess a few inches away from his face.

"Is there anything I can do for you?" she asked.

He looked down and saw with a subtle mixture of disappointment and relief that he was dressed.

He accepted everything that the airplane had to offer: drinks; little corrugated trays full of nuts, lunch, dinner; bedsocks, eyemasks; even a film of the kind that would find it hard to command an audience outside an airliner. In spite of fatigue, Edie's excitement grew as they began to approach their destination. The pilot's observation that the lights of Belfast were intermittently visible through banks of cloud inspired her to dig her nails painfully into Krumnagel's freckled wrist, to push her mouth into the shell of his ear and to sing "When Irish Eyes Are Smiling" in a version of her own, making up in brio what it lacked in tonality.

London, true to tradition, was entirely invisible until they were nearly on the ground, when suddenly it lay beneath them. Krumnagel laughed with delight.

"Son of a bitch," he cried as he looked down on the necklaces of traffic. "Will you get a load of that. Look at them, all driving on the wrong side of the road! Jesus, I'd take in enough writing out tickets in one evening to retire comfortable!"

[56]

He made several attempts to share his surprise with other passengers, but they had all evidently been abroad before, and either looked through him, or else nodded indulgently.

A fine drizzle was falling as they disembarked, and went through into Immigration. Krumnagel felt slightly disgruntled that there should be what appeared to be preferential treatment for citizens of the Commonwealth, but he kept his feelings to himself, only wincing at his first contact with English disinfectant, that no-nonsense and ferocious smell which permeates so many chill corridors and cheerless stairways, a dark brown odor which seems to be a first cousin of beef tea.

He gratuitously told the British immigration officer that he was a police chief. The officer in question, who had caked yellow hair just long enough to lie on the ridge of his shoulders, handed Krumnagel's passport back in silence after a colleague with even longer hair had leaned over to study it with him.

"Are you boys allowed to wear your hair that long?" Krumnagel asked.

"It's a free country," the officer replied, already opening the next passport.

This lack of civility, the unwillingness to take time out to be friendly — friendly, not merely courteous — galled Krumnagel.

"God save the Queen," he said, expressionlessly, as though it were a password.

The immigration officers didn't bother with him.

"What are you guys, naval officers?" he asked the customs officer.

"Customs and Excise, sir," the latter replied, as though one was worse than the other, and the two together were virtually unmentionable. His inflections were so mannered and so filled with obscure insinuation, that he had probably been invalided out of some corps de ballet in order to qualify for his present position.

"Well now, and what have we to declare?" he inquired. "If anything," he couldn't help adding, waspishly.

"We're U.S. citizens, see," Krumnagel said.

"No!" The customs officer exhaled in mock amazement.

Edie risked a small smile, but the customs officer just gazed skywards in a celestial aside. Without looking at them he spoke. "I somehow don't think we have anything worth declaring to the insolvent British, have we? I mean, why waste money on a bad thing? I mean why do it — when there are still undeveloped countries clamoring for our obsolete cannons? I mean — it's true isn't it?" The customs officer executed an arabesque on the luggage with his piece of sky-blue chalk.

"That'll be all, Maitland-Cleaver." It was an older colleague with a lantern jaw, who had turned up as silently and as efficiently as M.I. 5 itself.

"Oh, it's Maitland-Cleaver today, is it?" the customs officer hissed.

"That'll be all, Maitland-Cleaver," the older one said in an identical tone to before, but with a bit more spine to it.

"Yesterday it was Ronnie."

"Maitland-Cleaver!" A very much higher customs officer called out, his face disfigured by a grin as savage as it was insincere.

"I do hope you've been caused no undue bother," the older customs officer said to the Krumnagels. How British it was to associate the word undue with bother, but the Krumnagels had no ear for discords, and anyway, they had been in the land only for a few minutes.

"What's the matter with that guy? He a fag or something?" Krumnagel did a painful imitation of a homosexual. Edie tugged at his arm, and looked around defiantly.

"Let's just say that he's a little overworked," the older customs officer replied tactfully. "Now, sir, you know our currency, do you?"

"We have a booklet, yes."

"Ah, yes. That'll give you all the details, sir. May I take this opportunity of welcoming both you and Mrs. Burrowes to the U.K."

"Mrs. Burrowes? Who in hell's Mrs. Burrowes?"

"You are Mr. Burrowes, aren't you? The V.I.P.?"

"No. I am not."

"Oh, surely," M.I. 5 said doggedly. He was not easily thrown off the scent. "Jericho Steel?"

"Jericho Steel! Christ, if that was me —"

"Winkworth!" The very much higher customs officer, his grin having lost hardly anything in savagery, approached and with a gesture of supreme negligence replaced the wretched M.I. 5, who retired, fiddling nervously with his virgin chalk.

"Now, Mr. and Mrs. . . . ?" He left the phrase hanging and echoing with inquiry.

"Krumnagel."

"Very good. Very nice indeed. May I take this opportunity of welcoming both you and Mrs. . . . to the U.K."

"We already been welcomed."

"Well, you can't be welcomed enough these days, can you, sir? I mean courtesy's in short shrift all over, isn't it. Courtesy, toujours le politeness as the pundits have it — a wonderful thing, really — wonderful in many ways."

"Aren't you going to open nothing?"

"Why cause you annoyance at the very port of entry, sir? I mean, if you're transporting anything illegal, I'll never find it, will I, without your collaboration? And if you're the kind who's going to be transporting something illegal, you're not going to be the kind who's willing to collaborate, are you?"

"So what are you doing here?"

"What are any of us doing here?"

"We're here to see Great Britain."

"In how many days, if I may ask?"

"Three days."

[59]

"What are you going to see in three days that you couldn't more profitably cull from a picture book in your own home?".

"We was given the tickets," Krumnagel said defensively.

"Ah, that's different. That's human nature, isn't it, sir, of which, I need hardly add, I am a student. Human nature all over. If they gave me tickets to a hanging, I'd be forced to go, wouldn't I, out of courtesy. And we're back again to toujours le politeness. All roads lead back there sooner or later."

"Tickets to a hanging? Is that public here?" Krumnagel asked dramatically.

"It may come back. It may do. They vote it on and off. In search of a deterrent to the paltry amount of murder we have over here, they're capable of trying anything. As a student of human nature, as I previously had cause to remark, I am amazed that there aren't more murders. Coming into contact with a cross section as I do, I think murder is a pastime to encourage rather than condemn."

"You're crazy!" cried Krumnagel.

"I can't say if often enough, sir, toujours le politeness." The very high customs officer squiggled on the luggage with his chalk.

"Cloudesley!" It was the highest of the customs officers. Cloudesley, whose face had taken on a look of melancholy worthy of a Spanish monk, called out that he was on his way. The savage grin reappeared, banishing introspection and philosophy, and sent the Krumnagels on their way, while in the background a corpulent old man in a camel's hair coat fumed and fussed.

"My name is Burrowes, and —"

"Ah yes, sir, open these bags, will you please? All of them."

"They're all crazy," said Krumnagel to Edie in the cab. "A couple of hippies in Immigration, a queen and a pair of nut cases in Customs, wow, Arnie Brugger'd sure have a field day over here. And will you get this cab? How's it feel to be riding standing up, Edie? We must be doing all of ten miles an hour, and on the wrong side of the road. How much did the driver say the fare was into town?"

"Four pounds," Edie replied.

"What's that in real money?"

"Oh, I don't know. Ten dollars? Does it matter?" She gripped Krumnagel's arm. "We're in England, do you realize that? Where the Pilgrim Fathers set out from?"

"With Customs the way they are, I'm not surprised."

Upon arrival at the Lexington Towers Hotel, a subsidiary of the Friskin Chain of Des Moines, Iowa, the door of the cab was opened by a doorman in the uniform of a Civil War trooper.

"What the hell you supposed to be?" asked Krumnagel as he reached for his wallet.

"Civil War private," replied the wall-eyed Cockney. "Search me why. I only got the job yesterday, see. I reckon it's to put the Yank visitors at their ease. This is a wholly owned subsidiary of Friskin Hotels. The top echelon's all Yank, like everything else in Britain apart from the Pakistani restaurants. Now if you'll proceed to the desk, your baggage will follow you with the least possible delay. If you need anything, do not fail to ask. We are here to assure your comfort and your well-being in an atmosphere of relaxed and tasteful luxury. Gratuities are only accepted at the termination of your stay. Thank you, and it has indeed been a pleasure to serve you. Don't ask me what all that means, but I had to learn it by heart off a little Friskin brochure."

"I think it's most gracious," Edie said, with a trace of a royal nod.

"How much?" Krumnagel asked the taxi driver.

"Eight quid," replied the latter with heartwarming gentility.

"What's quid?"

"Eight pound."

"I thought you said four."

"Four's the fare for one way. I got to get back."

"We're not traveling back with you."

"Exactly. I got to go back empty."

"I don't get what you're saying. Why d'you have to get back at all? Why can't you pick up a fare in town?"

"I'm an airport taxi, see. We fall under a different scheme. I'm *not allowed* to pick up a fare who is not going to the airport. It's not worth my while. I'd lose my license."

"Give him six," suggested the doorman.

"Yeah?" Although doubtful, Krumnagel counted out six single notes. It was late, it was raining, Edie was cold.

Once the Krumnagels were inside the hotel, the taxi driver gave the doorman a pound.

"That's very generous of you, I'm sure. Ta."

For a couple of days the Krumnagels did all the things that Edie had marked on her memory pad. They stood in awe before the Albert Memorial, and seemed to hear the Roman legions thundering into the heart of the metropolis. They visited Parliament for a few moments and heard a section of a thrilling debate on the subject of local government and housing, which opened their eyes to the functioning of an even more venerable constitutional democracy than their own. They saw the crown jewels and the dungeons in the Tower, and trudged around Hampton Court with a guide. The third and last day Edie had reserved for herself. Her half brother, Major Batt O'Fehy, was stationed at an American air base somewhere in Hertfordshire. Krumnagel had no great affection for Major O'Fehy, perhaps because there were certain similarities between them. The bottle was enjoyed by both as a launching pad for the missile of social grace; although Krumnagel favored the softer stuff like beer — there was nothing on earth which gave him such an acute sense of well-being as a good, rollicking belch — Major O'Fehy had a preference for the whiskey as a more rapid form of transport into the euphoria enjoyed by those who hear without listening and speak without saying anything.

This third day began disastrously. Krumnagel, confident of his pathfinding ability, rented a car in order to search out the air base. The only car available was a tiny British vehicle which had been subject to fairly rough treatment during its life, and the gearshift felt as though it had been left in a pot of hardening glue overnight. The clutch slipped. The engine occasionally raced because the accelerator stuck to the floor. Every time the brakes were applied, the driving seat rolled back or advanced a notch, according to mood. In trying to find their way out of London, Krumnagel stalled the engine six times because he never knew when the engine was in gear, let alone which gear it was in.

By the time they were in the suburbs, Edie sitting beside him, a map resting on her knees, Krumnagel was bellowing mad.

"What have I done to deserve gettin' stuck with this friggin' toy?" he cried. "And all because you've got to go and see this goddam — he isn't even a real brother. If he was — if you was close — I could understand. But to come all this way — what is it? Five thousand fockin' miles to visit with Major Batt O'Fehy — that's carrying family relations just a little far." (And as an afterthought.) "Fockin' cretin." (Pronounced as though O'Fehy was of ancient Greek stock.)

Edie sat there, wrapped in a small thundercloud, either refusing to answer Krumnagel's questions about their position on the map, or else answering coldly without consulting the map at all.

"Listen, you want to get to see this friggin' major of yours or you don't? I'm only the guy at the wheel, you know. Don't think of me as anything else. Just tell me where to go, and I'll steer this fancy limousine in that direction. Maybe I'd have preferred to have spent today at Windsor Castle or the Edinburgh Festival or someplace, but that is neither here nor there. Do you have relatives in Paris, too, or do I get to see the Eiffel Tower?"

Edie settled it by beginning to cry, at first discreetly, then bitterly. It was Krumnagel who now turned to stone, the only indication of his inner turmoil being his driving style. This reached its apotheosis in a small village. Edie screamed when she saw the truck bearing down on them.

"What the hell —?" Krumnagel yelled.

"You're on the wrong side of the —"

There was an immense conflict of interests between the huge eight-wheel truck, transporting part of a house, and the little car. Luckily the truck was hardly moving at all at the moment of impact, and Krumnagel managed to apply his brakes, but nevertheless the damage was considerable. The car looked like something a monstrous child had dropped out of its pram, its works strewn over the road.

The driver of the truck came from some remote region of the North, and spoke in a truncated telegraphic manner, and with such a peculiar accent that Krumnagel understood not a word. However, it was clear from the inflections, even without understanding a word, that in the driver's opinion, Krumnagel was an imbecile at least, and probably several other things a good deal worse.

Krumnagel was slow to react because he was still pale and frightened. Edie was leaning against a doorway, her eyes shut. As Krumnagel explained rather pathetically to the policeman who ambled up, "I'm an American, see, and I clean forgot about you people driving on the wrong side of the road."

The policeman was very helpful, an unknown brought Edie some hot tea, and the driver of the truck calmed down. It was quickly decided that a local taxi would take Edie to the air base, while Krumnagel would have lunch by himself at a pub, then take in a movie, as he put it, and they would rendezvous in the same pub in the early evening, when the same local taxi would take them all the way back to London.

Edie kissed Krumnagel gratefully as she left, and he kissed her back. A breakdown truck came and dragged the rented car away. The crowd dispersed. Krumnagel was all alone in the village of Winkworth Travis.

5

The village was a typical one, a slow improvisation throughout the ages suddenly impaled on an arterial road which mercilessly bored its way through the quiet intimacies, but not without resistance in the form of dangerous corners, perilous crossings and hidden exits. To Krumnagel it was something rare and curious, especially since traffic problems attracted him more than romanesque architecture. He stood at street corners and watched with fascination the lugubrious discipline of the traffic, with its occasional romantic lawbreaker who flaunted the roadsigns with assurance and irrefutable initiative which must have given the old country its high tradition of piracy in times more ample. Impelled by his compulsive need to communicate, he approached a young policeman who gazed owl-like from the depths of his helmet, occasionally half-heartedly stopping traffic to let an accumulation of shoppers cross the road.

"Howdy," he said to the policeman.

"I beg your pardon, sir?"

"What's new?"

"New? — Excuse me, sir."

He strode out manfully in front of the traffic stream in order to shepherd an army of prams across. Krumnagel felt ignored again. In his heart, he believed he had priority over pedestrians.

"Now sir, were you looking for something?"

The policeman had returned to the sidewalk.

"I'm a policeman too," said Krumnagel.

"It's a rum kind of job, I reckon," the policeman said. "I don't intend to stay in it for life."

"No?" replied Krumnagel, penetrating the accent with difficulty. "What's better as a life for a man?"

"I'm keen on architecture."

"Architecture?" Krumnagel was incredulous.

"Yes. You know, building."

"I know what architecture is," Krumnagel insisted.

"I've always been keen on it. Where d'you come from? Canada?"

"Canada? The U.S.A. The United States."

"Oh, yes." The young policeman didn't seem impressed. What's this with Canada? What was the matter with this guy, to guess Canada first, before the United States?

"I'm police chief," Krumnagel said, "I got over a thousand guys under me."

"Well, then, you're hardly a policeman," the young man said. "You're more of an office worker."

"I am like shit!" cried Krumnagel. "Most times I'm out with the boys — I got other people in the office to do the paper work. I never forget I started a patrolman like you. Yessir, I was a rookie, started at the bottom of the —"

"Excuse me."

[66]

The young man had seized on another opportunity to halt the traffic in order to let a gigantic school crocodile through. As the giggling, chatting mass of schoolchildren cascaded across the narrow road in an apparently endless stream, Krumnagel moved away, disgruntled. The attitude of the policeman gave him no pleasure, and above all no succor for a strange feeling of loneliness, an emotion he was unused to, and which he found unwelcome at his time of life. It was as though part of his nature which had lain dormant, a part of nature with which the majority of men become acquainted during childhood, their noses glued to rain-flecked windows, was suddenly and unexpectedly back to torment him. At home he was respected, known, feared. He didn't have to wear a uniform to be recognized. Even during uneventful times, his head was held high. Krumnagel was used to reactions to his presence, recorded in the corner of his eye, and it was enough to sustain him in his attitudes. In fact, it was everything. It was a permanent reminder of the way he had come; it afforded him the pleasurable vanity of flaunting his humble beginnings, and as a consequence, it was a mark of quality.

Here, in this village which minded its own dull business in total ignorance of his august presence, he felt the pangs of premonition, as though some hideous mistake had been perpetrated, as they are in dreams. Nobody even looked at him. Either they were plain unobservant, or else there was something calculated in their hostility. Oh, they were civil enough when accosted, but it was not the same thing as the kind of civility which came as a result of recognition. He even began to miss Edie, not really out of a sense of deep attachment, but more because Edie was the one person around who knew who he was.

He halted before the war memorial, a mean little obelisk with a palm leaf etched on its flank. It mourned eight men who had died between 1914 and 1918. Of those killed in the more recent war there was no sign, as though men had given up

[67]

remembering because they had lost count. A clergyman emerged from the church behind the war memorial. He wore a grim vocational smile on his face. Krumnagel remained immobile as an ambush.

"Good morning," he said as the clergyman passed.

"Good morning," replied the clergyman, surprised, "or rather — it is morning?" He consulted his watch. "I suppose so, at a pinch."

"How come there are no names from the last war on this slab?"

"Are there not? Gracious. I never noticed. Thank you very much for pointing it out. Fancy that. Well, if you'll excuse me —" The clergyman raised his hat, and hurried away.

"Fancy that," Krumnagel echoed. "Jesus."

Gradually perplexity at the insulting abstraction of manners in this bleak village began to turn to anger, that most faithful ally of those who fail to understand. It was therefore in a mood which had lost all receptivity that Krumnagel entered the Tudor Tea Roome for what was advertised as "Light Luncheons." He began his flirtation with history by hitting his head on a low beam, and setting in motion a hysterical bell, which only stopped announcing his entrance after he had sat down at a table and removed his coat.

"Why the hell don't you have that beam moved?" he asked the waitress.

"What, American are you? No wonder you don't appreciate it," she replied acidly. He noticed with displeasure the rancid odor of her black dress, and stared with disbelief at the lace cap which tried to lend a little grace and style to the shriveled head with its sparse hair, querulous mouth and bigoted expression.

"That's right. You said it. I'm American and I definitely don't appreciate it."

"Well, it's been there since 1508. It's got every right to be there, I reckon. In any case, we can't move it."

[68]

"Why not?"

"It falls under the Ministry of Works. Most of the village does. It's 'istorical. There was fighting here."

"Fighting? Here?" Krumnagel didn't remember the Germans having invaded in either war.

"Oh, yes. Prince Rupert had an 'orse shot from under him where the graveyard now is."

"Prince Rupert?" Krumnagel racked his brains and searched mentally among all the films he had ever seen. "When was that?"

"October the ninth, 1647. It was a bay," she added gratuitously.

"What was?"

"The horse."

"How in the hell do you know?" Krumnagel could no longer stand this meticulous pedantry, especially from a woman.

"There's no need to be rude, you know," she warned him, her stone-colored schoolmarm eyes glinting behind her rimless glasses.

"I'm not being rude. Where else can I get lunch in this village?"

"The Bay Horse and Prince's Head."

Krumnagel rose.

"But they don't do lunches any more."

"I asked you where I could get lunch," he said, exasperated.

"If you'd let me finish, you'd be much better off, you know. They don't do lunches any more, but they did do lunches. If you'd have come before November last year, you could've had lunch there. Nice lunch, too."

"I didn't come before November last year. I came now. I want to know where I can get something to eat."

"Here. But you'll only get a light lunch, you know."

"So I'll take a light lunch. Later I'll take me a light dinner or two to make up for it."

"We don't do light dinners, you realize."

[69]

"O.K., so I'll have a heavy dinner."

"We don't do dinner at all. You'll have to go to the Bay Horse and Prince's Head."

"Now, or before November last year?"

"Before November last year, they didn't do dinners."

"Not even light dinners?"

"No dinners at all. *Now* they do light dinners."

"Listen, lady," Krumnagel said, exhausted, "we'll cross that bridge when we come to it. Just tell me what you do have." He sat heavily.

"Soup of the Day, Egg Salad. Steamed Suet Pudding."

"What else is there?"

"There is nothing else."

"That's all?"

"That's all."

"Christ."

The waitress looked at him as though he was guilty of some heinous social indiscretion.

"What's the Soup of the Day?"

"There's no name to it."

Krumnagel, in his own parlance, was beginning to blow his cool.

"It's got to be made of something, lady. All soup's made of something. It's not just hot water. It just has to have a goddam flavor."

"I haven't seen the soup yet, if you don't mind."

"Christ, there's only three items on the goddam menu. If you work here, it's not too much to expect that you'd know a tidbit or two about whatall's going on in the kitchen. Egg Salad. O.K., that I can guess. Salad with an egg in it, right? Steamed Suet Pudding. I don't eat dessert, so I don't give a . . . I don't care, see. That leaves the soup. Could you find out about it? Is that too much to ask?"

"Whatever flavor it is," the waitress replied icily, "it's the only soup we have, so it won't matter what flavor it is, it's the one you're going to get. As for your not taking sweets, you'll still have to pay for it. It's included in the menu, and we're bound to serve it whether you want it or not. Now, d'you still want to know what the soup is, or shall I serve it?"

Krumnagel sat again.

"Just bring me a beer," he said.

"We don't have a license. If it's beer you want you'll have to go to the Bay Horse and Prince's Head."

"That does it," said Krumnagel, rising again.

"But it doesn't open until five thirty."

"You mean I can't get a goddam . . . ?"

The waitress nodded triumphantly.

Krumnagel sat again, humiliated, near to tears of frustration.

"Bring the soup will you, and make it hot."

"You want it hot, do you?" the waitress replied, noting the request and miraculously succeeding in making it sound unreasonable.

Two old ladies entered, and began whispering in conspiratorial tones at another table. They were followed by a gaunt couple — a tall bald man who had cut himself shaving, accompanied by a large woman. They did not exchange a word throughout their meal. A father and son also came in, both of them elderly, and once again not a word could be heard except a high-pitched senile wheeze from the father and the deep drone of the son's voice. If it had not been for the slurps of soup and the tinkle of cutlery, Krumnagel felt he might as well have been in church.

The soup failed to reveal the secret of its ingredients. It was even impossible to guess what had been printed on the can. It was hot and brown and opaque. The egg salad was merely the two halves of a hard-boiled egg with a bluish ferrous tinge to it, lying in state on some leaves of lettuce turning autumnal gold at the edges. A couple of slices of dry cucumber and a few slivers of beet and a Spartan peppering of watercress completed this temptation to gluttony. And all around him, the others were eating with the application of Dickensian school-children, investing every movement with indescribable dainti-ness. The very old man had forced his napkin into his shirt collar, and was shoveling the lettuce leaves into his mouth with an agued hand. Occasionally a leaf would fall onto the table-cloth or onto his trousers, and the son would replace it on his father's plate with the elegance and speed of a conjurer. The large lady divided each half of her egg into at least eight seg-ments before hazarding the passage to her mouth, which hardly opened at all, but was merely discreetly left ajar to re-ceive the tiny morsels, which she then masticated politely for a seeming eternity, only to swallow them with evident pain or displeasure. The tall man was tidy to a fault, arranging his meal so that every item represented on his plate was equally represented in each mouthful. Occasionally, after egg, lettuce, beet, and cucumber were already present on his fork, he spent several tense minutes chasing a single blade of watercress around his plate.

Krumnagel watched all this noiseless industry with growing alarm. The silence was unnerving. He could not see the old ladies without turning in his seat, so he turned around and stared at them.

They stared back indulgently, seeming to pity him for being a foreigner to the mysteries attached to English rural gastron-omy. They smiled from somewhere beyond the quietness, and the ticking clock sounded like the beating of a heart. Krumna-gel felt deprived of breath.

"Don't you people have a radio or something . . . some-thing?"

He heard his own voice and was surprised to hear how loud it was. He seemed to have lost all sense of volume. The thin man arrested his chewing, and looked up like an animal alerted to danger. Then he smiled abruptly, as though humoring a lu-natic.

"Yes, I have a radio. At home," he said in a high and over-modulated staccato.

"Don't it get on your nerves, you people? This creepy silence?"

The old man wheezed a question. His son murmured some kind of reassurance while picking a couple of pieces of lettuce off the floor. The old ladies smiled sadly, a couple of super-annuated priestesses of this weird rite. The tall lady twisted her minute mouth into a kind of scar of social conscience, and stared at the lace curtains with a mystic intensity. The clock hissed with a sudden flatulence, and hesitantly released two distant cathedral chimes. Krumnagel called for the check. He asked whether a pound covered it. Without confirming that it covered it, the waitress told him it was fifty-seven new pence. He left the pound. The waitress took away his untouched suet, waited in the kitchen for a count of three, and then served it to the old man.

Krumnagel walked over to the cinema, hoping to find something familiar to look at.

His luck was out. As his eyes became accustomed to the dark, he saw the Queen inspecting some sort of guard of honor, accompanied by several men who appeared to be blinded by a profusion of white feathers which blew into their faces. The Queen was smiling doggedly, while the officers were entirely expressionless owing to the play of the feathers. Some poorly dressed but cozy ladies curtsied as the Queen spoke to them, and a lot of children waved flags as if they had been rehearsed.

"Holy mackerel," Krumnagel said aloud. Hearing his own voice was like rediscovering an old friend. And it didn't offend anyone, since he was virtually alone.

A member of the royal family whose name Krumnagel didn't catch galloped hither and thither on a polo pony, and the prime minister made a portentous statement about the balance of payments in the flash-laden darkness of a large hotel. This was evidently a selection of the hottest and latest news available to Britain at that moment.

The house lights went up after the news, and while music of mid-thirtyish rhythm played, local advertisements flashed on the screen, the lighter ones carrying large thumbmarks, and a girl dressed as a hussar passed through the empty house with a tray of boiled sweets, mascara oozing out of her dead eyes. Krumnagel looked at her and smiled, but she did not seem to have the energy to respond. He looked at her figure, which was gross. One of her net stockings was torn. Women. He sighed, and then whistled the tunes with a sense of relative well-being. He even remembered some of the lyrics of the songs, and intoned them while beating a rhythm with his foot. It was innocuous enough as far as pleasures go, but it gave him a warm feeling of recognition, and for that he was grateful.

The film was a British one, permissive and doggedly insular, set in the outskirts of Darlington, based on a best seller by a young man of the region. The critics recognized authenticity when they saw it, even though on the whole they had very little experience of the outskirts of Darlington. They had been, as a result, ecstatic in their praise of the film's brilliant observation, although naturally, observation of such brilliance was wasted on Krumnagel, for whom the actors might as well have been talking in Swahili.

Every now and then, when it was said slowly enough, he did manage momentarily to crack the film's code. For instance, when the young girl with the cheap foulard over her head cringed against the wall of a council house and said:

"I can't make loov tonight loov, I've got my period." Krumnagel understood, and even announced to the house, "I got no time for this shit."

Sex he could understand and approve, but life was anathema to him. "What's that got to do with friggin' entertainment?" That a girl should be in love was the stuff of which movies are made, but that the camera should capture her moments of embarrassment, why that was fit for the commercials, where it was tackled with taste and tact at least. As for the young man, there was an explicit scene of him in a government clinic for venereal disease. Since the doctor was played by a well-known regional comic, the scene made the four or five other occupants of the cinema rock with laughter.

"Makes you want to throw up," Krumnagel called out into the darkness. The young man's father spoke to him severely, and threatened to thrash the living daylights out of him if he ever caught gonorrhea again — at least so Krumnagel gathered. In the very next scene, the self-righteous father of a moment ago was rolling about in a brass bedstead with a huge woman whose vast nakedness smothered the screen with the heaving masses of palpitating flesh.

"Let's have your tits then, Mabel," the father seemed to say.

"Take 'em, if you can find 'em."

Again the house, what there was of it, roared.

The camera roved momentarily over a row of dingy dwellings, stopping at a lighted window. Inside, the young man's mother, who had been established as a pious, Bible-clutching fanatic, lay under the weight of a hairy Italian worker, her lips parted in passion. All this to indicate that promiscuity breeds promiscuity in this world. Back to square one. Broken homes. This was strictly a movie for the likes of Arnie. A load of crap.

As Krumnagel left the cinema, he announced to the few people studying the stills in the entrance, "You got to be sick to go for a picture like that. Just a load of crap. Filth. Filth."

To his amazement, this statement of his was enough to decide those who were still undecided. They lined up at the box office and bought their tickets.

"What's the matter with this friggin' country?" he asked. They regarded him with complicity, meeting his outraged stare with guilty and suggestive smiles. He went his way, deeply shaken in his equilibrium by the events of the day.

The Bay Horse and Prince's Head was not yet open. Krumnagel rattled the door, and tried to see through the glazed window, shading his eyes. It was growing prematurely dark. There was no sign of life, and it was cold. He walked up and down the cheerless sidewalk, eventually deciding to pace more briskly as the blue damp of the evening penetrated his marrow, and a haze lay on the outlying fields like a blanket. The acrid smell of manure rose from the puddles and bit into his nostrils. It was his idea of hell. The mud clung to his shoes, and the crawling traffic splashed him gently. He entered a field and relieved himself. It had been an awful day, a day towards which the entire police department, in its infinite duplicity, had contributed, and the governor's smiling face with its pluperfect teeth appeared like a Cheshire cat in the sky of Krumnagel's imagination, impervious to the ghastliness of the terra incognita which stretched away into the gloom from the isolated highland of God's own country. Obsessed with his unexpected loneliness, Krumnagel began to sing "America, the Beautiful," stopping suddenly when he discovered that the dwindling stream of urine was cascading convulsively onto his shoes. He shouted aloud in sheer exasperation, and tried to dry his shoes on the back of his trouser legs, succeeding in streaking them with mud at the same time. He reached out for his pack of mentholated cigarettes, and found he had run out. He threw away the empty pack as though he were throwing a stone to bounce on the water. To make matters worse, he found several boxes of matches in his pockets.

It was now dark. The Bay Horse and Prince's Head, now lit up from inside, looked like a Christmas card. He entered and found four old men and an old woman in the bar. They gave the impression of having been there a long time, even though the pub could only have been open for a couple of minutes. Three of the old men were sitting on a bench, and looked at the newcomer with that melancholy which can easily be taken for hostility in the aged. The old lady had a masculine tawdriness to her, a tarnished look, the battered, toothless, munching look

[76]

of one who has outlived her world and whose vice, black beer, is, alas, no longer considered evil. The other man leaned on the bar, and there was something about his stance which proclaimed his isolation. He wore his cap at a jaunty angle, whereas the others had placed their headgear squarely on their heads as symbols of conformity, of balance, therefore of decency. The man at the bar also wore a tartan muffler, both ends of which fell to the floor. His face, with a hint of madness to it, was red with past violence, his eyes suffused with intolerance, and his lips, stained with nicotine, twitched occasionally as some savage thought staggered through his consciousness. A drop on the end of his nose shuddered as he sought the strength to drag it back into the shelter of his nostril.

"Hi," said Krumnagel as he entered. The three old men looked at him in surprise, while the old lady munched away at nothing. Only the man at the bar started at the sudden intrusion, without, for the moment, committing himself to words.

"Got a beer?" Krumnagel asked the barmaid.

The barmaid's answer was entirely incomprehensible to the uninitiated.

"What's that?"

The barmaid repeated with painful slowness what she had said previously, without managing to cast any new light on its meaning.

"Look, all I want is a cold beer . . . ice-cold beer."

Krumnagel managed to glean from the reply that there was no ice, that the fridge was out of order.

"Christ — no ice?"

"You a Yank?" asked the Scotsman, blinking with malice.

"I'm an American if that's what you mean."

"I thought so . . . coming in here with your blustering ways . . . marvelous I call it."

The three old men began to cackle.

"That's right, give it 'im, Jock," one of them called.

Krumnagel felt for some unaccountable reason that he had

fallen into a trap, and looked around measuring his opponents.

"Never mind him," said the most conciliatory of the old men. "It's only old Jock."

"Only old Jock," spat the Scotsman, "the voice of common sense in the corrupt world of bourgeois values, and that's all the recognition it desairves, only old Jock . . . well, let me tell you something, old Jock may not be a major prophet like Vladmir Ilitch Lennan, but he's got a tidy enough ration of the good word to be able to tell Mister Fooking Edward Briggs that the days of his corrupt society are numbered, and what is more you dinna hae to be a mathematical fooking genius to be able to count on the fingers of one hand how much longer the capitalist-royalist conspiracy has life in it before the relentless tide of popular reprobation and disdain overwhelms it."

The old lady glanced up malevolently from under her battered trilby.

"Kindly moderate your language, Jock, there's a lady present." And she winked.

"The whore of Babylon could na' hold a candle to you, Lily, when it comes to ladyship."

The old woman cackled with pleasure.

"What in the hell are you all talking about?" asked Krumnagel, taking delivery of his warm beer. "And who's Edward Briggs?"

"I am," said one of the old men. He winked too. It seemed to be a malady of these parts.

"Glad to know you. I'm Bartram C. Krumnagel."

"Oh."

"Foreign sounding name if you ask me," Lily grumbled.

"Every name's foreign sounding to you, you chip of old Edwardian Imperial block, you —" cried Jock.

"That's me," said Lily, and winked.

"Ain't you going to buy me a beer, darling?" she asked Krumnagel.

[78]

"Sure. Sure. Hey." He attracted the attention of the barmaid. "Let's have some service here, lady. This round's on me."

He was blossoming as an ambassador among these strange people. He needed their friendship.

"Not for me, Agnes, if you dinna mind."

Jock's talk was of variable Scotchness. Like many people under the influence of their own folklore, he made appeal to blarney when indulging in dialogue likely to shock.

"What's the matter with you. Don't want a drink?" Krumnagel asked.

"I hae my principles," Jock replied darkly.

"Principles?"

"I'll no take drink with a representative of the exploiters of the toiling masses."

Krumnagel smiled grimly, and nodded.

"Don't mind him. It's only old Jock," he echoed.

The three old men expressed approval, and winked. Krumnagel played for time. He placed his beer to his lips, and almost vomited.

"What the hell's this, warm piss?" he roared.

The old woman almost died with mirth, and the three old men gazed at him with twinkling amusement and whimsicality. Few things tickle the English fancy more than to be misunderstood in an abrupt and picturesque way. If most tastes are acquired, the English have gone to great pains to acquire those not shared by any other people. Consequently their joy is heightened by the spectacle of those who make the attempt to follow them into their prejudices, and fail. In such cases, all eyes are focused on the banana skin.

"For once I'll agree with you," said Jock, the inveterate chatterbox. "The Sassenachs like to torture their palates with tepid dishwater and pretend it's nectar just because no one else wants it. I'll hae a malt whiskey, but I'll pay for it myself."

"It's your loss," said Krumnagel, who was not offended because commercial stupidity was involved.

Jock was evidently annoyed by Krumnagel's sangfroid. It was no fun baiting a placid bull. He searched his resources for a rag red enough to spur this alien hulk out of his complacent lethargy.

"Tell you what," Krumnagel said suddenly. "I'll join you in a whiskey. Lady! A double Scotch." Krumnagel looked at Jock as though he'd made an elegant concession. Jock studied his quarry.

"Cheers."

"Here's mud in your eye."

They drank, and the others hailed their host in their luke-warm beer.

"That's better," declared Krumnagel. "I'm not one for the hard liquor, but that beer's straight out of the washing machine — one glass of that is enough to pollute Niagara."

There was chuckling and winking.

"What d'you do for a living then, mister?" Jock asked.

"Call me Bart."

"Bart?"

"Bart. I'm a policeman."

"Oh —" It was a long Oh, as though this intelligence fitted into some slot in a secret pattern.

"What does that mean?"

"You control the traffic of those chrome-plated monsters, do you? Those huge cars purple-haired widows take shopping with them?"

"I control the men who control them," replied Krumnagel, sure of himself. "I'm chief of police."

"Chief of police?" Jock's eyebrows vanished momentarily into his hairline. "Well, we've really landed a big fish here, haven't we? A big fish in those waters filled with the sharks of Wall Street and black-faced tiddlers there for the eating."

Krumnagel looked up at Jock with interest. The inflated dia-logue, the forced imagery of the quarrelsome old fellow had something engaging about them. Every man, at a certain age,

[80]

has a right to his share of lunacy, and if there was a mental road, he'd see Jock safely across it.

"And what did you do for a living, old-timer?" he asked.

"What did I do? What *did* I do?" Jock cried incredulous. What *do* I do, man?"

"Still active at your age — why that's wonderful. Put it there."

Jock refused the gesture of solidarity.

"I'm shop steward of the Electrical Trade Union, the E.T.U. of fabled memory and glorious achievement, local 916, at the Parker McKinnon Iron Works doon the road, makers of Invincible brand of domestic boilers and cooking ranges."

"Is that right?"

Krumnagel caught a turbulence of more or less discreet negative gestures from the three old men.

"He *was* that," one of them ventured.

"And still is, Muster Bristow, the agreement was never rescinded, and owing to this, it still stands and is entirely operative according to rules, regulations and bylaws." Anticipating further argument, he raised his voice to even further stridency. "I've had a rewling from the ministry itself. April of the ninth instant. Operative heretofore and from then onwards till fairther notice!"

"Parker McKinnon don't exist no more," Mr. Bristow proffered mildly.

Jock shut his eyes in order to pontificate. He sang his words like a psalm.

"Parker McKinnon are in the course of reorganization and what you might call consolidation. I'll admit it. I'm the fairst to admit it. Fair's fair. There's a deal of mergers going on, and it's only reasonable that a fairm like Parker McKinnon should come in for its share of it. We're going in with Intex."

"That's an American corporation," said Krumnagel.

"It is no'."

"It is too."

"It is no'."

"Listen, International and Texas. Make sense to you?"

"International Television Exchanges Company Limited."

"Jesus Christ, man, it's one of our giants. They've got head-quarters all over the goddam place. Delaware. Delaware, that's it. Dover, Delaware, for tax reasons. It's a gimmick, see. They make the Starsparkle surface-to-surface rocket, the Spraychief submarine missile and the Totem anti-anti-ballistics ballistic missile and one hell of a lot of other hardware. It's a real big one, Intex."

"We canna be talking of the same Intex," said Jock huffily.

"Take it from me, there's only one Intex, and that's the U.S. Intex. International and Texas. Stands to reason, don't it?"

"International Television Exchanges Company Limited . . . of Aberdeen."

It was curious that grown men should excite themselves over the origins of a company that neither had ever served, and for which neither had any feelings, deep or shallow. They had come close to insult undisturbed, but suddenly the feathers began to ruffle for reasons which lie obscured in the darkness of human motivation. Krumnagel was really angry about the effort to denigrate an American industrial mammoth, while Jock burned with sullen fires because in his heart he suspected he was wrong, but didn't see what business that was to anybody but himself. They both drank another whiskey to help them calm down.

Suddenly Jock asked to be excused, and left the bar.

"Who is that old punk?" Krumnagel asked.

"Oh, he don't know 'is arse from 'is elbow," said Mr. Briggs.

"I'd not go as far as that," added the other old man, whose name was Bailey. Like all these rural sages, he was a great one for assessments, evaluations, everything in its place.

"I'd go a bit further, an' all," suggested Bristow.

"No, no I'd not go as far, I wouldn't," insisted Bailey.

"I still say, 'e don't know 'is arse from 'is elbow," said Briggs.

"All events, he was quite a big shot, you know, in the early days of the trades union movement, up on Clydeside, in the shipbuilding industry," Bailey explained.

"I find that 'ard to credit," muttered Bristow.

"No, 'e was. Friend of Will Gallagher and all that crowd. Ernie Bevin. The soup kitchen days. The 'unger marchers. The International. All that. Then he come south with Parker Mc-Kinnon, but they've been out of business for nearly a year, see. I think they keep 'im on as a kind of night watchman at the empty works. For old times' sake, I s'pose."

"Fine night watchman he is. Spends all 'is wakin' hours in 'ere," cackled the woman. "Still, 'e's got a fund of spicy stories, I'll give him that. Lovely dirty mind. Must 'ave been quite a stud in 'is day."

"I don't think he never 'ad much time for that, do you, Bert?" asked Briggs jovially.

"No, I don't. 'Course, he never married, so he must 'ave 'ad *some* time for it."

There was laughter.

"He looks kind of shabby for a union leader," Krumnagel suggested.

"Shabby? I wouldn't call 'im shabby, really," said Bailey.

"No, I think he's more Scottish than anything, really."

"He's shabby, all right," insisted Bristow.

"Shabby Scottish," Briggs compromised, "but then, you'd hardly expect a pin-stripe suit from a Communist."

"Communist?" Krumnagel asked in a hushed voice.

"Oh, yes," said Briggs, "he once ran for Parliament as a Communist candidate . . . Leith, I believe it was . . . lost 'is deposit."

Just then Jock reappeared, tripping slightly on his muffler, and ordered another whiskey.

"Make that two," Krumnagel growled, and saw Jock in a new light. He saw Intex, International and Texas, in all its infinite mercy and charity, a trusting, gentle giant, which gave stock bonuses to its better workers and promoted blacks to positions of responsibility if not of decision, a great force for good in the world, as blind as justice herself, and taking to its broad and open bosom a card-carrying member of the Communist conspiracy. It was too bad. It had to be stopped. And thank God, he was there to stop it.

"They tell me you're a Communist?" he asked, subtly.

"I am, and prood of it."

"Proud of it, huh? Tell me. What makes a guy be a Communist?"

There were groans from the old men. "Oo-er, now 'e's off."

Jock looked at them with disdain, while Krumnagel made a gesture demanding silence. He wished to handle this investigation his own way.

"A sense of history," Jock said magnificently. "A sense of social injustice, of social inequality. A desire to put things to rights."

"If every man put himself to rights, wouldn't that put things to rights?" Krumnagel asked.

"By God, you're a Communist without knowing it," cried Jock in mock surprise.

"I've never been a Communist. Never will be."

Jock frowned at such terseness from a slave in defiant defense of his servility. His mouth curved into a satanic smile of pity, while one eyelid billowed down over one eye.

"How sure you are o' yoursel'!" he said. "The captive showing off his shackles as though they were jewelry of the highest order."

"What the hell you talking about?"

"You know what you are, Muster Policeman? Clay. Clay. The stuff which the ruling classes mold at random into all the shapes human degradation has to offer. When the bugle sounds, you're the first to go running off to war, waving your boater in the air. To Berlin, to Paris, to New York, to the arsehole of the airth! When one of your politicians calls for sacrifices, you're that fairst of the donors, be it blood, money, or life itself. When the same scrofulous politician lifts a baby to his lips, he's got your vote there and then, hasn't he? And when he puts on a cowboy hat and strums a tune with one finger on his banjo, you regard him as a man o' the people, don't you? Brings a tear of patriotism to your eye. You're the ideal subject for the hypnotist. A man with a dog collar only has to come in here for you to watch your tongue, and start a sickly smile going, and when a voice, never mind which voice, says, "Let us pray," your knees hit the deck just a split second before anyone else's, don't they?"

"What are you trying to say?" Krumnagel asked, determined to keep serenity up his sleeve as his secret weapon. "Are you trying to say I'm not my own master?" He paused, and ordered another round of drinks, just to show cool. By now nobody cared who paid for what. "Ever heard of democracy?" he asked at length.

"Oh, we're going to get that old chestnut, are we?" cried Jock.

"Are you trying to tell me —"

"Why the devil d'you make out I'm trying to tell you anything?" Jock roared, suddenly out of sorts. "Either I succeed in telling you something or I don't. If I don't, it's because you're too fooking stupid to understand. If I do, it's because by some miracle, you do understand. I'm not *trying* to tell you anything, mon. I'm *telling* you."

Krumnagel waited for the outburst to end with his eyes shut, and his lips puckered. When it was over, he opened his eyes.

"Are you trying to tell me that democracy is — what was it — an old chestnut?"

"I'm telling you that democracy is an old chestnut."

"Cheers," said Mr. Briggs.

"Cheers," they echoed.

"Here's mud in your eye," said Jock, on his own, when they had all finished their demonstration of servility to tradition.

"Do you vote?" Krumnagel asked.

"What are you up to noo? Are you going to start a lot of drivel going about the American War of Independence and how you invented democracy before Socrates and the Greeks? Listen, you dunderhead. I stood for Parliament. D'you know what Parliament is? It's the wicked uncle of Congress. And it's about as useless. Vote? You make it a kind of moral obligation over there, don't you? You won't admit that an abstention is an expression of opinion same as any other. No. If you've got a couple of lousy candidates, you're expected to vote for the one who seems to you the least lousy. Well, that, to me, is a betrayal of democracy! No, I've never voted. Never. Why? I've never had a Communist candidate to vote for, that's why. The fact that Labour purports to be halfway there doesn't bamboozle me — I'd be more likely to support the Tories. I prefer an undisguised bandit to a disguised one. There's something mildly honest about a wolf in wolf's clothing."

"You mean you wouldn't vote if you didn't have a *Communist* to vote for?" laughed Krumnagel, shaking his head hugely. "Jesus Christ, you won't use the advantages of democracy unless you can vote for a guy who's sworn to destroy those advantages. There's logic for you. Commie logic."

"Well of course it's logical," cried Jock. "You people use democracy in order to limit the choice of the nation to those within the status quo —"

"The what?"

"Status quo. Things as they are. Capitalists. Middle class. Last and very much least, the Workers. Could a man like me stand for election in the United States?"

" 'Course you could."

"Could I win an election?"

"You didn't succeed here, did you?"

"Precisely. It's the same rotten system as yours. Here's where you got it from. Now, in the Soviet Union —"

[86]

"In the Soviet Union they don't have elections."

"They most sairtanly du!"

"They don't either. They don't have parties."

"We hae parties, do we? And what's the difference between the confounded parties? None what so fooking ever! The Communist Manifesto is the only alternative to the great complicity of the capitalist parties. Why do you suppose when the '14-'18 war was over — I beg pardon, '17-'18 war for you — the moment the great conflagration was over, with its monumental carnage, the Powers still found it within themselves to send armies to invade the Soviet Union? They knew the real danger in the long run was not some rival imperialism but the new conception of man's place in society as voiced by the youthful voice of international socialism. British troops, my friend, intervened in Murmansk, French troops, and — am I leaving anyone out? Yes, indeed I am. United States troops, sir. United States interventionist troops invaded the Soviet Union in order to try and nip the Red Menace in the bud. They failed!"

Krumnagel felt a rush of blood to his head.

"Let me say this," he said, his voice, choking with emotion. "First of all, the United States never invaded the Soviet Union, and you know it. Secondly the United States has never lost a war. Never, never."

"The United States never invaded the Soviet Union?" cried Jock. "What d'you call a landing on foreign soil effected by the troops of another nation? Presumably you only call it an invasion if it succeeds? Is that what I am to understand? I stand corrected in that case, Muster Policeman. Your invasion failed, so you tactfully draw a veil over it in the history books, so that kids can continue to be fed the fiction that the great United States has never lost a war."

"That's a dirty lie!" cried Krumnagel.

"Temper, temper," muttered Mr. Bailey.

Magnanimously, Jock ordered another round of drinks.

In the charged silence, they all stared at the floor with the exception of Jock, who stared at the ceiling. The old woman licked her lips in search of the last residue of bitter foam.

"O.K., O.K.," said Krumnagel, in a more conciliatory tone, "let's rule history off limits, shall we. Let's talk about now."

"Noo's a part of history — that is, soon will be."

"O.K., so what about the labor camps in Russia? What about the prosecution of the Jews —"

"You mean pairsecution, I take it —"

"Never mind what I focking mean," declared Krumnagel stoutly. "Are you denying it exists? And the arming of the Arabs. How about that? And the writers can't write the way they want. And the secret police buggin' hotel rooms and private apartments? And wild dogs at the border with barbed wire — I seen them on the newsreels. Are you going to deny all o' that?"

Jock shut his eyes.

"There's nowhere in the world where what you might call pairfection exists," he said. "I'm sure that the Soviet Union has its share of potential criminals, low characters, and subvairsive elements. All I am claiming is that they control them better. That's why labor camps exist, my friend. In your country, these same elements are either in prison, or else lounging round the streets waiting to commit a felony which will land them in prison. As for writers you claim cann' write the way they want —"

"Cheers," said Mr. Bristow.

"Cheers," they echoed.

"Here's mud in your eye," Jock said. "As for the writers — let me ask you a question — what writer in the world writes exactly what he wants? He writes to sell, doesn't he? Just as a woman makes hairself up to look attractive — to others, not merely to hairself, to others — and once a writer does na' write for a capitalist market, he fails — and if he fails, he starves. If a Communist writer does na' write to please a Communist market, he

[88]

likeways fails, but no one starves. We don't carry freedom that far, you see."

Jock's irony was wasted on Krumnagel, who noted the fluency of his opponent's arguments with increasing irritation, but without being able to get his teeth into any clearly understandable phrase in order to refute it.

"You mentioned the police bugging hotel rooms and private apartments. Well, I saw a film about the F.B.I. doing just that. Finally, I believe you uttered some stuff about the Soviet Union arming the Arabs. What on earth do you know about them?"

"Plenty," said Krumnagel, "and no amount of your twisting the facts is going to help you there. The Jews got a right to a National Home, right? Well, for many centuries, see, they was prevented from having it. Six million of them were killed in concentration camps. That's all they want, a National Home, and the United States is right in there to see they get it."

"Is that all?"

"Isn't that enough?"

"No. What has all this got to do with the Arabs? Did the Arabs kill six million people in concentration camps?"

"You know better'n that, don't you? It was the Krauts. The Germans."

"So what's wrong with the Soviet Union arming the Arabs? Aren't you arming the Israelis?"

Krumnagel sighed and grimaced with irritation. He ordered another round of drinks, as he scratched his head.

"Are you a Jew hater?" he asked at length.

"How can a Communist be a Jew hater?" laughed Jock. "Even I don't pretend Marx's real name was McKinnon. According to the religious authorities, the Jews were chosen by God. That's all right by me. But isn't that enough? Do they have to choose themselves as well? Or are they merely as doubtful of God's choice as I am?"

"You're an atheist?" accused Krumnagel.

[89]

"Of course I am."

The gall of the man, to have no shame admitting it.

"I'll go further, and say that the choosing of the Jews was the first example of racism in history."

Krumnagel blinked a bit. He could see two Jocks, very close to one another admittedly, but there they both were, hideously accurate in their unison.

"That's a load of shit!"

"You are certainly producing the most incontrovairtible arguments in response to mine."

Krumnagel attempted a huge and generous laugh, recognizing a hint of something intended to be amusing even through the haze which suddenly enveloped him. He tried to rise, but fell onto the old woman, causing her to spill some of her Guinness. The old woman laughed generously. She knew her way around drunkenness.

"Cheers," said Mr. Bailey.

"Here's mud on your prick," stammered Krumnagel, and then was seized with a paroxysm of laughter at his own undiminished capacity for quick repartee.

"Cheers," said Jock. His bloodshot eyes were none too steady, but he was filled with disdain for the man who could not hold his liquor. He held onto the bar as though it was the rail of a ship in a frisky sea.

"Zionism is a European idea, formulated by European Jewry in their sairch for lost dignity at the end of the last century. And when — listen to me, damn you — I'm nae imparting this knowledge for ma ain pleasure — I know it all, I know it all — and where does a sairch for lost dignity lead you? Tae Fascism's door. Take Benito Muscle-ini —"

"You don't know what the hell you're talking about," Krumnagel said softly, dangerously.

"Take Benito Muscle-ini," Jock insisted, spitting a great deal as he took excessive grip of every word and tried to combat his growing inebriation by sheer precision. "Contemplating the tombs upon the Appian Way! Joseph Schickelgroom, ah, is Adolf Hutler —"

"You don't know what the hell you're talking about," Krumnagel repeated.

"How about Cuba?"

Krumnagel sprang to life.

"Leave Cuba out of this!" Jock was on the point of infringing the Monroe Doctrine.

"Ach, you dinna frighten me," Jock yelled suddenly, his pride irked by the bullying conceit of the drunken policeman. "Ye'd do well to read a few pamphlets published by the Society for Friendship with the Soviet —"

"God love me, if you wasn't so small 'n old, I'd sure teach you —"

"Where's yer spirit noo? In the shambles of some napalmed village in Veet Num?"

"Oh Christ, now you done it." Krumnagel shuddered, and then his hatred for the vast incomprehensible overflowed. He tried to advance on Jock, but the variable angle of the floor wouldn't let him move.

"Come here, you motherfockin' gook," he roared.

"Wash your mouth out," ordered the old woman, suddenly revived.

"Come here, God damn you."

"See the great helping hand stretched oot tae the world!" cried Jock in a hail of saliva. "You great gorilla you, farting your platitudes —"

"Gook, gook, gook!" shouted Krumnagel.

Each was anchored to a piece of convenient furniture, unable to advance or retreat, as bellicose and as impotent as ancient warships on a windless day. Jock, suddenly aware again of the drop at the end of his nose, reached into his pocket, presumably for a handkerchief.

Through the haze, Krumnagel saw Jock dig into his pockets, and it must have been sheer instinct, for a revolver fired twice in rapid succession, without even Krumnagel knowing much about it. A second later he looked down at his own hand, and saw his gun there, a wisp of smoke snaking its way out of the barrel. Jock looked in surprise at his arm and his chest. His cap had been blown up to the ceiling and had fallen behind the bar.

"Jesus Christ," muttered Jock, "you're worse than I thought you were," and slid slowly down the bar onto the floor.

The old men staggered to their feet, the old woman kept repeating, "What have you done?" as to a child who should have known better. Krumnagel was the first to fully realize what had happened.

"O.K.," he said. "Someone get the police . . . and a doctor."

Sobered by the incident, he realized that the people were petrified by the revolver, which was still in his hand. He put it back in its armpit holster.

The young policeman appeared after about five minutes. A doctor arrived.

"Right," the young policeman said to Krumnagel. "Did you actually see what happened?"

"Sure, I shot the guy."

The policeman looked at him in disbelief.

"You did, sir?"

The three old men and the old woman confirmed it nervously.

"May I have the weapon, sir?"

"I'd rather keep it," said Krumnagel, producing a document in a cellophane envelope. "See, I'm a policeman myself. Police chief. You'll see all about me there — I talked to you, remember in the village — well, that's me." He pointed to a photograph of himself on his identity card. "This guy —" he pointed at Jock, "was going to pull a gun on me. I shot him in self-defense."

"Self-defense, eh?"

The policeman knelt by Jock.

"Is he alive?" the policeman asked the doctor.

"Yes, but he's pretty bad. I'll have to get an ambulance right away."

"There's no gun in his pocket, sir," the policeman said after a moment. "Only a handkerchief."

"A handkerchief," Krumnagel echoed, a little rattled for the first time. "Try the other pocket."

"A key and a box of matches."

The policeman rose to his feet, and brushed his knees.

"I'd better have that gun, sir."

"Do I get it back? I'll sign anything you want. Like I'll say it's me shot the guy in self-defense. It was I called you, understand. I —"

"Have you a license for that gun, sir?"

"Sure I do, I'm chief of police —"

"An English license, sir?"

"Shit no, what do I want with an English license —"

"In that case I'd better have that gun, sir. It'll be better in the long run. It's illegal, you see, sir."

"How can it be illegal —"

"We don't carry guns, sir."

"Don't . . ."

Krumnagel dissolved into laughter. It could have been hysterical, even ironic. All that was sure about it was that it was laughter, and that it came as a relief. He handed over the gun, making sure that the safety catch was on.

"And now, sir, if you will come with me."

"After you."

"I feel I ought to warn you that anything you say will be taken down, and may be used in evidence."

"*Evidence?*"

Krumnagel swayed slightly, and frowned like a victim of treachery. What the hell . . . ?

6

Sir Neville Nym was a bachelor, and far too brilliant for his job, probably a little too brilliant for any job. As director of public prosecutions at the Home Office, he was in permanent contact with the seamier side of human nature, and managed to steer a central course between the double temptations of excessive callousness and excessive harshness with a kind of sardonic mellowness. He rose early and breakfasted in his dusty misanthropic chambers in Victoria. The breakfast was furnished by his housekeeper, Mrs. Shakespeare. He wasn't in the habit of speaking a great deal during it, because he read the paper, did the *Guardian* crossword puzzle in the time it took to run his bath, and then spoke to her kindly and complicatedly for five minutes about various topics before leaving on foot for the Home Office. Today, however, he had no sooner opened the paper than he said, "Oh, dear God."

Mrs. Shakespeare sensed his exceptional need to communicate. "Anything I can do, sir?" she asked.

He frowned, smiling at the same time.

"You know, Mrs. Shakespeare, the world has become so small that different standards and different concepts are forced into good neighborliness when they have absolutely nothing in common. There are so many anomalies these days that the quantity of conceivable disasters has increased to a frightening extent. I am haunted by any amount of eventualities, and open my paper every morning with a gathering sense of foreboding. Now, one of my recurring fears has actually occurred. Now, today."

"I'm sorry about that, Sir Neville, I'm sure."

"Thank you, Mrs. Shakespeare. I suppose you'd like to know what it is."

"I would, yes, if it's all the same to you."

"An American policeman has opened fire in a Hertfordshire public house and has wounded a local Scottish trades union leader."

"Ah, well, I wouldn't put it past them — the Americans I mean. You've seen the films, haven't you, Sir Neville?"

"I haven't been since Harold Lloyd was on top of his form, and in those days the so-called 'cop' was a figure of fun, of amusement, of good-natured ridicule."

"All that's changed now," grumbled Mrs. Shakespeare. "I know, I got to take my youngest from time to time. It's all a big bloodbath these days, with the fuzz — that's what they call them now, not cops no more."

"Fuzz?" The name made Sir Neville wince.

"Fuzz, yes. With the fuzz shooting their way out of trouble."

"There, Mrs. Shakespeare, you have put your finger on the very nub of the problem."

[95]

"I have?" Mrs. Shakespeare was a little abashed at her achievement.

"Yes indeed. We can't change the American way of life. That would be the greatest presumption, even were such a thing possible. They evidently attribute a quality of gaiety and adventure to death which is their absolute right, and perhaps it is a failure in us that we can see nothing in it but a rather tasteless bore or, at other times, a distinct relief. The very same man who shoots his way out of trouble in America could easily be the one who shoots his way into trouble over here. And this is the exact description of the case we have on our hands, I feel. Understand me, I base my criticism of his behavior on no very high moral level. A Scottish trades union official in the heart of rural Hertfordshire already sounds so improbable that, for all I know, he may have deserved death, even at the hands of some imported fuzz. Be that as it may, my worries are of a purely technical nature — as are my recurring nightmares. Here we have a case which no English judge, no English advocate, no English jury and no English public is qualified to judge." He paused. "Ask me why, Mrs. Shakespeare."

"Why, Sir Neville?"

"Because none of us know what it is to be an American fuzz in an American city. Try and translate into English terms the motivations which lead a man like that to use his gun, and you will find it won't make sense. English liquid has a much higher boiling point than its American counterpart. This is going to be one of those desperately unfortunate cases where an error of judgment is inevitable."

"Inevitable, sir? Surely not. In England?"

"If I were reduced to shooting a man in Des Moines, Mrs. Shakespeare, I should hate to be judged by American standards — or worse, by American standards adapted out of sheer goodwill to accommodate the spirit of David Copperfield and Mrs. Miniver."

"I see, yes sir," Mrs. Shakespeare muttered, in a grave reverie. She didn't understand a great deal of what Sir Neville said, and that was why he said it. For him, there was a wonderful feeling of liberation in being able to warm his mental machinery early in the morning before a witness who was incapable of any initiative that would complicate the issue.

"And now I am going to take my bath, Mrs. Shakespeare."

"You haven't finished your egg, Sir Neville!"

Sir Neville vanished into the bathroom without making any excuse for not eating the egg.

Later, in the office, he received Bill Stockard, his assistant, and a high-ranking officer from Scotland Yard, Chief Detective-Inspector Pewtrey. They sat drinking midmorning tea.

"It's not as though he were just a rank-and-file policeman," Pewtrey said, "he's chief of police of a city of nearly a million people."

"I didn't realize that." Sir Neville stirred his tea thoughtfully. "Gracious, that makes the whole thing much worse, doesn't it?"

"Does it?"

"Well, it makes it more difficult for us to judge."

Stockard smiled slightly. He knew the subject of his chief's introspections.

"Oh, my Lord," Pewtrey remarked, lighting his pipe, "if we stop to think what's easy, what's difficult and what's impossible to judge, we'd all be nervous wrecks long ago. I mean, what about these odd tribal cases we've been getting — ritual murders and cannibalism in Notting Hill Gate? Scores being settled in Berkhampsted for a feud begun five hundred years ago in northern Nigeria? D'you think Lord Justice Beckwith or Mrs. Justice McQuiston were capable of meting out justice in those cases? What? We really needed a witch doctor in full war fungus to cut the culprit's balls off and no questions asked."

"Well I suppose there'd have to be an appeal later," Sir Neville added with a wry smile. Pewtrey laughed.

The office intercom buzzed. Stockard flicked the switch.

"A gentleman from the Foreign Office."

"Oh?" He looked questioningly at Sir Neville, who nodded.

"All right." Stockard flicked the switch back. "What now?" he asked.

"I suppose the Yanks will be threatening to send the Sixth Fleet unless we release their man," Pewtrey joked.

"Not the Sixth Fleet. Not for a police chief. Ronald Reagan perhaps, or Shirley Temple, but not the Sixth Fleet," Stockard said.

The door opened, and a short and very untidy man entered, with a strange apologetic affectation of the head, as though he were playing an imaginary cello and listening to its tone. He plunged and bridled and screwed up his eyes, and simpered. His face, when he left it alone, was very fine and noble, but he seemed embarrassed by his own distinction, and did his best to create an impression of uncouth worthlessness. He introduced himself as Gyles de Montesano. He came from one of England's old Catholic families, and he rolled his r's like a distant roll of drums.

"We've had a communication from the consulate of the United States this morning about the case of Mr. Krumnagel," he said.

"Already? That's quick work," Sir Neville remarked. Montesano smiled the agonizing smile of a burning saint.

"Well, it was an unofficial communication, that's why it was so quick in coming," he said. "But mark you, it is unofficial only in that it has not yet been followed by a more official aide-mémoire, or something of the sort."

"I don't follow," said Pewtrey.

"Well." Montesano screwed himself into a new and derelict shape. "Well, you see, it took the form of a phone call from Mr. Alberts, who is the personal assistant to the consul general, and he made it quite clear that his phone call was not to be treated as something entirely unofficial, since it would doubtless be the precursor of a written communication of some sort. I don't know if I make myself clear —"

"Mm. Perhaps we should be told what the message contained," said Sir Neville with gentle precision. "I presume your purpose in coming here was to tell us about it."

"Quite. Quite." Montesano choked with mirthless laughter.

"The Americans evidently wish to assure us that they expect no special treatment for this man. To quote Mr. Alberts, he should have known better. It's his own fault if he didn't."

"In other words, no pressure," said Pewtrey.

"What's no pressure if it isn't a form of pressure?" asked Sir Neville.

"Ah," said Stockard, wisely.

"That was our first impression too, I must say," admitted Montesano. "It seemed so rapid a communication — and yet, I had the feeling they're genuinely embarrassed by what has happened."

"So they should be," said Pewtrey.

"There's a feeling he's let the side down."

"Only because he's abroad," Sir Neville reflected. "At home he'd probably have got a medal."

"Oh, surely not." Stockard was always doubtful that there was such a great difference between the English and what he liked to call our American cousins.

The phone rang.

Stockard picked it up, and listened.

"I see," he said at length, and replaced the receiver. Sir Neville did not look up.

"The Scotsman's dead, isn't he?"

"Yes."

"That does it," said Pewtrey.

"Yes, I've been waiting for that. I had a feeling we'd have our problem solved for us by the substitution of another one. Now, Mr. de Montesano, all speculations about pressure become academic. I can't ignore any part of what happened now. I can make allowances, but only within the framework of a homicide."

"Naturally. Of course."

"May I ask what you hope to do?" asked Pewtrey.

"I'll go hammer and tongs for manslaughter. It's clearly not murder. There was no premeditation there."

"Why was he carrying a gun?"

"Why do the rest of us carry toothbrushes when away from home overnight? Force of habit."

"D'you think the fellow's as idiotic as that?"

"He's a policeman, remember."

"Mm. One of theirs."

When Krumnagel was informed that Jock had died, he wept unashamedly, to the embarrassment of the police.

"He was just a sweet old guy," he reiterated like a litany. Every now and then he would ask if Jock had any family. When told that there was no family to the police's knowledge, Krumnagel would mutter his thanks to God for that. It was the extent and consistency of his sorrow which disturbed his captors. They treated him more like a distinguished prisoner of war than as an arrested criminal. Considering that the justification for his act was based largely on the claim that this vicious old Communist agitator had insulted the United States, and done everything he could to provoke a normally placid police chief into an act of violence, this sudden solicitude for the victim just because he was dead confused and bewildered the men at the station.

Gradually, as the day passed, Krumnagel began to recover his composure. A visit from Edie boosted his morale, even though she was accompanied by the unloved Major Batt O'Fehy, who chewed gum moistly during the emotional embraces.

"Go in there and tell them, the way you did at your testimonial lunch," Edie said, thumping him on the chest.

"Sure will. I'll look after myself. If only that poor little old . . ." he faltered as his eyes filled with tears at the very thought of Jock.

"He's not the first guy to die and won't be the last," said Edie, who resented the effect this old Scotch corpse was having on her man.

"That's right," reflected O'Fehy, transferring the gum to the other side of his mouth.

"Remember the day you brought me the news about Chet . . . Chet Koslowsky . . . how he was my husband and I could be expected to cry, isn't that right?"

Krumnagel rippled his jaw in a masculine way.

"I know it, Edie. It's just that I didn't sleep too good."

"Sure, I know. Edie knows." She kissed him on the cheek by standing on tiptoe.

"Hey, you don't have a cigarette, do you Batt?"

"Sorry, feller. I got some gum if you want it. I don't smoke no more. Cigarettes and skydiving don't go together."

"I don't care for gum. Not right now."

The atmosphere was like that on the eve of the big fight, except that the characteristics and record of the opponent were absolutely unknown quantities. The hero and his entourage could not even guess what the challenger was like. They could neither mourn nor scoff, neither laugh nor properly cry. Batt O'Fehy added nothing to Krumnagel's sense of security by his eternal sticky munching and his occasional glances at his watch. It should happen to him. Bastard.

The next day there were two developments. First of all, the name of a lawyer was suggested to Krumnagel. Maud Epsom, Q.C. In his own words to Edie on her daily visit, he hit the ceiling.

"What the hell they offering me a dame for? Who ever heard

of a dame attorney anyway? I guess these sons of bitches just don't want me to win this case. The whole focking charge is loaded anyway. I'm friggin' sure that old Commie shit-heel was packing a gun someplace — maybe he slipped it behind the bar — that cop, he was only a young guy, a greenhorn, too young to trust with a gun of his own — he didn't even look back there — it's too late to search the focking joint now — they're all in cahoots anywhichways you look at it — that just about proves it. Shit."

"What the hell they send him a broad for?" flared Edie, who had visions of her Bartram in his cell, the attorney, her hair in wild disarray, held in his gentle brutal mitts for a petting session.

"Miss Epsom is one of the finest lawyers around, I'll say that for her," said the police sergeant. "I've never heard her to take no nonsense from no man. I suppose that's why she's still single," he added as a good-natured afterthought.

Actually the idea of inviting a woman to defend Krumnagel emanated from the brain of Sir Neville. He had received the visit of the personal assistant to the American consul general, Mr. Alberts, brought by Gyles de Montesano, and he had made his fears regarding the case abundantly clear, to the satisfaction of Mr. Alberts — putting forward at the same time the idea of a brilliant female advocate as a method of cunningly redressing the balance in this impossible trial. Talk of gunplay in a mellow contralto voice would somehow even further remove it from reality.

It was Mr. Alberts who now came to pay a visit to Krumnagel to establish a necessary contact, and to convince him that the idea of a female lawyer was a bona fide effort to help him, not a crude maneuver to sap his Samsonlike strength in the trial to come.

Unfortunately, the differences of opinion and predilection which separated the Krumnagels from Mr. Alberts were even greater than those which separated either party from the English, who at least tried to be accommodating. One glance was enough to put both sides on the defensive. Krumnagel was all that irritated and depressed Alberts about his country. As he sat in the small room put at their disposal by the police station, draped over the shaky wooden chair with the grace of an Afghan hound, Alberts studied this malefactor from under his drooping eyelids.

The sheer inefficiency of his grammatical syntax, the inability of his mind to follow a logical train of thought even at a respectful distance, the coarseness of feature and of expression, the sheer loathsome vulgarity of the man, and of his wife, were enough to fill Alberts with a sense of sullen outrage. The thought that this oaf was in a position of some local importance made Alberts reflect yet again that apart from some areas of New England, his United States was still a largely undeveloped country.

"I really think you ought to seriously consider accepting Miss Epsom," said Alberts, with a swishy wobble of the head.

"Listen, are you married?" asked Krumnagel, cruelly.

"I happen to be," replied Alberts, with a weight of unexplained nuance.

"Then you got to know there's things you can't tell your own wife you can tell a total stranger. Keep out of this, Edie," he said to his wife, who hadn't even the intention of opening her mouth.

"Think of the impression a female lawyer would make on the court, especially in a case of manslaughter by gunfire. I happen to know that that is in the forefront of the minds of those in charge of the case."

"They've got to be full of shit to go for that thinking," snarled Krumnagel, while Alberts winced. "And what's their equivalent of the district attorney like?"

"They don't have district attorneys."

"I said equivalent didn't I? I know they don't have D.A.'s, I'm educated."

"I haven't any idea. It's not every day we have a citizen in court, you know, on a felonious charge. I'm no expert on their legal system, or on any legal system, thank God."

"Well, it's got to be a man, right?"

"I imagine so."

"Right. So what chance has my dame in the infighting?"

"Infighting? I can't imagine what you think an English courtroom to be like."

"Our traditions come from here? Right?"

"Yes," Alberts conceded patiently.

"O.K., so the courtroom scene's got to be rough, like it is back home, once we got it from here. There's none of that ladies first horseshit. A lawyer's there to win cases, and if he's any good, he don't care much how he does it. Listen, I spend half my life in court, I know what the fock I'm talking about. And I'll tell you this, mister, a court's no place for dames. Oh, it's O.K. for the good-looking broad who's killed her husband, all dressed in black and awful sorry for what she done, but kind of relieved all the same. I'll give you that. But some jobs just isn't for women. Bishops maybe is one thing, attorneys is another. And you can tell that to whoever you goddam like, compliments of Chief Krumnagel."

Alberts unwound himself with a sigh.

"I just know everything's going to be all right," he said with a smile as magnanimous as it was insincere, stretching out his hand.

"It'd better be, I tell you."

"Mrs. Krumnagel. Don't worry now."

"Listen, I've lived through worse," said Edie.

"That's the spirit."

His head wobbled on its tall neck with a final gesture of suspect solidarity, and he went off to be present at the Jackson Pollock retrospective at the Tate Gallery.

Miss Epsom's candidature was withdrawn at Krumnagel's request, and he received the visit of the substitute, Lockwood

Cramp, who was a Member of Parliament for a constituency in Northern Ireland. He was not quite the kind of ally Krumnagel had been expecting, since even his appearance tallied with no terms of reference known in the United States. Nevertheless he looked as though he had been selected for the infighting if for nothing else. His face, which had been lacerated, crushed, run into, and disfigured in both war and peace, was a patchwork of different shades of red with heatherlike outbursts of ginger hair erupting from his ears, his nostrils, and his cheekbones.

("Why don't he have some of that crap removed?" Krumnagel was to say to Edie subsequently.)

He affected long and prickly sideburns, framing a large mouth, in which tusklike teeth stood at intervals, leaving ample room for the gnarled black pipe which belched asphyxiating fumes endlessly, and which caused a trickle of saliva down his chin. The center of interest, however, were boyish blue eyes of extraordinary credulity and innocence, great round buttons of no depth whatsoever, peering from under his orange eyebrows with a frankness both amusing and impressive. Here was obviously a man who had never had to find an alternative to physical courage, and that characteristic was probably both his strength and his weakness. He may have been born to lead; he was probably not born to be followed.

Painfully he and Krumnagel sat in the latter's cell, like schoolboy and tutor struggling through a backlog of homework.

"Did you serve in the armed forces at all?"

"No, sir, I did not."

"Oh, that's a pity. Never mind."

"You mean, if I'd won a Purple Heart, that would melt the jury's heart?"

Cramp smiled grimly.

"It shouldn't, but it helps. I've known quite a few war heroes in my time, and as a rule they're pretty unreliable peacetime citizens. You can't have it both ways, you know. Still the courts

[105]

never realize that. Was the reason for your not going into the armed forces a medical one?"

"It was, sir, yes."

"Was it a malady we could get any sympathy out of? Tuberculosis? Cancer? Anything which left its mark on your stability?"

Krumnagel swallowed briefly.

"No, sir."

"Right. Right. I don't want to know about it, then."

Oh, hell. Now the guy had the wrong impression.

"It was something any guy could contract."

"Oh, one of those," Cramp grunted, "better keep quiet about it in that case."

"No, not one of those," Krumnagel protested. "One of the others."

Cramp looked at him sharply.

"Which others?"

"Not them . . . the others."

"I don't follow. You're not a homosexual, are you?"

"Jesus Christ." Krumnagel threw a box of matches across the cell.

"Now, sit down, and don't be childish," Cramp reprimanded. "There's really no time for any behavior other than completely and utterly functional cooperation. We've a lot to get through, and by just shooting a defenseless man in a pub, you haven't given me a great deal to go on by way of defense. We've only got one of two chances. The one is to prove that you're a maniac. The other is to prove that it was all the result of a tragic misunderstanding. Frankly, it's much easier to prove that you're a maniac."

"I am *not* a maniac! I was loaded!" shouted Krumnagel.

"That's not the best of defenses, believe me."

"So was he loaded!"

"He's dead, unfortunately. It is no longer any concern of ours whether he was loaded or not."

"Well, I'm not a focking maniac," cried Krumnagel, resentful.

"I very much regret it."

"I want to go home, see, take up where I left off. I'm chief of police, and that's what I intend to go on being. Chief of police, and there isn't a guy in the world can take that away from me!" And Krumnagel thought abruptly and uneasily of Al Carbide, to whom he had not given much time of late.

"You mean to tell me that you anticipate an acquittal, and the possibility of going straight home and resuming your functions?"

"Sure. Why not?"

"You have much more confidence in me than I could possibly afford to have in myself," muttered Cramp.

"Listen, what happened to me could have happened to 'most anyone, and you know it."

"No, I don't know it," said Cramp. "It couldn't have happened to anyone at all over here except a criminal or an American policeman. And what I have to do, if I can, is to convince the court that there is a difference between the two."

7

As the time for the trial approached, Sir Neville found himself thinking more and more about it from every angle, strategic, tactical, humanitarian. It occasionally happens with men of achievement, who have managed to tame and master a subject of vast complication, that their magnanimity and entertainment of new ideas is increased instead of diminished by their success in their professions. Sir Neville was such a man, whose vision was no longer fettered by the letter of the law but merely by its spirit. Only a man ignorant of things legal, or else a man of Sir Neville's mental purity, could have suggested going "hammer and tongs after a manslaughter charge." It was clearly impossible, since nobody in England could conceivably believe that a man — a Zulu or a Malgache or a Maldive Islander, let alone a police chief from the U.S. — would mistake the gesture of reaching for a handkerchief for that of reaching for a gun.

As Bill Stockard put it, "No child, on seeing a Western, could think for a moment that the cowboys on Main Street of Carson City are reaching for their handkerchiefs. Why should the opposite be more credible?"

Sir Neville laughed. He liked Stockard. His youth and directness pleased him, because he knew that with the going of one from a body the other soon abandoned the spirit. Stockard reminded him of what it had been like on the way to the top.

"I agree," he told a relieved Stockard. "The charge of manslaughter will have to be arrived at in court, and it will have to be arrived at because proof will have been given that a charge of murder is not apposite in this case."

"Exactly." Bill Stockard smiled at his own presumption, and then added, "You knew that the whole time. You've just been pulling our legs, haven't you, Sir Neville?"

"I knew it all the time," Sir Neville replied without levity, "otherwise I wouldn't occupy this chair in this office, but I assure you that I am not pulling any legs with the possible exception of my own. It is the usual democratic agony I am suffering, Bill, I know exactly what should be done, not for the sake of justice — oh, no, I haven't those qualifications — but so that justice is not miscarried. Unfortunately I am not empowered to do much but watch and trust those in the arena. I don't trust them, Bill. I don't trust anyone but myself." He smiled at last, and added, "I say this, of course, with all humility."

"You're right, of course, to describe that as the usual democratic agony. We all suffer from it."

"Yes, and once we all suffer from it, it'd all be much more restful under a dictatorship."

"I can't see you under a dictatorship, sir."

"There's no point at all in a dictatorship if you are compelled to be under it. I would have absolutely no objection to a dictatorship if I were dictator."

"I don't believe you, sir. Saving your presence, you'd be a bloody awful dictator. You're far too complicated."

"Really?"

"Oh, yes. You're too courteous for a start."

"I flatter myself I'm sometimes very rude."

"Only a courteous man has the technique for really glorious rudeness. And dictators have no time for that. They have to be insensitive. And they can't afford to listen."

"Hm. It seems to me you'd be as bad a party member as I'd be a dictator. On that uplifting note, may I offer you lunch?"

Bill knew what that meant. He hesitated for a moment. He was too modern to enjoy club life. He'd have preferred a quick snack. And then he was married, with three kids. He really had no time for these common rooms where elderly prefects sipped their port and muttered the latest rumors of school to one another.

"Yes," he replied, "with pleasure."

As they walked, Sir Neville spoke.

"It's really very good of you to accept my invitation, Bill, since I know that you really have no time for club life."

"Oh, that's not true —"

"It is indeed and it's quite understandable. You're a married man. You've opened your life to other possibilities. Socially a club is merely a solace for aging adolescents — but there is, of course, another side to it. England is a country without a constitution. Practically nothing is put in writing — we destroy evidence as we go, leaving nothing but a residue of unexplained tradition, and what we do, we do with a seeming negligence — but actually there are unspoken and unwritten rules to our mysterious conduct which make the Mafia look like a public service corporation rather than a secret society. The orderly British executive mind knows by a sort of instinct acquired by habit, nuance, prejudice, and God knows what other condiments of the soul, which of his friends or enemies are liable to be at which club at what hour. It is on those rare occasions when he makes an error, that he sighs about the final unpredictability of existence with a bitter, "You never know, do you?" Well, that is so rare as hardly to matter. It is, however, for that political reason — policy is not decided in Parliament, or in the ministries, but in the clubs — it is for that reason, and not because I think it will make you pass your spare time pleasantly, that I insisted on putting your name up for Black's."

"I did understand your motives, Sir Neville, and I'm very grateful, even if it does set me back seventy-five quid per annum."

"Oh, you're not accepted yet. That'll take another four or five years, no doubt. So you see, it's rather more economical than you think. However, we're not going there now."

"I know that."

Sir Neville looked at him sharply.

"How do you know?"

"Well, largely because we're walking in the wrong direction."

"Ah, yes."

"I imagine we're going to the Kemble."

"What on earth should make you imagine that?"

"I imagine you want to see Sir Aaron Wellbeholden. He usually gets there about this time."

Sir Neville nodded with satisfaction.

"You're learning," he said.

Sir Aaron Wellbeholden was a Treasury Counsel, a large man with a lower lip so prominent that the wetness of its interior was almost always in evidence. Occasionally he grunted and sniffed like an old bulldog, and he possessed the nobility of extreme ugliness, making even his occasional bad temper lovable, or at least eminently excusable.

"Why on earth bother to come and see me?" he asked, as he sipped his pink gin noisily and gratefully.

"I didn't come here specifically to see you, A.W.," fibbed Sir Neville. "I just thought I'd give young Bill Stockard, my assistant here, lunch. I'm a member of this club too, you know."

"Rumor had it we'd lost you to Black's," Sir Aaron grunted, spilling a little gin on his waistcoat, on which there was evidence of other delicacies lost in flight.

"Semper fidelis."

"What?"

"I said, semper fidelis."

"Oh yes, Latin." Sir Aaron puffed appreciatively. "Well, come on then, let's not spoil our luncheon with business, what? Get it over before we go in. Why bother to search me out in my lair?"

"There's really no reason, A.W., except to put my mind at rest."

"Mind at rest? When can your mind ever be at rest . . . or mine for that matter? What?"

"Spoken like a lawyer with a conscience."

Sir Aaron wheezed and heaved agreeably, his lower lip aglitter like coral in shallow water.

"Knowing you, D.P.P., I'd say you're worried about this American fellow."

"We've both been in the profession too long," said Sir Neville quietly, after a moment.

"Can't pretend to understand his motives or his character. Makes no sense whatever to me. None whatever. Nothing I hate more than dealing with a case I don't understand. You lose sight of your own sense of justice, don't you see? Or at least, it puts you mentally on the defensive."

"Perhaps it's just as well?"

"Why d'you say that?" asked Sir Aaron. "We tend to forget — and that's the only pleasant surprise I feel we may be able to give our American guest — we forget that the role of prosecuting counsel in England is not to win cases, but merely to present the facts as coldly and accurately as possible. There's no slur attached to our losing cases. Some of us would like to lose every case."

"Well, of course, you are correct when you say that we tend

to forget this — and I am so gratified, although not at all surprised, A.W., that you should have reminded me of it. Some of the best advocates in the land cannot resist the heightening of the temperature in the courtroom."

"That's why they're thought to be the best," murmured Sir Aaron insidiously.

There was a pause while Sir Aaron swilled his second pink gin around in its glass, staring at it as though seeking clairvoyance.

"Do you have an inkling why a normally constituted man should fire at another one in a public house?"

"Do you know why Chinese women should mutilate their feet, or Africans elongate their necks with rings, or Buddhist bonzes burn themselves on the pavement in order to underline a point they had been making?"

Sir Aaron battled with his sinus cavities.

"In other words, you think it was so natural to him it really bears no explanation?"

"Perhaps."

"But then why has it never happened before?"

"It probably has."

"Over there, you mean?"

"Oh, yes."

"Frightful."

There was a moment.

"You've got grandchildren, haven't you, A.W.?"

"Four of the little beggars. Don't say that you want to see their photographs? I make it a point never to carry the photographs of any relatives on my person."

"That's another aspect of your character which makes it difficult for you to understand the Americans."

"Oh, never mind the Americans — there are Englishmen who go traveling. First thing they bring out when they're unpacking is a kind of collapsible altarpiece featuring all their physical achievements. Gracious, if you can't remember what

[113]

your wife and children look like, you don't deserve to have them. But why did you ask me about my grandchildren?"

"They watch Westerns, don't they?" Sir Neville asked, with a grateful glance at Bill for having put that line of country in his mind earlier on.

"Never mind my grandchildren, old man, *I* watch Westerns. Life would be poorer without those easy ways out and facile solutions. However, that's fiction, not life."

"However far away it drifts, fiction's always remotely based on life."

"Yes, but I mean, there aren't *people* like that!"

"Somewhere in the world there are. Almost like that."

"I don't believe you."

Sir Neville changed his tack.

"If you like opera, you usually go for the music, don't you? Not really for the story."

"I don't like opera."

"Nor do I, but if we did, we'd rather go to listen than to wonder who's going to get the girl or who's going to get the knife between the ribs. I mean, even a philistine can be carried away on a great sweep of melody, whereas the story of a clown transporting his dead daughter in a sack during a thunderstorm is frankly absurd."

"Yes it is — and yet, wasn't there a case like that only the other day — an out-of-work comic or something — the most ridiculous murder of the century —"

"Exactly. You've made my point, A.W. It even caused the gutter press to go intellectual, and to refer to it as the Rigoletto Murder Case."

"I see your point. I walked into that one. Nothing is so absurd it can't happen in life."

"Who's defending?" Sir Aaron asked, out of the blue.

"Cramp."

"Cramp."

The inflections of both men meant nothing, and yet it was a

nothing redolent of everything, as though each was able to read the other's mind. There was nothing unkind about the inflections. There was even a ring of admiration about them, and yet there was a lingering aftertaste suggesting limitation, a lack of horizons — but then, of course, the very sound of the name lent itself to a feeling of restriction and the earthbound. Each man meditated.

"I thought it was going to be Maud Epsom."

"It was. The man you refer to as our American guest wouldn't have her."

Sir Aaron pulled a face.

"He was wrong."

" 'Course he was."

"Must have been your idea, Maud Epsom, wasn't it?"

"I admit it."

"Thought as much. Lunch?" he said, really coming to life for the first time.

After lunch, and back at the office, Sir Neville said he was reassured as far as he possibly could be by his contact with Sir Aaron. In any case, the food had been edible. Six months ago the Kemble had passed through a culinary crisis, but seemed now to be recovering. He was glad, even if he was one of the few members to have noticed the decline, and now the renaissance. There was left only one unknown, or practically unknown quantity, and that was Lord Justice Plantagenet-Williams, who would try the case at the forthcoming quarter-sessions in Hertford. He was an old man, one of the oldest, with a reputation of being very good, but it was almost impossible to tell whether this very good should be considered in conjunction with his extreme age, or whether it was a true assessment by any standards. Sir Neville would have preferred George Cladbourne or Howard Fitzandrew, one of the more modern judges, pragmatic within the obvious limits, bright, quick, with a wide and alarmed vision of a rapidly changing world. There was no evidence that Lord Justice Plantagenet-

Williams moved with the times, indeed that he moved at all. He was not a clubman and never had been, and it was therefore extraordinary and rather frightening that he had advanced to the pinnacle of his profession. It suggested to Sir Neville that he had probably achieved this as a result of inflexible integrity, a quality which has led to as many errors of judgment as any other.

There was nothing to be done on a practical level, however. It would be quite out of order for the director of public prosecutions to seem to be attempting to influence a judge before a trial. That was where friendship was so useful — and the clubs, which made mere acquaintanceship seem like friendship for a few important moments whenever the need arose. If a man chose to be aloof, and imagined that such isolation lent itself to an open mind, that was his business. Nevertheless, Sir Neville suspected that the majority of those determined to preserve an open mind made their effort some time after their minds had been hermetically shut. Damn democracy.

The day before the trial, Sir Neville made a decision. He told Bill Stockard that he would not be coming into the office the next day. Bill was quick to guess the reason.

"Don't say you're going to Hertford, Sir Neville?"

Sir Neville looked at him with a trace of irritation. Not to answer would give the matter too much importance. To answer in the affirmative made him feel unaccountably guilty.

"Why not?" he asked.

"I hope this trial isn't becoming an obsession."

"Justice may well have become an obsession, Bill. If that obsession expresses itself through this trial, I'll just have to let it take its course."

"What shall I tell people? A slight chill?"

"That sounds a deal too much like Buckingham Palace. Just say I'm out."

"D'you want me to come?"

"I'd rather it was you said I'm out than it was someone else. It'll sound truer."

"Fair enough. Thanks."

Personal freedom doesn't increase with a man's altitude in the hierarchy of society. Sir Neville knew this all too well. Had he been an ordinary prison warden, he could have satisfied his curiosity about Krumnagel to his heart's content. As director of public prosecutions, this just wasn't possible. He had to rely on sources as well-meaning, but as utterly different to himself in makeup and in the horizons of the mind's eye, as Detective-Inspector Pewtrey.

"Extraordinary kind of fellow," was the extent of Pewtrey's contribution. "He's like a man disturbed by some incident in the war, that's the best way I can put it. A sergeant. Sergeant-type, or better, sergeant major. One moment he's absolutely lucid about his job, and has a pretty profound knowledge of police work, with some ideas which, although diagonally opposed to our way of thinking, might still very well work — in other words, he's a hundred percent policeman, a professional. That's one side of him. Then, suddenly, without any warning, he'll start getting violent — oh, not physically; personally I believe that was the damn alcohol at work — no, mentally, which is almost more alarming. He uses very salty language, usually when there are ladies present. While we were conducting his psychiatric tests in the hospital, it only needed matron or nurse to enter the room for a choice selection of four-letter words to make their appearance —"

"You're sure he wasn't pretending to be crazy?"

"It's the last thing he wants," Pewtrey cried. "He anticipates being acquitted, and taking up his police work again next Monday. He explains to matron and me in no uncertain terms that you can keep the rest of the world — he's seen enough of it in England, and he can guess the rest, and it's lousy, inefficient, bereft of know-how, raddled with Communism, and no place for an American who isn't armed — not with a revolver in his armpit, mark you, but with a tommy gun at his hip and a deal of civilization to sell."

Sir Neville sighed. "That's what worries me. I have no objection to this kind of talk myself. I find it picturesque and refreshing. But there's no guarantee a British judge in his late seventies will take it in any other way except the spirit in which it is meant."

Pewtrey laughed. "It's quite exhausting, Sir Neville. One has to listen to you so carefully in order to understand exactly what you mean. I got that. I got it. The spirit in which it is meant. Very good."

"I am glad you liked it," Sir Neville admitted, "but your delectation of my little jokes hardly helps us with our problem. It's miserable that it had to be a murder charge after all."

"Well, it was technically a murder."

Sir Neville winced slightly. "I am sick and tired of technicalities," he snapped. "If I had my way, it'd be manslaughter. I hate to be forced to take the risk of allowing it to be called murder even for a moment."

"Oh, there's really no risk, Sir Neville. Cramp's bound to put up a fairly good case; Sir Aaron's no fool — ten years ago, Lord Justice Plantagenet-Williams was very, very good indeed."

"And today?"

"Today? — As far as I know, he's still very good, but he's old."

"He was old ten years ago."

"He's . . . he's older."

The case was marred at its opening by an occurrence which nobody could have foreseen. When Krumnagel emerged from the darkness into the courtroom, he saw the lion and the unicorn upholding the coat of arms of the realm, a sight which had chilled the hearts of innocent and guilty throughout the centuries, for it meant they were confronting the nation itself, naked before regiments of muskets, steaming horses, the rock and spew of ironclads, and the awful ritual of heraldry — a single isolated figure at a time, standing accused. All this was lost on Krumnagel, however, because his reflexes had been conditioned otherwise. He glanced at it as though it were some curiosity from a lost culture in the jungle, and then let his eye fall on Lord Justice Plantagenet-Williams who was pretending to busy himself with some documents. He saw an aged patrician, muttering to himself, who seemed to have put a mop on his head, a kind of mass of tangled material hardened into a mold and caked with white matter, as though someone had cleaned it mistakenly as a tennis shoe. Krumnagel frowned, then smiled. He looked at Sir Aaron Wellbeholden, who was also busy sorting papers, his lip brilliant and his eye clouded. On his head he wore the same peculiar headgear. Krumnagel laughed softly to himself. Then he spotted Lockwood Cramp, whom he had got used to either bare-headed or else with his battered bowler on his head, the cardboard visible in places where the brim had worn thin. Now the blue button eyes were staring at him, friendly and encouraging, and yet preserving this implacable distance under a replica of the other mops. The red of the face with its flourishes of carrot-colored hair was framed in white curls, and this was too much. A roar of uncontrollable laughter erupted from Krumnagel.

The judge and Sir Aaron looked up, surprised, and a murmur went up from the public gallery. Cramp was alarmed and mystified by this turn of events. The judge was tempted to call for order, but was a little hesitant until he understood the reason for the mirth. Since it was the habit of judges to pretend to be easily shocked in order to impress wrongdoers with the immensity of their crimes, Lord Justice Plantagenet-Williams immediately adopted a look of facile outrage, but this was the result of force of habit, and he found very little to do with this attitude once he had adopted it. Like the schoolmaster faced with a classroom of giggling children, he inevitably entertained the horrid thought that perhaps there was something scandal-

[119]

ous about his personal appearance. His horny fingers patted the top of his wig for a brief moment as though there might be some rude object attached to it by a pin. He found nothing, but took the opportunity to straighten a wig which had been straight in any case. He felt his face in a manner at once negligent and thorough and flapped his gown like a bird preening itself. He looked behind him, above him, at Krumnagel, who held the rail before him as though it were the handlebars of a motorcycle, twisting and turning over it in an attempt to check the tumult of laughter.

"What is the matter with you? Are you ill?" inquired the judge.

Somehow when those under the mops spoke, it made them even funnier. Very often people are irresistably comic in the shower rooms of sports clubs, when they walk about naked but with the expression of the well-dressed. For the same reason, a face endowed with eloquence under a ludicrous headdress, and demanding to be taken seriously, was quite irresistible.

"Is he ill?" demanded the judge of whatever third party chose to answer.

Only Sir Neville shut his eyes, like a man expecting the worst whose every fear had been instantly gratified. He had understood in a flash that even the most sacrosanct and time-honored of symbols could not remain forever untouched in a world which had been content to walk for centuries, but which had suddenly, within living memory, broken into a canter, then into a gallop, and then had suddenly begun to take flight — and was now flying so fast that the eye could hardly take in anything of the ever-changing landscape. All the old men who doggedly believed they were in charge of things still went through the traditional gestures, getting in and out of planes, cars, and doorways, saluting, shaking hands, and laying wreaths on tombs of unknown warriors. They still issued statements to the press, and replied to questions with the most elaborately rehearsed and consequently deeply felt sincerity. And yet they were largely ignored without even realizing it. They were like actors playing in empty theaters, and bowing to the thunder of silence.

Krumnagel, when he found words, was defending himself in some other court, somewhere else.

"It's this way, Your Honor," he tried, but had to laugh again.

"You refer to me as My Lord, not as Your Honor," the judge declared, for something to say.

Krumnagel frowned for a second, then decided against it, since My Lord had a blasphemous ring to his ear. Suddenly, irresistibly, the second wave of laughter attacked his diaphragm, and set off a series of oscillations, like the nerve of a dead rabbit, and he howled.

"I must instruct you to pull yourself together," cried the judge, and appealed to Cramp.

"Can I ask you to influence your client to pull himself together?" he asked.

"M'lud, may I remind you that my client is a foreigner, and is no doubt overcome by the gravity of his situation in surroundings which are unfamiliar to him?" Cramp pleaded.

Could they not face the fact that they were figures of fun to those who had not been brought up from youth to shudder at the sight of them? Eventually, of course, Krumnagel did manage to put an end to his outburst, although all through the trial a bilious smile would occasionally make its appearance on his lips, threatening a recurrence. He realized that his attitude was not one to endear him to his captors. When seized by cannibals, you don't make jokes about calories.

Sir Aaron presented his case with tact and consideration, making it clear that the prosecution was not after a head, but was carrying out a sad, if necessary duty, simply because a quirk of fate had put an end to old Jock's life. The three aged men, called as witnesses, stressed the fact that good nature had been the keynote of the evening up to its very closing moments, although, under cross-examination from Cramp, they all admitted, as did the old girl in the trilby, that Krumnagel had been under considerable provocation from Jock.

"You've got to remember," said Mr. Briggs, "Jock was a Communist — and there aren't many of those about — he was enough to provoke anyone, even a Socialist — the kind of Socialist we got today — and it wasn't politics with him — it were a religion — I mean it, a religion."

Sir Neville looked with affection at Briggs. Here was an old simpleton who thought for himself, and almost made himself understood, heroically.

"You mean, Communism was his substitute for God?" Cramp asked.

Oh idiot, idiot, Cramp. You're taking all the goodness out of Mr. Briggs's assessment with that hypocritical question!

"I'd not be prepared to say that, sir, not being able to enter into his thinking — and, 'course, it's too late now —"

"That was the impression he gave, at all events?"

That's better, Cramp, but the harm's done.

"That's the impression he give *me.*"

"I see. Can you remember some of the ways in which he provoked the prisoner?"

"Oh, no . . ." Mr. Briggs concentrated hard. "No . . . but he did. We all know he did, but then none of us was exactly . . . I mean. No, I can't say the words."

Krumnagel, in his own defense, was inclined to be garrulous. But then, he was not used to being in this position, nor was he used to a legal system in which the evidence is presented as often as is at all possible in the form of monosyllables, presumably in order to protect the ignorant, and leave the burden of their defense or prosecution on the shoulders of those with the power to plead in ringing tones, and the devil take those facts to which a yes or no can only be qualified and inadequate answers. Often Krumnagel just ignored the instruction to confine himself to affirmation or denial, and plowed into the argument with gathering stridency. He was not used to being treated as a fool, and the moment when his future was in peril was no moment to attempt the experiment. No amount of gavel drumming or ominous admonition was able to stop him, and at times an open clash between the ruffled majesty of the court and the rampant indignation of the man on the murder charge seemed inevitable.

"Can you remember some of the provocations?" Cramp asked him.

"Well, of course I can. What do you think?" Krumnagel barked.

"There is no need to take that attitude," the judge rebuked.

"Have you ever been on a murder charge, Your Honor? No? If you had, and it was a trumped-up" — gavel, gavel, gavel — "let me finish — trumped-up phoney charge" — gavel, gavel — "You'd try any attitude" — fortissimo — "to see which one worked!"

"If you go on like this, I shall charge you with contempt of court," cried the judge in his small yet cutting voice.

"I'm on a murder charge, and I've got to worry about that?"

Krumnagel looked around for approval for his particular irony, but found only an awestruck and obedient silence.

"Lot of stuffed shirts," he muttered.

"Could you describe some of the provocations which you say you endured?" asked Cramp.

"Do I have to stick to yes and no?"

"I strongly advise you to change your attitude," said the judge, "especially towards your own advocate. We are here to help you, within the limits imposed by the charge on which you find yourself."

"Oh sure, sure. I forgot," replied Krumnagel, with his own form of bitter sarcasm.

"Oh, Bart, don't get so ornery," Edie muttered.

Major Batt O'Fehy put an arm around her, gave his head a philosophical shake, and chewed deeply into his gum.

"You want to know what that old guy said to me?" Krumnagel asked. "Well, I remember him saying that democracy is an old chestnut."

"And what do you suppose he meant by that?" Cramp inquired.

"Isn't it clear?" Krumnagel asked, frowning with disbelief.

"I want to know what *you* suppose he meant."

"He meant democracy was a dead duck, that it had laid an egg, that it was a lemon. Want me to go on?"

"Did he say anything specifically anti-American?"

"Sure did. He said the United States invaded Russia. He said we had no business to be in Vietnam. Said he was a Communist." And there Krumnagel had to pause. It didn't sound very provocative, and he realized it. He changed his tone. "It wasn't so much what he said as the way he said it — you got to believe me. There was a sneer in his voice — he was like trying to bait me, know what I mean? People back home — diplomats and the military, often get warned this kind of thing's going to happen in some foreign countries where the people are jealous of us, see — and they get booklets given out, like *How to Be a Good American Abroad.* 'Remember every citizen is an ambassador just as much as an accredited ambassador of the U.S. is' — that's a phrase I remember — I seen the booklets, and I did my goddamdest to do what the booklet said, see, but I guess it was just human nature or something — when I hear my country attacked, 'specially by an admitted card-carrying member of the Communist party — and an atheist, too — yeah, that's another thing, he was an atheist — said he had no time for God and prayer — said it, right in front of everyone." Krumnagel lowered his voice like that of a guilty child. "Well, I guess that and the beer and Scotch and being in a strange place — I just didn't have the self-control I should have had,

[124]

that's all — so when that old guy dug in his pocket, I just didn't have the time to think it all out — we get regular target practice in the police before we get ourselves into executive positions — but I never gave it up, even though I'm police chief — I still work out in the gym twice a week — get a rubdown, keep in shape, and go in the armory for target practice — maybe I'm still too active for the job I hold down — I don't know — but when I saw that old critter going for his gun — going for what I sincerely thought was going to be his gun — why, I didn't hesitate."

"He's doing great," murmured Batt O'Fehy.

"Oh, Batt, he can be so brilliant," cooed Edie. "I love him so."

"I know, honey, I know."

"And is this the first time this has happened to you?" asked Cramp.

"No, sir, it is not," Krumnagel replied.

The judge leaned forward, wide-eyed.

"Will you kindly describe to this court the previous occasion on which this occurred?" Cramp requested.

"Sure will. It was in the late forties . . . forty-eight, forty-nine, in that area. I was on patrol in the downtown area of our city, where there'd been a lot of violence . . . you know, boys coming back from the army, trained to kill, no place to go nights, bored with the daily grind . . . and we was all on our mettle. It was down on Monmouth and Seventh, where Zigler's Jewelry Store is — still is to this day. I saw the sunlight catch the door, see, out of the corner of my eye, and of course, I swung around. We'd gotten so jittery, any quick movement made us jump. Then I saw this guy, see, a young guy, in his early twenties I'd say, fair-haired young guy with a crew cut, running out of the jewelry store and racing down the sidewalk. I'd seen this kind of thing in movies — so had the public, and it was beginning to lose faith in us. Before I had time to think, my gun was in my hand and spitting out lead, and there was this young guy, Cass Chalkburner his name was — I'll never forget him — lying on the sidewalk with his brains twenty yards farther up the street. That's all, I guess."

"Had he robbed the jeweler's?" the judge asked, with the intensity of a child listening to a bedtime story.

It would be so easy and so pleasing to say yes.

"No, he had not, sir. He was . . ." Krumnagel faltered. Cass Chalkburner and old Jock were beginning to mingle in his mind, his own canister of spilled milk . . . "He was engaged to be married, sir . . . Your Honor . . . and he was just purchasing the wedding ring, sir . . . he had a fine service record, and he was going to get married to a wonderful girl . . . I killed him, Your Honor."

A hush had fallen over the Court. Krumnagel had all the dignity of a Dreyfus as he accused himself with massive simplicity — more dignity, for Dreyfus was merely stoic, whereas Krumnagel had the opportunity for a cool understated mea culpa, and with an instinct produced by the moment and the situation, he took it.

It was Cramp who broke the silence.

"Will you now tell the court what happened to you as a consequence of your action?"

"Nothing, sir."

"Nothing."

"Nothing?" asked the judge, incredulous. "There was no trial?"

"No, Your Honor, there was not."

"Why not?"

"There was an inquiry, naturally."

"No trial, although the victim had done absolutely nothing to provoke you?"

"No, sir. Like I said, there was an inquiry."

"And what was the outcome of the inquiry?"

"I was reprimanded, Your Honor — but I remember the then chief of police, Chief Ritchie McCarron, a wonderful guy and a great policeman, but great — he called me into his office, and I felt the sh . . . the excrement was really going to hit . . . anyhow, I thought I was going to wish I was dead instead of the other guy, way things looked. Well, he said this. He said — and I'm quoting here to the best of my memory — 'Bart, you done something could well bust a guy — you know this, and I'm not going to harp on it — I don't like thoughtless shooting — we can't have it in the City — that's one side of the story — now that that's said, I want to tell you I'd have done the same thing — any policeman who's going places has a couple of mistakes in him, and I'd trust him more than I would the guy who never puts a foot wrong. All this is strictly off the record of course,' he said — and he offered me a cigar. It was greener than I was used to, and I threw up. Next promotion list, I was on it."

"Are you suggesting," the judge asked, in a voice of porcelain, "that this is the second of the two mistakes which any policeman worth his salt is *bound* to have in him?"

"I'm not suggesting nothing, Your Honor," Krumnagel replied soberly. "I'm just telling you what happened the way you asked." The judge thought it prudent to recess for lunch.

8

Finding a place for lunch in a smallish country town on market day is not easy unless a reservation has been made ahead of time. Sir Neville had had this foresight, and he now squeezed through the milling crowd of farmers, holding their drinks aloft as they spiraled away from the bar with rude delicacy, calling out to their guests that their mission had at last been successful. In the maelstrom he suddenly found himself face to face with Sir Aaron, and like shipwrecked sailors, they spoke while the anger of the human sea allowed them to.

"The start was disastrous, but he pulled himself together remarkably for a strong finish, I thought. Curious cove. Another world. Another world, what?"

"You deserve a great deal of gratitude," Sir Neville replied, as he was jostled. "You could have been much tougher in your questioning, even within the limits prescribed."

"Oh well, we do what we can. I agree with you, though, D.P.P., we're not fit to judge a man like that. And after a bit of time, we inevitably begin to ask ourselves what we *are* fit to judge. A fellow like our American guest has that effect on us."

"How d'you think it's going?"

"If I were the judge, it would be going fairly well. It's sometimes good to create two as widely divergent impressions as Krumnagel did. It's all up to old Plantagenet-Williams. I don't know."

Mr. Alberts had been pushed into their creek by the tide and had overheard the conversation. He now followed Sir Neville into the dining room. On their way, they passed Cramp sitting in a haven he had found by the wall. Preventing himself from being pushed into Cramp by holding one arm doggedly against the wall, and using his body as a buttress, he asked Krumnagel's defender how he thought it looked.

"Haven't the foggiest. Fighting the Hun was a deal easier than defending the Yank. It's like trying to drag the truth out of a child — he's absolutely genial, and he does all the work himself. Then you meet a knot in the cord, and he gets himself stuck on some monstrous piece of stubbornness. I thought he was rotten when he was trying to fight — simply because you can't win, you can only create a bad impression — *we* all know this — unfortunately *he* had to find out. On the other hand, he was absolutely magnificent when he began to plead. Magnificent. Noble, in the Roman sense. Don't know what came over him."

"Well, however different our traditions and our problems may be, a man who has risen to his position in society simply must have some qualities."

"I agree, but the ones he showed were the least I expected from him."

"Yes. Fair enough. What's your impression now?"

"Old Plantagenet-Williams gives nothing away. Just sits there like an icebox. I frankly don't know." He smiled mischievously. "I'm surprised to find you here, D.P.P. Is the case as riveting as all that?"

"I can't very well say I just happened to be passing, can I?"

"Hardly."

"Have you talked to Sir Aaron?"

"Oh, yes, we talked in the toilet. Old lawyer's trick. Unfortunately the one in this hotel has three compartments in the urinal — know it well, of old — and number three was occupied by a gentleman from the *Daily Mail*. Well, it's a little tricky to pretend to be peeing for over twenty minutes, although it seemed like a full quarter of an hour before he gave up pretending — he surrendered first to the outcry of bursting bladders behind us — we were too distinguished to be jostled, you understand, and so we did get a word in. We're very much in agreement."

Sir Neville was compelled to ask Mr. Alberts to join him, since the latter was without anywhere to go, and Sir Neville could hardly hog even a small table merely as compensation for his foresight. His courtesy gave him no pleasure, since Mr. Alberts was not his favorite transatlantic character, with his slightly spiteful elegance and his knowing ways.

"Well," said Mr. Alberts, "not a day passes but I marvel more at the wonder and beauty of your great country."

"That's very good of you, I'm sure," Sir Neville muttered in reply. Flattery of such crushing magnanimity was the weapon most likely to find the Achilles heel of the English. Sir Neville would far rather have fenced his way out of some justified criticism. He was on his home ground there. He was so full of criticism himself that he knew the chinks in the armor, which he could attack or defend at will.

"I could have gained some futile promotion, and become counselor in Mauritius or cultural attaché in Mali or something, but I preferred staying on in London, and just basking in the British way of life, for want of a better phrase," Mr. Alberts went on.

"Really."

"Yes, I mean the Guggenheim or the Museum of Modern Art may have finer collections, but where is the heart?" His head wobbled in emphasis, and he answered the question himself. "No, give me the old Tate any day, with all its lousy lighting and its occasional doubtful attribution." He tapped his chest with two fingers. "Heart," he said. "It runs grudgingly through every artery of British life."

Sir Neville was startled. He rather liked the phrase, but it was upsetting to hear a true word or two from a man you had made up your mind to dislike. In his way, Mr. Alberts promised to be as surprising as Krumnagel. Odd lot, these Americans.

"And what is your impression of the trial?" Sir Neville asked.

"That's just it. I don't know how much you had to do with it, Sir Neville."

"Me? Nothing," Sir Neville snapped.

"Well that's just what's remarkable. There's no way of saying that Krumnagel is an idiot without upsetting the applecart, and yet the insinuation that this is not a normal case is implicit in every question of counsel and of the judge. If any of this atmosphere could be put into words, it would be nailed as collusion, and yet it is there all the time — an unspoken understanding that here is an oaf who acted according to his own flickering lights in a moment of stress, and who cannot be judged by any standards except his own. I felt this atmosphere so strongly that it came as a shock to hear counsel put it into words just now. It was a shock because it was unnecessary. The court had already understood."

"The court may have done, but has the judge? That is our only worry now."

"Oh, surely."

"You think he'll get off, do you?"

"I think he may well. Whether I think he ought to is another question."

"Do you think he ought to?"

"No."

Sir Neville raised his eyebrows.

"That's an original thought," he admitted. "Why not?"

Mr. Alberts smiled a little grimly, like someone who knows he is embarking on the defense of a point of view which is bound to be unpopular.

"I hardly know how to begin, Sir Neville. There's an awful lot of talk about racism these days back home."

"Everywhere."

"Everywhere, yes. This is usually the result of a somewhat ruthless assessment, based on color alone. Blacks, whites, yellows and reds. It's like a kind of sinister and silly game which, alas, any number can play and do. But there's much more to racism than that. The anchor of America is her Englishness; that's my prejudice, and I'll stick with it through thick and thin. And I think myself that there is just as much difference between what England has given America and what Germany has given her and what Ireland and Italy and the Jews have given her and what Sweden and Holland and Japan have given her as there is between the contribution of any of these peoples and what the blacks have given her. In other words, there is a racism between whites which is just as intense as that between black and white — 'specially since we tend to judge the blacks not by their unique qualities as blacks, but by their ability or inability to do a white's job. The racist who believes a black to be less good a cop than an Irish one is not a white bigot, but an Irish one — since the Irish have the same prejudice about the Armenians and the Puerto Ricans. All races are tolerated in the police force, because that's American, and democratic, but this intellectual tolerance only makes the secret prejudices more acute. And out of these secret prejudices come a kind of crazy

[132]

folklore, which is accepted by everyone if it's potent enough —
once again because that's American, and democratic, and the
rest of the blarney. We talk about the fighting Irish. For some
reason we accept the Irish fighting, but the fighting Lebanese
would not be tolerated for a moment. What is healthy high
spirits in the one is a sinister brawl with jackknives when the
others are involved. We talk about Jewish humor. Who ever
heard of Finnish humor, or laughing at the antics of a Turkish
momma?"

"Perhaps the Turks don't have mommas."

"They sure do. I was there en poste, boy, filial piety is something quite horrendous in those parts. Every Turkish general
worth his salt has a ferocious mother in her late nineties."

"From what I know of your country, which is disgracefully
little, it seems quite obvious that you have been especially hos-
pitable towards small peoples, who have found a kind of second personality on your shores. I refer in particular to the Irish
and the Jews. At home, the Irish have no one to fight except
each other, or occasionally the English. This is hardly sufficient
nourishment for the hungry fist. They had to go to America in
order to really become as Irish as they wished to be. It's the
same thing with the Jews. They're better talkers than listeners
— it's written all over their history — and perhaps Jesus
wouldn't have come to such a tragic end if the Jews in his audience had been listening more and talking less, and if the Romans had been talking more and listening less. Whatever the
truth of this, the fact remains that it was useless for the Jews to
practice their humor in Israel, with the Arabs as their only audience. Their humor needed a wider canvas, so they came to
America in order to spread their bittersweet view of life like a
profane gospel for everyday. But minorities like the Russians
have all the local color they wish back home, ranging from
Dostoevski to Siberia and back, and they really have no need
to be particularly Russian in America."

"Yes, you have a point, but it's not quite true, Sir Neville."

"Nothing is quite true, otherwise there'd be no need for laws."

"There'd be no conversation either."

"Exactly."

Mr. Alberts smiled.

"It's impossible to be serious with an Englishman."

"It is *always* possible to be serious with an Englishman," Sir Neville corrected sternly. "What is more difficult is to be earnest with him. Hence Oscar Wilde."

"He was Irish."

"He wrote for the English and about the English. The Irish would have been too drunk to understand."

Mr. Alberts toyed with his cottage pie.

"Krumnagel," he said, "is just the kind of blinkered local autocrat who talks endlessly of rights, of equal opportunity, helps friends, makes things tough for those who haven't paid him tribute, hits below the belt when nobody's watching, waxes tearful over the flag, mistrusts Negroes and Mexicans and Jews, talks of the fraternity of all races, wears green on St. Patrick's Day and a bit too much ash on his forehead on Ash Wednesday. He contributes nothing to society, takes a lot out of it, and respects himself as a symbol of all that is virtuous and pure and masculine."

Sir Neville laughed. "My God, you've really got it in for him. Your Krumnagel (I hope I pronounce him right) seems to me to be one of these sentimental, brave, ruthless men, what the detective-inspector in charge of the case described to me as a sergeant major type. And you know what a warrant officer is like when associating with those he believes hold higher stations by luck of birth — he affects the conceit of merit, and exudes a feeling of having achieved everything himself — unlike others he could mention, unlike others — that is the operative phrase. Now this, to my mind is a trait germane to such people the world over, and we can recognize it quite as readily as you. I see a man who has been taught to think for himself, and does so by imagining what he would be expected to think by those that taught him, if you follow me. A man who has been put in a position of authority, and who, before issuing orders, remembers the kind of orders he used to be given, and issues those as though they were his own. Perhaps I am maligning him, and perhaps I am judging him by what I know of his English equivalent. And consequently, I can't see that the reasons you have given for condemning him are adequate. We need dogs to defend houses; we need men to fight wars. It's our own damn fault. Occasionally the dog will err by excess of zeal, and bite his master. Occasionally the sergeant major will get his signals mixed, and fight a war in the public saloon of a pub. As I say, it's our own bloody fault. We wanted such people; we got them."

Mr. Alberts shut his eyes in what looked like reverence.

"All of which only confirms my high opinion of this country."

"What does?" Sir Neville was irritated now. Hang Henry James and his confounded bowler and standing for the Queen or King, or whatever it was then.

"Why, the fact that you can still have such a magnanimous mind after all the evidence we have heard, and all the rough mountain justice horseplay in court."

"You sound like the first of the Pilgrim Fathers to utilize the return half of the ticket."

"Which — under the guise of the personal assistant to the consul general of the United States, with the local rank of consul first class — is just precisely what I am," and his head wobbled at the irony of it all. His eyes refused to meet Sir Neville's.

In the silence which ensued the eloquence, Sir Neville wondered about the judge. A personal opinion in a public matter is never of much value, since it is too fragile. How often, when attending a play, had he thoroughly enjoyed the first act, and gone into the bar in high good humor, only to find that the general opinion was much more reserved than his own. He had therefore to spend his time either defending his viewpoint or else cravenly conceding a few points for the sake of politeness. His attitude to the second act was inevitably colored by the discussions of the intermission. Thereafter all purity was lost. At the end he would applaud roundly if his personal enjoyment still warranted such expression, or else begin to understand the strictures of other intellects, and leave the theater a little less depressed and, as often as not, annoyed with himself. After that, all social discussion of the play in question would be like the opening of an old sore. He would grow weary of rising to its defense or of condemning it with thoughts which were not originally his own. And, surprisingly soon, he could no longer remember clearly what had happened on the stage, or what had aroused his enthusiasm or made his hackles rise, and he took to merely repeating what had been his opinion on the previous occasion on which the subject had cropped up. And so gradually stamina plays havoc with memory. It was for this reason that Sir Neville, although frequently invited, avoided first nights like the plague.

In law, every night was a first night, and there was no avoiding it. And here now was the intermission, and over their cottage pies and sausages with pickle they were all trying to guess what the great critic was scribbling on his program. Sir Neville scanned the other tables quickly. There was no real possibility of finding Lord Plantagenet-Williams there, but he looked all the same. The judge was probably locked in his chambers, away from influence and drafts, nibbling at a crustless sandwich and sipping beef tea, and reducing everything to its unrecognizable shape in the crystalline geography of his mind.

The trial was a short one. The witnesses were few, and owing to circumstances beyond their control, they could remember nothing with that succinct clarity which a good trial demands at the expense of things as they really occurred, blurred, confused. Sir Aaron and Cramp both did what was expected of them, Sir Aaron harping on the bad luck the prisoner had suffered because his training in small-arms drill had survived his inebriety, and the bullet had found its mark. He even went as far as admitting that the case had the elements of a personal nightmare to it, elements which might make them all uneasy with the invariable thought which every normal man must entertain at some time or other, "What are the limits of my patience?" "What are the limits of my endurance?" "Of what am I capable if all I hold dear comes under attack?" "What control do I still exercise over myself when I drink too much?" "When I drive home after excessive drinking, is what I see through my windscreen the truth, or is it some dreamworld in which alcohol has played havoc with proportions?"

Lord Justice Plantagenet-Williams blinked with disbelief on occasion, because it was hardly clear on whose side Sir Aaron was exercising his Victorian power for evoking horror, and if this went on, there would be very little left for Mr. Cramp to say.

Cramp asked the jury to put themselves in the shoes of an American policeman abroad, an invitation which the jury resisted to a man. He described with baleful insistence the workings of a mind seeking solace in a single drink after a terrible road accident — and how this single drink had become a multitude of drinks out of social obligation, and how the conversation, at first merry and innocuous, had turned sour as the spirits inflamed their minds.

"The spirits, the whiskey, stirred up the quiet waters which lie at the core of every one of us, waters which are tranquil under the influence of what we have learned, our social graces, our civic sense — but which, when stirred, bring all the confusion of our primitive beings to the surface, all the sentiment of hatred, aggressivity, childhood memories, bad dreams, all the atavistic blackness of our soul's stretching back to the mark of Cain, and to the conscience." He left a terrible pause, and swept the jury with his expressionless blue eyes, fixing each member for a brief embarrassing moment. "We all have these waters within us."

"This is no place to relieve ourselves, however," Sir Neville whispered to Mr. Alberts, who rocked with such excessive, if silent, laughter, that Sir Neville soon regretted having voice to this little pleasantry.

Cramp ended his defense of his client by dismissing the charge of murder as ridiculous under the circumstances, even if there was technically no other charge which could reasonably have been brought. It was, he supposed, possible to regard the act as one of manslaughter, but one has to have a particularly tough, unrelenting, and inhuman mind to insist on this. He glanced at the judge, who expressed nothing at all. Obviously, he admitted, it was impossible to condone gratuitous killings in public places, or anywhere else for that matter, but here we had the case of a distinguished public servant, a man of achievement and responsibility in his community, lauded by the citizens and awarded an enviable diploma (here Cramp quoted the text of the award in full, flinching a little at some of the grossest neo-medievalisms). This man, by some accident of circumstance, had never been out of the United States in over half a century of life. Whereas his experience of his own civic problems was extensive, his knowledge of other ways of life was nil. Even if it were merely out of deference to our great ally, who had been the most important, sometimes even the only bulwark of democracy in a bitterly divided world, it was their solemn duty to acquit one of her more important public officials ensnared in a tragic trap far from home, and faced with fearful recrimination for what was, by all evidence, an error of judgment.

"Would you like it if the local chief constable were arrested and judged by an American court for a silly crime of this nature?"

There was something about the silence of the court which

suggested that quite a few people thought this might be a very good idea. Cramp quickly passed back to a less speculative, more rhetorical form of argument, and ended with a display of grandiloquence which would have matched Sir Aaron's cavernous style, but which in his mouth sounded like exasperation. Flushed and twitching, and waving a few blank sheets of paper in the air, he sat down, and urgently placed a yellow pencil between his teeth to compensate for the absent pipe. Immediately the saliva began to flow down his chin, and he looked like a huge baby in his white bonnet, his eyes seemingly as yet innocent of any experience.

The judge summed up. His voice was utterly passionless, and yet his manner of caressing word suggested a desiccated sensuousness about things which for the majority of men hold no voluptuous appeal whatever. Sir Neville felt that if you punched the old boy, a cloud of library dust would rise from him, and hang about in the air for an eternity afterwards with nowhere to go.

"If you decide," he said to the jury, with the rising and falling inflections of the nursery rhyme, "if you decide that here was a man who entered the public house with the desire to kill, and who accomplished his aim on the body of his unfortunate victim, then there is only one verdict, and that is one of guilty of murder. Witnesses have said that the prisoner gave no evidence of having known the victim before, so that their meeting was no doubt one of chance, the meeting of two people who happened to slake their thirst — or else indulge their weakness — in the same bar. Since there is nothing abnormal about the prisoner, apart from a predilection for rapid decisions with his firearm, which we learn he is allowed to wear on his person when in his own country, there is no suggestion that here we have a madman whose idea was to kill the first comer. There is, therefore, no suggestion that he would kill a person he did not know previously, with premeditation.

"On the other hand, you may decide that here is a man who

is, as counsel for the defense has proposed with no mean eloquence, and in which he was somewhat surprisingly seconded by the Crown, a man who is a high official of a friendly power and who has by mischance strayed away from his usual grazing ground. If they are to be believed, we have here a lost lamb of sterling rectitude and irreproachable reputation — apart from a previous error of judgment of a similar nature, perpetrated in an area in which he should have known better, and in which the reproof seems to have become confused with congratulation and promotion. However, be this as it may, it falls, happily, outside of our jurisdiction and therefore of our judgment, although we may perhaps be permitted to remark within the relative safety of our own sphere of existence, that congratulation and promotion are questionable deterrents to arbitrary killing. If the prisoner has been brought up on this kind of intellectual diet, it is little wonder that he finds our food for thought indigestible. No doubt the characters of *Alice in Wonderland* would have the same difficulty in adapting themselves to life in Great Britain, and it would be our duty to temper our reprehension with pity. A man who attempted to play golf using a flamingo as a club would rightly have the R.S.P.C.A to contend with, and would in any case not have much of a score at the golf club. Human nature being what it is, it is probably the latter reason which would cause him to abandon his flamingo.

"There is, of course, endless delight in fairy stories. Especially as one grows older, the literary and human value of these flights of fancy begin to gain in profundity, and the frontiers between them and reality become more uncertain. I am willing to believe them more than most people, and yet we must ask ourselves nevertheless whether it is credible, feasible even, that a foreigner can be so ignorant of life in other countries that he draws a gun on a perfect stranger, using this gesture as a final argument in a political discussion? And even if it is credible, or feasible, must we be especially considerate towards a man with high local responsibility, or must we, on the contrary, expect a higher standard from him? If we condemn a man in the street for not knowing better, should the law be different for a public official because he should have known much better? Should the law be different at all under any circumstances? Send Alice to ask the Queen of Hearts.

"If you believe, as we have been asked to, that this highly placed innocent abroad entered into a political discussion of rare acrimony in a public house, and that he used his gun in order to make his point, for the reasons that this was his habit, for which he had been congratulated and promoted before, then it is your duty to acquit.

"There is, however, a third alternative. If you believe that here is a man who did not have the common sense to declare his firearm at the Customs, which would have removed all temptation — a man of such naïveté that he considered that a police chief in one part of the world was automatically a police chief in every other part of the world — a man of limited experience, of an uninquiring mind, a man of vanity, a bit of a bully, a bit of a cad, a bit of a good-hearted fool, and quite a lot of a spoiled child, then it is necessary to think in terms of a verdict which is both stern and merciful. If you believe that he entered that public house with the intention of passing the time while awaiting his wife's return, and that there he began to drink heavily, undoubtedly under the provocation of the kind generosity which applies to chance meetings in taverns and alehouses, and that he then became involved in a political discussion of gathering rancor and incoherence, which culminated in his shooting a defenseless man to death, then it is your duty to return a verdict of manslaughter.

"One final point. If you believe that the prisoner sincerely thought, in his ignorance and in his drunkenness, that the victim was reaching for a gun in order to do him harm, then there is still the possibility that his act could be interpreted as an act of self-defense. If, however, you believe that the gesture of searching for a handkerchief and reaching for a gun differ in speed, in intention, and in manner, even to the eye of a man in his cups, then there is no other verdict but manslaughter. Remember, an innocent man entered the public house just as the prisoner did. One came out alive; the other lost his life there."

The jury was not long out of the courtroom. They returned a verdict of Not Guilty of Murder, Guilty of Manslaughter. Lord Justice Plantagenet-Williams sentenced Krumnagel to seven years' penal servitude. Krumnagel was led away shouting obscenities, which were not part of the record. Edie yelled at the judge, but his mind was already elsewhere.

"It's still a great country," Mr. Alberts said to Sir Neville, smiling in his most aggravating way.

Sir Aaron was gloomy.

"It's all my fault, I'm afraid. I rather overdid it."

"It's not your fault at all. It's democracy," Sir Neville said. "When there are too many people on one side of the boat, they tend to gravitate to the other in order to keep the damn thing steady in the water. They pay lip service to the importance of the individual, but it's the boat that counts. It's the boat, all the way."

"If the boat weren't there, we'd all be in the water, drowning."

"I know."

"So you can't think of a better system?"

"No. Not yet," he added modestly, with a sad smile. "But it's not a neat story."

"You're asking the impossible."

"Unless you ask for the impossible, there's no point in being alive."

9

The immediate consequences of the trial were several. Edie gave a press conference, tears streaming down her face. All the repressions of her emotional life drained freely away as she stood alone, looking tinier than ever, in the conference room of the Lexington Hotel in London. Major Batt O'Fehy had not accompanied her. She had wanted to be alone. Once resigned to the inevitable, Joan of Arc wanted to share her pile of faggots with no one. The privacy of glory was the least one could ask under such circumstances.

Journalists from the tabloids and the Sundays who specialize in trial thrills asked most of the questions.

"What do you think of our English justice?"

"Ask me what I think of your English law. English justice, I haven't seen any."

"Fair enough. Do you yourself believe your husband ought to have got off?"

"There's a crazy question. How long you been a reporter, son?"

"What are you going to do now?"

"What am I going to do? Fight. That's what I'm going to do. Seem funny to you? Funny a woman should want to fight? Listen, we do it better'n some of you guys. And you know why? We got a bigger choice of weapons, that's why. I'm going to fight for my man, that's what I'm going to do."

"Just exactly how are you going to do this?"

"You think I'm going to tell you 'just exactly how,' you got another thing coming, and then some. Listen, you think my hometown's going to stand for this? You think America's going to stand for it? I'm going to do everything ever I can to make it tough on you people. I'm going to go on the air, on television, walk the streets if need be, telling people what it's *really* like over here. All about your kind of hospitality, of Christian good neighborliness, seven years in the goddamn clink."

"Are you, in fact, Christian?"

"You got a nerve. I'm Catholic. Born Mittelhauser, from Alsace, Germany, and my mother was a Grace O'Reardon."

"Irish?"

"What kind of mental age do you boys have? What should O'Reardon be then, Puerto Rican for Christ's sake?"

"Are you going to see your husband before you go?"

"I sure am. And I'm only going in order to come back again finally and get him out of there. I'm going home to raise money, see, for a fighting fund — and to go on the air, like I said. I intend standing by my man."

"No matter how long the fight?"

"No matter how long the fight."

"All seven years if need be."

"Seven years, seventy years — you name it. Listen, I love my man. I want you boys to make that part of the record."

"Doesn't it worry you — I mean, has it ever worried you, living with a man who is capable of shooting others?"

"I wouldn't respect a guy who wouldn't be prepared to shoot it out if need be. I wouldn't respect a feller who didn't know how to handle a gun. I don't go for pacifists and fags."

"Do you have to be a pacifist or a fag not to care for gunplay?"

"Sure you do. I'm not saying there aren't exceptions — the Pope for instance — but of the available guys, those who talk about peace on earth, brother, they want peace in bed too."

"Can we quote you?"

"Can you quote me? What are we here for, fellers? Social gossip? I been married more times than one, see, and I guess you could say I know what I'm talking about."

"How many times have you been married actually?"

"Me? Four times. And it's always been to policemen. And I'm proud of it."

"Four times? You told us just now that you were, in fact, Catholic. Are these marriages quite compatible with your beliefs?"

Edie paused. She nodded dangerously, and let her questioners suffer under the intensity of her gaze.

"Wise guy," she said at length. "I was married when I was fifteen years old to Patrolman Warren C. O'Harity. We wasn't compatible, but I stuck it out till he got killed in a seven-car pileup on State Highway 173, between Beckford and New Wittenberg, while chasing a suspect in a stolen Graham-Paige roadster. Yellow, it was. I was a widow at seventeen." She shouted at dictation speed. "Then I hitched up with Larry Bunyan, of Homicide. He was a fine officer, but he cheated on me. I don't want to say nothing against him on account of he passed away, see. Want me to go on? He was taken with leukemia. He was about gone before they identified what it was. O.K.? Are you all with me? Then Chet Koslowsky began taking me out. He was wonderful to me while he was courting, but afterwards — Well, nothing's perfect, is it? You ought to know that over here. He shot it out with a gangster outside Barney's Cellar-on-the-Roof — that's a rooftop dive we got back home. They both died. And Chet went with a smile on his lips. 'I got him, didn't I? Tell me I got him.' 'You got him, honey,' I said, and he lay back and passed on, still smiling. And then Chief Krumnagel began paying attention to me. And that about brings us up to date, don't it? Now there's nothing in the Good Book which says a Catholic can't marry again if one or the other gets knocked off. Till death do us part, remember, or ain't you married?" she sneered.

The journalist was without conscience. Unembarrassed, he pursued his line of cool questioning.

"Isn't it rather unusual," he asked, "for a woman to be married to four consecutive policemen?"

"What d'you want to make of it? Get me into Ripley's *Believe It or Not,* and make a quick buck for the information? No, it is not unusual. If I didn't have bad luck, I'd still be married to one policeman, wouldn't I? My dad's a policeman, see, Lieutenant Caspar H. Mittelhauser, Junior. He's retired now. In the line of my parents' social life, I didn't meet mostly nothing else but other policemen. That I got married to them was natural. Listen, it was as natural as that I'm fighting for my man now."

"Will there be an appeal?"

"If I ever see that old son of a bitch of a judge with that soiled towel on his head, I'll spit right in his goddam eye — is that the kind of appeal you mean, boys? I'm here to fight — and where I'm in to fight, I'm in to win!"

Two of the papers carried huge pictures of Edie the next morning, one with her mouth wide open, maliciously selected, under the headline "I'm Here to Fight," the other with her fist to her forehead, her eyes shut, under the words "I Want Peace on Earth, Not Peace in Bed." The wave of permissiveness which was sweeping the world evidently included the permission to misquote.

Sir Neville had ordered all the papers that day, and Mrs. Shakespeare found him strangely silent at breakfast. He was disgusted with what he read, as much in the pallor and rigidity of the more distinguished papers as in the stereotyped schmaltz of those which purported to reflect the viewpoint of the average man. None of them could do more than report the facts of the trial, or at least embroider on the human debris which all trials leave in their wakes. As he looked at the pictures of Edie, wedged between photos of a nude scuplture which had just been banned by the town council of Fishguard as obscene, and the smiling faces of three English hippies lost in a forest of hair, who had been asked to leave the Azores for having celebrated a midnight black mass around a public fountain, he felt a deep surge of disillusion. It was not his habit to take any but the two most famous newspapers, and perhaps in doing this he had blinkered himself voluntarily to all the incredible things that were going on around him. Not that existence itself had changed that much, but the way in which it was presented — or was the word of the publicists, sold? — began to look like both a projection of a presumed public wish and a distillation of the most colorful aspects of an event at the expense of all others. It was as though every item were bowdlerized for the consumption of morons, or else seen through the sleezy eyes of the moralizing lecher. There was no balanced information as such in the papers, but curious breathless little articles of telegraphic concision and utter grammatical license, one more incredible and childish than the other, each done up in stylistic cellophane, tidy as sweets, and reeking of artificial flavor.

Sir Neville wondered of what point the careful education of children was, the lessons in debate and its civilized rules, the rudiments of citizenship, when they were exposed to the great leavening of mediocrity early in life? Why struggle for standards of comprehension, why pursue mirages such as justice, equity, the rights of man, when the dice seemed so utterly loaded in favor of the facile and the superficial? It was one of those rare days when Sir Neville was glad he had no children. He felt effete, useless, pedantic, a luxury no modern state could or should afford. He made a resolution as other people frequently do about smoking, and owing to his great strength of mind he managed to do no crossword puzzles for a week. When he resumed, however, it was in the form of a veritable orgy of them, since he had carefully preserved every copy of the *Guardian,* in case he weakened.

Krumnagel was at the beginning of his personal Calvary. He was automatically subject to all the humiliating rituals of initiation into prison life. His personal effects were taken away from him, catalogued and marked for their eventual return, and he himself left naked and shivering for an unpleasant medical examination by an impersonal doctor, who lavished whatever humanity he had in his expression on every part of Krumnagel's body but his eyes. Then the prisoner paraded in a white sheet, like a Ku Klux Klan member who had lost his hat in a race riot, until his rough prison garb was issued to him. He tried hard to keep his head, and it is to his credit that he largely succeeded. He did it by trying to study what was happening with the eye of a sociologist. He imagined, at times convincingly, at others mechanically, that what was happening to him was really happening to someone else, that he was a kind of privileged observer, comparing the details of penal usage on both sides of the Atlantic.

He had heard that a seven year sentence was one which would be examined after four years and six months, and that his case would come up before the parole board in two years and three months, and in any case Cramp had told him of his determination to appeal. Consequently, there was no definite sense of time stretching before him. The future was still peppered with hope, and the concept of the scope of his confinement had not had a chance to harden into a dark inevitability. He had not acclimatized to this half life within a life, and with luck, he never would.

[148]

All the same, it was during the loneliness of the first night, a night which lasted an eternity, that the recurrence of his anger gripped him every now and then as his mind raced, avidly poring over every impression, reliving the murder, the trial, episodes of childhood and maturity, all interspersed and shaken up in a silent and fretful cacophony of the mind. Occasionally he woke himself and others with a garbled shout, an imprecation, an appeal, or a train of filthy words, carriage clanking against carriage on their circular track.

There was no sense of air, no sense of light, except for the small weak bulb in the ceiling, like the eye of a watchdog glazed with the shallowest of sleeps, ready to brighten with awareness at the slightest troubled movement. There was no rest that night, just plungings into monstrous hour-long fantasies which lasted ten seconds, blinding flashes behind the closed eyelids, thumps and explosions and a singing in the ear — a terrible blinding, bottomless world, body and mind in open revolution, a chaos of the soul.

When dawn broke, it did not grow lighter. There were just stirrings from the others, those in the grip of habit. The noise of bodies turning on mattresses, the noise of men clinging to sleep as though clinging to childhood, as a refuge from the miseries of reality. Krumnagel was quieter now as he felt the presence of a community — he was beginning to be alone with others; he was no longer alone with himself. He even fell into a short (or was it long?) sleep.

By the time he was freed to get up and prepare himself for breakfast, he was beginning to calculate. His resentment was as deep as ever, but he began to realize that he would be lost if he allowed the initiative to be taken from him. As a dog will hide a bone against the day of disaster, so must men hide their initiative somewhere deep within their resilience — at no time must he make the best of a bad job, for that entailed surrender to the inevitability of prison; that entailed a fracture of the spirit, which was exactly what the society was after, what prisons were for. He would not make friends, for with friendship the disease of the spirit became contagious. He would not enter the communal life of the temporarily underprivileged, because such a surrender to the desires of the punishing authority would leave a residue after, when he was out. Behind a barrier of sullenness, he would dispose his reserves, cunningly marshal his forces in depth, and begin the battle of attrition.

The padre came to see him, a smiling figure with a deceptive mildness of manner, and a clipped athletic way with him, as though life had a score and was played to the whistle.

"Had a rotten night, I suppose. We all do the first night."

We? He had a nerve.

"Slept like a baby, Reverend," Krumnagel replied.

"Did you now, did you — is this your first time then?"

What the hell does he think I am? Hold it. Ho-old it. Krumnagel preserved his cool.

"Sure is my first time. Why d'you ask?"

"Well, it's usually those who make it an unfortunate habit to be inside, those who treat H.M.'s prisons as hotels, who sleep well the first night. But, mark you, they didn't sleep well, either, the first night of all."

"Is that right," Krumnagel said, with so little interest that he declined to make a question of it.

"I'm afraid so. I had a report you'd been heard to call out in your sleep, so I thought I'd come along and make sure it was nothing worse than the usual new-boy symptoms."

"Calling out in my sleep?" Krumnagel asked incredulously, but without much real surprise. "No, sir. You got yourself the wrong man. I didn't do no calling out. Don't make a practice of it."

Since the padre looked unbelieving, Krumnagel narrowed his eyes in reminiscence, overacting rather, and murmured slowly —

"Oh, yeah, come to think of it I did hear some guy calling out during the night. Seemed like in pain. It came from down that corridor."

"There's no disgrace entailed in feeling homesick, or lost, you know. After all, it is rather like the first day at school for a young boy."

This creep had to be put in his place, coolly. Young boy? What's he making with young boys for? Don't he have no sense of what's what?

"I don't believe you know who I am, Reverend."

"Here we're all equal. Nobody cares who anyone else is, or was. We're one family in misfortune, facing up to the reality of our life, with God's help."

"That go for you too? Then why ain't you dressed like us?"

"There is no difference between us," he said, "except that I'm allowed to go home at night. I know that may seem a big difference, and yet nearly all my waking hours are spent here. When we are asleep, do we really know where we are?"

"There's other differences, Reverend. You can talk down to me. I'm supposed to talk up to you."

"Not really. It's only because I wear the cloth. Only because in a sense, I represent God, very inadequately. Are you a practicing Christian?"

Krumnagel frowned.

"Sure am. There's not a man can say I'm not. I got my own preacher I go to, Reverend Delricks, of the Sunny Valley Lutheran Episcopalian Church, out in Sunny Valley, and when I get back home, there's certain questions I'm going to level at the big man up there."

"Big man up where?"

"Big man up there — in the clouds. The big man moves the sun and earth, and reads our minds like an open book."

"Oh yes, I see."

"If He can read my mind right now, He'll be able to tell that I'm kind of mad."

[151]

"Mad."

"Yeah, mad," Krumnagel said reasonably, as though it was a word he'd been searching for for some time. "Maybe you like to think that you're all equal here, and all the jazz about buddies in misfortune — I don't, and I don't intend to, and my God has never led me to believe I was the same as everyone else, except in the way laid down in the Constitution, that we're all equal before God."

"That's all I meant —"

"Oh no, it isn't. You wanted me to forget who I was before I came here. You wanted me to knuckle under and start thinking that because we're all in the same stinking prison clothes, we're all the same in mind and body. Now I don't go for that, and my God has never indicated to me that that's what he expected, otherwise why would he have let me get to be chief of police, with a hell of a lot of civic responsibility, and near a million people ready to greet me in the street? 'Hi, Chief!' 'How's it going, Chief?' 'Take it easy, Chief,' that was all I heard, wherever I went, any time of the day and night. I was respected. I'll even go so far as to say I was loved. No shit, I'm not trying to fool you. Those people out there loved me, and they often said as much. Why? Because they knew that, with God's help, I was doing my job to the best of my ability. That's why."

"What does God mean to you? I mean, how do you see him?" asked the padre.

Krumnagel cocked his head in consideration of this grave question.

"I'll tell you," he said at length, slowly, and with measure. "I see him as an elder brother . . . the elder brother I never had, I guess. I'm kind of his shadow, and yet, he wants me to stand on my own, up to life, and do his work in the way I'm most fitted."

"Then why are you mad?"

"I'm mad on account he had no business letting me wind up here."

[152]

"After all you've done for him, is that it?"

"Yes. Sure, that's it."

"But when you pray — I presume you do pray?"

"Every day, twice, morning and evening."

The padre was a little taken aback at the glibness of the reply, and wondered for a split second whether he had not, in a moment of aberration, asked Krumnagel how often he brushed his teeth.

"Well, when you pray, do you really open your heart to God — I mean, are your wishes in the form of a humble supplication, or do you present him with a kind of shopping list of your desires?"

"I never ask for nothing," Krumnagel snapped, declaring his independence of God within the framework of his confessed dependence on him. "I like to consult him, tell him what I've done, and I intend doing."

"Do you do this in words?"

"I don't do it by talking out loud, if that's what you mean. You want people to think I'm crazy? No — I meditate."

"You talk to God with an inner voice."

"Yeah, that's right. That's good. I like that. That's precisely what I do."

"And now, last night and this morning you've been busy ticking him off, have you?"

"Listen, what gives between me and God is my business — I beg His pardon, our business."

"Because you're a big police chief, doing the same kind of work God does, but a bit more on the scale of human possibilities."

Krumnagel's eyes narrowed again.

"I don't like the way you said that, Reverend."

"I'm not frightened of you," the padre said, somehow oozing the self-confidence of a man with quite a bit of pious judo up his sleeve.

Krumnagel forced a smile to his lips.

"And I'm not trying to scare you. I'm not going to kill another guy just because I don't know my own strength with little punks that get loud in the mouth and start claiming they know it all. I'm too big for that. I'm too big and this time I'm not loaded, as they haven't told me when the bars around here open up. Only I got a word of advice to you. This is a big cooler by the looks of it. There's room for both of us. Just keep out of my way, that's all I ask. I don't need the aggravation. And nor does my God."

The padre grinned. He was one for looking ahead, and seeing potential moralities everywhere. In his mind's eye, he could already perceive this great hulk of a man on his knees, sobbing bitterly at the discovery that his God was but a reflection of himself in a gigantic mental mirror, and that the still small bleat of the lamb had never found an echo in his heart. He saw a magnificient sermon in it eventually. All that was needed was patience, because God for God, if not man for man, he felt he outgunned Krumnagel.

None of the prisoners created much of an immediate impression on Krumnagel, although they all stared at him with unashamedly calculating eyes, having followed the trial in the papers, and wondering what this new addition to the "family in misfortune" was really like. In church, a Gothic nightmare of a building, he rose and knelt with the others, but in the middle of "O God, Our Help in Ages Past," he fancied he caught the eye of the Rev. Dobbs, standing in the pulpit with a look of odious serenity about him, so he immediately stopped singing and sat down.

Only one prisoner made a consistent effort to create a contact with Krumnagel. He was an old and cheerful fellow with a painful cough and a pleasantly disreputable face who would occasionally aim a finger at the newcomer, and, while agitating the finger as though it were firing, make a passable imitation of a machine gun with his mouth. Then, in explanation, he would say something like "Chicago" or "Wise guy" or "I filled yer full o' lead, baby" in an accent purporting to be gangsterese, but which was in fact snarled Cockney.

This was just the kind of old crackpot who was calculated to worm his way through Krumnagel's defenses, and therefore constitute a real threat to his ultimate tranquillity. After all, the shooting of Jock had begun with a sudden tenderness for the old and their innocuous follies. Krumnagel turned over his attitude in his mind, and decided that there was nothing incompatible between his toleration of this old fool, and the hardness he would continue to show towards all others. He decided this because he had been made optimistic by the first of a barrage of letters from Edie, enclosing the press cuttings of her defiant conference. The sudden mellowness which this show of solidarity and belligerence on his behalf had engendered, required an outlet, and so he fell into conversation with the ancient, whose name he learned was Harold, Harry for short.

Harry had a single tooth, which stood lonely as a rock in the entrance of his mouth, deflecting spray left and right as his tongue crashed into it like a breaker. Most men with practically no teeth can do quaint things with their mouths, seeming to button them like an old lady's handbag or shrivel the whole of their faces up like the bellows of early cameras, and Harry was no exception.

He never failed to fall back on these tricks when he felt the need to ingratiate, and when playing a gangster in old Chicago, a recurring theme in his dreamworld, he would clutch his chest, make like a Graflex, send his eyes out of sight under the upper lids, and sink to his knees saying something like "They got me, buddy." Krumnagel would help him to his feet, with an "I'll tell them you died like a man." The secret of this undeniable and curiously quick friendship was perhaps that the world of childhood and make-believe was not very far away in either man, and in an atmosphere austere and grim enough to be bereft of the physical elements to feed these dreams, they had to create their own playthings, and to overemphasize the reality of such playthings to themselves.

In reply to a phone call from Sir Neville, the governor of the prison, Major Attlesey-Gore, reported that the prisoner was having some difficulty settling down, that he was sullen and uncommunicative, that the padre, who usually brought out the Cub Scout in most men, could get nowhere with him, but, on the credit side, he seemed to have struck up a kind of friendship with a habitual criminal in his late seventies, one Harry Mothers, who had spent over thirty years of his life in jail.

"A habitual criminal in his late seventies?" Sir Neville reiterated in disbelief.

"Yes, he's not quite all there. Half of it is senility, I believe, but half of it is congenital stupidity. He's been in and out all his life."

"For what reasons?"

"Oh, petty crimes, you know — but of late he has become more ambitious, and attempted to rob banks, an activity for which he has no aptitude whatsoever. I shouldn't think he's robbed more than a couple of thousand quid's worth of goods in thirty years of hard crime."

"How depressing. Still, I'm glad Krumnagel has found a friend."

"Yes — it won't be for long I'm afraid. Harry comes out in two weeks."

"Oh, dear. But he won't be out for long either if what you tell me about him is true."

"He may die. He's seventy-six, and was gassed in the First World War."

10

In the week that followed, Edie's campaign back home was in full swing. She visited the mayor, who listened to her with profound attention, and even lent her his initialed handkerchief to dry her tears on. Her description of the trial began to be really hair-raising by the third telling, so that by the time she told it to Arnie Brugger, it sounded as rigged as the condemnation of Socrates. The judge appeared in this patriotic version of events as a bitterly partisan figure, obviously anti-American by virtue of his lack of knowledge of that greater freedom which citizens enjoy, smugly content with his little bookish existence, locked away in the creaking old world where air conditioning was called a draft and liberty merely license, and where the horizon was a pea-soup fog. The advocates were, in her telling,

creatures out of a Disney forest, the one with sprigs of wild
weeds growing out of improbable places, the other with his
coffeepot spout. Which sides they were on hardly mattered.
The witnesses were three of their dwarfs, with the old woman
who lived in a shoe thrown in for good manners, while the
police were strange creatures blinded by their helmets, who
plodded around in lugubrious boots and communicated in
monosyllables.

The sequence of events in Edie's highly charged mytho-
manic style was too extreme to convince many of her listeners,
but it was all improbable enough to make good copy, and she
commanded even more space in the local press than she had in
the London papers. The morning paper, the only one, the *Cross-
Examiner and Free Speaker,* even came out with an editorial
on "The Nature of Justice," in which sources as diverse as the
Bible and Judge Felix Frankfurter were quoted, and the reader
was reminded that it is the State Department's duty to protect
Americans in countries which profess their friendship, such as
South Korea and Great Britain, as well as in countries hostile to
the idea of personal liberty. "There's not much for accredited
ambassadors to do in these days of sophisticated communication. Let our man in London go in there and ask a few searching questions. Not only the City, but America, and Justice herself, ever blind, but we trust not deaf, demand it," the article
ended, and the message was taken up by the large evening
paper the only one, the *Insider,* owned by the same family, in
an editorial entitled, "The Strange Case Of Chief Krumnagel,"
beginning with the words, "It is only a bare three months ago
that Chief Krumnagel, our controversial but generally respected Number One Policeman received, at the hands of Governor Darwood H. McAlpin personally, an illuminated scroll
testifying to his great service to this, our wonderful City . . ."

Once this tendency had been expressed in the papers, it was
not difficult to form a committee, nor was it difficult to find a
figurehead for it in the shape of one of the City's more contro-

versial personalities, the retired Major General Cleaver T. Cumbermore, a raddled nut of a man, bad temper written all over his face in slashing downward strokes, with a mouth like a gash from which the stitches had not yet been removed.

This General Cumbermore had several things going for him, as they say, public-wise. First of all, he was a general, and generals in America are like phoenixes who rise endlessly cleansed and pristine from the flames of wasteful battle, consistently blameless and authorities on everything. Opinions of generals on every subject under the sun, including education, architecture, the fine arts, and sociology are consistently solicited, and widely quoted in newsprint. Naturally the space devoted to any specific general is in proportion to his distinction, and here General Cumbermore seemed to suffer a fault of personality. Whereas General Patton had once struck a soldier, and got into trouble for it, General Cumbermore had struck several, and nobody had taken any notice. Even the victims had not thought of complaining. There was no reason for this other than some indefinable quality which made General Patton's single cuff historically important and the lack of which made General Cumbermore's repeated backhanders ephemeral. Nevertheless, the intention of wickedness was there in Cumbermore, even if consistently frustrated by events, or the lack of them, and this counted for something.

"The affair of this . . . of the arrest and imprisonment of this . . . this . . . of Chief Krumnagel . . . is a goldarn disgrace . . . and if I had my way . . . my way . . . I sure wouldn't take this kind of . . . kind of insult from the . . . from the cotton-pickin' Redcoats lying down . . . For God's sake, we know enough of . . . of Redcoat justice, don't we? Ask Gen'l Wash'ton," General Cumbermore declared in a television interview, purple with intolerance, and one would say, a little loaded to boot. This was enough to inflame certain extreme elements in the City, men and women whose life lacked clean excitement, and for whom, like Krumnagel himself, the irresponsibility of the playground was fading too quickly, before they were ready for it.

A group of these (it was presumed, because the police were slow to express even a suspicion) planted a bomb in the British consulate in Houston, which was the nearest British agency to the City. It went off, wounding a Negro girl who was delivering a tray of coffee and Danish pastry from a snack bar. The local Sachs and Friedenberg department store in the City, part of a large, prosperous and enlightened chain of wholesalers covering the entire South and Middle West of the United States, had just opened a British Cheese Week, in an effort to help the British and show that the French weren't the only ones, damn them; and this Cheese Fair, for the exploitation of which a London bus and four Beefeaters had been imported, came to a sticky end, Cheshires and Cheddars and Wensleydales and Caerphillies and Union Jacks rolling all over the place, among broken glass and pictures of the Queen. The bus was overturned and partially burned, and the poor old Beefeaters manhandled. The British consulate in Houston cabled the Foreign Office suggesting that no further cheeses or Beefeaters or busses should be sent for the moment, until conditions were normalized, and the Beefeaters were sent home to the Tower via Montreal.

As the news of these events became known in prison, Krumnagel's stock soared up. He became something of a mystery man, and his aloofness now found a positive echo of awe among the inmates. It is not every day that a British house of detention is honored by the presence of a man capable of inspiring riots five thousand miles away. Perhaps, even more than the prisoners, it was the warders who were impressed, and with them, no doubt because they were in positions of relative authority, the reaction was cautiously jocular rather than silent. To them, the ice had been broken, and they began to treat Krumnagel as somebody who had suffered bad luck rather than bad judgment.

Even the padre sidled up to Krumnagel and said, "I see from the newspapers that your disciples are up in arms in far corners of the earth."

"Maybe my God heard my prayer," Krumnagel snapped, as he loped off majestically like a latter-day King Lear, his aged clown at his heel making rubber faces at the padre in consolation.

Back in his office, Sir Neville found himself quite openly and with childish stubbornness hoping that the hooligans would destroy more British property in order to prove his point of view. A destruction of cheeses was hardly an adequate platform from which to launch a demarche; even an overturned bus could hardly claim attention in a day and age when hundreds of busses a day were being overturned the world over by enraged students, sulking bus drivers, bitter passengers, inflamed Moslems, crusading Catholics, self-righteous Protestants, lamenting Jews, barricading bonzes, or any of a million sects, groups or unions with a grievance. And as for the manhandling of the Beefeaters, it became clear that this item of news had been exaggerated for the sake of a more substantial story, and that they had been no more jostled than by the usual crowd of American tourists within the Tower itself.

Nevertheless, Sir Neville exerted himself in his lunch hour, trying to take in one club for his preprandial gin, another for food, and a third for coffee, and at each he tried to turn the conversation in the direction of the Krumnagel affair. As is not unusual in England, the majority of those with a reputation for being well-informed replied —

"Oh, I didn't see that. Which page was it on?" or else, "Local cranks, I wouldn't be surprised," and then, incredulous, "Where did you say this happened?"

With one or two of those he talked to, he did have more luck, but on the whole the going was tough. The rioters had destroyed too little, and the City was too remote. If only it had been New York, or Washington, even better.

As Sir Neville said ruefully to Sir Aaron, "It used to be too little and too late; now it's too little and too far away."

Sir Aaron grunted. "While we're still allowed by circumstances to live with illusion of comfort and the mirage of wealth, governing the country through Parliament, administering it through the offices, but ruling it through clubs, it'll always be too something or other and too something else."

"Yes," said Sir Neville, with his quiet mischief. "Long may it last. Cheers."

"Cheers."

And they drank to the dark background which set off the sweet colors of life.

Back home, in the City, Edie's committee, launched hopefully, began to run out of steam. Unfortunately, there is no holding back other events, and in the general clamor of murders, rapes, holdups, kidnappings, sit-ins, sit-outs, marches and countermarches, sexual malpractices, dopings, druggings, sluggings, muggings, there was very little in the sob stuff about a police chief, of all things, and his gallant widow to hold the public attention. The committee met once or twice, made elaborate plans, which were as always contingent on money, grudgingly given and in small quantities, and eventually the whole ambitious scheme began to sink by the stern. General Cumbermore became strategically sick, since he had got as little mileage out of this adventure as was his habit. Edie attempted to interest people outside the City, without success. The papers felt they had already done their bit by writing leading articles, but told her that the response to them had been disappointing, and that even great papers like theirs couldn't continually push an unpopular measure for fear of antagonizing the readers. Red Leifson, writing his syndicated column from the pontifical immunity of his wheelchair, did not help much by snidely asking, "Whatever happened to the great 'Help Chief Krumnagel' campaign launched with such hoo-hah by none other than General 'Meat-Cleaver' Cumbermore and whilom Police-Bride

Edie Krumnagel, and which cost late-Great Britain half of next year's national income in Cheddar cheeses? Could it be that my friends and partners the public (Hiya, pard!) has gotten itself fed to the proverbial teeth with this outa-date sob stuff, and would just as lief (no pun intended, folks, honest) let has-beens be has-beens?"

When Edie complained about the vicious tone of this piece, the editor merely shrugged his shoulders.

"Space is space, Edie, you know that. Christ, you got what you wanted, didn't you? No one cares what the papers say so long as they say it — that's Walt Whitman or Orson Welles or someone, but it's no less true for that. Lookit, Red Leifson's got many enemies around town. That's why we keep him on. Most people read him just to get mad. I'll bet he's gotten you a hell of a lot of sympathy with this piece. Honest."

Honest. The fact was that few people cared for Krumnagel when he was up, and the fact that he was down was not calculated to change their opinion. Even among the leaders of opinion — another source of income with greater sums of money from fewer donors — there was not much support. A so-called free society has never been remarkable for its feeling towards its casualties. It is invariably richer in charity than in compassion, probably because charity is taxdeductible whereas compassion is merely time-consuming. With their minds bent to ease and profit, and the social graces which are the outward signs of success, they had very little time for anything but successful and profitable ventures, more especially since the interim police chief, Al Carbide, was now showing none of the teeth he had shown as a deputy, but was, on the contrary, treating Joe Tortoni, Boots Shilliger, Milt Rotterdam, and other well-known and socially respectable racketeers with all the circumspection their elevated position in the hierarchy demanded. The mayor was even able to arrange a small dinner and swimming party at his ranch to which all the notable racketeers as well as a few accommodating legal and political figures were invited, and include Al Carbide among the guests, an initiative he had never dared take with Krumnagel, because he had always seemed to him too stupid to be reliable as a force for either good or evil. Since the mayor felt, sincerely at times, that he was managing to do a lot of good through evil, by the kind of logic which declares that counterfeit money will pay for hospital supplies just like good money, providing nobody knows it's false, he naturally felt more at ease with the evident awareness of Al Carbide than he ever had with Krumnagel's clumsy slyness.

The only positive gestures which Edie were able to wrest from any of those present at the triumphal lunch of three months ago was a letter of regret at what had occurred from the governor, signed in his absence — his absence in an adjoining office probably — by his secretary, and a promise from Monsignor Francis Xavier O'Hanrahanty to send Krumnagel a small volume of comforting thoughts for those who have fallen by life's wayside, collated by himself, with a foreword by the Cardinal Archbishop of Boston.

As his brief star faded, however, another was rising for Krumnagel, who used old Harry as a kind of confessor for all his sourness. They used to sit in various secluded spots in the prison, Krumnagel talking without end, Harry listening like a child. Whatever Krumnagel didn't know, he made up, so that he became a beacon of all knowledge for the old man. Jesse James, the Cisco Kid, Dillinger, Capone, Elliot Ness; Krumnagel spoke as though he had known them all, exchanging words and bullets in that feeling of romanticized euphoria which has by now cleansed the air war of '14–'18 of all sordidness, and made it seem like an epos of legendary loveliness.

The old man, whose education had been comic books, would sometimes grow melancholy.

"All my life, I guess," he would say, staring at nothing and diminishing his face by half, so that his chin covered his nostrils, "I bin a loner. Never found a pardner to go in wiv' me, share the swag."

"There's no disgrace in that. I'd say there's glory in it. Dillinger was a loner. They finally caught up with him coming out of a movie house — alone."

Harry did a machine gun, and died.

"That's right. That's precisely right," Krumnagel went on without smiling. "Now Capone — Al always needed people around him. Without his gang, he was nothing. A child didn't have to be scared of him. But when the boys were around, you better lock up your daughters — they was rough, and I mean, rough."

"I'll fill you full o' lead, baby."

"That's right, and there was no shortage of bullets — when those babies said full o' lead, they meant just that, and no kidding. Today we might consider them wasteful — we got tidy-minded today, and we shoot straighter — but those old-timers, they shot through their pockets, often as not — anytime you went down into the Loop in Chicago, and you saw a guy with a hole in his pocket, you could bet your bottom dollar that guy was a gangster."

Harry whistled with disbelief.

"That's correct. I knew one feller in Chicago about your age, bit younger maybe, name of Israel Mendelssohn, Jewish, a tailor, called him Izzy for short, on account his name was Israel, see, and he made a fortune just mending pockets for the gangs. A fortune. I'm not kidding. When he retired, he bought himself a large place in Miami, know where that is? Florida. Large place with an organ in the living room. Passed away there not too long ago. Richer'n all hell, and you know something, neither he nor Mrs. Mendelssohn played the organ. They had no children."

After they had pondered for a moment on the irony of life, Harry suddenly asked, "Any of those guys rob banks?"

"Sure they did, but most of them didn't have to. They got so rich they bought banks."

"How do they do that?" Harry was aghast.

"By framing bankers."

Harry whistled again.

"That's right. But the loners, why, they had to be real good to do a bank job on their own. Guy like Jesse James — first rule was, never go in by the front door."

"I always go in by the front door!" cried Harry. "With a file, a piece o' wire . . ."

"Are you crazy?"

"Where would you go in?"

"The back door."

"I'm never sure I can find it."

"A window."

"I'm too small. You can't start putting ladders up. Not if you're a loner."

"Well, I'll tell you. Some of today's loners, they realize times are changing and they figure that, well, even a loner got to go along with progress. No use being Jesse James today — not with hidden cameras and all that crap, and I don't care how many stockings you put over your face, they'll always get you in the end. So some of these new . . . I call them the new wave of criminals, they're not going in by windows or doors."

"How they get in then? Don't tell me . . . skylight, right?"

"Nope. They get them an explosive charge, see, and they blow a hole in the wall. They get it all planned before, you follow me? Then they blow the front of the safe off with another charge, and if anyone gets in the way, why that's just too bad, they carry three or four of them Molotov cocktails — that starts fires, and there's nothing scares people away more than fires. I know one guy, we caught him eventually, but he had a run of ten months, name of Joe Corilli, Joe, short for Joseph, he got in a bank that way, and he was a loner. The Great Lakes and Medical Bank down Artillery Road, a quiet, residential neighborhood . . . Well, Joe had it all planned — around seven o'clock in the evening he turned up dressed as a plumber, see, and laid the explosive charge, timed to go off at one, six hours later . . . 0100 hours, get me . . . well, at one it went off like planned, and he got right in at the bank, laid the second charge under the safe, blew that open — now right then, a patrolman drove up, and come into the bank through the hole in the wall — the bank was wired against intruders — and you know what Joe did? Called out in a broken voice, see — 'Quick, officer, get help . . . there's been an explosion . . . there's a fire in the vault . . . I'm the night man,' and with that he threw a Molotov cocktail. Well, the mention of the word fire would have been enough — that patrolman, 'stead of coming right in and shooting it out with Joe the way he ought to have done, why, he got right out of there and radioed the fire department. And while that patrolman was in his automobile, you know what Joe did? Unlocked the front door of the bank from the inside, and walked right out of there sixty-five thousand dollars richer, like he owned the place. And we didn't catch up with him, like I said, until ten months later, when we got him on a technical kidnapping rap, taking a broad across the state line for immoral purposes, and we found five thousand bucks of the dough on him, still in the bank wrappers. I know that story real good because I was the guy had to reprimand Patrolman Kelly for not going in there and killing Joe." He laughed. "I guess I scared Kelly bad, because next time he saw a plumber, why he didn't ask no questions. Just started shooting." He became grave again. "That was the end of Kelly. The headshrinkers busted him."

Old Harry, wheezing away every now and again, was lost in a cloud of wonder.

"I don't know how he done that," he muttered.

"Who? Kelly?"

"No, not Kelly. Joe. Joe, I don't know how he done that."

"I told you," Krumnagel said, a little out of patience after all his effort.

"I know you did. That's why I say I don't know how he done it. I mean, you got to make a bomb, 'aven't you? You can't go to 'Arrods Bomb Department and order one, can you? You got to make it yourself. Then you got to make three of them cocktails you was talking about —"

"That's easy. Listen, in an hour I can make a bomb large enough to blow a hole in the prison wall."

"Why don't you?"

"Are you out of your mind, Harry? Where do I get the materials, will you tell me that?"

"What do you need?"

"Well, I'll tell you . . ."

And Krumnagel began enumerating the ingredients on his fingers, and started making a diagram on the ground with a twig. Joe took it all in like a child learning the alphabet. A world of golden achievement was opening up before him.

When Harry was released a day or two later, the farewell was one of genuine and touching emotion, a sad yet inspiring incident on the range. Harry had tears in his eyes as he extended his hand to his mentor, and at the sight of tears Krumnagel gulped hard, and in spite of himself his lip began to tremble.

"I don't want to go, you know that, don't you partner?" murmured Harry.

"Go out there, and show 'em — from me — from Big Bart."

"I guess this is it, Big Bart . . . where the trails part."

And the old man was led away by a warder towards the freedom he dreaded.

To Krumnagel, the departure was disastrous. He hardly realized how much he had begun to depend on Harry, as everything from a friendly if lunatic ear to a mental punching bag. The silence he left was immense, and Krumnagel began to recapture the horrid emotions of the first night as he noticed his fellow prisoners again, and found he knew every structural detail of his cell with sickening accuracy, for want of anything better to do. Still no news of the appeal, and the letters from Edie were decreasing in number and length, and the smile of the padre was growing more confident.

Then six days later, at about seven in the evening, a most enormous explosion rocked Knightsbridge, and the entire Edwardian façade of the local branch of the Manchester Cotton Bank, cornices, gables, crenelation, castellations and all, crumbled and fell into the street, blocking it entirely. Luckily there were no passers-by, although the first people on the scene did find an old plumber with a rubber face coughing his guts out in the huge cloud of brick dust which enveloped the disaster. At first the police assumed that Harry was an innocent bystander who happened to be there at the time, until the constable grew suspicious of the three canisters he was wearing around his waist on a rope.

"What are you going to do with these, then?" The constable asked, but Harry was still coughing too profoundly to answer coherently.

"What d'you make of these, Bill?" The constable said, and another policeman said, "They look like them Molotov cocktails to me," and the two policeman looked at each other, and that was that.

At the station, there were those who knew Harry, so he was allowed to sit, now wrapped in blankets, sipping hot, sweet tea, while answering the questions of Detective-Inspector Pewtrey, who had hurried from the Yard on the assumption that this incredible act of vandalism must have some political or racial implications — nothing else could explain its scope, or violence, or the feeling of inefficiency that surrounded it.

"But why the Manchester Cotton Bank of all places? You didn't mistake it for some other building, did you Harry?"

"Mistake?" Harry spat. "I knew what I was doing."

[169]

Pewtrey altered the tone of his voice.

"Were you in this alone, old man?"

"I always bin a loner."

"I know you always were in the past, but a man of your age just doesn't go and blow the front off a bloody bank for no reason. Who were the others, Harry?"

"There wasn't no others," Harry glared.

"What did they pay you then? And who are they?"

"Me. I was goin' to pay myself out of what I got out of there."

Pewtrey rose.

"Don't waste my time, Harry, I'm a busy man."

"I was busy too, before you brought me in 'ere."

The detective put his face very close to Harry's, and tried a very soft approach, very delicate.

"Are there politics involved?"

"What you talkin' about?"

"Were you paid by Arabs? Irish?"

"Wait till I tell 'im. I got something to tell 'im now."

"Tell who, Harry. Tell who?" Pewtrey asked urgently.

Harry halved his face, his mouth disappeared altogether, and he was mum.

Pewtrey sighed.

"This is not going to be easy for you, Harry boy. You're seventy-six. This is your twenty-ninth offense. Before, the courts have always been lenient — because you were a loner — just because of that — but if you come before them now as a part of a gang — and the silliest part of a gang if you'll pardon me — the part that takes the rap while the others get off scot-free — they're not going to be lenient again. On top of which, this time it isn't just money or silver candlesticks, you've destroyed an awful lot of private property, worth millions of pounds I wouldn't wonder —"

Pewtrey stopped because Harry's eyes were agleam with accomplishment. They had millions of pounds written all over them, to such an extent that Pewtrey had an unpleasant suspicion for the first time that he might be a loner after all.

"All right," Pewtrey said wearily, "let's say you were a loner."

"That's better. More like it altogether," said Harry.

"Why were you pretending to be a plumber?"

"What d'you want me pretend to be?"

"Why weren't you just dressed as yourself?"

"I'm too well-known. I wouldn't risk that. No. Any'ow when they go for banks over there, they most times go as plumbers."

"Over where?"

"Dixie."

"Over in Dixie, most bank robbers dress up as plumbers. Is that what you're telling me?"

"Right."

"Where the hell did you get that from?"

"Grapevine."

"Grapevine. Where did you get your plumber's outfit?"

"Abrahams, the theatrical costumer."

"At least that's one thing settled," Pewtrey said to his assistant. "The plumber's outfit goes back to Abrahams. Now what were you going to do with three Molotov cocktails?"

"I was going to set fire to the bank once I got in there."

"You realize what you're saying, do you? Sergeant, don't write that down!"

" 'Course I know what I'm saying! If the police tried to force an entrance by the hole I'd made in the wall, I was going to explain that a fire broke out, and if there was any doubt in their mind, I was going to let one of them babies go, prove it, see."

"But how on earth did you come by the idea of Molotov cocktails and bombs? Who made them for you?"

"I made 'em," Harry shouted.

"You never made them," Pewtrey shouted back.

Harry laughed incredulously, a rhetorical laugh. " 'E don't believe me," and he halved his face, and his mouth vanished again.

Pewtrey looked at him in irritation.

"Oh, not that again, for God's sake. All right, you made them."

"That's more like it."

"But who told you how to make them?"

"I made them. Never mind who told me."

"I do mind who told you."

"I made them."

"You've never made anything in your life."

"Want to bet on that?"

Exasperated, Pewtrey lifted Harry by the arms, and yelled at him.

"Who told you, Harry?"

" 'E did," said Harry in a tiny voice.

"Who's he?"

"Bart. My buddy. Big guy. Yank. With freckles. The greatest gun in the West. Fought it out with Dillinger. Cornered Dutch Schultz in the 'ooch still."

"Krumnagel?" Pewtrey asked in disbelief.

"Yeah, that's 'im." Harry was eager to correct any wrong impression. "Don't blame 'im for it not goin' right. 'E told me what to do in every detail. It's not his fault. I got the timin' of the bomb wrong. I must've connected the wrong wire to the halarm clock — or else the wire got loose — or else the halarm clock was too cheap altogether. Any'ow, the bomb was only supposed to go off at o one 'undred, that'll be after midnight, but it went off the moment I put it down."

"How did you travel to the scene of the crime?"

"Bus."

"Was it full?"

" 'Ad to stand."

Pewtrey shut his eyes, and felt himself shudder.

"Even so, goin' off when it did, I should've been able to get in through the 'ole and collect the money. There's only one thing I didn't foresee."

"And what was that?"

"The dust. I got gassed in the First War, and then I got T.B. Only one lung. I didn't foresee the dust. I couldn't breave enough to go in through the 'ole and 'ave recorse to them cocktails whatever they call 'em."

Signals to end from Scotland Yard. Major Attlesey-Gore made inquiries of his warders, and one of them remembered the buddies' farewell.

"Yes, sir, I remember distinctly Krumnagel saying to Harry words to that effect. 'Go and show 'em — from me,' he said. 'From Big Bart.'"

"Did he indeed," remarked Major Attlesey-Gore grimly. "And have you noticed Big Bart talking to anyone else?"

"No, sir, keeps very much to himself," said another warder, and his colleagues agreed, with the exception of one, who said he'd seen Krumnagel get a light for his cigarette from Ned Pratfold on more than one occasion. Major Attlesey-Gore tensed. Ned Pratfold was one of the highest hopes of the British underworld, as yet greater in promise than in achievement. The governor didn't like this cigarette business. He seemed to have an obscure mental impression of American crooks invariably discussing any desperate move while they lit each other's cigarettes at interminable length, burning finger after finger from the matches. This might merely have been a rusty reflex from the gangster films of his youth, but who knows how half the baggage of the human mind gets there? Suffice it to say that Major Attlesey-Gore was influenced by this image, and at his request Krumnagel was moved to the maximum security wing of a prison located on an offshore island — on the very day his appeal was refused.

11

When Sir Neville heard what had happened, he was beside himself — not exactly with anger; he had never learned to surrender to emotion in moments of stress — but rather with a hopeless feeling that a basic injustice was being perpetrated with his knowledge and even, partly, in his name. Throughout history there have been cases similar, and more dramatic. Justice has often been rough and expedient, the letter of the law is seldom adequate, and legion are the orders for execution given in unsteady voice or with uncertain hand.

This, of course, was not execution. Already Sir Neville was spared the verdict of a hundred years ago — and yet judicial error is not less excusable if it is a whisker's width away from what is just than if it is summary and gross. On the face of it, there were redeeming features. Krumnagel hardly possessed

[174]

the stature of a hero. Here was no André Chénier, able to express himself immortally at the very moment his mortality was proven. And yet the public sense of what is heroic had changed so greatly in terms of what is felt rather than what is accepted, that Krumnagel, the great, coarse, bumbling, verbose, mentally short-winded oaf, stood a far better chance of invading the human conscience than did a chiseled poet in an open-necked shirt. Lawyers, like administrators and the military and the clerics, had on the whole failed to keep in touch with the rapid growth of a public sense of paradox. They are stranded in coves and backwaters, issuing instructions to deaf ears, and believing that all is well. The Emperor is long since dead; it is the courtiers, the cream, who wear the new cloth; and it is youthful men and women who see the nakedness, and it is even more unsightly a state for such minds than for such bodies.

Sir Neville felt the undertow of unrest very strongly, and he sensed that it was luring him into unpopular attitudes at a time of life when he was expected to know better. This late awakening had its dangers, and he was aware of them. English intellectual life, more than most others, is obsessed with the fear of seeming out of date, and so much that is written in the form of criticism betrays this desperate anxiety to be in tune with youth. The very terms "in" and "out" are eloquent, and some of the middle-aged are shyly letting their hair turn unaccustomed corners and wearing sunflowers on their ties.

Sir Neville had immense sympathy with the young, and agreed with a great many of their complaints, and if he did draw the line at policemen being hit on the head, it was largely because he thought the wrong heads were being hit. And he did not feel this pull towards rebellion because, like some of his contemporaries, he imagined that contact with youth would pollenate his moribund faculties — on the contrary, like most bachelors, he felt older than he should, and looked younger, and was resigned.

But it did disturb some of his friends that such a brilliant

[175]

man should be growing symptoms of unrest. He was never boorish, and yet he had a very perceptible tendency to quarrel. Some of his friends suggested it was the result of change of life, which perhaps it partly was, and yet the roots for the malaise were so clearly intellectual that it would have been unperceptive to blame the manner for the matter, when the opposite was clearly the cause.

In truth, he had been director of public prosecutions for nigh on three years, and his prescribed time was nearly up. What happened after that was his business, but until then there was the prison of his office, the cell of his clothes, the greater agony of a substantial, yet partial responsibility. There were days when he strode into his clubs as though he were going to strike someone, only then to run into a congenial acquaintance, and fall into introspection tinged with that humor which is both a saving grace and a brake on all action.

Once or twice he did run into a blustery gale, however. Some character like Sir Inigo Cheverneix (pronounced Chinny), an ashen crackpot from the old Colonial Office, or Lord Paul Hore, a crimson crosspatch from the world of business, all crushed up like a puppy, and shivering with malice.

"It really is too bad to hear an active D.P.P. talk the way you do, N.N. Too bad. What would your foreigner think if he heard you? Here's dear old Blighty filling up with effing colonials — God knows what my dear old grandfather would have said — I can imagine — he'd have turned to Asquith or whoever he thought responsible, and he'd have said something crushing like 'Are we being a little liberal with the tarbrush, perhaps?' He was never rude, was the first Lord Hore, but absolutely withering nevertheless. Always made himself understood. Had that gift, you see. Yes, well, he wouldn't have spared you, N.N., I can tell you that. He was much more talented than I am, even though I'll leave considerably more money than he did — but there you are, I suppose, can't have everything. As I was saying before I got on the subject of my pater's old man, the country's

[176]

filling up with effing colonials to the extent of changing the bloody place's character. I motor in to my local of a Sunday to have a sherry before lunch, and what do I find there? Pakistanis, Ghanaians, even the girl behind the bar's a Yugoslav. We're getting more American by the minute, every day you read of another old established firm being swallowed up — and then when one of their policemen comes over here and tries to make an historic English village into Chicago, you want to let the darned fellow off. I tell you what I'd do. And I don't doubt my grandfather would approve. I'd import a dozen registered gangsters from Sing-Sing and condemn this policeman with the unpronounceable name to be shot by his peers."

Sir Inigo was more economical in his means of expression, perhaps because he had spent a high proportion of a long life in tropical climates instead of rampaging over damp moors like Lord Hore, who always gave the impression of talking to keep warm rather than to communicate a meaning.

"The birch is more effective than the gallows. There is dishonor attached to the gallows; merely humiliation to the birch," Sir Inigo rasped. "There should be a pickled rod in every household, and your places of correction would be as quiet as Chelsea Hospital."

"That may have been true of British Honduras in 1870, when you were young, Sir Inigo, but it holds no meaning for us today outside the brothels. Those who so lacked maternal affection that they perforce fell in love with their public schools might agree with you. No one else," Sir Neville replied, and made another enemy.

He did not even bother to reply to Lord Hore, except to remind him that one of his own companies, Horex, the makers of light bulbs, batteries and electric toasters, had just become a so-called Proud Member of the American Morningside International Corporation of Conglomerates, best known for their prefabricated funeral parlors and plastic parking meters.

"I don't claim to be different from everyone else," Lord Hore bellowed. "I'm no Pharisee, for God's sake, striking my breast and claiming I'm not like my neighbor. All I am saying, N.N., is that you're one of the few people we still look to for an example."

"Would your grandfather have agreed with you, I wonder?"

The allusion was too fragile to do anything but baffle Lord Hore. Unable to make head or tail of the remark, he came to the conclusion that his grandfather had been insulted, and stalked out of the room muttering something ferocious about not wishing to drink with bolsheviks.

"Why don't you give those clubs a rest?" Bill Stockard asked Sir Neville back at the office.

"You don't think they're good for me?"

"I think they're bloody awful for you at the moment."

"At the moment? D'you think I'm unwell?"

"Unwell, I don't know. But you're not quite yourself these days. And I've noticed that you're better in the morning. You seem to look forward to lunch, and then you usually come back disappointed, and can't settle down to anything, and leave at five to six. And then I can see you from the office window. The way you walk has changed. You stoop, your steps are smaller even from this angle."

"By George, you have been sleuthing."

Bill produced a handful of blotters.

"Look at these, sir. You used to leave the office exactly as you entered it. There wasn't a speck of dust on your desk. Your blotter and your notebook were always absolutely untouched. You kept every message and every phone number in your head. It was a matter of pride, I believe. Now look at these —"

He spread the blotters like a deck of immense cards.

"You use one a day — and just look at them."

They were covered with doodles, geometric designs of tremendous complication, decapitated heads, forms like sinking ships, lines of such intensity that they had gone right through the blotter in places.

"Yes, if you put it like that —" Sir Neville mused. "All the same, it's wasteful to give me a new blotter every day."

"I always hoped it might remind you."

"A smoker's conscience is more likely to be touched by the sight of a full ashtray the day after a party."

"Well, you can have the old blotters back —"

"No, no, no," Sir Neville laughed, and then subsided into a very human, a vulnerable and gentle mood. "You're very solicitous, Bill," he said.

"You can't work with a man without — that is —" Bill looked at Sir Neville and took his courage in his hands. "Helen, my wife, and I were wondering if you wouldn't care to break your great social whirl and dine with us one evening."

"I'd love to, Bill," Sir Neville replied quietly.

"Helen thought that, since we only have a tiny flat in one of those huge modern blocks, we should get a baby-sitter in and take you out to a restaurant, but I disagreed. I told her that in your present state it'd be much better for you to be in a functioning home, however modest."

"When is it to be, nurse?" Sir Neville twinkled.

"Tomorrow?" Bill was really daring, but he recognized a kind of emergency.

"Very well."

"Great. I'll write the address on a bit of paper."

"Just tell me, Bill. I'll remember," he replied. "I will, really."

And he not only remembered the address, but also remembered to get out of a soiree of the Lincoln's Inn Wine Tasters Society, giving as an excuse a migraine.

Perhaps it was the smallness of the flat, crammed with sleeping life in darkened rooms with the doors ajar, perhaps it was the proximity of a woman other than Mrs. Shakespeare, but the evening began to have its therapeutic effect. Mrs. Stockard rose frequently from the table, since she was cook and waitress and hostess — an able, efficient, and soft creature with an open wistful look, green eyes flecked with black and yellow, and a

[179]

noble nose, flared at the sides and ever so slightly turned up at the end. There was a not-too-distant feeling of tweed and station wagon about her, but there was nothing affected about her voice or movements. She was quite clearly a dear woman, a woman who knew the value of love, and who gave of herself without a thought of distrust, without a thought of the possible complications of life. Such a person was easy to live with, and easy to hurt. She brought out the best in a man, and had no knowledge or suspicion of the worst.

Whenever she rose, Sir Neville could not help noticing the exquisite balance of her body, so personal as not to resemble a Miss Britain, but all the more desirable for that. She was thin, but not too thin, with a beautifully proportioned neck, and the first few faint lines of age on the face and under the chin. Sir Neville looked at her with pleasure, and this unexpected sight made Bill smile with discreet delight and without a trace of jealousy.

"Your husband has been like a nanny to me," Sir Neville said, "and I must say, he is a deal better than Miss Matthews, whom I had when I was a child."

"I feel sometimes I'd rather have Miss Matthews in the house than him. Perhaps he's better with older children, Sir Neville."

Sir Neville basked in the warmth of the welcome. He liked being teased under these conditions.

"I've told Helen all about Krumnagel," said Bill, "and she very much agrees with you."

"Oh?"

"It's a dreadful case," Mrs. Stockard said. "And it's all the more dreadful because it's almost funny. I mean it's a case one can only take seriously because it has happened. If it hadn't, it couldn't, if you know what I mean."

"Exactly. And the trouble is that almost everything could happen, as we inevitably find out to our horror when it does."

"Yes. There's nothing more aggravating than some of these old union leaders. I've often felt like shooting them."

"So have I, Mrs. Stockard — the trouble here is that Krum-nagel didn't feel like shooting this one, but did. How are you going to explain that to a jury?"

"Oh, a jury might understand. At least one or two members of it. But it's the legal authorities I mistrust."

"What did I tell you?" Bill laughed.

"A woman after my own heart," Sir Neville cried. "Mark you," he went on more soberly, "many of those in the legal profession are extremely brilliant, perspicacious and broad-minded. I feel one is weakening one's case if one does not admit this."

"But isn't that half the trouble?" Mrs. Stockard suggested. "I mean I'm only a woman, an amateur, but it does seem to me that there is a danger that there are certain very simple human reactions which one can very easily be too intelligent to under-stand. The law appears to me to have a pretty thorough ability to deal with either intelligence or crass stupidity, but it's far less happy in between. I mean, how would you describe Krum-nagel? As a highly placed cretin?"

"It isn't even that, Mrs. Stockard, it's that intelligence has different weights and measures in different parts of the world, and, unlike money, there is no possibility of relating one set of values to another. Krumnagel defies description by our stand-ards, which are no higher or lower than those in America, but utterly and entirely different. I've never been over there, and I really have absolutely no intention of going — but it does seem to me at times that they have never really recovered from hav-ing wrested their liberty from us — an achievement which it is easy to exaggerate, remembering the condition we were in at the time — but perhaps we will understand them better when the moment comes for us to wrest our freedom from them. Be that as it may, our concepts of liberty are at variance. We know that liberty, like nicotine and alcohol and gossip, is pleasant and even necessary in small doses, but lethal if taken to excess.

"As a consequence, and perhaps a little unfortunately, we

have learned to live with a little less of the precious stuff than we really need. Over there, they use up all stocks of it wherever they find it, and may appear to us like doctors who inject such quantities of the antidote that they give the patients the disease. As an illustration of this, I may say that I have discovered in the course of the investigation that over there, many of the judges and police chiefs are elected, and the way things are going, it wouldn't surprise me in the least to discover that their victims are elected also."

The dinner refreshed and rejuvenated Sir Neville, but it did serve to make him a little melancholy as well, in a healthy kind of way. Before turning out the lights that night, he stared at the ceiling and floated off on a cloud of abstractions which gradually focused into an honest and surprising picture. He imagined the space beside him occupied by Mrs. Stockard, and the idealized conversation stretched away to infinity. He had by his side an imagined warmth, the attractive nose, the eye of wet stone, the mouth with the dimple scratched in the skin as by a fingernail, the long thin neck, the birth of the breasts growing out of a gently freckled chest, the arms enveloping him, the pulse, the heat; he closed his eyes. He opened them again to find Mrs. Shakespeare beside him, her white turban on her head, and the straps of her gingham apron against the scratchy gray of her woolly. He shuddered. She understood at once (this was her virtue), and vanished. He fell asleep, relieved to be alone. Hardened bachelors often ruin the particular by invoking the general; even the most exquisite of particular cases cannot survive for long.

The next day, Sir Neville was at the office punctually. His blotter retained its purity all day. He lunched in a restaurant with Bill and worked late. Among the men he telephoned was Pewtrey, whom he told of his annoyance that Krumnagel should have been victimized because he had told an old nitwit how to make a Molotov cocktail.

"It could be argued that Krumnagel was responsible for the

disaster, since he had had adequate knowledge of Harry Mothers's childish, impressionable makeup."

"It could be argued in that way, but it won't be argued in that way," Sir Neville said cuttingly. "Krumnagel himself is quite as childish and impressionable as Harry Mothers, and it could be argued that since Harry Mothers is older than Krumnagel, he ought to have known better."

"He's so old, he's senile."

"You might say the same about Lord Justice Plantagenet-Williams, but it has not yet stood in his way."

From now on, Sir Neville was waiting for the opportunity to take the matter to the Home Secretary. Time was running short for him, and so was patience.

Krumnagel found a different atmosphere in his new home. The warders seemed younger and more aware, while the prisoners were far fewer, and of a different stamp. In spite of the fact that the letters from Edie had dwindled to a mere trickle, and that they were short and depressed whereas before they had been long and delirious, Krumnagel was a little happier than before, perhaps because he had slipped into a kind of sullen way of survival, but probably also because he felt he was with the cream of some world, even if only that of crime. Edward Tyhoe was there, the spy, sentenced to forty years in prison for giving away some of the few secrets Britain had left. He didn't look like Krumnagel's conception of a spy, with his wavy yellow hair and receding chin. Then there was Jeremy Sabak, one of the Maltese brothers who had been responsible for the deaths of an estimated forty underworld characters. They were reckoned to be so dangerous that nearly every prison had a member of the Sabak family, other brothers of the parents, but no prison had more than one. There were Porter Ellison, Noel Burpage, William Gunsmith and a few other smart motorcar-salesmen, who had absconded with four million pounds in a spectacular coup during which a bullion-carrying Boeing had been hijacked. The pilot of the Boeing,

Percy Cowley-Middlethorpe, a Battle of Britain ace, was still at large, and formidably dangerous. There was a degree of snobbism in this prison's maximum security wing, not only because the inmates felt themselves to be exclusive, but also because many of them were growing wealthy by serializing their stories or even publishing their memoirs. Tyhoe irritated them all by setting standards no one was qualified to follow. He had coolly refused to be ghosted, saying in his quiet, careful voice that he didn't feel inclined to let some hack's journalese disrupt his literary style.

His book came out just after Krumnagel's arrival, and the other inmates were all scanning the literary pages of the papers for critiques. The Sunday *Times* and the *Observer* both were most flattering, while the *Telegraph* was more reserved, mainly, it appeared, because this reviewer thought that a spy should not be allowed to make a profit out of a forty-year sentence. The book began to do well and Tyhoe sent a signed copy to the governor of the prison, Mr. McIntyre Bird, who read it and called a conference to redouble the security precautions.

The Sabak brothers' notorious career was being serialized by the *News of the World,* while the Boeing hijackers were telling their story to the People. Krumnagel was not looked up to at first as he had been in his original prison, largely because English crime had reached a degree of maturity independently of its American example. In fact many of its more hardened perpetrators considered that American crime was in a decadence, not because the F.B.I. had succeeded in clearing up the country, but because its clearly defined motive of profit had got somehow entangled with political and racial issues of no financial interest whatever. And as if that were not sufficient, the English prisoners felt that hippies were giving drug addiction a bad name. The fact that he was there at all gave Krumnagel a considerable standing, however, and when an offer for serialized memoirs came in due course from a weekly with a huge circulation called *Lights Out,* Jeremy Sabak was pleased to welcome him into the inner sanctum of literati, and even gave him some tough and shady hints about his contract with the paper.

"I Tell It All, the Way I Know It" marked the first installment of the Krumnagel story in *Lights Out*. Edie's picture was resuscitated, as well as the photograph of a small Huckleberry Finn type which resembled Krumnagel not at all, but looked as though it were a still from a silent film. "When old folks used to ask the tousle-headed barefoot swamp kid I was then what he was gonna be when he grew up, the little freckled face looked up at them, and said proudly, 'I gonna be a policeman, an' kill gangsters.' Little did I know then, as I do now, looking out at the gray English sky through the bars of my cell . . ." It was clear that the living Krumnagel had a British ghost.

Against the advice of Jeremy Sabak, but encouraged by the majority of the hijackers, Krumnagel had accepted a fee of £500 per article, and directed that the money be sent straight to his bank in the United States. But he did listen carefully to the implorations of Sabak about the serial rights in other countries. "Italy's very hot on success stories in crime, and you can make a mint in lire if you box clever. This may not mean much in the open market, but you can live in comfort in Sicily for years, bribes and Mafia protection included, if you happen to be lying low for any reason. Germany's good too, but they're bigger on crimes with a political or sexual edge — if you can work fur-clad Amazons with high boots and a whip into the story, so much the better, and if she was Goering's mistress on the side, you got it made. Holland, Belgium, small markets admitted, but millionaires make their fortunes counting pennies after a while, the big stuff comes by itself. America? There's too much competition, and then they find it cheaper to make the stories up. They get sued less."

In reply to Sir Neville's usual phoned solicitude, the governor said that the atmosphere was unusually quiet in the maximum security wing of his prison, a phenomenon no doubt due .

to this being the height of the literary season, but of course the sight of a group of schoolchildren doing their exams with application and discipline did not mean that their usual sense of mischief had deserted them forever. He expected a resurgence of trouble eventually when enough money had been paid into their banks for the authors to feel a desire to go out and spend it.

And indeed, after a week or two, Krumnagel discerned an unexplained tension in the place. No doubt someone without the training and habits of a policeman would not have noticed any fluctuation, but men like Krumnagel, while remarkably insensitive to a whole range of atmospheres, are seismographically sensitive to the imminence of human eruption; similarly, at the very moment of entry into public places where there has already been conflict, they assess what has occurred with uncanny speed, arresting all those with the invisible aura of guilt. As old men's aches and pains foretell the approach of bad weather, so Krumnagel's police sense told him that there were undercurrents beneath the smoothness of the surface. He looked from eye to eye, and tried to assess the strength, direction, and purpose of these currents. It was too soon to tell.

One evening towards the end of a recreation period — it was that indeterminate time of day when motorists begin to put their lights on — he noticed the members of the hijack gang exchange looks of such emptiness that they were full of meaning. Curious human species, always overacting or underacting — never quite on the beam, even the masterspies. Now they all began sidling over to one side of the courtyard with so obvious a lack of intent that their gesture shouted larceny.

"Something's up," said Sabak out of the corner of his mouth.

"You didn't have to tell me," replied Krumnagel, tense and very quiet. Everybody had begun to notice except the two warders. From far away came the noise of a helicopter, that beating of great, vulnerable, prehistoric wings. A warder looked up. Now he was alert. Then another looked up. The

[186]

noise came from such a curious direction, and it was growing in volume with such uncanny rapidity. There was something wrong. This was not the kind of noise tolerated in a town. Louder and louder grew the iron flapping, and then, like horror-struck men in a science fiction film, they all saw the helicopter appear, a vast black insect crawling over the wall, its single bulbous eye reflecting the setting of an orange sun, and seeming to be replete with malevolence and wit.

A few canisters dropped with a clatter, and clouds of smoke belched out of them the moment they hit the ground. The warders fired once or twice, were answered by a machine gun. One of the warders reeled and fell; the other began coughing, unable to breathe. Some cardboard cartons fell out of the helicopter. Krumnagel sprinted forward into the cloud of smoke and tear gas.

"Where are you going?" Sabak shouted.

Krumnagel's lungs were too full of fresh air to answer. He reached one of the boxes at the same moment as one of the gang, Bill Gunsmith, had begun to undo it, and was withdrawing a gas mask from it by the straps. Krumnagel felled him with a massive blow on the jaw, and Gunsmith dropped the gas mask. At that moment, a rope ladder came snaking out of the helicopter, and two figures, both wearing gas masks, began climbing up through the fumes of the smoke bombs which had exploded at the same time as the tear gas, and which now blanketed a considerable area. Gunsmith rose, and rushed at Krumnagel, who was trying to get the straps of the gas mask over his head. For a moment the two grappled, then fell to the ground. One of the men on the rope ladder hesitated, then made to climb down again but was restrained by the other. The pilot was shouting silently inside his glass bubble while the blades champed and rasped. One moment Gunsmith was up, tears pouring out of his eyes, stifling, groping, then Krumnagel had him by the ankle like a dead weight and held him immobile. The pilot had had enough. The chopper moved away. The smoke was denser than they had calculated, and the pilot knew they had to keep low. Ellison had climbed up into the fuselage, but Burpage, more compassionate, less callous, loitered on the ladder. The helicopter passed perilously near the top of the prison wall; Burpage hit the wall, was dragged up against its rough surface, across the iron spikes and the broken glass; lost his grip as the hideous lacerations wracked his body, and fell into the road outside the prison, distorted and curiously flat, his gas mask already assuming the cheerless grin of death.

As the smoke began to clear, a ring of warders armed with automatic weapons, closed in on Krumnagel and Gunsmith, still wrestling, although Gunsmith was vomiting from the effects of the gas. Krumnagel was astonished that the warders used such violence in separating them, and became very angry when they smashed the rifle butts into his ribs in an attempt to force him to walk towards the cells. His voice could be heard dimly shouting inside his mask. They were nervous, and they were going to tolerate no nonsense. Into a small cell he went, and Gunsmith followed him. After a moment, the governor came in, pale and agitated. The warders looked far from cheerful. They practically tore the mask off Krumnagel's face, which was scarred with red semicircles where the eyepieces had bitten into his skin.

"Try to escape, would you?" the governor spluttered.

"I didn't try no —"

"Shut up! It won't do you any good, you know. I'll see to that. No good whatever. I could've been your friend, put in a word here and there with the parole board — but there's no chance of that now. Not on your life. You're in for twenty years, Gunsmith, and you know what that means in your case — just what it says — no remissions, none of that — how old are you now, twenty-five, twenty-six? What a waste! As for you —" He turned on Krumnagel who was frowning in bewilderment. "We don't want any of your dirty American methods here. Seven years you got, didn't you? Well, it's too little as far as I'm concerned. They tell me you were chief of police in some God-forsaken hole. I'm not surprised the world's in the state it is."

These gratuitous insults were quickly bringing Krumnagel to the boil. His face, painful where it had been hit, twitched and flickered with indomitable hatred.

"That's the thanks a feller gets!" he roared.

"Thanks?" the governor shouted.

"What the fock d'you think I was doing fighting with this guy?"

"I thought the governor told you to shut up," the chief warder snarled.

"You keep out of it!"

"What were you doing?" the governor yelled, beside himself, brushing the chief warder aside. "You were in a panic, weren't you — like cowards at sea, you were struggling to get into the lifeboat, knocking yourselves off the ladder in your selfishness? Well you needn't have bothered. We'll get the lot of you. The lot of you. And Wing Commander Cowley-Middlethorpe into the bargain. Now both of you are going into solitary for a week. At the end of that time, we'll talk again."

"Tell him I tried to stop you making a getaway," Krumnagel ordered Gunsmith.

"No more talking," cried the chief warder. "Come on, move, move, move. Off you go into solitary."

Krumnagel backed into the corner of the cell, while Gunsmith just looked at him, expressionless.

"I got news for you fellers," Krumnagel said quietly, braced. "You're full of shit. And I ain't going into no solitary."

The chief warder was equally quiet. "You're not what? And what is that we're full of?"

After a moment of mutual appraisal, the warders rushed up to Krumnagel and began to bludgeon him. He fought back furiously, with a ration of righteousness to use up. There was a shout down the corridor.

"Sir, sir!

The center of interest shifted instantly.

"What is it?" called the governor.

"Burpage's dead, sir."

"Dead?"

"Dropped off the ladder into Balaclava Drive."

"Poor stupid bugger."

"He was alive when we got to him, but he wasn't conscious."

There was a sudden scuffle. The warders, who had relaxed their grip on Krumnagel for a moment in order to hear the latest news and learn if their presence was urgently required elsewhere, were surprised by the precipitate attack of Gunsmith, who, without any warning, flew at Krumnagel. Fists pummeling like pistons and shouting, "Bastard, bastard, bastard," he had to be dragged away by force, while Krumnagel's blood spilled onto the concrete floor with an initial splash as it cascaded from his nose.

The warders and governor looked bewildered, while Gunsmith began sobbing hysterically, accusing Krumnagel of killing his friend, and chanting his litany of bastards, each having a new inflection and new intensity.

"Do you mean . . . ?" asked the governor, but stopped because he dreaded the consequences of his question. He need not have worried. In any case Krumnagel was now in no condition to answer.

"We could have got away," moaned Gunsmith, "if it hadn't been for that bastard —"

The warders looked at the governor like retrievers anticipating the whistle, but the latter, furtive and embarrassed, avoided their scrutiny.

"Well — help the man up!" he burst out, as though it were the most natural thing in the world.

"Is he to go in solitary, sir?"

"Take him up to my office. Gunsmith goes into solitary."

"Right. Come on, Gunsmith."

Gunsmith shot Krumnagel a look which was beyond loathing as he was led away.

Krumnagel's eyes were closing as he sat on the governor's chesterfield, leaning forward, a fighter still in his corner after technically knocked out, uncomprehending and still eager to do battle with the red shadows in his blood-flecked field of vision.

"Cigarette?" Mr. McIntyre Bird asked.

Cigarette. When he'd shot Cass Chalkburner it'd been a cigar, but this was England, a country without style. He tried to talk, but his lips hurt. He just shook his head negatively.

"It's awfully unfortunate . . . but I think you'll understand that it was hardly logical to assume that you, a convict, were actually helping the prison authorities. When you were fighting with Gunsmith . . . and with a mask on your face at that . . . I mean . . . put yourself in my shoes."

"Why don't you put yourself in mine for a change?" Krumnagel lisped painfully. "See how you like it."

"My dear fellow, if I hadn't the capacity to do that, I wouldn't have asked you up to my office, would I now?" the governor said testily.

"I don't know whether you would or not," Krumnagel replied, cool but tense. "You think it's such a goddam honor to sit in your office? Listen, I had an office, the anteroom was twice this size. And I had wall-to-wall carpeting and an icebox built in a Marie-Antoinette commode —"

He stopped and touched his festering lips. The effort had been too much. He was raw in mind and body.

The governor didn't relish this assault on his standards of comfort, but felt he must swallow his pride in the light of his dangerous error of judgment.

"It only remains for me to thank you," he said, rather foolishly, looking around instinctively to be sure they were alone.

"For what?"

"Well . . ."

"For what?" Krumnagel reiterated, cruelly. "Those boys

know what they're doing, you got to hand it to them. They had it all timed to the split second — a great piece of planning — low-flying helicopter, same as them Jews done, in under the radar screens out there 'n Far East — so damn close you can't hardly get a bead on them — tear gas and smoke bombs —" He dabbed his lip, licked it, and flinched — "all figured out like they'd practiced it under different weather conditions — chose a windless day — worked out how long it would take to disperse — great plan — rope ladder — great — only one thing wrong with it."

"What's that?" asked the governor, in spite of himself.

"It's no good if it goes wrong. It's too perfect. It's not human. It only needed one thing to be miscalculated for the whole goddam package to go out the window."

"What do you suggest was miscalculated?"

"Are you kidding or something?" Krumnagel asked. "Was they expecting me to stop them? You know that's what happened, don't you? If I hadn't gone in there and tackled Bill Gunsmith, they'd have been out of here before any of you people knew what hit you. They hesitated, and that was enough. They blew it. Panicked. The pilot tried to make up for lost time, got out too close to the wall, killed Burpage. Is that what you got to thank me for? The lot? The whole lot. Every frigging thing."

"Yes, well, that's what I did," mumbled the governor, embarrassed.

"Yeah, but don't just thank me on account of I *helped*. I *did* it all. I *did* it." He pointed to himself with a blunt thumb. "Number six one six stroke one nine five seven. Krumnagel, Bartram T., Police Chief of Some God-Forsaken Hole in the U.S.A. And while we're on the subject. Your guards was just lousy, just pitiful. It was *they* didn't help *me*. That was some of the worst guardwork I ever saw."

"Don't say that," said the governor resentfully, more discountenanced than angry, as though he'd heard a blasphemy.

[192]

"The first to know something was going to happen was us, the convicts. Your guards was still yapping together. Even after we could all hear the chopper, one of your boys was still looking at his focking fingernails, wondering if they were going to have to be evened up. I never seen nothing like it."

The phone rang. The governor, exhausted by the emotional strain of the day, and by now so thoroughly on the defensive that he was sure of none of his reactions, lifted the receiver with trepidation as though a newer and even viler method of taunting him was about to be set in motion.

He listened for a moment.

"I see . . ."

His face gave away very little.

"Into the sea?"

He listened again.

"Thank you."

And he hung up. Krumnagel looked at him inquiringly. The governor held his peace, hardly knowing how to communicate this new information, or whether it was necessary to take the prisoner into his confidence at all. He decided against it. After all, he was governor, and for a prisoner to be in his office in the first place was a luxury, and not to be taken as an everyday occurrence.

"What fell in the sea?" It was Krumnagel asking. "The chopper?"

"What? . . . No, no, nothing."

"The chopper fell in the sea? What happened to Porter?"

"They've got him."

There was a pause.

"Aren't you going to thank me?"

"I've thanked you as much as I'm going to," the governor suddenly said, with childish stubbornness, and then felt a surge of annoyance that circumstances should have placed him in such a very awkward situation, and even inhibited his powers of thinking lucidly.

Krumnagel rose.

"Where d'you think you're going?" asked the governor.

"I guess you seen about enough of me for one day."

"I'm not sending you away. I haven't done with you yet."

"Oh, come on," Krumnagel said with a sudden weariness. "It must be tough having me in here, telling you how to run your outfit."

The governor wasn't prepared for this unexpected solicitude. He was prepared for nothing these days.

"Yes, it is," he admitted.

"I can imagine," Krumnagel grinned. "You need it like a hole in the head, me telling you what you done wrong — and then, how the hell does a cop thank a convict — it has to be off the record, don't it?"

"Not necessarily. I happen to have an idea which is quite official. I believe — especially in view of our — em — momentary misunderstanding of your motives — that you deserve every consideration. I am consequently in favor of sending you away from here."

"Away out of here?" Krumnagel asked. Total liberty was too much to hope for — was that what this idiot governor meant? No, couldn't be. Hadn't the authority.

"Yes, I feel that you no longer should be detained in a maximum security prison."

"You know something? One prison's a lot like another. I'll go further. You got a better class of felon in here than you got in that first crummy outfit you guys put me in."

"That's very good of you, I'm sure." The governor cleared his throat. "It's always nice to hear that . . ." The governor interrupted himself. Mustn't get in too deep with this fellow. He'll be sitting in my seat if I let him. "Actually, my idea wasn't only the result of wishing to acknowledge your conduct on our behalf, but I also felt that perhaps you wouldn't be quite as popular here from now on as you were before."

Krumnagel frowned.

"What you got against me?" he asked.

"It's not us," the governor said hastily. "I think you'll find that you're quite popular with us — but that isn't going to help you with your fellow prisoners. On the contrary, I'd say."

Krumnagel seemed to pale.

"Yeah, and with the kind of hepcat guards you got yourself in this cooler, I ain't got the right to expect much protection. I'd be a stiff already while that creep out there's figuring on evening up his nails."

The governor thought furiously of how he could defend the warders, but eventually hoped that silence had the virtue of a certain colorless dignity which is about the only substitute for constructive ideas on unhappy days.

"Jesus, I'd be happier if I had a gun," Krumnagel said.

The governor looked up. He didn't think he had heard right, but Krumnagel was already on his way to the door.

"One final question," the governor called.

Krumnagel stopped and turned.

"Why did you do what you did?"

"I guess . . ." and Krumnagel pondered, his jaws rippling as though his molars had become embedded in a sea of gum and he was trying to liberate them. "I guess, once a cop, always a cop. Sir."

He opened the door, and before the prison officer waiting in the corridor had time to say anything, Krumnagel spoke. "O.K., let's go," he said.

The next morning, they found Krumnagel more dead than alive in a far corner of his cell. He was nowhere near the bars, and there was no sign of foul play. He spoke to them in a small voice.

"Get a message to the governor, will you. Tell him to get me out of here, like he said. Tell him quick, or there'll be too many questions to answer . . . too goddam many . . ."

"One good thing," the governor said, as he sat awaiting a phone connection with the Home Office. "If there are any questions about how Krumnagel got his face smashed in, all we have to say is that it was done by fellow prisoners."

"Yes, there's that, sir," the chief warder agreed. "Every cloud has a silver lining."

12

The newspapers were full of pictures of the helicopter in the water, of frogmen and of police. The reconstruction of the escape was shown in nearly every edition, either in diagram or else in old photos of the prison yard with superimposed arrows. Of Krumnagel, however, not a word. It was only when Bill Stockard called Mr. McIntyre Bird on Sir Neville's behalf, ostensibly on some quite other business, that he learned, in response to a casual question, that Krumnagel had been moved back to his original prison.

"I'm very glad to hear it," said Stockard, "but d'you mind telling me why?"

"We just — thought it was better."

"Better?" There was a pause on the phone. "I know it's

hardly in our province any more, but Sir Neville has shown such interest in this case that I really think that out of courtesy, if for no other reason —"

"Frankly, he became rather unpopular with the other prisoners."

"Why?"

"Oh, you know . . . uppish . . . know-all kind of cove . . . and then, there is a certain amount of anti-American prejudice among maximum security prisoners . . . it's unfortunate, but there it is."

"Why is this, can you guess?"

"It's a difference in method, I think. The Yanks used to have a monopoly on crime, but all that's over. Others, and especially the British, have made enormous strides in this direction, using a great many new methods perfected in warfare, and the Yanks are regarded as definitely old hat, but as arrogant about their prowess as ever."

"Is that enough to justify the lack of popularity of a single individual? Excuse me, one last question if you don't mind, Mr. Bird — how did this unpopularity express itself? Was there . . . I mean . . . unpleasantness?"

"Unpleasantness?" grunted Mr. Bird. "A few scratches only."

"A few scratches? How many scratches?"

"Is this a cross-examination or something?" The governor was becoming his usual rattled self. "Do I have to take this from the D.P.P's department?"

"Of course not, but there's nothing in the rule book to the effect that questions can't be asked interdepartmentally, is there? If there is, I'm not aware of the article."

"I am answering your questions to the best of my ability."

"Right. Thank you, Mr. Bird. Now one final question if you have no objection."

"Fire ahead."

"Aren't your warders able to prevent prisoners from scratching each other?"

The governor began shouting.

"Since I came here, I've been asking for more warders. It's the old business. I've got too few of them, and those that I have are either too old and set in obsolete ways or else too young and irresponsible. You find me the young man who wants to make H.M.'s prisons his career without having been turned down for a dozen jobs before!"

"Thank you, Mr. Bird, for your courtesy."

Bill hung up, and told Sir Neville about the incident. Sir Neville telephoned Major Attlesey-Gore.

"No, he's not here yet, but I'm expecting him before long. Frankly, I'm not at all keen to have him back. Can't they send him somewhere else?"

"But why is he being sent back to you in the first place?" Sir Neville inquired.

"I gather from McIntyre Bird that he's in a pretty bad way."

"We were told he had a few scratches."

"A few scratches? He's being brought in an ambulance."

Sir Neville started.

"An ambulance?" He made up his mind. "I say, do you mind if my assistant, or someone from my office, has an interview with Krumnagel as soon as he arrives?"

"Not at all. If you can conspire to get him off my hands, I'll be jolly grateful. As far as I can see, he spells trouble wherever he goes. Shoots an old man in a pub, then is instrumental in blowing up a bank, and now gets himself half-killed by fellow convicts."

"Tell me," Sir Neville suddenly asked, "when did this happen, d'you know? The assault on Krumnagel."

"Yesterday. They say there's some urgency getting him out."

"Yesterday. And before yesterday was the attempted escape, wasn't it?"

"I never thought of that."

"Were the members of the hijack gang taken back to the same prison?"

"I imagine so. That is what would happen, automatically."

"Thank you."

Krumnagel was carried on a stretcher to the room where prisoners check out. He attracted practically no attention in that strange aquarium world of silence and of undercurrents as he was transported from the infirmary, where he had spent the night under guard. Now his personal effects were being collected, and an ambulance was being backed into the yard. He lay on the floor, his eyes closed.

"What happened, buddy?"

He opened his eyes with difficulty, and saw vaguely the form of an old man, his face halved, leaning over him.

"Don't make me laugh, Harry," he murmured. "It's too goddam painful."

"Did they get you?"

"They got me, pal."

"I'll get even with them for what they done to you," Pew-pew-pew went the finger-gun, shooting it out with the bad men.

"You sure laid an egg with that bomb, pardner."

"I did everything you tell me, but something gone wrong, don' ask me what." The old man beamed. "But never mind. They tell me I done something like twenty million quid worth o' damage. Imagine that? Cor. That's a lot of damage, that is." He was happy and relaxed. "Thanks to you, old-timer. I'll get to end me life in maximum security. Never, in my wildest dreams — Harry Mothers, in maximum security? — They'd have laughed a few months ago — but now, thanks to you — I can 'old my head 'igh."

"You've got no right in there! What you doing in there? We've been looking for you everywhere!"

Goddam warders. Krumnagel shut his eyes again, more in disgust than in pain. He could have been massacred ten times over while they were having their surreptitious smokes and paring their fingernails outside.

"See you on the range," said Harry, as he was led away.

"Right by the cook-house door."

"Yes, sirree."

Then they took Krumnagel to the ambulance, and drove him off.

Bill Stockard traveled up that afternoon, and visited Krumnagel in the prison hospital where he had been admitted on arrival. He was shocked by what he saw, and heard.

"Do you mean to tell me that all this happened to you after you helped prevent the escape of the hijack boys?"

"That is correct. Sure did. Oh, you know, sir — I hardly got a right to blame them. I ought to have remembered what prisons are like — I guess the world over. In Greece and Guatemala they may be a little cruddier, in California they maybe have TV by now in the better cells, in Red China you get the works of Chairman Mao shoved up your ass instead of breakfast, but they've all got to be pretty much the same — places where fellers hope for the best but expect the worst. That goes for everybody, prison officers and convicts. I was crazy to come out and help. I guess I just forgot I was inside, see. I guess I tried to forget so hard I maybe succeeded."

In this mood, Stockard really rather liked Krumnagel.

"Well, maybe it wasn't quite in vain, Mr. Krumnagel. After all, you attracted attention to your case."

Krumnagel seemed to be writhing in pain.

"Hey, don't make me laugh mister, will you?" he implored. "That hurts."

"What did I say?"

"What's with the Mr. Krumnagel?"

"Oh, we believe that a man's misfortune should not remove his right to ordinary courtesies."

"Please!" (Renewed attempt to laugh.) "The name's Bart. Bartram T. Krumnagel." He extended a hand from the bed-clothes with the imploration, "Don't shake it too hard. It did a lot of damage."

Bill took the hand and exerted moderate pressure while himself being crushed as in a mangle. Krumnagel's eyes became watery.

"You know, that's the first handshake I've had since I said goodbye to my lawyer — the creep — and it done me a hell of a lot of good."

Stockard was embarrassed by the directness of the sentiment. He was not used to it.

"What's the T stand for?" he asked.

"T?"

"The T in your name."

"That T don't stand for nothing. It's just a middle initial."

"But it must stand for something."

"Why should it?" There was a trace of the unreasonable now. "I like it the way it is."

"That's certainly your privilege. How d'you spell it?"

"T. Don't you know how to spell T?"

"But on a document — when you have to spell out your entire name?"

"I put down T," Krumnagel said with growing annoyance.

"Not TEE, or TEA, or even TEIGH?"

"Just T," Krumnagel insisted his eyes blazing. "Why you got to make fun of a person's name?"

Bill understood why people sometimes got shot. The pretexts were minimal, and the heart of gold hidden by storm clouds of excessive adrenaline. He said goodbye, and Krumnagel looked at him as though he'd spoiled it all.

Back in London, Bill told Sir Neville of his visit, and answered the most detailed questions. Sir Neville was not annoyed, but rather relieved. What had occurred seemed to him to vindicate all his previous bad temper in the clubs. As in court, after a shaky start, Krumnagel had done his protector proud. Now Sir Neville picked up the phone and asked for an urgent meeting with the Home Secretary. This was naturally accorded two days later, over lunch, in a private room at the

Junior Veterans Club, to which the Home Secretary belonged. The Right Honorable Clive Belper was a relatively young man for such an exalted office, being in his middle forties, but this was an era in which youth was much favored in high places, and even seemed a virtue in itself. He was a man tall enough to stoop a little, with yellow boyish curls over all his head except the upper plateau on which a shiny scalp was visible under the hair, making him seem fairly bald from some angles, not at all from others. He wore quite heavy glasses, and his eyes behind them often became glazed when he was listening; it was disconcertingly unclear whether this was due to the intensity of his concentration, or whether, in fact, his mind and faculties were elsewhere.

Sir Neville told the Krumnagel saga — an, alas, unfinished story — with his own particular persuasiveness, telling it all as it happened, and yet not attempting to disguise his prejudice in the matter.

"One thing is abundantly clear, isn't it, D.P.P., and that is that there must be an investigation of what goes on at our maximum security prisons. If necessary, put the governor on the mat. This would, actually, be quite an expedient moment for such an initiative, since there is a discernible tendency at this time for Opposition members to ask awkward questions. The rising quantity of spectacular escapes and the mounting crime rate make me an automatic target for this kind of thing. They are, in fact, trading on public fear. I'd do the same if I was in opposition."

"May I point out," replied Sir Neville, with a honed edge to his delivery, "that you are not in opposition, Mr. Belper, but in the Government. Consequently your responsibilities are not to create confusion by asking awkward questions, but, on the contrary, to prevent awkward questions from existing by the wisdom of your judgment. I did not come here to plead for an investigation at a maximum security prison. That is hardly the business of my department, however relieved I may be as an individual if and when such an investigation takes place. I am here to point out to you that a man is in prison who really has no place there, and to consult you about means at our disposal for eradicating, or at the very least, alleviating his condition."

"I take your criticism of me in the avuncular spirit in which it is no doubt intended," Belper said, showing quality and smiling, "but I do feel, Sir Neville, that you are being perhaps a little sentimental as regards this American cop. After all, he did kill a man, an Englishman."

"A Scot."

"Was it? Well, in any case, a British subject in England. Now the law surely says — correct me if I am wrong — that he must stand trial for that crime, and once the man dies, there is no possible charge other than murder."

"That is correct."

"Now this man did stand trial, and was found guilty of manslaughter and condemned to seven years' penal servitude. A degree of mercy and of modern intelligence was already shown in court. With a judge from the past, and a jury of fifty years ago, he might easily have been hanged —"

"My point is not legal, Home Secretary, but human. Or rather, it is only legal in that I am convinced that if, say, Maxwell Learoyd or Lumley Jacobs had been judging the case instead of Plantagenet-Williams, we'd have stood a good chance of acquittal —"

"Even with a dead man, a victim?"

"Self-defense? Even the illusion of self-defense in a man accustomed to defending himself against firearms? Certainly. All it needed was a judge with imagination, a lawyer able to dramatize the more improbable aspects of the case without making them seem impossible, and a couple of more moviegoers in the jury. Few cases have relied more on elements of luck in the composition of the court than this one."

"I hope you're not expecting to eliminate the element of luck in court?"

"There is only one weapon against the element of luck, and it is infallible," Sir Neville said slowly.

"What is it?" Belper was compelled to ask.

"Compassion."

Belper smiled in disbelief.

"Really, Sir Neville, I expected something a little more technical from you. After all, you're a highly professional man, and a highly brilliant man within that profession."

"What do you mean by professional, sir?"

"Professional is to my mind the description of a man who searches for his solutions within the realm of possibility, not beyond it."

It was Sir Neville's turn to smile.

"We must not forget, Mr. Belper, that the realm of possibility is a mortal kingdom; what lies beyond is divine. If professionalism entails a detachment from all divinity, then I am opposed to your definition. And if you had expected something more practical than compassion as a solution, then I must remind you that the law is merely an ever-inadequate human endeavor to divide justice, which is divine, into categories. The law is a servant, not a master. So that if I have disappointed you, it is because I exhausted the law and now take a fresh look at the justice it was designed to serve. It may seem to you that compassion is too simple a word for a man of sophistication to employ, and yet there is a great deal in common between the clarity of discovery in the young and the clarity of rediscovery in the old — between first and second childhood you may well say — and so I do not apologize for my use of the word compassion. I have just found it again, and realize I hardly missed it for forty years, and I am ashamed. All I ask for Krumnagel is compassion."

Belper examined Sir Neville's face with intensity, sensitive to an unexpected and disturbing human warmth, and yet wondering whether sanity was not saying a slow farewell.

"How would you wish me to express this compassion?" he asked at length.

"I don't know yet. Let's examine the facts together, and see whether the result of our examination doesn't lead us to some conclusion. The trial we know about. The court, guided by Lord Justice Plantagenet-Williams, sentences Krumnagel to seven years' penal servitude. He goes to prison, where he befriends an old codger who's been in and out of the jug from adolescence onward. In the course of conversation, he spins a yarn or two, satisfies the curiosity of the old numbskull about Chicago, the Wild West, and in the course of this hokum explains how bombs and Molotov cocktails are made. By chance the time for the old man's release comes up and, with the formulas for the infernal machines fresh in what passes for his mind, he blows the front off a bank. Krumnagel is blamed for this, quite erroneously, and is sent off to a maximum security prison. Here he helps the warders to stop a multiple jailbreak, and his reward is a beating from some of the warders and ultimately even more severe treatment at the hands of the other inmates. Now what's going to happen? You'll inaugurate an investigation of the governor and leading prison officers at the maximum security prison, and they're bound to be axed when the truth comes out, or at least severely disciplined. Then Krumnagel will have implacable enemies both among the criminals and the prison officers. His life, what's left of it, won't be worth living. Was this in Lord Justice Plantagenet-Williams's mind when he passed his equitable judgment of seven years' penal servitude? I hardly think so."

Mr. Belper laughed helplessly. "Oh, you're very persuasive, D.P.P., but I simply do not dare do anything official to alleviate this unfortunate gentleman's predicament. After all, I am a political animal if ever there was one. Somehow, in our system of government, common sense comes out of neither the wisdom of the man in power, nor the vigilance of the man in opposition, but out of the clash of the two divergent points of view, ex-

[206]

pressed with humor, and with passion. I simply can't try to accelerate the decision of the parole board, nor can I decree that his behavior is so golden that he be released as a reward for good conduct after a few weeks of a seven year sentence. We live in times in which the public is increasingly nervous about crime, and, as I indicated previously, members of both political parties are catering to this public nervousness, and trying to turn it to their advantage at the polls. Christopher Clewley is going hammer and tongs for a reintroduction of the death sentence for murder of any sort, Colonel Proudhead is pushing through a bill introducing the cat for dope pushers, and may well succeed, while Lady Lovilow is lobbying for enforced abortions for English girls rendered pregnant by foreign workers, meaning black workers, of course. It's a miracle to me she still gets elected, but she does, with monotonous regularity, and she has a faithful following of cranks and gauleiters manqués of which you will find many among the molesters of small children and the loiterers round public lavatories. If I come out for Krumnagel now, I'll have all this host of vigilantes after my blood, each in his own way, but with similar energy and commensurate ambition."

"And yet something must be done," said Sir Neville categorically.

Belper thought for a moment, frowned, and then spoke with great care and intensity.

"I understand your problem better than you imagine, but, if you will permit a criticism from a man a little younger than yourself, Sir Neville, I believe you are weakening your position by voluntarily abandoning your professionalism, and by opting for purity as an only weapon instead of relying more heavily than ever on your Machiavellian talents for imbroglio. After all, you wish to save a man. With me as an ally, you don't stand an earthly chance. I don't know if you have a chance at all, mind you, but I do know you have more of one alone — or with Machiavelli."

"What do you suggest, O Prince?" Sir Neville asked.

"Well, an idea that is patently absurd, but it could serve as an example of what I mean. You could, for instance, send this Krumnagel to one of the new experimental prisons without bars, like Lyburn or Trussmore, and then encourage him to escape."

Sir Neville's face lit up after a moment of reflection.

"You're quite right," he said, "larceny is much more fun than high principles, and in any case, it makes high principles work."

"For heaven's sake, that was only a crazy and exaggerated example of what I vaguely had in mind."

"On the contrary, it's a very good idea. Lyburn is only about twenty miles from Liverpool, and the docks and the freighters. Scotland Yard could probably be talked into following Krumnagel not too closely, and missing him by inches as the boat edges over the three mile limit."

"I am no longer listening, Sir Neville."

"What did you mean when you said that with you as an ally, I didn't stand an earthly chance?" Sir Neville asked maliciously.

"So long as everybody appears to be doing his best, Sir Neville — it is that that counts. There's no argument against that. It's all I ever ask."

"I agree," said Sir Neville, now with the straightest of faces. "No man can do more than his best."

13

Krumnagel, his face now somewhat healed, sat opposite Angus Peverell-Proctor in a very modern office constructed out of rural materials. Peverell-Proctor was an idealist of shattering intensity, a permanent evangelical smile underlining the hypnotic mildness of his green eyes, which lay like stagnant pools under the high ridge of his eyebrows. His voice was high and elflike, carrying his whispered words on gossamer breath, while his hands grasped each other like lovers. He was a man with a mission.

"Lyburn," he murmured, "is unlike any other house of correction in the world — in fact, it is not a house of correction at all — but more, I like to think, a house of reflection, of reorientation, a laundry of the spirit. A man has done wrong. Is that a reason for him to be degraded, rejected, immersed in sordid surroundings, bereft of aesthetic satisfaction? I think not. On the contrary, he should be lifted out of the moral quagmire of society's making, and be shown beauty, utility, glimpses of the majestic possibilities of life. It is for that reason that I prevailed upon the powers that be to permit me to create Lyburn, a prison that has largely been built by the prisoners themselves. We are building a church this year, designed by a prisoner who is a qualified architect. Next year, we will undertake a heated swimming pool — so you see, our activities embrace the whole gamut of human endeavor, sacred and profane. And verily, it is sometimes difficult to know which is sacred and which is profane, so grand is the canvas upon which life is painted, and so infinite its range of colors. In the sense that the mind may wander during divine service, it is possible for a cathedral to sink into profanity, whereas a swimmer, glorying in the free movements of flotation and aquaceous propulsion may easily feel himself the beneficiary of a sacred gift, and discern in the freedom of his movements a message from on high."

The smile gained in intensity as the focus of the green eyes suddenly diminished from the all-embracing to land gently on Krumnagel.

"I hope you will be happy here. You're a little late to be much help with the church, but I hope you will muck in when we begin digging for the swimming pool. We often have lectures and theatricals and concerts, and these are, of course, compulsory. They are in fact all that is compulsory here." He consulted a list on the desk before him.

"Tomorrow the Whitechapel Quartet are performing three of the last quartets of Beethoven. On Tuesday, Major General Sir Gordon McVicary is lecturing on "Ceylon — What Next?" and on Friday we are beginning rehearsals for a production of *The Importance of Being Earnest*. I doubt whether there are any roles still open, but now that you are with us, we may change our plans and do *Petrified Forest* next. We've always wanted to perform it, but we never had anyone quite up to playing the gangster."

Krumnagel could hardly believe his ears, and now, a few minutes later, he could hardly believe his eyes either. Most of the other inmates, who stared at him with a winsome, pouting curiosity, seemed to him either subnormal or else very queer indeed. He had hardly dared exchange a word with Mr. Peverell-Proctor, since the tenor of the interview was so very unexpected, and the whole atmosphere so overwhelmingly dainty. He had an extraordinary feeling that he had been relegated to a home for the elderly by mistake. Even though quite a few of the convicts were young, they exuded a sensation of impotence and handicap.

For a while things threatened to go wrong again when he was shown his room (in Lyburn they were called rooms, not cells), which he was expected to share with a Negro drummer who had been caught with cannabis on him. Krumnagel was used to black dope addicts and raised no particular objection, but the Negro was racial as all hell, a bit of a panther on the side, and demanded to be called Mustapha Abdul instead of Meadcroft Arthurs.

"Get that fuzz outa here," he yelled. "Mustapha Abdul ain't gonna share his livin' room with no whaaite fuzz."

The fact that liberalism condoned reverse racism, as though every black has ten centuries of personal wrongs to right against any old white, whereas every white must have been personally guilty of some nastiness against his brother of a swarthier pigmentation, seemed ludicrous to Krumnagel.

"Don't give me that horseshit," Krumnagel yelled back at Abdul, who came from Trinidad, where he had led a poor but relatively happy existence, but who was thirsting for something to complain about, and as a first step to petty martyrdom, chose to be considered American. "You don't know me, you

[211]

haven't even set your goddam eyes on me, you got no right to talk the way you're doing."

"I don' have to know a Yank fuzz to have an o-pinion," Mustapha jeered. "I got Chicago to remember, an' Lil' Rock, and Beh-min-ham, Al-bama."

"One more crack out of you, and you'll have Lyburn to re- member, too — a little smear on the tile floor, that's all that's going to be left of you."

Mustapha began rolling his eyes in a drunken manner, his yellow whites, seemingly rotten with nascent cataracts, passing and repassing in rhythm with his feet and the toss and plunge of his torso; quickly a creamy foam began to appear on his lips, and he shook his shoulders as though trying to free them from some unseen weight, going through limbering and swimming motions, and eventually shivering and shuddering while mut- tering musically in a strange clicking tongue.

"What the hell you doing?" Krumnagel asked, a little nerv- ously, above the ritual.

"I'm laying a curse on you," chanted Mustapha, and stamped away in his frenzy.

Krumnagel contemplated his roommate for a moment, saw that he was psyching himself into an irresponsible state, and opened the door briskly.

"Hey!" he called out to a couple of long-haired warders who were chewing the cud further down the corridor. "There's a guy in here laying a curse on me. I don't care for it. Get him out of here — either it's him or me. Things is tough enough without curses. I don't need them."

"Oh, crikey," said the rather effete warder, breaking off his conversation, and walking towards Krumnagel, "is he at it *again?* He does it to every roommate. It doesn't actually mean anything, you know. He's very friendly once he gets to know you."

"I don't intend to get to know him that good. He's foaming at the mouth, and as far as I'm concerned that means you can't

[212]

even argue with the guy. Go talk to the tall party I saw when I got here, and get me another cell, will you?"

The warder banged on the door with the palm of his hand, trying to force his way into Mustapha's trance.

"What are you doing then? Behaving nasty again? Mr. Angus won't be pleased to hear that. He'll confiscate your guitar, he will." But it was clearly no use. The rhythm had gone out of him, and he was now broken in two, but stiff as a ramrod in this normally untenable position, quietly frothing away and occasionally convulsed momentarily as he stared up at the ceiling with unblinking eyes. Krumnagel peeked at him from behind the door, and had the unpleasant feeling that perhaps this tortuous rigor had set in because the curse was beginning to work. There was a sudden stabbing pain in his chest, which threw a shroud of ice over him, followed by a sensation his head was going to burst, and other trivial but exhausting assaults on his imagination.

"It's no use," said the warder, fed up. "I'll have to call Dr. O'Tool. Come on, we'll see Mr. Angus."

Krumnagel was taken to another "room," and introduced to his new roommate, a bald, corpulent man who was already in bed in spite of the fact that it was only five o'clock in the afternoon. Beside him, on a neat bedside table covered in chintz, was a headblock, and on it reposed a ginger toupee.

"What are you doing in there, lazybones?" asked the warder.

"I felt a twinge of a cold, and I said to myself, bed for you, old man. It's the only place."

"Have you told Doctor O'Tool?"

"Keep him away from me! He's got the evil eye!"

"Oh, rot."

"Well anyway, he's got cold hands." He gave a sensuous shudder.

"Here's your new roommate, Mr. Krumnagel. Mr. Krumnagel, Mr. Livingstone."

To which Mr. Livingstone added, "I presume."

"Hi," said Krumnagel, assessing his new neighbor.

The warder left. Krumnagel wandered to the window, and looked at the plowed field which stretched away to a distant hedge. There were no bars.

"I've read about you."

Krumnagel turned to face Livingstone.

"Oh."

"I'm surprised they sent you here. After all, you shot a man, didn't you? This place isn't for violent people, oh dear me no. Should I be scared of you?"

"What you want to be scared of me for? If you stay on your side of the line, we'll get on O.K. What are you in for?"

"Offenses against minors."

"No kidding. You one of those sick people wait outside for the little girls to come out?"

"I'm under Dr. O'Tool. Oooh! That's dirty, that is. Who said I waited for little girls?"

"What, you mean you're a *fag*?"

"I am a practicing 'omosexual, and practice makes perfect as my dear old mother used to say."

"Christ almighty, now I seen everything. First I got to share my cell with a Black Muslim, and now they give me a super-charged faggot to set up house with. Now listen, first wrong move from you, and you'll have cause to be scared of me."

"I may like roughness."

"You may like what?" Krumnagel said, incredulous.

"Roughness. There's nothing more thrilling than a little roughness at the hands of the loved one."

"Brother, what you'll get at my hands won't be roughness. There'll be nothing left of you but your hairpiece if you try anything funny. Why you smirking?"

"I'm not smirking, I'm smiling. You wait till you've been here a year or two. You'll be glad of a little comfort. A goodnight kiss, a little fondle . . ."

[214]

"That'll be the day. Jesus, what's come over me already? Any guy talked to me like that normally, I'd murder him."

"Is that what happened? Was that old Scotsman a fairy? Come on now, you can tell me, you can tell Coral."

"Coral?" Something about this suddenly found Krumnagel's funnybone, and he began laughing in sheer disbelief.

"You got a focking nerve," he said, "talking that way to me. And what's that you called yourself, Coral? You got to be kidding. Who gave you that name?"

"I gave it myself," said Coral, with dignity.

"Come on, come on, what's your real name. I ain't going to call any guy Coral."

"My real name is Coral. I don't answer to any other. Coral, or the Queen Mother. There are some who prefer that. I suppose I've been here a long time and given a lot of advice to a lot of young people I've shared things with."

"O.K., O.K., Coral, you win. My name's Bart. Bart. And unless you want me to call you Charlie, don't start calling me Beatrice."

"Beatrice is a lovely name for a boy."

Actually Krumnagel became acclimatized quite quickly to the proximity of Coral, who turned out to be a heavy and frequent sleeper, and quite harmless. Like many such people, he was also basically an extremely kind person, sheltering under a protective cover of bitchiness. He understood loneliness and its problems better than most, because he had been born with secrets, which had blossomed within him in the fullness of time, and which, because of his unprepossessing and flaccid appearance, he had always found a difficulty in sharing. Now he listened to Krumnagel's story with an equilibrium which was not moral, as a priest's would have to be, but much more partisan, out of sheer camaraderie. It was a damn shame, another trick of nature turned hostile, Krumnagel reflected, that Coral should be queer. He could have been the buddy of a lifetime, and yet, no buddy would have listened with such feminine, such motherly, such Queen Motherly patience without attempting to compete with anecdotes of his own.

In the daytime, Krumnagel worked on the church, his technical knowledge of masonry coming in useful, and his great swings with hammer and lunges with saw watched with awe by the majority of the workmen, who were afraid of damaging their hands. Soon he was in command of the group, even telling the warders and the architect (who was inside for fraudulent income tax returns) where better effects could be produced, and how structural rigidity could be increased. Mr. Peverell-Proctor watched the building from his window with liquid wonder in his eyes, and in his mind he saw an infinity of spire piercing the empyrean like a hypodermic needle rich in the serum of faith, and he marveled. He was one of the few people left who knew what it was to marvel, and even, in rare moments, marvel greatly. Krumnagel appeared to him like a gladiator who had been blinded by the great light at the moment of victory in the arena, and who had followed the light not to the heights of mortal triumph, but into the gloom of the catacombs, there to bend his ferocious fingers to the tasks of gentleness.

There was nothing mystic in the satisfaction Krumnagel derived from his activities; the fact that it was a church he was building held no particular symbolism to him for the moment. What mattered was to be in charge, to lead, to bellow once again, to be humorous and dangerous at the same time, to show off.

What he found more trying were events like the concert of chamber music. He found very little discernible rhythm in Beethoven, and an orchestra of only four strings an error of misplaced economy. Four brasses, or three basses and a percussion section would have given twice the results at no greater cost. It was only during the scherzo that he found justification for clicking his fingers, and even this innocent participation was met

[216]

with stares and shushings from those who knew what store Mr. Angus laid by beauty. The reactions were even more outraged when he attempted to speak during the slow movements, and there were eyes lifted skyward and tut-tuttings when he suddenly asked, "What kind of music is it you can't talk through, for Christ's sake?"

Peverell-Proctor smiled indulgently at his great Ursus, his great gentle giant who was walking the stony path to loveliness.

The lecture on Ceylon by the retired general was not quite so overwhelmingly boring as Beethoven, mainly because it was accompanied by slides, so there was something to engage the eye other than four men fretting away interminably. In any case, Krumnagel had always thought of Ceylon as being an insular appendage of Africa, not of India — perhaps confusing it with Madagascar, which he had heard of but couldn't place at all, other than it seemed to him Humphrey Bogart might have once made an adventure movie with that name or something similar. The general was a pedantic man who told them that the name for the island in Sanskrit was Singhala Dvipe, that the majority of Greeks and some Romans referred to it as Taprobana, and that the Arabs called it Serendib, and then left long pauses as though to give them time to make written notes of these valuable bits of information. He showed them slides of Colombo taken by himself, usually from such a distance and with such an aggressively grainy quality that they might quite as easily have been views of Columbus, Ohio.

Krumnagel was mercifully not cast for any role in *The Importance of Being Earnest,* but as a courtesy he took time off from overseeing the construction gang to drop in to rehearsals, and watch Coral prepare himself for future adulation in the role of Lady Bracknell, a role for which he was admirably suited by nature, if lacking a trace of the masculinity and energy the role requires.

It looked as though Mr. Peverell-Proctor's great experiment

[217]

was working, at least in so far as a certain category of prisoners was concerned. Undeniably some of the homosexuals had set up comfortable little ménages, à deux, trois, quatre, and they were better off here than penniless in sordid digs, surrounded by prejudice and cruelty. Undeniably also, it was difficult as yet to conceive of Lyburn as a haven for hardened criminals with outside connections in the underworld. Krumnagel was treated as a kind of test case, quite erroneously as it happened, and it seemed like a vindication of his life's work to Mr. Peverell-Proctor that a murderer, by definition a roughneck of great natural wickedness, should now be the most responsible, vigorous and methodical of all inmates. The governor went his casual rounds wreathed in alleluias.

Back in London, Sir Neville received the visit of Chief Detective-Inspector Pewtrey, and was pleasantly surprised and not a little shocked at the same time that Pewtrey approved his nefarious plan for liberating the country of this man it could not judge, but merely punish.

"I was going to bring some such idea up myself sooner or later if you hadn't, Sir Neville," Pewtrey said.

Sir Neville, a new hand with larceny, was amazed at how close to the surface of each man's makeup the dishonest lies, and wondered, after talking to Belper and Pewtrey, whether he hadn't misjudged the entire human race all his life, and gone through his career with blinkers of holier-than-thou. The highest moral standards are inhuman. That is their greatest drawback when dealing with the men for whom they are intended.

"Yes," Pewtrey went on, wearily, "in the heat of the moment it seemed to us all that Krumnagel had no doubt carefully instructed Harry Mothers in bomb-making in order to get his revenge on British justice, but on reflection our whole assessment of the thing was probably quite unfair. Harry's a cunning old rascal underneath all that bull, and Krumnagel's a bit of an ass when it comes to character assessment — he probably romanced away, and told Harry all the wild and wonderful

[218]

things criminals got up to over there — he's pretty patriotic about all things American, including crime, is Krumnagel — and old Harry probably made mental notes of everything he heard, hoping to get an exclusive lead over all the other super-annuated loners in the business. So that we had no right letting Krumnagel go to maximum security, and certainly it was most unfortunate that he was beaten up there as a reward for allowing his police instincts to come to the fore, and then half-killed by an inside vendetta job. Curiously enough, that bore the stamp of the Maltese, not of the hijack gang, but then, alliances in crime are as mysterious as they are in love, and no one can stomach a traitor. Krumnagel merely forgot how he was dressed. Now we've got to get rid of him. I agree with you one hundred percent, Sir Neville. I didn't before, now I do. We've got to get rid of him before something else goes wrong, and we have that great oaf on our consciences for the rest of our lives."

"Is it hard to get out of Lyburn?"

"If I know him, he won't stomach it for long. There's nothing there but a lot of pansies and perverts, and a few minor fraud cases, and the governor's a pain in the neck."

"And then it's only about twenty miles from Liverpool."

"Quite. We're going to watch Lyburn from now on. I'll go up there and talk to the local police. Whatever happens, everything has to be verbal. Not a word of any of this must get in to writing."

"Of course not. Whatever happens we can't risk implicating the Home Secretary," Sir Neville said hypocritically, avoiding Pewtrey's eye.

"That's a point," Pewtrey conceded, as hypocritically avoiding Sir Neville's eye.

And yet, the days passed and Krumnagel was still inside, urging the slaves on to build the temple, giving advice on the playing of Lady Bracknell, whose dialogue he found it difficult to understand, and feeling bronzed and fit. From Edie, not a word.

[219]

After the collapse of the local campaign, Edie suffered a re-
lapse, drinking too much and staying the whole day in her
dressing gown. The excitement, the heroics were all behind
her, and now the City hustled and bustled all around her,
minding other businesses and bent on newer and better desti-
nies. The final blow was struck when Al Carbide was promoted
to police chief, and the event was celebrated by a big luncheon
in the Buffalo Room of the Gateway-Sheraton Hotel, to which
Edie was evidently not invited.

When Al got back to his office, Krumnagel's office, now re-
decorated to suit Al's taste — American Colonial, white and
slatted with prints of ancient firearms on the wall — he found
Edie seated in the anteroom, dramatically dressed in black, veil
and all.

"Edie," he said, smiling nervously. For some unaccountable
reason, she looked as though she had come to shoot him. These
were the kind of clothes women wear when they have decided
to shoot a fellow. And yet, there was no quick movement, no
sudden appearance of a mother-of-pearl-handled handbag revolver with a wicked snout, like a pug dog, in the black glove.

"I come to congratulate you, Al," she said in a broken voice.
She had evidently been crying.

"Why, thanks, dear."

"And I also come to remind me what a shit looks like."

"Now, Edie," Al's smile became glacial. "That's no way to
talk to me, to Al Carbide, your old pal."

"Ever since I got back, not so much as a goddam gesture.
Not a phone call. Nothing. That's what one old pal does to
another?"

"I was in a bad position, dear, you understand that, surely,
dear? Bart got himself in a fix. That was unfortunate. You came
back home and you ran a wonderful campaign, just wonderful
— I should deserve such loyalty — but I couldn't support that
campaign officially. I sent money — honest — I'll show you the

receipt — but I'm employed by the City, same as Bart was. I got to keep aloof of campaigns."

"Campaigns. Who cares for campaigns? Couldn't you have called? Just to say hello? Just to say, Edie girl, I'm behind you. Just to say nothing but it's me, Al, remember?"

"Sure I could, dear. But I got troubles of my own. Not like you — not troubles like that — but still troubles."

Other people, not important enough to have been at the banquet, gathered to congratulate the new chief, and stopped embarrassed when they noticed the presence of Mrs. Krumnagel.

"Tell you what, Edie, how about dinner tonight? I'll fetch you early, six thirty say, dear, so we can go out to the Silver Spur, or some place across the state line," he said softly.

"Aren't you going to celebrate your moment with Evelyn?"

"Evelyn and I are — estranged. Like I said, you think you got troubles — 'course they're not troubles like yours, but for want of something better . . ."

At six thirty sharp, the big green and mauve Oldsmobile coupe pulled up at the curb outside Edie's house, and Al got out, in a summer suit the color of an oyster, with crocodile buttons. He found not at all the black widow of the early afternoon, but a carefully groomed, calculating little female wearing her sex on her sleeve, all fluff and undulation and challenge. They drove off to the Silver Spur, a place eighty percent gimmick and twenty percent gastronomy, made up to look like a piece of authentic Americana, with waiters dressed as Buffalo Bill and hostesses hard as horseshoe nails. They took their places, and consulted menus with the dimensions of the New York *Times*, listing a small number of items in gigantic capitals. Cocktails were taken with relish, with Al showing off a little by specifying the dryness and the twist and just how he wanted everything served, while Edie looked on with a grudging admiration at the demanding male animal at work.

Once they were at their table, half lost in suggestive gloom, with a faintly flickering brazier as the only immediate source of light and soft music spreading its symphonic treacle over their senses, the conversation began in earnest, Edie aware of the proximity of a living male for the first time in weeks, accessible and frank and attractive as possible.

"What happened between you and Evelyn?" Edie asked. "The word always was you were such a great match."

"What happens between men and women?" Al said, knitting his brow with an unconvincing show of introspection, which broke into too glib a smile too soon. "One day there's no mystery — one day it's all answers and the questions go with them are just used up, I guess."

"Was it your fault?"

"Yes . . . and no."

"Was it?"

"Yes, I can't help it, Edie. I'm highly sexed. Lots of guys envy me, but it's not all fun and games. I only have to look at a girl to get a hard on — most times it don't even have to be a good-looker — just any girl. I hope you don't mind my talking like this?"

"Why should I. It's natural," Edie lied, fighting the blush which had prowled right up to the roots of her hair.

"Gosh, if ever Evelyn had said it was natural, chances are we'd still be together. But she was different, jealous as a tiger cat, with less and less to offer. Told me I was wearing her out, that I talked filthy, that I only wanted one thing, and ignored her spiritual qualities, but what the hell . . . I told her, when I want spiritual qualities, I go to church."

"You maybe scared her," said Edie, toying with her fork, and showing all the solicitude one woman will show for another woman's predicament when she feels that things are safely hopeless.

"After seven years, I scared her?"

"Women change. They change more than men." She sighed. "They get older sooner."

Al veered like a bird in flight.

"Why don't you get no older, then?"

Edie bit her lip trying not to smile, or cry.

"Me? What should have been the best is gone for me. Four policemen. You understand what that means?"

"Who better? You're a kind of a mascot for the force, you know that? But for me . . . why, for me you're more than that . . . always have been . . . you're a woman of flesh and blood . . . and a heart and . . . a body . . . with needs and desires and Christ knows . . . you was always wasted on that great slob . . ."

"Don't talk ill of those who aren't here to defend themselves," Edie panted, swallowing to moisten her throat.

Al played his trump card.

"You want the Cherries Jubilee?" he murmured.

"Cherries Jubilee?" she echoed, and looked straight at him, from mouth to eyes, first one then the other, then both with a squint, then mouth again, a long time.

"Let's go home."

Their mouths drifted together, only for him to avoid actual contact.

"What's the matter?" she asked, with innocent deference to the commercials. "I got bad breath?"

"Not here," he said, and tried to hide his head behind his hand.

"What's the matter?"

"Red Leifson."

He had caught a glint of chromium in the dark, and now the invalid carriage with its smiling occupant drew alongside the table.

"Why, what have we here? On the eve of his installation as chief of police, Alan Carmine Carbide dines over the state line with the wife of his deposed predecessor? What is this, police business, private business, or mere elegance?"

"You ought to know better than ask questions like that, Red. Edie's pretty upset. Jesus, it's the least I can do."

"We'll put it down to elegance, shall we? This once," said Red, writing on a pad. He went on, grinning, "I hope you're not going to tell me that you'd knock me down if I wasn't down already, or cover my car with tickets like your predecessor in high office?"

"I don't have to, Red, I trust your sense of personal decency."

"No kidding. You must be the only one. But seriously, why take the lady over the state line? I trust there's no innuendo there?"

"I just happen to like the kitchen here."

"What did you order?"

"Christ, Red, what is this?"

"It's just for my cookery corner, Al. I like this joint too. I think it deserves our custom. I like the clean American atmosphere. I can't explain it. It's — wholesome? It's like —"

"Apple pie?"

"Yeah. You like it better than any place in town?"

"I like a change, Red, like anyone else."

Red looked at Edie and smiled.

"I see that," he said.

"You are just the lowest little slimy worm that ever crawled out from under a stone," Edie hissed.

"Aha. The quotable stuff, at last," said Red, writing furiously.

"Edie!" Al admonished. "She's overwrought."

"I am not either overwrought. This little creep makes me want to throw up, hiding behind his injuries." She flared, "How d'you lose those legs anyway? I'll tell you how. You fell off a chair when you was a baby, trying to see through a keyhole into a bedroom. Now, is that quotable stuff?"

"Sure, sure," said Red briefly, livid, and wheeled himself away. It took a broad to hurt him.

When he had gone Al said, "I wish you hadn't done that, Edie, and I'm awful glad you did. Come on, I'll take you home."

They drove back with more sweet music on the cassette, and

Edie felt wanted in a subtle way. Every now and then she'd steal a look at the icy profile, with the light blue eyes staring at the road, and all those attractive lines around the voluptuous mouth, and she thought how, if her wild dream came off, she would be envied, and other women would wonder what she had, to make it possible.

The car drew up by her residence. Curiously enough, he did not leap out and open her door. She waited a moment, then she got out, rather angry, realizing at the same time she'd been a fool to entertain such fantasies, but as age crept up, what's left? Fantasies —

"Aren't you coming up and have a highball for the road?"

Maybe her tone of voice in this despairing last effort would touch him.

"Sure, sure," he replied. "I'll just park the car."

"You can leave it here."

"No I can't, baby."

"Why not? It's my space."

"That's just why not. I'm chief of police now," he said, rather grossly Edie thought. "And Red Leifson's on the prowl. Go on in."

Edie obeyed him, and once she had closed the front door thought rather routinely of the folly she was committing in inviting this notorious lover up to her place, with his shining badge, his bulging holster, and his extra chromosome. She switched on the mood music, dimmed the lights, and ignited a stick of incense. Then she put the front door on the latch, and went into her room.

Suddenly, to her dismay, she heard the television above the mood music.

"Help yourself to a highball," she called.

He did so without replying, and settled down in Krumnagel's chair to watch an old film about Charlie Chan in Hawaii. Just as he was beginning to get the hang of the mystery, Edie made her entrance in her diaphanous drapes with exposed nipples

[225]

and the Mata Hari cigarette holder, and said, "Sex, anybody?"

Al roared with laughter.

"What's so funny?" she asked angrily.

"That's just about the greatest entrance I ever did see. Yowie!" He made a cowboy rodeo noise. Then his eyes caught sight of the nipples, and he stubbed out his cigarette meaningfully, stabbing it against the ashtray for a while after it was dead, Charlie and Confucius things of the past.

"Hey, that's some garment, know that?" he said hoarsely, "I seen them in the novelty shops. Turn round. You got a bare ass also?"

"One thing at a time," she said, approaching him slinkily, and blowing a heavy stream of smoke into his face.

Al coughed, waved away the smoke in irritation. The approach was altogether too subtle for him, and there was no need to spur his sensibilities with suggestive externals. He seized Edie and tried to turn her around in order to satisfy his curiosity about the garment. She struggled, but it was of no avail. He stroked her body for a moment, then rose unsteadily and forced a huge and greedy kiss on her, seeming to wish to take a bite out of her. As soon as the kiss was over, he looked at her, the knotted veins on his temples standing out like mountain ranges seen from the air. She was breathing deeply, with a look on her face which might have expressed resentment, but it could quite as easily have been the outward sign of sex aroused and bright feathers ruffled.

"You and me's going next door," he hissed.

"What's next door?" she panted.

"You're next door," he confided, "or you will be in sixty seconds if you know what's good for you. You'll be next door, bare as the day you was born. I don't want no more clothes on you."

"What you going to do during them sixty seconds?" she murmured, hypnotized by his lips.

"I'm going to turn off the television — and I'm going to the john."

[226]

"God, you're romantic! Why d'you have to tell me?"

"Politeness, that's why. You asked. Now git!"

Pretending she was still mistress of her destiny, she walked slowly out, wiggling her hips, dropping the ash off her dying cigarette into an ashtray, helping herself to a candy out of a large box and shooting him a farewell look of studied independence. His nostrils twitched with impatience. He glanced at Charlie Chan, who was just on the point of proving that the chief of the Hawaiian police committed murder out of motives of revenge. With a vague feeling of outraged lèse majesté, Al turned off the TV, and snuffed out the joss stick between his forefinger and thumb. He felt this gesture had eliminated Charlie Chan for good. Then he slipped out of his pants like an athlete discarding his track suit. It was interesting that he took his pants off before his jacket. His tie soon followed, his shoes, his socks. He hung them all up tidily in the cupboard in the hallway. Then he bolted the door, placed the chain in place, and took one penetrating look through the spyhole. A moth flying blindly towards the porch light was the only sign of life he saw.

Satisfied, he discarded his underwear, and went into the toilet naked. He emerged after a moment wearing nothing but a wristwatch and a contraceptive, paused for a moment by the cupboard, took his gun, wrapped it in his underpants, turned out the lights, and entered Edie's bedroom.

In obedience to instruction, she was lying on her bed in the nude, her eyes closed, imagining perhaps that she was the village maiden on the stone slab, offered up in sacrifice to some sun god or other. He glanced at her in satisfaction, pushed the gun and drawers under the bed, took his wristwatch off, made sure it was working, and set it up facing the bed on the night table. Then he shut off the lights, crossed to the window and peeped out between the slats of the Venetian blinds. The street was empty.

Edie heard his movements with growing excitement. The sun

god really was taking his time, and the sweet agony of uncertainty was the sexiest thing that had happened to her in years. In the darkness, he began to assume monstrous shape and towering dimension, a creature with avid eyes and the inanimate pelted face of the standard Hollywood super-ape, staring at the tiny struggling female in his grasp with a mixture of pity, curiosity and desire. Before she had time to elaborate her dream, reality was upon her, and she felt herself impaled on an arrow which shuddered in its target. Her legs flailed about dramatically, fighting shy of this late awakening out of a sense of form. There was no escape. Turn and twist as she might, a sharp-boned man, spare and rigorous, held her in place. Her mating song began, a series of ahs, breaking at some secret signal of nature's into a series of ohs, and then blossoming into half-tones and quarter-tones, a whole tonal odyssey of unresolved chords, culminating abruptly when Al suddenly said, vigorously and far from amorously, "Quit pinching me, will you?"

She evidently quit pinching him momentarily, for the ballet continued, and the intensity of her gasping threatened to burst into climax when without warning Al fetched her a great clout on one side of the face, and then another with the back of his hand.

"Don't ever do that again!" he shouted.

"What I do?" she sobbed.

"You bit my goddam ear . . . it's bleeding. Do that again and I'll tan the hide off of your fanny so you won't be able to sit for a month."

"Sorry, sorry, sorry, sorry . . ." she intoned, pleading for the rite to continue.

Perhaps he suspected he had allowed his anger to get a little out of hand, because he now settled down to organizing her chaotic array of emotions, and making sense out of them. That's, after all, what great ice-cold lovers do, the ones whose organs are trained like sheep dogs to the whistle. He began murmuring into her ear, and she felt she was learning the se-

[228]

crets of intercourse for the first time, although from the tone of voice he adopted, a passerby might have guessed he was helping to park a car in a narrow space. "Come on . . . come on . . . come on, now . . ." he remonstrated. "Don't let her go too soon now . . . hold it right there . . . easy . . . that's my girl . . . you're a great lay, you know that?"

Edie made garbled noises of gratitude.

"Hold her on that course now . . . don't force nothing . . . just keep her coming on that track . . . easy, she's getting away from you . . . you're not going to get your full mileage if you let go now . . . that's better . . . hear the jungle drums? . . . O.K., O.K. . . . this is it!" A note of urgency crept into his voice, "Take her away then . . . give her the gun . . . give her all you got!"

Edie trumpeted her triumph, and her head fell sideways, blotched and mottled, gasping for breath. Al tried to lift himself off her, but she grasped him as though she might lose this newfound treasure.

"Let me go," he said.

"No," she whispered. "I'm going to keep you here forever."

"Remember what I said?"

"I don't care. Beat me black and blue, you're just not going out of my sight again, ever."

Al smiled, and kissed her. She took the whole of his mouth in hers and began sucking, but it was too late for this sort of thing. Al might be a great lover, but he was functional. It was typical of broads that as soon as they'd had an orgasm, they tried to behave as though the best was yet to come. Al wrenched himself free and went off to the john again. When he came back, Edie had already fallen into a sleep, the serenity of which was punctuated by reconstruction of her ecstasy. In the dim light, Al saw her seize the pillow destined for him, and dig her fingers deep into it, placing it on her chest, rolling about under it, and eventually sinking her teeth into its plumpness.

"Holy mackerel," he said aloud, for want of something better. He had no doubt who the pillow was supposed to be, and began to feel resentful on its behalf, as though some part of him were being molested. Brusquely he seized the pillow. She half woke up.

"Is that you, lover?" she crooned.

"Sure is. Lover wants his goddam pillow."

"Take everything, lover. Take it all."

And she clung to him as though shipwrecked, with a tepid sea lapping sensuously all around them. He smiled in spite of himself. The proximity of a woman was a sensation he could never have enough of for moments at a time. The warmth, the perfume, he liked, as a fiddler likes his fiddle. She was asleep, which made her just about perfect. He shut his eyes, heavy with satisfaction, chalking up an imaginary trophy on his mental fuselage before falling off into the immense cradle of postorgasmic peace.

He woke at six thirty because that was his habit. To his surprise, he found Edie already awake, her eyes gray, sad and discreetly alarmed.

"Hi," he said. "Where am I?"

"Oh, Al," she muttered heartbrokenly. "I been thinking of Bart."

"Shoot!" he said, trying to moderate his language.

"That wasn't kind."

"What wasn't?"

"To say shoot when I mentioned Bart."

"Oh hell," grumbled Al. "O.K., so I'll say shit, like I originally intended. Is that better?"

"It's better'n shoot where Bart's concerned. Poor Bart. Thousands of miles away in prison."

"It lessens the possibility of him walking in here right now."

"I never lived until I met you."

"I bet you say that to all the fellers."

"I'm being sincere, Al. Gosh, it's awful."

"What is?"

[230]

"I feel I'm falling in love with you."

"Hey, hold on there!" Al sat up. "We hardly know each other."

"I've known you for years . . . without knowing you," she said, as though it were poetic.

"What in the hell does that mean? Listen, Edie. Don't hold out hopes, see. I'm not worth it. I'll make your life a misery."

"Maybe misery from you's better than the other feller's bliss?"

"Say that again?"

"Bart," she said sadly, "that poor slob."

"That's democracy," Al declared. "You come round to the majority viewpoint eventually."

"Did you always think that?"

"Always."

"Right from the start?"

"Right from the start."

A moment passed in silence.

"I'll make you breakfast."

"Don't bother," he said. "I'll pick up some at the drugstore."

"I'd *like* to make you breakfast," she insisted.

"I can't wait that long," he said, putting on his wristwatch.

"What's the matter with you, Al?" she cried. "It's half past six in the morning."

"I got to go home first," he explained patiently, "go to bed — so that Mrs. McAllister thinks I slept in. I got to take a shower, so the footboard's wet. In other words, I got to fix the place so it looks like I stayed home."

"Jeez, is that what they got to go through every time a detective commits adultery?"

"Don't mention that word!" Al commanded, crossing himself briefly, and slinking to the window.

As he stood looking out through the slats, Edie switched on the light.

[231]

"Put that light out!" he cried, dropping to the floor like a sack.

Edie began laughing. There was something irresistibly comic about a police chief, dressed in nothing but a wristwatch, lying under a window and bellowing orders.

"What's the matter?" she asked.

"Put that goddam light out!" he yelled in a whisper.

She began singing "Twilight in Turkey," and doing a belly dance, nearer and nearer the window and her recumbent master.

"For Christ's sake," he appealed. "There's a red convertible out there wasn't there when we went to bed. There's a guy in it."

Edie bent down a little to look through the slats. The man in question was standing by his car, and appeared to be looking straight at her. She retreated slowly towards the bedside table, and switched off the light.

"I don't think anyone can see in here," she said.

"Listen," he replied as he began easing himself forward on his elbows, as though carrying out an attack in 1914, "if you want to see it, you can see it, take it from me. It depends how much you're getting paid."

"Anyway, it's not who you think it is. This guy's standing by his car. He walks."

He was fed up with her stupidity.

"Hell, Edie," he said, "if I want to keep my eye on a whore-house, I don't stand out there on the sidewalk myself, do I? No. I order a cop to do it. So it's the same with other big shots. Red's not going to sit out there all night in his wheelchair, is he? Not when he can send a cub reporter."

The doorbell rang.

They froze.

"Don't answer that!" Al hissed.

"It may be a telegram from my mother," Edie whispered.

[232]

"Yeah . . . it may be Bart, or the President of the United States," Al whispered back. "At six thirty in the morning."

"What if something's happened to Mother?"

"In that case it's too late to worry. Now if something were *going* to happen to your mother, I could understand your worrying."

"I'd never forgive myself —"

"Is the guy still by the car?" Al appealed.

Edie bent down an inch.

"No," she said.

"So it stands to reason, the guy at the door's got to be the guy who was by the car."

"It could be another one."

"Oh sure, sure. The street's full of people. Take your pick."

The doorbell again.

Al took a decision.

"Is there a back way out of here?" he asked, while climbing into his briefs.

"Through the kitchen."

"Answer that guy. Keep him talking, while I get dressed and get the hell out of here."

"When do I see you again?"

"Now you ask me! A man from Red Leifson's columns at the door, and the lady has to wax sentimental! I'll tell you what. I'll call you."

"No, Al. You got no right to go out of my life just like that."

"I told you. I'll call you."

"I don't believe you."

"Baby." He pretended to be shocked.

"Swear it."

"I swear it."

"On your mother's head."

"I swear it."

"On your mother's head."

[233]

"Where d'you get that from?"

The bell rang again with insistence.

"I swear it on my mother's head," he whispered, and they tiptoed into the hall.

While he got dressed with rapid and silent gestures, she looked through the spyhole, then nodded to Al.

"What is it?" she asked, hoarsely.

"Oh, we're looking for Chief Carbide, Mrs. Krumnagel," said the voice. "Can I come in?"

"Who are you? Police department?"

"No. Not exactly. We're . . . helping the police."

"Helping the police? Aren't they able to help themselves no more?"

"There's been a big armed robbery downtown, you understand. Everyone's looking for Chief Carbide."

"Have you looked at his home?"

"Mrs. Carbide says she hasn't seen him all night."

Edie looked open-mouthed and furious at Al, who shrugged it off with a gesture of irritation. He was nearly dressed.

"What was that you said?" the voice asked.

"I didn't say nothing," Edie snapped. "You haven't told me who you are yet."

"Butch Krenowitz from the newspaper."

"From Red Leifson's column?"

The voice answered after a moment of hesitation.

"I sometimes work with Red, sure. We had this report, see, you'd been seen with Chief Carbide at dinner at the Silver Spur, and we figured you might know where he is."

"Well, it so happens I don't," she replied curtly, "and I'd like to know what right you have to come knocking on people's doors before dawn."

"I wouldn't have done, lady, if I hadn't seen a light on, and figured there was people up and about already."

As Al zipped his fly, he tried to kiss her good-bye, but she pushed him away. For a moment he looked hostile, then

[234]

thought better of it, and left towards the kitchen, tying his tie as he went.

"I didn't catch that last remark," said the voice.

"I didn't pass one," declared Edie. "I just think you ought to go away and not bother me no more." She suddenly remembered she had to play for time. "The fact that I was having dinner with Mr. Carbide is a tribute to a very beautiful person —"

"Who's that? Mrs. Carbide?"

"I'm referring to Mr. Carbide, if you don't mind." Edie barked. "He didn't want me to feel bad the day he got to be chief of police — after what happened — so he asked me out to dinner."

"Across the state line?"

"He asked me out to dinner." She was back to her dictation speed venom. "I went. At a certain hour, he said to me — Edie, it's been wonderful, but now I've got to get back to Evelyn — he drove me home, and then —"

"This must have been a few minutes ago in that case — because he's not back home yet."

A ferocious barking interrupted him.

"I got to go now," said the voice cheerfully. "One final thing, you do a great belly dance for an American, Mrs. Krumnagel."

Edie listened to the dogs barking, and suddenly smiled. She had forgotten to tell Al about the neighbor's Doberman pinschers. There had been no time or opportunity. She hurried through the house to the kitchen door. It was open. She caught a fleeting glimpse of the man in the raincoat, running through her garden and disappearing. The sun chose that moment to burst out majestically, spilling its light and warmth on the glistening grass and shivering leaves, blinding Edie. She shut her eyes, breathing the unaccustomed air of the early morning, her head bursting with pleasure. She hoped that the dogs, now reduced to silence, had taken a bite out of those bony buttocks. He deserved it, the deceiver, with his melancholy talk of

[235]

estrangement, and his serfdom to his own demanding genitalia. She closed the door softly on the outside world, and did not bother to lock it. She loved him. Now that she was alone, she was sure of it. And even if he did not love her at the moment, Red Leifson might easily force him to change his mind. It was good to be alive, in the land of the free.

14

Sir Neville was reaching a dangerous pitch of disillusion-
ment. It was hardly conceivable. Three weeks and more had
passed, and the reports from Lyburn were of a contented man,
busying himself with the refinements of a church predestined
to be hideous by the extreme vulgarity of its architect and the
dull symbolism of its inspirer's mind, which saw everything in
life as a battle between sunburst and shadowy night, with the
inevitable victory of the former. According to report, Krumnagel was occasionally sent to toil the fields, planting potatoes
and spinach and sea kale. And on these days, the huge trudging
figure could be seen returning to its voluntary captivity before
nightfall, aglow with achievement and a pious aura of angelus.

"I can no longer understand this man," Sir Neville moaned.
"He reduces the most saintly of impulses to the self-gratifying

Pharisee-sermonette of the do-gooder. I wish he'd never shot his way into my life. I wish he'd had the decency to spare me the effort. I wish — what's the use of wishing?"

"Well, I've been thinking," said Bill.

"With what result?"

"Once a man has the psychological makeup to help the authorities to frustrate an attempted jailbreak, without any thought of ingratiating himself toward them, but purely by impulse, then it's also conceivable that a prison without bars is the very thing to bring out all his sense of honor. I mean, once he is trusted not to escape, he cannot break that trust."

"Now you are plunging me into the depths of gloom."

"Why?"

"Because I recognize the awful accuracy of your assessment." Sir Neville doodled hopelessly on his blotter. "You mean," he went on after a moment, "that in order to encourage him to escape, it will be necessary to send him back again to a normal prison with bars?"

"There's no guarantee that'd work either," Bill said.

"You mean he'd be torn to pieces by the Mafia of mad Maltese?"

"Or else rise through the ranks until he's governor of the prison."

Involuntarily Sir Neville smiled.

"You always were an optimist," he declared.

"I don't think it's safe to bank on his trying to escape at all. It's far too arbitrary a solution, and it's putting the onus back on him."

"It's a very British solution, put it that way. It's a compromise. But it may just work because it's the last thing people would expect from a morally incorruptible person like myself."

"But will you get the adequate satisfaction out of having allowed him to escape, when you feel you should be able to make a positive contribution towards his freedom?"

"Oh gracious," snapped Sir Neville, "I hope I'm not such an

[238]

old woman that I need my ounce of satisfaction daily. I'm much too pragmatic for that, thank you very much. All I want is him out of my hair. I want him out of my jurisdiction, not because my jurisdiction is right or wrong, but because he has rendered it incapable. I'm not even tenderhearted about him, I'm just colossally embarrassed. It was the moment he began laughing at the wigs in court that I realized the full awfulness not only of his predicament, but of ours as well. I suddenly saw ourselves through his eyes, and I felt ridiculous. Why did I feel ridiculous? Very simply because at that moment I was ridiculous, and so was everyone else."

"Yes, but once he's gone," Bill insisted, "won't you feel that setting him free should have been done constitutionally?"

"Heavens," sighed Sir Neville. "That'll be the day, when he's gone. No, no. We have studied every avenue, as they say, and left no stone unturned, as they also say, and we have come up with no constitutional method for getting rid of him. It was that strange American gentleman, Mr. Alberts, who pointed out to me over lunch, in an atmosphere of contained hysteria, that even the most brilliantly worded of constitutions are made inadequate by the passage of time and the unpredictable march of progress. The arrival of an American police chief in England with a gun in a hidden holster is one step in this unpredictable march of progress, and if he turns out to be the forerunner of a mass of his fellows who come over to these shores in order to mow down elderly Scotsmen in pubs, then no doubt in the fullness of time adequate machinery will be set in motion to deal with such cases — once our legal system staggers forward from precedent to precedent like a man crossing a torrent stone by stone. But for this moment this is an isolated case, and poor blindfold justice cannot distinguish between Krumnagel and a workaday murderer. Consequently I have no great pioneering urge to shift the law. It's much easier to shift Krumnagel."

"Is it though?"

Sir Neville thought for a moment, then puckered his nose. "Oh, it must be, Bill."

Pewtrey was equally amazed by the high reputation acquired by Krumnagel in Lyburn.

"It's a hotbed of vice, is Lyburn," he was to say to Sir Neville. "I suppose it's out of the question that a chief of police could be a suppressed homo, or whatever the word is, a latent pansy. There's been some trouble of that kind among Chiefs of General Staff and Roman emperors and so on, but I've never heard of it high up in the police. If he's not, and if he hasn't settled down to have a whale of a good time with some mincing auntie in a cell with flowered curtains, then there's no other solution than that the American police has sunk into utter decadence. Not even to try and escape is utterly reprehensible, once you think of him as a kind of prisoner of war rather than as a criminal. I can't understand it. I could never trust a man like that in any unit of mine. Anyway, we can't go on watching Lyburn for ever. The local police resent our interference, and my men are getting bored."

It was the very day Pewtrey's vigil was relaxed, a day of glorious sunlight fading with crystal clarity into untroubled night, that Krumnagel came in to supper, and received a letter. He had worked hard and well all day, fitting a perfectly obnoxious stained glass window into place over the altar, an object of obvious reds and blues, depicting the Creation or some such incident.

As he spread vast quantities of margarine on his bread, Krumnagel read the letter. Almost immediately, he stopped doing anything but read. When he had finished it, he read it again, following each line with his fingernail so that nothing should escape. Then he folded it, placed it in his pocket, and continued eating automatically. He gave nothing away, but took no part in conversation. His mind was working furiously. He could have understood that the uncertainty and loneliness was too much for Edie — if she had affairs, he didn't want to know about them — they'd keep her calm and happy — yes, he approved of them — but to divorce him now that he was down, that was playing dirty — and on top of it, out of all the male animals in the goddam world, to plump for that runt Carbide, with his lousy moralizing attitude about the rackets, that was just the last goddam straw. This camel's back was broken, hump and all, no question. The steam built up in Krumnagel till he was blinded with rage and anguish. Tonight was the night of *The Importance of Being Earnest*. He'd promised to help Coral with his makeup. He strode out of the mess hall, and down the corridors, and into the latrines. They were empty at this time of the evening. Once he felt himself alone, all restraint vanished. He let out a great howl, and hit the wall till it was too painful to go on. His face had collapsed, and big tears squeezed their way through the folds of flesh, running fast and salty into his mouth. He leaned on the partition between the toilets, sobbing bitterly and occasionally seeming to coax a final tear from the now empty ducts. Slowly the sobs subsided, and although his lungs were occasionally shaken with squalls, he had begun to think.

Got to get out of here. Not now. Not tonight. Broad daylight. Perhaps. Play it by ear. Element of surprise. No church tomorrow. Those damn vegetables. Way out by myself. Got work to do tonight though. Dough. Passport. Etcetera. Can't think what it is, but there's got to be etcetera. Always is, and most times it's forgotten.

Now that he had the makings of a plan, he began to be overtaken by a feeling of savage well-being he had not experienced for months. It was as though an ulcer had burst and he sensed the same marvelous relief. The confusions which had governed his behavior in various places were suddenly nightmares which belonged already to the past. Gone was his sullenness, his piety; all those false protective skins were shed, and he rediscovered his old truculent self. He even blessed Edie and Carbide. They had brought about his precipitate redemption, and

[241]

saved him from surrender. His mind was irrevocably focused on a distant point. Revenge, he reflected, was sweet. If that had never been said before, it ought to have been.

"You're very jocular tonight," said Coral, as he made himself up as Lady Bracknell. "Is it because you know I'm nervous?"

"Sure you're nervous," Krumnagel replied. "Jesus, you're playing a big part with a lot of fancy dialogue. Stands to reason. You're lucky in one respect, though."

"And what is that?"

"You could be playing a guy."

"Oh, you are wicked, honestly!"

Coral liked being teased, and liked pretending to be offended.

"How do I look?"

"You look just great, Coral . . . only you'll look better when you get your wig on. All that rouge on your face and mascara, that don't go too good with a bald head."

"My head is not bald, it's shaved."

"Like your armpit."

"I'm not talking to you if you say things like that. They're rewd and vowlger!"

As curtain time approached, Krumnagel accompanied Coral backstage and gave him the final encouragement. He also saw Mr. Burgess, the prison officer in charge of theatricals, for whom he was going to play the gangster in *Petrified Forest*.

"Oh, Krumnagel," said Mr. Burgess, "the very man."

"Yes, sir?"

"I asked the costumiers to send a couple of *Petrified Forest* suits down with the clothes for *Earnest* so that we could try them on you in plenty of time. After all, you're an uncommonly big man, and we want to be sure that we avoid a panic in the last moment."

"Sure. Yeah. That's clear thinking. Where are the suits, sir?"

"Oh, they're here somewhere, among all this stuff."

"D'you want me to try them now?"

"No, not now. There's only ten minutes to curtain time."

"I could do it real fast."

"I think not."

Hell. Krumnagel looked at the pile of clothes, and saw that there were three or four cardboard boxes still unopened.

All the prison seemed to be there. Mr. Peverell-Proctor sought out Krumnagel.

"I've just been in to church again, and I couldn't take my eyes off the window," he said. "It is truly an object of glory. How do you feel after your devotional handiwork?"

"I feel O.K., governor, sir — great really, uplifted."

"Yes . . . yes . . ." said the governor, with understanding.

"Only I get this occasional diarrhea."

Mr. Peverell-Proctor seemed vaguely surprised that the conversation should have taken such a turn.

"You must see the doctor."

"If it goes on, I'll take the liberty, sir. It's funny, really. I've always been regular as clockwork, all my life, and then, bingo!"

"Yes, it is odd," the governor admitted, thinking of something utterly different.

"Yeah, I get these, more like cramps."

"Well, I hope you enjoy the play," said the governor, bringing the conversation to an end.

Krumnagel found the play quite desperately pedantic and unfunny, but then he wouldn't have laughed much even had it been a riot. He bided his time until he deemed that practically the entire cast was on the stage, when he rose, gripping his stomach, and made his way out of the theater, taking care to catch Mr. Peverell-Proctor's eye and to register his inner turmoil. Once in the open air, he ran backstage. The unfunny lines could be heard again. He could hear Coral say, "A handbag?" which, for some reason, got a laugh. He entered the changing room. It was empty. Frantically he eased open a cardboard box. It contained the clothes of a clergyman, and a small clergyman at that. He replaced them. He tried the next box. A pearl gray suit lay there, with huge lapels, a shirt and a loud tie of the twenties. The complete gangster. Krumnagel rolled the suit hastily into a bundle, shut the box and left the building in the direction of the latrines.

Once there, he stripped down to his underwear, and put on the suit. It was almost too big for him. Then he changed back into his prison clothes, and made his way back to his room. He lifted the mattress, and eased the suit underneath it. Then he went out in the open again. If only he knew how long the goddam play lasted.

"What are you doing out here, Krumnagel?"

It was a warder.

"Got this diarrhea, mister."

"The lats are the other way."

"I thought I'd lie down a while. Didn't feel too good. Kind of weak."

"You know the play's compulsory, don't you? If you feel better now, I'd go there if I were you."

"I been in there. The governor knows I'm out here. I told him."

"Oh. What's the play like then?"

"A load of horseshit."

"Go on!"

"Coral's having herself the time of her life."

"Caw. Good for 'er. She's been on heat all this week."

They went their several ways. Once the guard was out of sight, Krumnagel sprinted over to the Admin. Block, keeping out of the light. There seemed to be no one about. He knew his way about this prison by now, and he thought he knew where everything was kept. It was with a sigh of relief that he let himself into the darkness of the governor's office from the flat light of the corridor. There had to be some kind of filing system in the room next door, where the secretaries worked. He looked around. The Queen looked down from the wall with indulgence and appeared to approve his actions. Silently he moved to the room next door. There was no safe. Thank heaven everything in this place was based on trust. "Trust in the Lord is trust in thy neighbor," was the motto of the stinking place, but in Latin, of course, which was Greek to Krumnagel.

He opened the filing system. He found himself under "K." There was a key and a locker number attached to each card. He found locker 317, and opened it with a shaking hand. There, before him, lay a familiar green passport. He opened it, and a younger, keener Krumnagel stared back at him, face frank and determined, ignorant of humiliation, yes, and of tragedy. A light moisture of self-pity shuddered on the surface of the older Krumnagel's eye. He took some money, almost a thousand dollars he had had on him. He took some keys and documents. After a moment of hesitation, and a pang of regret, he left his revolver in the locker, almost like a visiting card. He shut the locker, and locked it. Once more he crossed the Admin. Block, and was about to plunge into the open air when he saw the crowd gushing from the theater. The play was over. Now he'd have to lie to Coral, tell him he'd been just great. He did not dare risk emerging from the Admin. Block while there were people, convicts or warders, in the area. How could he explain his presence? There were voices in the corridor. He stood flush with the wall, breathing deeply. It would be just terrible if his plans were frustrated now that everything had gone so well. The crowd was scattering. Soon there would be no one left. Eventually he dared it — opened the door a crack — eased himself out — stood still. He moved forward cautiously.

"There you are!" It was a warder. "Christ, you had us worried."

Instinctively Krumnagel's hand flew to his stomach.

"Gee, I'm sick!" he groaned.

"It's all right, sir!" cried the warder. "He's here. Says he's sick."

The governor and a few warders appeared, walking quietly towards him.

Mr. Peverell-Proctor smiled ruefully.

"My goodness, Krumnagel, I don't know how I could have doubted you — I thought it wasn't possible that you could have escaped — after all the work we have done together on the house of God. It wasn't like Saint Christopher, I thought, to drop the infant in the water when only halfway across. You have vindicated my faith in you. Thank you. And you missed a wonderful show. What a delight Oscar always is! And how happy he would have been at Lyburn." He sighed. "But that was before his day. Oscar Wilde was a Reading man, was he not?" The governor's voice became more authoritative, possibly because there was a chill in the air. "Go on sick call tomorrow morning, Krumnagel. And good night to you."

"You heard that, did you?" said a warder.

"Sure I heard it."

"It was an order."

Some men are just vocationally disagreeable. Now he had to change his plans. The key was out of the filing cabinet. The gangster outfit was out of the wardrobe. He went to his room, holding his stomach in case anyone was watching. Coral was sulking.

"You weren't there when the curtain came down, were you?"

"Hey, what I saw was just great — just great, Coral."

"But you weren't there at the end, was you? I looked for you as I took my curtsies."

"I had diarrhea."

He was getting tired of the game, and of the excuse. Coral had eroded his way into Krumnagel's life, because they were housekeeping together, and the absence of anything physical in their relationship hardly made any difference to the tone of mildly quarrelsome domesticity which prevailed in their cell. Now that Krumnagel had decided to escape, it all sounded and felt so utterly absurd and unreal, this endless badinage with an aging queen, who always wanted to be hitched, unhitched, zipped, unzipped, comforted and rubbed up the wrong way.

"The governor told me he thought you was just tremendous, Coral."

"The governor? Been sucking up to him then, have you?"

"Oh hell — I try to be nice —"

"It's your own fault. You told me you'd be there clapping. You wasn't."

"O.K., O.K., so you're greater than Sarah Bernhardt, greater 'n Katie Hepburn, greater 'n Minnie Mouse, and with a little help from nature, you'd be greater 'n Mickey Mouse as well."

Coral drew in his breath sharply, pursed his lips, and those were the last words they were destined to exchange.

They went to bed in silence, each waiting for the other to use the sink with elaborate consideration, so that no word had to be exchanged. Krumnagel listened in the darkness, and for an age Coral still twisted and turned in bed, excited by the performance, reliving it in detail. At last he fell into some very unladylike snoring, and Krumnagel began to calculate. It had to be round about midnight. Liverpool was twenty miles away. At four miles an hour that would take him into the dock area round about five — say half past five in the morning. The hue and cry wouldn't be raised till after six. He had to move fast. He slid out of bed, onto the floor. As quietly as possible he dressed. He piled the prison garb under the covers, then, as a final malicious nicety, he took Coral's toupee off its block, ruffled the hairs a bit, and placed it on his pillow, just visible, from under the bedclothes. It was great to be wearing collar and tie again, to be in possession of your own passport, and to have close on a thousand bucks, and some more in traveler's checks. Quietly he opened the door, and carrying his shoes in his hand, he passed silently down the corridor, and out into the night.

The best way was across the church building site, over a low wall, and into a plowed field. There was no one about, just an occasional light at the corner of a building, with the usual hectic night life surrounding it. Krumnagel entered the church, made his way across the rubble, emerging by the unfinished vestry, leaned on the wall to put on his shoes, panted as he eased his heels into them with his forefinger. He was getting old and heavy. He assessed the wall, took a jump at it, and failed to cross. He dusted his hands on his pants and looked around guiltily for having failed. Once again he ran at the wall, easily, unhurried, and imagined himself a famous pole-vaulter, only to land once again on the wrong side. Too damn idiotic to be stymied by a low wall in a prison without bars. A dog began barking somewhere. Krumnagel was sure he was the cause. He tried a third time with the speed of desperation. This time he clung to the wall, refusing to fall. He could not rise, either. He just hung there doggedly, recovering his breath. With a sudden movement, calculated to take the wall by surprise, he got one hand over the top, and slowly forced his left leg up the gritty surface. With a final effort he managed to get himself astride the wall, and lay on top of it, his forehead on the scratchy brick and concrete, and if Great Danes had made their appearance at the moment, he would have given up without a struggle. After a while, the instinct for self-preservation took over again, and he dropped his packet of aching bones on the other side, and began plodding through the disheveled earth of the rich black field.

He followed the signposts towards Liverpool, eventually entering a freeway. He preferred country lanes to these vast exposed highways where a lonely pedestrian attracts attention. He figured that if he walked against the stream of traffic, there was less likelihood of the cars or trucks stopping. The sooner he reached the harbor area the better — not only because he would attract only minimal attention in a large seaport, whereas a man in a navy blue shirt, white tie with a preening peacock on it, and a wide-lapeled, double-breasted business suit in metallic gray, smelling strongly of mothballs, walking on the freeway at night, seemed out of place. Suddenly a car stopped. He stood his ground, impaled by the headlights. Police.

"Where d'you think you're going?" in a flat Lancashire voice.

"Am I heading for Liverpool, fellers?"

"Yank, are you, then?"

"Sure I am. I got drunk. Wow! Did I get loaded! Hey, where in hell am I? And where's that girl? The redhead?"

There was good-natured laughter from the police.

"D'you know what country you're in then?"

"Sure do. That much I know. Don't tell me, now. Don't rush me? U.K.?" he ventured, squinting with effort.

"Where you from then, Shiddington Air Base?"

"Nope, I'm a seaman . . . technician . . . radio operator on the U.S.S. . . . Jeez, I've forgotten the name of the focking ship."

"*Titanic?*" one of the boys suggested, to laughter.

"Uh-uh."

"Will you remember before we get there?"

"Get there?"

"Jump in, we'll take you into the edge of the Port Area. Can't take you any further, see . . . it's not our bailiwick."

As they drove, the car radio was alive with news of petty thefts and suspicious loiterings. Krumnagel became more and more nervous as the minute hand edged its way around the clock, feeling that any moment that silly old Coral might wake up to take a leak, and get hysterical when he noticed his hairpiece had gone. Trust him to wake the confounded joint for a goddam hairpiece. It hadn't happened, but Krumnagel got angry at the thought. His face worked nervously as the odor of camphor permeated the police car. He put his hands in his jacket pockets, which he had not done yet, and found them alive with little balls, like marbles.

"Where that smell of mothballs come from?" asked the driver.

"Oh . . . it's me, I guess," said Krumnagel.

"Like the smell, do you?"

Was this some sort of sarcasm or what? The ghost of the police chief threatened to break out of Krumnagel and ask the young man what the hell he meant by such a remark, which was mysterious enough to sound unfriendly.

"I spend most of my life at sea, young man," replied Krumnagel, with moralizing dignity, "and I only got one going-out suit, see, so I got to preserve it — and the moths out in the China Seas, they come big as bats out of hell round sundown."

"Out in the China Seas?" asked a third policeman, "I didn't think you fellows went out that way no more."

"When I refer to the China Seas," Krumnagel glowered, "I mean the waters around Taiwan, you understand."

Meanwhile the litany of petty larcenies crackled unrelentingly on the intercom, suspicious characters loitering, an attempt to break and enter, even an assault with intent to ravish. Krumnagel ran a furtive finger over his forehead, and dislodged several drops of iced sweat. This he interpreted as fear. Jesus, give a man a chance. He simply couldn't be overwhelmed in a police car if the message came through now. What kind of strategy was that? Nobody'd believe the story when it came out. "You know where they caught him?" the inflection already tremulous with laughter on the way. "Krumnagel? They caught *Krumnagel* that way? I don't believe it? Who? And it wasn't even the F.B.I.? The limeys? The li-meys!"

"Let me out of here!" he bellowed.

"We're not there yet," the driver said.

Krumnagel steadied himself. Spoke softly.

"Think I'm goin' a throw up."

The police car braked harder than in any gangster picture. Krumnagel lurched out and began coughing, holding his throat, doubled over.

"Want us to wait for you?" the driver called.

Krumnagel waved the car on, sank to his knees. Hold it there. Mustn't be too dramatic. He stood up again and breathed. Don't want to end up in the hospital through sheer overacting. He heard the car drive away. The performance had really made him feel queezy. He gripped his stomach and the tears glinted in his eyes like diamonds. "Christ," he said.

Dawn was beginning to break, uncertain and wistful, a couple of orange gashes on a full-bosomed sky of gray, when Krumnagel's pointed black and white gangster shoes accosted the first damp cobblestones of Liverpool's bleak docks. He was footsore, and the shoes were designed for the smooth surface of ballroom and boudoir rather than for these slippery and bulbous uncertainties. He looked for a ship with a welcoming personality. He had nothing but first appearances to go by, and a hope of beginner's luck. As was natural for a man of his temperament, he searched for the American flag like a homing pigeon. There didn't seem to be one, except for a large craft which looked like a troopship, called the *General Augustus B. Savage*. That was not the kind of ship to make a getaway on. That was just a large floating squad car in Krumnagel's book.

He became more anxious as the day grew slowly lighter, although he was reassured by the manner in which those already around at that early hour ignored each other. There is something functional and impersonal about docks, much as there is in hospital corridors, where it is never clear whether the members of the staff know each other or not. The characteristic which would have been interpreted as a form of unexplained hostility by Krumnagel in normal times, he was grateful for now.

Coral turned in his sleep, opened an eye, and closed it again. The messages flashed back and forth along his inner lines of communication. They sped with such dispatch while the apparatus was still cold that they brought a frown to his forehead. The eye opened again, shortly followed by the other. He stared at the block while he grew accustomed to the half-light. It was

[251]

as smooth and shiny as his own head. He sat up in panic. His hair was gone. He looked over at Krumnagel. A little tuft was on the pillow, but the body had diminished. He rose silently, as though in the presence of the supernatural. With a sudden movement, he ripped off the bed covers and screamed.

Mr. Peverell-Proctor was on the phone several minutes later, telling his story to the police and a little while after that, having acquired the number from Scotland Yard, he was in touch with Chief Detective-Inspector Pewtrey, who agreed that what had occurred was regrettable. "He won't get far," Pewtrey heard himself saying.

He immediately dialed Sir Neville's number.

"I hope I haven't woken you, Sir Neville. The fact is, Krumnagel's gone, scarpered."

"Thank God!" cried Sir Neville.

"I thought I'd tell you, but I don't think we should sound too enthusiastic."

"Why not?"

"You never know who's listening."

"Who could possibly be interested in Krumnagel?" asked Sir Neville.

"The police," Pewtrey replied with considerable irritation.

"You don't mean to say we use methods like that?"

"There are crossed lines and crossed lines," Pewtrey murmured.

"Well, thank you for the tragic news. Is that better?" Sir Neville asked gaily.

"Don't mention it. I'm off to the office as soon as I've shaved."

Things moved rather more rapidly than Pewtrey had dared fear. By the time he reached New Scotland Yard, he found a generally jubilant mood, since a squad car had reported giving a lift to a man answering Krumnagel's description, and this man was apparently set on reaching the docks. Pewtrey lit his pipe in order not to have to express any emotion, and cursed Krumnagel roundly behind the blue smoke. With that man's

luck and savoir-faire, he'd probably be taken asking a policeman the time, not because he wanted to know it, but out of a
desire for human warmth.

At that moment, Krumnagel was actually aboard a cargo
ship, the *Agnes Stavromichalis*, which was in the habit of limp-
ing around the world like a beggar, carrying rust and filth
along with its other cargoes. Its flag had something in common
with the Stars and Stripes, so that its concept produced a certain sense of harmony on Krumnagel, although it only possessed one star instead of the proud myriad. Monrovia, the
ship's port of registry, Krumnagel had never heard of, although
he guessed it must be in Texas, the lonestar state. Sons of
bitches, they got a navy of their own then. To confuse him even
further, the master turned out to be Greek, Themistocles Makarezos.

"Sounds Scottish to me."

"Do I look Scottish?" asked the master agreeably, gazing at
Krumnagel with two little eyes, like currants, only just separated from one another by the razor-edge prominence of his
nose.

"You sure act Scottish, I'll say that for you. Say that figure
again?"

"Five hundred dollars — in cash."

"Do you realize what you're asking?"

"Why didn't you compare the figure with cabin class transport in a normal regular transatlantic liner?"

"Where do you expect me to get hold of the documents I
need?"

"Ashore. We don't sail for a couple of hours," the master said
easily.

Krumnagel hesitated, licked his lips. Makarezos smiled.

"You don't have the time to go?" he asked. "I understand. So,
I'm saving you the trouble by giving you the facts. All you have
to do is trust me. O.K.?"

Krumnagel fidgeted again, tapped his pockets.

"Listen," said the master, as though to put an end to badinage, "weigh up the advantages and disadvantages. You have a reason to get out of England, I have the means to get you out. A comfortable bed, clean water, food you can eat — that I can't offer. For that you're better off with a regular ocean liner. If you don't want to go through customs, however, you're better off with me. And all I ask is five hundred dollars, and maybe a little easy work."

"Work? I got to work on top of half a grand?"

"Easy work." The master derided it with an elaborate play of his shoulders and a pained lifting of eyebrows. "Swabbing the deck, cleaning dishes, a little polishing here, a little scrubbing there, it won't kill you. I'd do it myself, only I'm master, and it don't heighten the respect of the crew if I do any work myself."

"How about the unions?" asked Krumnagel doggedly. Between the church and the vegetables, he figured he'd worked enough for a while.

"This is a nonunion ship."

"Nonunion ship?" Krumnagel echoed with outraged disbelief.

"You sound as if it's not your habit to serve aboard nonunion ships," observed Makarezos coolly. "If that is the case, if you have scruples of that sort — in other words, if you're a troublemaker — you'd better look elsewhere."

Krumnagel took lightning stock of his position. Why did he always sound self-righteous with the wrong people? What insane urge had sent him galloping across the prisonyard like the U.S. Cavalry to engage an escaping criminal in combat? Why the hell did the policeman keep showing through the cracks in the man? What do you mean, policeman, patriot yet, clean-living, high-minded, God-fearing missionary on behalf of the rest of the countries — and what place was there for such a wonderful guy in a dirty segment of the world?

"I don't give a shit for no unions," he said, trying to destroy his troublesome image.

[254]

The master smiled.

"I was not quite accurate when I said we were entirely non-union."

"Now what?"

"We are subject to the Liberian unions," the master went on.

"What in the hell are they?" Krumnagel asked.

"I don't know," the master replied. "Now, have you made up your mind?"

"You're bound for Galveston, Texas, right?"

"Right."

"And the asking price is five hundred bucks."

The captain had no time to reply before an Oriental opened the door, and spoke in some strange Eastern tongue. Since most Eastern tongues have an in-built note of alarm and anxiety to Western ears, it was not clear to Krumnagel whether this was due to the message the man was imparting or to the language itself. The master seemed to understand. He turned to Krumnagel.

"The police is here," he said curtly. "So it is understood. One thousand dollars."

"One thousand —"

"I'll be generous, seven fifty. Be reasonable. I have to give something to the crew. They know you're here."

"Why you low-down —"

"In that case, please follow me." He spoke to the Oriental in clipped monosyllables. Krumnagel had a fleeting vision of himself and the wall, and this final indignity tipped the balance.

"It's a deal," he hissed. "Seven fifty."

The Captain ordered the Oriental out, locked his door, stood briefly on his swivel chair and removed a panel of rotting wood from the ceiling, painted light blue in places to disguise its hopeless condition.

"Get up there," snapped the captain.

"Up there?" moaned Krumnagel. "I'll never make it."

[255]

"I'll push from behind. Can you hear the voices? The police."

Manfully Krumnagel got into place on the wobbling chair, and prepared to make the gestures of effort, but he felt as unreal about it as a paratrooper trying to reenter the aircraft after having leaped into space.

"Don't you have no other place I can hide?"

"Don't waste precious time. I got not only you to think of, but my reputation. Now one, two — up!"

Krumnagel felt it was the agony of the wall all over again, but in front of a witness. He hung there until the master's hands on his rear made him start like a horse. In his effort to escape this irritating and suspect contact he suddenly found himself head and shoulders through the hole. With the Greek still goosing him, he pulled himself out of reach, and lay gratefully on the creaking timbers.

"You see, the only way to help you is to goose you. I haven't the strength to push you," smiled the master as he replaced the floorboard.

"Hey, what's this God-awful stench up here?"

"That's from the kitchen."

For a short while, all was silence and a cocktail of evil odors. Then Krumnagel heard voices, and through the multiplicity of apertures, he saw the top of the flat blue caps of the police, accompanied by a helmet, the apex of which practically scraped the ceiling. The police looked around for a moment. One of them tapped the roof with a torch.

"What's up there then?"

"That's just decorative — the metal structure is a few inches behind it — there's just room for a rag or two and a pot or two of paint. Cigarette?" The master suggested quickly.

"We can't smoke while we're on duty."

"They're Egyptian. Take one home. They're good, for after lunch."

"Thanks very much."

The policemen helped themselves and went to search elsewhere. Krumnagel lay there for what seemed like hours. As his eyes became accustomed to the darkness, he imagined he saw two glints of light, close to each other and unflinching. Unhurriedly the two shining objects moved closer, and revealed themselves to be the eyes of a rat so filled with the riches of the pantry that its feet were quite inadequate to keep its billowing mass off the floor.

"Get outa here!" hissed Krumnagel, suddenly possessive about his tiny cache.

The rat looked at him with eyes hurt rather than unafraid, and Krumnagel saw the wigless Coral, staring at him reproachfully.

"Escape, all well and good, that's up to the individual — if you didn't care for my company, that's one thing — but why ruffle my hairpiece?"

"Out! Out! Back to your hole!" Krumnagel tried to be frightening on an intimate and noiseless scale. The noises he made seemed to correspond to words of kindness and trust in the language of rats, because the huge creature came closer, its nose twitching with joyous mischief. Krumnagel shuddered with horror, and felt the hairs of his body raise themselves in alarm. It was the clatter of the chains which distracted the rat from an active pursuit of this new friendship, and it turned its back on Krumnagel, recuperating its energies while lying like a huge beige pincushion. The noise of the chains was accompanied by splashes and shouts and the groans of machinery attempting to turn over. Then the noise became deafening, and a tidal wave of Diesel fumes engulfed both Krumnagel and the rat, which returned into the darkness grumbling in a high, squeaky, Dickensian voice.

Krumnagel saw the master return to his cabin. He tapped on the loose board.

"Can I come down now?" he asked furtively.

The master looked up with a grin.

"What's the matter? Don't like your quarters?"

"My quarters?" Krumnagel pulled the board out of place. "These are my quarters?" he asked angrily. "For seven hundred and fifty bucks, these are my quarters?"

"If you hadn't complained, they might have been."

What kind of a guy was this? With what kind of sick humor?

"Hey, you got a rat up here, you know that?"

"I got several. Which one was it? A very stout one?"

"Are you trying to tell me they're household pets?"

"Not exactly. Ever heard of what the Russians call coexistence? Well, that's us with the rats, the rats with us. Armed neutrality. Was it the stout one?"

"I'll say it was stout. It was positively portly."

"That's Electra, the mother, grandmother, mistress, aunt. If you get on well with her, it speaks highly for you. Now see if you get on with me. I saved you from the police. How about my reward?"

Krumnagel half turned away from the master in order to count his money. With great regret, he parted with seven hundred and sixty dollars.

"You owe me ten dollars," he said.

"You owe me your freedom," said the master with a smile.

"If you think so little of ten dollars," Krumnagel cried, "give me twenty back and I'll owe you ten dollars."

"I owe you ten dollars," crooned the master. "Now don't move from here. I've got to go on the bridge and get this deathtrap out into the open sea where those goons up on the bridge will find fewer targets to hit."

"Deathtrap?" Krumnagel inquired.

"Fire hazard. Certified unsafe. Hull only one eighth of an inch thick in places. Defective engine. I could go on forever. Can you swim?"

"No, I can't swim," Krumnagel near shouted, but the master was already up the ladder and onto the bridge. Goddam it, that's some lousy sense of fockin' humor if ever I see it.

In London, Pewtrey had abandoned Scotland Yard and its optimism for Sir Neville's office.

"Surely no news is good news?" asked Sir Neville.

"I quite agree, but no news is not really no news if it runs the risk of becoming news at any moment. If they don't catch him on their first inspection of shipping in the port, they'll go through them all again with the proverbial fine-tooth comb, with special attention to all shipping bound for the U.S.A."

"D'you know the origin of the term fine-tooth comb?" asked Sir Neville expansively.

"With all due respect, I don't think this is the moment to inform me," Pewtrey snapped.

"I don't know myself," Sir Neville declared. "I was asking you."

The director of public prosecutions was at his most aggravating, at his most boyish today.

Pewtrey picked up the phone and asked for a Liverpool number.

"What are you going to do?" Bill Stockard asked.

Pewtrey smiled slightly. He'd smile for Bill, not for Sir Neville.

"I'm going to take a risk," he replied.

"Is that wise?" Sir Neville asked.

Pewtrey did not answer. The phone bell saved him.

"Hello, Detective-Inspector Golham please. Detective-Inspector Pewtrey, Scotland Yard." A moment passed. "Hello, Bruce? Any luck with Krumnagel yet? . . . I'm not surprised. They've picked him up in Stafford . . . What? . . . Yes, he would, he caught the early morning train from Liverpool . . . the train going to Stafford about twelve minutes ago . . . We picked him up . . . What? . . . Well, if you're as close to a seaport as that, chances are a criminal, especially a criminal with a police background, will try to avoid the obvious . . . he'll guess the police'll all rush to the seaport . . . No, it's no

[259]

feather in my cap, Bruce . . . the man who scores the goal often gets the credit, whereas it's the man who passes the ball to the scorer deserves it . . . that's life . . ." He replaced the receiver slowly.

"That is a risk," Sir Neville announced, as though recognizing one for the first time in his life.

"How will you get out of that if there should ever be an inquiry?" asked Bill.

"I haven't quite decided, that's why I referred to it as a risk. I only had time to do my homework as far as trains were concerned. There simply wasn't the physical time to think out the consequences in greater detail."

"You could deny it," Bill suggested, a little tensely.

"That would be the most ruthless, and in a way the safest way. It means pulling rank, as they say, up to a point. Golham's word against mine. Alternately, I could wait half an hour, and then say it was an error. It's more dangerous, that, since it may mean inventing a whole imaginary chain of developments, and sticking by them. It's the stupid way. It makes no sense. It's inviting disaster."

"And it's undoubtedly the course you'll take," Sir Neville said.

"I expect so," Pewtrey sighed.

"You could take Golham into your confidence," Bill suggested. "As you took the boys in the squad car into your confidence."

"Afterwards. Afterwards, of course. It's the only way to kill the story. Conspirators are always flattered to know something others don't."

The phone went. Sir Neville picked it up. His expression changed.

"The Home Secretary," he confided, his hand over the mouthpiece. His energy, his innocence, and his playfulness returned in anticipation of his conversation.

"Good morning, sir!" he called out. "Yes, for the time of year, indeed it is . . ." He became graver. "Oh, it's in the early racing edition of the evening papers, is it? . . . I couldn't very well, I only heard about it a few moments ago myself . . . oh yes, I don't think there's any doubt he'll be recaptured . . . that's right, indeed yes, he's never shown the kind of resource one would associate with a man in his position . . . no . . ." Once again, Sir Neville became studious, attentive, and then the light of battle flickered in his eye. When at length he spoke, it was with precision and with acid. "I am under the impression, Home Secretary, that I obeyed your instructions not only meticulously, but also in the spirit in which they were intended . . . I'd never have brought the subject up at all, but once you mention it again, I can only say that if I were put under oath in a court of law, I would be bound to admit that you had suggested that Krumnagel be placed in a prison without bars and be encouraged to escape . . . A joke? . . . It has to be an awfully good joke, Mr. Belper, to outlive the situation which occasioned it . . . Many jokes, especially of this kind, fail to retain their freshness when repeated . . . and there is no more effective death to humor than an oath to tell nothing but the truth . . . the truth is apparently devoid of all levity . . . Your word against mine? How strange you should mention it . . . no wish to be melodramatic — oh, believe me, Home Secretary, I am practically immune to melodrama — I will be retiring very soon in any case, and at this rate, I may very easily be tempted to write my memoirs . . . As for your word against mine, I am a Queen's Counsel, you a politician . . . I have no fear of the outcome . . . What? . . . I assure you, I am calm . . . Forget the conversation? . . . Only if I am free to remember it again if the need should arise . . . in this profession, one apparently never knows . . . I beg your pardon? . . . A risk? . . ." (He winked at Pewtrey and Stockard.) ". . . A happy choice of word, if I may say so . . . A risk?

What is a risk but a course of action which is reasonable in itself, but which fails to take into consideration the prejudice and the stupidity of others . . . Shortsighted? Perhaps . . ." He became very cold and ruthless, and was evidently enjoying himself to the full. He listened for a while to the hesitations, the maneuvers, the equivocations of Belper at the other end of the wire, gaining authority by the second with his charged and vibrant silence. Eventually he condescended to speak. "Home Secretary, you must have thousands of decisions to make all day long. If each one of them causes you the introspection and remorse of this one, then may I humbly suggest you find some other employment commensurate with your splendid gifts before it is too late. Perhaps the Prime Minister will see fit to move you to the Foreign Office. Certainly dealing with foreign countries does not require quite such high ethical standards as you bring to your work at the Home Office, and the tendency you have to blackmail might with luck bring great credit to your country, or at worst, they could be smoothed over by an astute translator . . . Am I being insolent? I beg your pardon. Every phoenix needs flames from which to rise. I am eternally grateful to you, sir, that you have provided them for me. The fact remains that you gave me certain instructions, which I have carried out to the best of my ability. I, in turn, conveyed your wishes to New Scotland Yard, and I am sure that the mission you entrusted us with will shortly be successfully accomplished in the highest traditions of . . . hello . . . hello . . . he has hung up." Sir Neville smiled savagely.

"We are all conspirators now," he said.

"Why did you have to go that far?" asked Pewtrey.

"I didn't really go far enough," replied Sir Neville. "All I have done is to hasten my retirement."

"On the contrary. You're much less trouble to Belper in office than out of it. Freedom must be denied you in case anything goes wrong," Bill said.

"What could possibly go wrong?" Sir Neville asked. "By

now, Krumnagel is on his way back to his own people, and good luck to them all."

"The ash is safely under the carpet," Bill reflected softly. "It is out of view. That does not mean that it has gone forever. Ask Mrs. Shakespeare."

15

.

The voyage on the *Agnes Stavromichalis* was not particularly
noteworthy from a maritime point of view, in that the events
were more redolent of Dostoevski's dank attics than of Joseph
Conrad's bridge or Melville's yardarm. If it hadn't been for the
sickening plunging and lurching of the rusty carcass, Krumnagel would hardly have known he was at sea at all. To make
matters worse, whenever another ship hove in sight, it seemed
to be riding with swanlike serenity, and with just enough foam
around the bows to give it a somnolent snarl, while the pride of
Liberia gasped and shuddered and belched black smoke erratic
as a Japanese tree, and made no progress whatsoever. The first
day was relatively uneventful. A motorboat came along side
and delivered several suitcases, and later in the afternoon, Song
Yi, the cook, had an epileptic fit while serving the soup. Krum-

[264]

nagel quickly took command of the situation, forcing a dishrag into the Chinaman's mouth, and holding him down like a rabid dog until the attack subsided. It was only then that he discovered that while he was demonstrating the benefit he had received from the first-aid classes, the others had finished all the food.

"I hope you're proud of yourselves," he yelled at them. They nodded as a man in recognition of the noise.

"They don't speak English," said the master.

"Hey, what did those swarthy guys deliver in the Chris-Craft?" he asked.

"I help all sorts, not just criminals on the run," the master replied pleasantly.

"Opium, was it? Heroin?"

"You might get your fare money back, and a little more, if you are willing to take some of it through."

"Through what?"

"Through U.S. Customs and Immigration."

Krumnagel took a deep breath. All sorts of glib moralities were on the boil in that great emotional cauldron, and he felt his cheeks burn with the fervor of uprightness.

"How much?" he heard his voice quaver as it went against the grain of his thinking.

"We'll talk about it later."

The second day out, Ali Bin Ibrahim stabbed Servaes, a seaman from the Maldive Islands. The motives were not clear, since neither spoke the other's language, but there was a general feeling among the Orientals that Ali Bin Ibrahim suspected his victim of being Jewish. It became necessary to put Ali Bin Ibrahim in irons, and Krumnagel was the only man with the sheer physical volume to succeed in this.

"I'm beginning to wonder what we would have done without you," the master laughed, during the second inedible dinner.

"How the hell can you eat this shit?" asked Krumnagel.

"You can't cook, can you?"

"Better'n this."

"How would you like to take over the galley? Then we can throw the epileptic Chink overboard."

"You're joking?"

"No. There are nearly eight hundred million of them. They'll never miss him."

Krumnagel grunted.

"I don't appreciate your humor," he said.

"What's the matter? Have you never killed a guy?"

"Sure I killed a guy. Listen I killed two guys . . . maybe more, but that's nothing to go boasting about. That's easy. I got news for you. That's easier than leaving them alive."

"I like your attitude," said the master. "You're not the brute you look."

"What's your racket?" asked Krumnagel suddenly. "A guy like you could make a fortune in the cathouse district of any medium-sized city. Why do you have to give yourself ulcers as captain of a hell-ship?"

The master smiled reflectively.

"Here, I'm the master. In the city? Compromise, compromise, percentages, bribery, dirt, dirt. All the figures you got to keep in your head. How much who gets. Who needs it? And then Italians. Sicilians. Everywhere you look. Preferential treatment. It's immoral. It's closed shop for uncles, aunts, cousins, brothers. At sea it's different." He grinned a triumphant, haughty grin. "Just let a filthy Sicilian show his face here. Here it's a Greek monopoly. Here I'm free to have uncles and aunts, and I would if I could trust them. Unfortunately, they're Greek too."

"The mayor of our city, he's Greek."

"Yeah?" the master asked. "Good boy, good boy. Hey, what'd you do? For a living, I mean. With your physique, I'm surprised they didn't want you for the police."

Krumnagel felt himself swell with authority, but then once

again his newfound power of duplicity took over. He invested his features with what he felt was a shifty look.

"I wouldn't be caught dead with the pigs," he said expansively.

"That's what I like to hear." The master's eyes narrowed in a kind of heavy-handed character assessment. "You know," he said, with the inflections of a fine judge of human character, "you and I could go a long way together."

"As what?"

"I transport drugs. You get them through the customs and distribute them."

"Fifty fifty?"

The master laughed heartily.

"What's on your mind?" Krumnagel asked.

"After all, it's my business," said the master. "I'm letting you in."

"Letting me in at what figure?"

"What does an actor pay his agent? I'm letting you in at ten percent."

"Ten percent for ninety percent of the risk? Go fock yourself."

The third day at sea was uneventful except for the fact that a deaf and dumb seaman from Trinidad, name of Ichabod Baynes, stabbed the first mate who was from Brunei, and the master upped his offer to fifteen percent.

"No dice."

On the fourth day they ran out of chains, and in any case the part of the wall on which the manacles were attached succumbed to dry rot, and the offenders had to be set free.

"Why don't you get yourself an English-speaking crew you can control?" Krumnagel asked, as he took a pause in sawing Ichabod Baynes out of his shackles.

"You think I'm a fool? The only crew I need in this business is one that can't communicate, see. The best of all's the deaf and dumb ones, but nature hasn't been all that generous. I know what I'm doing, believe me, and my employers don't mind what I do so long as I deliver what I'm supposed to."

"What are you supposed to deliver?"

"It varies. Mixed cargoes mainly. What others won't take. Overage horses from Galveston to the Spanish bullrings. Explosives. The leftovers."

"Jailbirds, rats, acid," Krumnagel added as he fretted away.

The master roared with delight. "You were the one to say it."

By the end of two weeks, Krumnagel looked as though he had spent most of his life at sea. His skin was golden, and his eyes had become lighter as a consequence, while his continual activity among backward people in the open air gave him an expression of vivacity which was animal rather than intellectual. He was in undisputed control of the ship, but by virtue of his mental makeup, he was not in control on his own behalf, but on behalf of the reprehensible master, who sat on the bridge getting slowly high on a mixture of sweet vermouth, ouzo, and retsina, and singing melancholy songs the Greeks had pinched from the Turks without acknowledgement, to the hesitant accompaniment of a cracked mandolin.

One day, about noon, a sulphuric haze wrapped in a cocoon of visible pollution heralded the proximity of civilization, and very soon the silver silos and water towers began to catch the light and respond with an evil glitter, and a little later, oilfields became visible, insatiable and scrawny hens pecking endlessly at the ground. Krumnagel filled his lungs with the foul air and beamed with gratitude. But for seven hundred miles in a Greyhound bus, he was home. At the same time, his duty became clear.

The surface Krumnagel had adapted himself to so many curious outside circumstances that the real Krumnagel sometimes wondered whether all this necessary playacting weren't eroding the essential man. For the sake of harmony he had kept house with an old queen and had played the game of the underworld with a latter-day parody of Ulysses; he had cast a narrowed eye over baked red horizons for the pleasure and instruction of a superannuated English bank robber, and he had made a carload of young policemen wonder what they should do with the drunken sailor; he had walked the freeways of the North in the pointed shoes of the Chicago hoodlum, and he had entered literary history with a series of autobiographical articles which he had neither read nor written, but for which he had received money, and if that's not glory, what is?

And yet the real Krumnagel had remained unchanged, or so he imagined as he opened his wallet and saw his police chief's identity tab nestling there in its cellophane home, warm and vibrant and real. He had an authority to brandish and an ability to threaten arrest anywhere outside the radius of people who knew that that creep Carbide — he killed the thought stone dead before it could run its course and decided that the document in his hand was the reality, the rest just a bad dream which could be flushed away like garbage once the facts were known. The facts. In his imagination he saw himself sitting on the back of a white convertible, a huge grin around his face, ticker tape falling like confetti around him, Edie in tears in a window, Carbide driven out of town. He made his decision.

As the *Agnes Stavromichalis* limped into Galveston harbor, Krumnagel climbed the ladder to the bridge, from where the bleary master was giving instructions to the engine room, and fixed him with a half nelson.

"What the hell you doing?" cried the Greek raucously. "This is no time for games."

Neither of the two seamen who were up there moved to their master's rescue, since they had both experienced Krumnagel's playfulness, both in and out of chains.

"I want seven hundred and fifty bucks back."

"Are you joking or something?"

"I'm not joking either," said Krumnagel, tightening his grip.

[269]

"You call that honorable? We had an agreement."

"I figure I more than worked my passage, Cap'n. And then, if I'm going to carry that grip through Customs —"

"Will you let me go, son of a bitch? The pilot's coming aboard presently."

"We'll ask him to arbitrate shall we? That's a good idea."

"O.K., O.K., it's a deal! cried the captain, who noticed his ship beginning to turn to port under the influence of the tide.

"And while you're about it, make it a thousand dollars, will you?"

"You son of a —"

"Bitch," said Krumnagel quietly. "Go get the money. Now. Else I'll break you in half."

"Let me give my orders first."

"No," Krumnagel wrenched a bit harder.

"Hard to starboard!" yelled the Captain. Nothing happened. He repeated his order in Mandarin.

"O.K. I know when I'm beat. Let's go," he said, his hair falling over his forehead in moist spirals.

Krumnagel followed him in the cabin.

Silently the Greek found the thousand dollars, and gave it to Krumnagel.

"There is no place for you in the rackets," he said quietly but venomously, "because you're dishonest. Our business is based on trust. I don't trust you."

"That is mutual, to say the least," Krumnagel said.

"We made a deal. You cheated. You are a cheat, mister. A cheat."

In spite of himself, Krumnagel blushed a deep crimson. It was the simplicity of the master's language which hurt, its lack of ornament, of adjective.

"That's a lie," he said, without conviction. Then he added, "O.K., if that's the way you feel about it, I'll give you two fifty back."

"I wouldn't accept it."

"Why not?" shouted Krumnagel, as usual taking refuge in power.

"You've got to make up your mind in life whether to be honest or dishonest," said the master, aglow with corrupt intelligence. "And once you've chosen, you've got to play the game to the whistle. Sure you can get a little shady when the referee isn't looking — that's in the luck of any game — but one thing you can't do is to keep changing sides. Nobody's going to stand it."

"Right. So I was wrong. Take two fifty."

"No. Out of my way."

"So where's the grip with the acid?"

"You think I'd trust you with half a million dollars worth of heroin now? You must be — not crazy — stupid."

"So you made your point!" cried Krumnagel, "So I've made my choice."

"Out of my way, or we'll lose the ship."

"No!"

The master hit Krumnagel a clean blow in the diaphragm, and followed it with a numb uppercut when the big man was doubled up and windless. Krumnagel fell to the floor, breaking a chair on his way. He sat there feeling into his mouth with a gigantic forefinger for the breakages. The master returned to the bridge, welcomed the pilot abroad, and brought the *Agnes Stavromichalis* to the quayside in an expert manner.

As Krumnagel prepared to disembark, he felt a kind of surly resentment against the master for having spoiled his homecoming, but this was only by way of a bandage to cover a much deeper hurt. He feared and resented the power of a man so sure of himself that he had no need to show his strength. Christ, if things hadn't come to a head, Krumnagel would never even have known of the accuracy and efficacity of the man's punch. It was wonderful enough to have the ability to hurt a stronger opponent with such cunning, but how much more wonderful to be able to hide this ability, to keep a secret which must set muscle and fist twitching during even the mildest argument.

Seeking an outlet for his humiliation, Krumnagel began to sense a growing resentment at having been used as a convenience by this lazy roughneck.

He saw himself slaving away, a captive gorilla at the disposal of the master for the rough stuff, so that the latter needn't soil his hands. But who had held the Chinese cook inanimate during his epileptic fits on previous voyages? Who had forced wild men into obedience and captivity? It had to have been the master himself. Were they so meek not at all in deference to the harsh bulk which Krumnagel brought to all conflict, but in fear of the subtler savagery which lurked on the bridge? Was he merely the master's hack, his replacement for drudgery and danger — and all for no pay, but for an unjust outlay of seven hundred and fifty bucks? The blood quickened with self-righteousness as the embarrassment was smothered by the usual mechanisms which people employ in order to transmogrify humiliation into honorable anger. There was only one thought which the master had expressed with which the rehabilitated Krumnagel found himself in absolute agreement, and that was that a guy had to chose which team he was playing for, and stick to it. There was such a thing as loyalty, for Christ's sake, as that goddam Greek would soon learn to his cost. He counted the thousand dollars with relish. The Greek might have his pride, but at what a price? Exactly two hundred and fifty bucks. And yet, could real pride be said to have a price? No, reflected Krumnagel, as he replaced the thousand dollars in his pocket.

The U.S. Customs officers hardly knew what to make of the big man who came down the gangplank dressed in a soiled suit of forty years ago. The Orientals and Levantines could wear such garments with impunity. Style travels slowly, and the dernier cri of Karachi, Port Moresby and Sidon may well be feeling the first impact of Chicago in the thirties; but what was so surprising about Krumnagel was his wholesome freckled face bursting out of the wasp-waisted daintiness and his black and white shoes emerging from the generous pants like the noses of Dalmatians under a tent flap.

"Are you a citizen?" asked the customs officer.

"Sure am, Mac. Hey, who's top man around here?"

"Top man? What d'you want him for?"

"That's between him and me."

"Suppose you tell me what you've acquired abroad meanwhile?"

Krumnagel looked at the customs officer, and reached for his wallet. He produced his identity card.

The customs officer whistled, as he was supposed to.

"What's a nice guy like you doing traveling on a ship like that?"

Krumnagel grinned.

"Nice guy, huh? That's classified information. Suppose I see your chief."

"Take me to your leader? Sure thing."

The customs chief was a slow moving skeptic who believed that in his life every man, woman, and child has more to declare than they are willing to admit. His name happened to be Roald F. Benediktsson.

"What can I do for you, Chief Krumnagel?" he asked. "Apart from examining baggage?"

"I haven't got no baggage," Krumnagel replied.

"No? That's kind of suspicious, isn't it?"

"Let's say I'm traveling light," Krumnagel said, with enough mystery to put Mr. Benediktsson on the defensive.

"O.K., so what else can I do for you?"

"Listen, I'm doing special work for the . . . the F.B.I. . . ."

"You didn't have to mention it. I guessed," Benediktsson said economically.

"Right. That's why I traveled on board —"

"I guessed," Mr. Benediktsson interrupted. "Let's get down to the nitty gritty. What can I do for you?"

"I don't want no questions asked."

"Am I asking you any?"

"Afterwards. Just let me go. I got my own report to make out."

"Shoot."

"There's half a million dollars worth of heroin on board that ship."

"I can take a hint. Ryan, take the chief through Immigration, and see he gets through real quick."

"Thanks."

"Line of duty."

Krumnagel bought himself a new suit and some clothes and was able to read about the arrest of Captain Makarezos the next day as the Greyhound bus thundered over freeways towards Atlanta, and from there towards the City.

He arrived in the City during the morning of the next day, and it was with gathering excitement that he saw his familiar grazing ground unfold through the window. The weather was neither good nor bad, since the true color of the sky was successfully obscured by the fruits of man's labor. All one could be sure of was that it wasn't raining. As the bus swung into its terminal, Krumnagel felt a great flow of achievement, a triumphal surge of emotion at his homecoming. It was only after he had alighted from the bus that it occurred to him that this joy was all very well while the City was still a dot on the map or a name on a signpost, but that now he was physically at his destination, he had nowhere to go. To stay the night at a hotel in his own hometown was unthinkable, and yet it might well be inevitable. There was no Edie available. There was no TV. There was not even a can of beer on ice.

After a moment of burning outrage, he pulled himself together. He had no desire, and he felt no need, to cut a pathetic

[274]

figure. He was here to fight, and, to borrow a habitual phrase from that miserable slut, Edie, when he fought, he did it to win. Solvency, he calculated, was that which would help him to hold his head high at this time. Naturally his first initiative was to take a taxi to his bank, the Pioneer and Merchants Bank, in order to see how he stood. He hailed a taxi. The driver indicated he was off duty, and drove on. God damn it, things had changed under Al Carbide, he reflected. A second cab just seemed to ignore him, so he stepped in front of it. The cab swerved, and the driver shouted an obscenity, which Krumnagel answered with interest. The driver heard it, and braked. Krumnagel braced himself and hitched up his trousers. The driver got out of his cab, snarling with fury. The two men approached each other like protagonists in a conventional Western. Suddenly the driver stopped dead, his mouth open. Krumnagel stopped also.

"Chief Krumnagel," muttered the driver.

"So?" replied Krumnagel dangerously.

"So? You ought to know better'n stop a cab with a party in it."

"A party?" Krumnagel glanced at the cab, and saw a lady with purple hair glaring at him through malevolent glasses studded with rhinestones.

"I beg your pardon, lady," he said, inflectionless.

The driver shook his head negatively, his disgust overflowing.

"Shit," he said without malice and spat into the road.

Krumnagel returned slowly to the pavement, sending surly looks at the few people who had collected there.

"What's the matter with you people?" he asked rhetorically, and they dispersed, reflecting on what was the matter with them.

Eventually he found a cab with a young black driver.

"Where you want to go, mister?"

[275]

"Pioneer and Merchants Bank."

"Where's that?"

"Midway at Pontecorvo."

"Midway at Ponnicorvo — I didn't know there was a bank there."

"Well, there is."

It was clear that the young man didn't know Krumnagel from Adam.

"You new in town?" he asked.

"I want to go to a bank you've never even heard of — why should that make you think I'm new in town?" Krumnagel grumbled.

"I d'know, just had that feelin' about you. I get these feelin's sometimes. They're that strong. Man, are they strong! Like I oftimes know when a fellow's gonna die. I can say to him like, man, no matter what you do, you can run this way or that, or hide your head someplace, it don't make no difference, you gonna *die*."

"I don't want to hear about it," Krumnagel said. He'd had enough with his first cellmate at Lyburn working himself up into a lather while setting a spell, to have a shuddering respect for elemental forces, even expressed in the conversational intimacy of a taxicab.

His squeamishness made the driver laugh, a great African recurring musical laugh, a laugh of huge generosity which got on Krumnagel's nerves.

"What's so outstandingly funny?" he asked.

"You ain't gonna die, not for a while." Suddenly the driver grew grave, and fixed Krumnagel with a smouldering clairvoyant eye in the mirror.

"But, man, you're the cause of a lot of activity. Man!"

"I told you I don't want to know."

"And you're not new in town?"

"I been away."

"Figures," said the driver soberly as he drew up at the bank.

As he paid, Krumnagel tried to avoid the driver's eye, but he didn't succeed. As they looked at one another, Krumnagel felt he was giving away thoughts he had not yet had.

"Remember what I said."

As he entered the bank, he saw the manager, Latham Hodnick, talking to a client at his desk. He waited, smiling, to be recognized. When a girl asked him if she could help him, he asked her to tell Mr. Hodnick that Mr. Krumnagel was here. She did so. Hodnick looked up, surprised. Then he got rid of his client and beckoned Krumnagel towards him.

He wore an expression of concern, hovering somewhere between commiseration and congratulation.

"Long time no see," he said safely.

"I just spent the best part of a month on a boat full of Chinks, L.H.," Krumnagel replied as though making light of hell. "So I can do without pidgin English."

"Yes? Where you been, Bart? That is, I know where you've been. Tell us all about it. At least, tell me anything you feel you want to tell me." Can't be more tactful than that.

"That's all old history," Krumnagel said grandly.

"Did they let you out? Finally let you out?"

"No. I just left."

"Left?"

"Took it into my head to go. Felt kind of homesick."

Krumnagel smiled at Hodnick's perplexity.

"Let's talk of something else," he said. "How do I stand?"

"How do you stand?" Hodnick asked.

"Financially."

"Financially?"

"Am I not speaking distinctly or something?"

"But Bart. When Edie and you . . . split up . . . she took her account elsewhere."

Krumnagel reacted.

[277]

"She did what?"

"The two of you had a joint account, as you know. Well, when she divorced you, she took her account over to American and Natural Gas."

Krumnagel glowered.

"That's what happens when you trust a woman," he said slowly.

"Well, it's possibly also what happens when you trust a man. I believe she has a joint account with her husb — with Chief — with Mr. Carbide now."

"A joint account with Mr. Carbide. Is that right?"

"So I believe."

"You know that was my money, L.H.?"

"It's not my place to know what money belongs to who in a joint account," Mr. Hodnick pleaded, waiting for the inevitable storm to break.

"That was the money I earned. Money I saved. She never brought no money when we got married. She never earned a nickel in the whole of her goddam life."

"No, I didn't know that," replied Mr. Hodnick, as though he was hearing a most interesting fact for the first time.

"And now she's taken my earnings — my life's earnings — and given it to that skunk Carbide by way of a dowry."

"I never cared much for Mr. Carbide myself," said Mr. Hodnick, literally beginning to quake.

"You know, there's other money too. Money I earned while I was away."

"Yes, I remember being surprised. D'you want me to look up the amount?"

"I know the amount. I want it back. I want it all back!" he suddenly shouted, creating a commotion.

"Now, Bart, we've known one another for a long time —" Mr. Hodnick reasoned.

"What the hell has that to do with it?" Krumnagel asked, calm again, dangerously calm.

"Do you want to use my phone to call Edie?" Mr. Hodnick suggested.

Krumnagel smiled humorlessly. "You're going to use your phone to call her," he said.

"What? What am I going to tell her?" Mr. Hodnick asked, petrified.

"Tell her . . . tell her . . ." Krumnagel consulted a piece of paper in his wallet, and made a quick calculation. "Tell her she owes me eighty-six thousand dollars and forty cents, from which I'm willing to subtract housekeeping money from the day of my arrest to the day she filed for divorce, but to which I'm going to add two thousand five hundred pounds at the rate of two dollars and forty cents to the pound, details to be worked out later. Tell her that."

"I can't remember all that," begged Mr. Hodnick.

"Tell her to give me fifty thousand dollars to go on with. The rest I'll bill her for."

Nervously, Mr. Hodnick looked up the number, and dialed. His eyes twitched once or twice, and his fingers drummed a noiseless tattoo on his knee.

"Hello, Mrs. Carbide? She's not at home?" he asked hopefully. "Oh." His voice dropped. "Is that you, Edie? I didn't recognize your voice. This is Lath Hodnick. Remember? Long time no — yes. To what do you owe the pleasure —? Listen, is Chief Carbide, your husband, that is, there? No! No, I want to speak to you, not to him. What's eating me? That's a good question. Lookit . . ." Mr. Hodnick tried to seek inspiration from Krumnagel's glowering face, but he found it a source of terror rather than encouragement.

"Edie," he said, "Bart's back." There was an evident pause on the line. "Oh, he's all right. Very tanned. Looks like a million dollars — which brings me to the subject of my call. You remember when you transferred away from here to American Natural Gas, I said to you what happens when Bart comes home? Well, I don't think we need to go into what either of us

[279]

said, Edie. The fact is, he's here, and he's in his rights. You'll sue? Who are you going to sue, Edie? Loyalty towards whom? I don't follow you, dear."

Krumnagel seized the receiver.

"Edie?" he cried, "It's me, Big Bart. I'm out, and you owe me some money. Now I want that money, and there's going to be no argument about it, otherwise someone's going to get hurt, and that someone's not going to be me. You understand? Now I'll let you off light. For the first installment, I want fifty thousand bucks. Fifty thousand —" he enunciated. "That's right, not five thousand. I want you to bring it this evening at six o'clock. It's not dark by six? Seven o'clock. The children's playground, Millard Fillmore High. By the Abelard Bridge. Where we used to go courting. You be there, with the dough. Or else. As Lath Hodnick is my witness. Roger."

He banged the receiver back on its stand.

"Bart," said Mr. Hodnick timidly, "don't do anything rash. Ever."

"Why should I do anything rash, Lath?" Krumnagel asked truculently. "I got right on my side, don't I?"

16

The place where Bart and Edie had gone courting was perhaps not the ideal site for romance, but it had its practical advantages. First of all, there are fewer things emptier than schools at night, especially school playgrounds. This one stood fairly high above the Platonic River, a filthy foam-laden waterway which swirled a grudging path under a series of vast toll bridges the size of which more than flattered the poisonous clay-colored stream so far beneath them. The panorama of depressed area, ghetto, and massive civic architecture was set off by the great harvest of refuse which broke the monotony of the steep grass banks leading to the water's edge like so many flowers, and on those rare occasions when the sun managed to burst through the opaque mist of industry, the beer cans and silver cigarette paper sparkled in the field like false jewelry in a counterfeit crown. Quite apart from the sheer poetry of the place, the road came to a dead end against the netting of the playground, which enabled the more sedentary, or in some cases recumbent amorosi, to copulate or at least neck, in the relative comfort of parked sedans.

At seven o'clock that evening, Krumnagel stood waiting there as he had of old, except that he held no flowers behind his back, nor was he lost for words. At ten past seven, he began to fume and rattle the metal grille of the playground, while at a quarter past, he became more philosophical, imagining all the thousands of reasons which could have kept her. He tried to decipher some of the graffiti on the concrete wall, but it was too far away for him to make sense of them. At almost twenty past seven, he was blinded by the headlamps of a car which seemed to be cruising cautiously. He suddenly felt exposed. His police training always gave him the suspicion that he was falling into a trap. He moved forward warily. The car stopped. He approached it. The electric window slid down. He bent down and looked in.

"Hi," said Edie.

"Hi," said Krumnagel. "Get out of the car."

"Isn't it better if you get in?"

It was annoying, but he had to admit that it was. He tried to open the door.

"I'll unlock it," said Edie, after he had struggled for a moment.

Bitch. He opened the door quite easily, and sat down.

"New car?" he queried.

"It's his. It's . . . Al's."

"Cadillac Eldorado. The police force seems more profitable these days." He sniffed. "What kind of perfume does Al use? And don't he need his car?"

"All right, so it's mine. I had a windfall."

"Windfall? My royalties!" Krumnagel blazed.

[282]

"It was not your royalties either. My aunt died."

"In the old days you never had no aunt."

"So maybe it was your royalties, I don't know." It was her turn to erupt. "What in the hell are you doing with royalties anyway? You never had royalties in your whole life before!"

"So I wrote the story of my life," he cried. "I got paid. And then you couldn't even have the trust or love or you name it of a toy dog, could you? No, you thought I was in there for life, didn't you? You psyched yourself into feeling that I wasn't never going to come out, didn't you? So you had to fall for the smooth talk of that third rate schmuck Al Carbide."

"Don't mention his name to me," Edie hissed.

Krumnagel was frankly taken aback, but all his defenses were out nevertheless. Now what?

"Oh, Bart, I'm so miserable," she managed to say, and then began to cry.

"I never asked who you was screwing in the past. I knew we didn't pull it off too good. Maybe I was, too — I don't know. I'd have forgiven you anything. Anything, Edie, I felt that sincere about you. I'd forgive you anything, your goddam biting and scratching and tickling and shenanigans and the way you'd give people you'd never seen before the come an' get it and the rest, God knows, the screwing — it must have gone on — but why Al Carbide? Why Al Carbide for the love of God?"

"I don't know why Al Carbide," she screamed hysterically. "He beats me. He's a sadist. And he's never home nights. Talk about screwing! Boy, he ought to get himself into the business weeklies, he's got an average like Dow Jones, I'm telling you. Jeez, what Evelyn must have been through! And then when I ask where he's been — wham! A left to the jaw or a right to the eye or I get a razor strap around the ass, and then, as if he was not bad enough the way nature made him, he's got his bathroom cabinet chock-full of Japanese erection lozenges and love elixirs made by a colony of Hindus in upper New York State. Do you want some? He'll never know they're gone."

[283]

Krumnagel was just about to refuse more or less politely when it occurred to him that the purpose of their encounter had been cunningly forgotten. He knew Edie too well to let her get away with it.

"Where is it?" he asked, quietly.

She ate him up with her sparkling eyes. The tears nestled among her eyelashes like raindrops among the leaves after an April shower.

"You've never stopped being my man. You know that, don't you?"

"It's a distinction I share with Chet Koslowsky and several handfuls of others," he said.

"You know damn well you're different," she insisted gallantly.

"Sure. I know we're all different. That's our charm. The more the merrier."

"You're a bastard," she said, casually.

"So where's my money?"

"I don't have it."

Krumnagel looked at her with icy consideration.

"You think Al hits you hard?" he asked.

"You wouldn't dare. I know you."

"I thought I knew you too, Edie. The me you know is the one who thought he knew you. I don't think either of us knows the other no more. I want my money, Edie. I don't want you, believe me. I think Al Carbide is a very lucky guy, but I think I'm just that bit luckier. Now, let's have it. Then I'll leave you in peace until I work out what you *really* owe me."

"I don't have any money."

Krumnagel stared at her, transferring his look from one eye to the other in search of a nonviolent solution. He hated wrangling with females except in self-defense, and his confrontation with Captain Makarezos had made him twice shy in any case. Edie looked back at him, also searching first one eye and then the other, and then she smiled disarmingly.

[284]

"I guess you're right," he murmured grudgingly. "I don't feel like hitting you."

"Yeah, like I told Al," she said gratefully. "If a guy can't get what he wants without violence, you know what I mean, he don't deserve it."

"So — where does that leave us?" Krumnagel asked.

"Kiss me."

"I'd rather pass."

"You want your money, don't you?"

"I'll take a raincheck."

"For old times' sake?"

There was a pause. Under her breath, and in the manner of the smokiest of blues singers, Edie began, a little flat, to sing "Should old acquaintance be forgot . . . de dum . . . de dum . . . de dum . . ."

Largely in order to put an end to the music, he kissed her ear.

"Now see what kindness does for a guy, kind sir?" she said perkily, and produced a check from her handbag. He took it, and his mouth dropped open.

"What in the hell is this?" he roared. "Two thousand bucks?"

"I can't give it to you all at once, Bart, honest," she pleaded. "That creep goes through the bankbook every week, I'm not exaggerating, and my life won't be worth living if he ever finds out."

"But that's *my money,* Edie!"

"I know it is, Bart. You know it is. You try telling him it is."

"I'll go right up there and tell him!"

"Please. Please Bart. I'm begging you. Give me time. If I can make it look like extravagance, I may risk a beating or two, but I'll settle our accounts. Give me time."

"You mean we got to meet here every evening for the next year, and you give me a couple of bucks a day — just to keep me going? I need capital, Edie. Capital. I may feel like investing. I may go into business on my own!"

[285]

"Two thousand dollars is not a couple of bucks," she replied hotly. She looked at her watch. "Jeez, I got to go now. But I tell you what. Meet me here at seven tomorrow, I'll maybe bring a bit more, see. Five thou. Even ten. Let me be the judge of how much."

"This is not going to last, this method of yours, on account of I'm going to get mad, Edie. Real mad."

"I love you when you're mad," she said negligently, starting the engine. "Now let me go. Otherwise he'll ask questions."

"In a day or two, it's going to be me starts answering them, Edie," he said, as he opened the door.

"I love you, Big Bart," she said, and backed into a lamppost. She nearly ran over Krumnagel as she tried to turn her huge white car, but in avoiding him she knocked over a pile of garbage cans which a local strike had allowed to accumulate there.

"Women," Krumnagel reflected as he watched the car gather speed and disappear on the wrong side of the road.

He spent the night in the Valley Forge Transient's Hotel, a nondescript building which seemed to be composed entirely of fire escapes, and the next evening at seven o'clock, he was once again at his romantic rendezvous. Since the strike was not yet over, the garbage cans lay precisely where Edie had left them. It was also raining slightly, a light, misty moisture drifting about like a veil and drenching clothes without seeming to.

Krumnagel had had ample opportunity to think. He had paid in the check to his bank, together with the traveler's checks, but had kept what was left of the money he had extorted from Makarezos in cash. He determined to be tougher with Edie on this occasion. It was his gentlemanliness which was at the root of every disaster, he decided. In a world of crooks, you have to be more crooked, more clairvoyant, and above all, faster to succeed. One of these days, he would change sides for good, and then society had better look out. Captain Makarezos had taught him a lot, come to think of it. That was that. The world was divided into two sides, the good guys, and the bad guys, but it was like with football, some temperaments just don't suit some playing styles — it was as unnatural as a Protestant playing for Crown of Thorns U. — and then you just got to get yourself a transfer. He figured he'd been a good guy all his life, even when society had gotten its information screwed up and tried to force him into a black track suit, but by God, if there was no place for his loyalties among his own kind, then he'd go where he was appreciated.

The appearance of the Cadillac interrupted these reflections. Krumnagel glanced at his watch. It was seven o'clock on the nose. That's funny. It was unlike Edie to be on time. He did not move forward, but stared suspiciously into the haze. The lights of another car appeared. Krumnagel could see it was a police car even though its red bubble was switched off. Trouble.

The Cadillac drove right up to him, blinding him and all but crushing him against the wire mesh. He walked up to the door. Al Carbide was at the wheel. Edie sat beside him, hiding her face.

"What's the idea?" Krumnagel asked.

"I'm taking you in, Bart," Al said.

"Taking me in? What for?"

"I'm not taking you in myself. There's a squad car in back. I'm on my way to dinner."

"Suppose you get out of the car?" Krumnagel suggested.

Before Al had time to reply, a voice called out from the darkness.

"Welcome home, Chief!"

"Who's that?"

"Marv Armstrong."

"Hi, Marv!"

Al Carbide leaped out of his car.

"I didn't tell you to come here personally," he snapped at Armstrong. "I just said for a car to follow Mrs. Carbide's."

"I thought I'd come myself, Chief," said Armstrong easily. "You didn't say not to."

[287]

"O.K." Al Carbide seemed in a very bad humor. "Take him in."

"Don't you think you owe me an explanation?" Krumnagel said. "This isn't the way I taught you to make an arrest, is it?"

"You owe me an explanation, Bart. You're a convict, and under state law you're compelled to register with the police department on arrival. You failed to do that."

"That don't apply to overseas convictions, Al, and you know it. I didn't think you were so stupid."

"No, but England may want to extradite you, and in that case we got to know where you are in order to ship you back if they should demand that you serve out your time over there."

Krumnagel suddenly felt sick to the stomach at such an idea.

"Another thing, Bart, I don't want you around town threatening my wife."

"I never threatened Edie."

"You said you'd hit her if she didn't give you money."

"Did I hit her? Did I hit you Edie?"

Edie came to life, pointing at her thigh, and gathering her skirt in her hand.

"Look what that bastard did to me —"

"Shut up!" commanded Al, in case it was to him she was referring.

"That's my money!" cried Krumnagel.

"That's not the decision of the divorce court. You'll have to fight a court order if you want a penny of Edie's money."

"Why, you lowdown shithead, you know that that money's my life savings —"

"Are you threatening me?"

"Come on, Bart, let's go," said Armstrong, with quiet authority. "You're not going to do yourself any good trying to settle this in the street. I'm only here as a witness, you understand that, don't you? And I don't want to have to see or hear anything that may prejudice anyone's character. We've had enough of that already. Right? So come on with me, feller, and we can arrange for you to see a lawyer, and just go through the motions back at headquarters, know what I mean?"

Once he was safely held in Armstrong's friendly grip, Krumnagel made a half-hearted effort to lunge at Carbide, while Lady Macbeth watched the proceedings with wide eyes from the depths of the Cadillac.

"Come on, Bart, this way."

"I believe you managed to extort two thousand dollars from Mrs. Carbide by threats and violence," Al said coolly. Krumnagel made every effort to attack him, but Armstrong held him manfully.

"Well, you just try cashing that check," Al went on. "And if you don't leave Mrs. Carbide alone, I'll have you up on every charge from vagrancy to extortion and back again. You saw him trying to attack me," he said to Armstrong.

"You want me to let him go, don't you?" Armstrong replied, rather surprisingly. "So you can slap an assault charge on him right now."

Carbide felt he had been stabbed in the back, while Krumnagel understood in a flash that this observation had been aimed at him. He stopped struggling at once. Armstrong let him go.

"O.K., Marv, let's go," said Krumnagel, looking down on the ground.

"Have a good dinner. Goodnight, Edie," Armstrong called out.

As their figures were lost in the darkness, Al nearly exploded with glacial fury. The veins at his temple stood out so clearly they cast a shadow as the bleak light of the streetlamp fell on him.

"Come on in. You're going to get wet, Al," called Edie from inside the car.

Al took a few steps away from the car.

"You want me to drive, honey?"

Al returned to the car, sat down, looked at his wife, and beat her over the head. He was in control of himself once more.

"What I do?" wailed Edie.

"You didn't do more'n usual, but why that schmo Armstrong had to come here himself when I asked for a patrolman — he did it deliberate, of course. Ambitious schlemiel."

Edie smiled diabolically.

"You police chiefs always have trouble with your wives and your assistants. When I think back on the trouble poor Bart had with you — and with me. Jeez, I reckon he deserves a break. Wives and assistants . . . they're so hard to get rid of . . ."

Al did an illegal U-turn amid a symphony of angry hooting.

"Where we going?" Edie asked alarmed.

"Home. I'm not hungry."

"I am," Edie said.

They drove home.

Armstrong had told Krumnagel all the latest news in the police car. Local elections were coming up soon, and Mayor Calogero was running again although arraigned on extortion charges, and the more his name was associated with shady elements in the City, the stronger his political position became. Various fearless columnists, or rather columnists who wrote as though they were fearless, attacked the rackets, but always without mentioning names, and every time they wrote, they exuded such an aura of democracy at work that all moral scruples were satisfied. People had become more sophisticated, and yet as gullible as ever; no longer did they necessarily melt to a politician in fancy dress, strumming folk instruments or spending ten minutes down a shallow mine shaft, or kissing babies who desperately wished to avoid the experience; but it sufficed for a corrupt poll to announce that the mayor was in an unassailable lead for many people to believe it, even if some individualists reacted against. Since there were five or six such polls, which came to conclusions not outrageously at variance with each other, it was very difficult to tell which was in the pay of the rackets and which wasn't. Guesswork has never been an actionable offense, and yet Armstrong felt that the pompously named Institute of Plebeian Comment, Incorporated, which consistently showed the tide of opinion swinging in favor of Mayor Calogero, was wholly supported by the underworld. Milt Rotterdam was a director.

"Did Al do anything to break the rackets?" Krumnagel asked.

"Off the record, I'd say he's done everything to help them," Armstrong replied.

"But who brought the extortion charges?"

"There was no avoiding them — things were getting that out of hand and scandalous. I'd go as far as to say the rackets encouraged the charges on condition they could be sure they could win in court."

"Are you kidding?"

"No. Everyone knows the rackets exist. What people don't know is that they can come out of court smelling sweet."

"Who's the judge then?"

"Judge Weyerback."

"I dig it. It's enough to make you throw up," Krumnagel said.

"Sure. And yet you know, Bart, I never thought much about it till I got made deputy police chief."

"That's the trouble, Marv. People don't." And he thought guiltily of his steak lunch with Al. Then his fury returned. Lousy hypocrite, Mr. Two-Face Carbide, with all his crusading talk about cleaning up the City. What had he done once he had the opportunity except carve himself a man-size portion of the dirt?

"What in hell you people going to do to me?" Krumnagel asked.

"Oh, it's only a formality," Armstrong sighed. "You can imagine it's not my idea. Al got to hear you were back a couple of days ago —"

Krumnagel started.

"A couple of days ago? How'd he do that? I wasn't even back yet."

Armstrong shrugged.

"Don't know. He came out of a meeting with the mayor around lunchtime, and took me aside to say Krumnagel's back, and that's all he said."

"That's all? There was no dialogue?"

"No. Seemed kind of worried though. You can always tell by them veins."

"Yeah, them goddam veins."

Armstrong hesitated a moment. Then he remembered that Carbide had put through a long distance call to Washington right after he'd got back to the office.

"He'd gotten the idea of telling the British, see. Through the State Department or the F.B.I. or someplace," Krumnagel said. "Think anything'll come of it?" he dared to ask.

"Pick yourself a good lawyer, and even if the British are just doing all they can to lay their hands on you, why, the case can go on for years."

"Yeah," Krumnagel admitted, "you got to hand it to American justice, the finest in the world, no case is ever so closed it can't be reopened."

"So long as there's money in it, there's no reason why litigation shouldn't last forever."

"That's right."

"Any idea which attorney you'll go to?" Marv asked.

"No."

Suddenly Krumnagel brightened.

"Mervyn Spindelman."

"He takes one hundred and ten percent of your income over the next fifty years."

[292]

Krumnagel hesitated.

"That's for sure," he meditated. "Still, I remember him saying that there was cases he didn't take for the money, but for the reputation."

"Defending a retired police chief in litigation about alimony and extradiction?" Marv asked skeptically. "That is going to improve Spindelman's reputation? For it to do Spindelman much good, you got to do something really bad, kill someone or something."

"What, again? Listen, I had enough for one lifetime."

"Then don't go to Spindelman."

Just then the police car swung under a huge concrete bowl which had not been there before.

"What the — hey, is that the —"

"Yeah, the MacDonald Schnitzler Ball Park."

"They finally built it?"

"Sure, in four months and six days. *Fortune* magazine says it's a national record, using new methods of prestructured plastic fragments bombarded by electric impulses, or some crap of that sort — any which way you look at it, it cost sixteen million dollars more than it was supposed to, even though they finished it more'n a month ahead of schedule. You don't have to guess where the money went. It's a nonprofit-making corporation."

"Are they using it?"

"Opens come Friday with a night game — big deal. Crown of Thorns U. versus the Great Lakes Apaches. The Honorable Darwood H. McAlpin, governor of the state, is throwing the first ball."

"Who's going to be there?"

"Just everybody."

"Gee, I'd sure like to go."

Marv Armstrong looked at Krumnagel earnestly now that they were getting very close to police headquarters.

"Why don't you go someplace for a short while? Colorado Springs or someplace . . ."

Krumnagel was surprised.

"What's wrong? Isn't this a free country no more?" he asked quietly.

"Sure it is," Armstrong replied, "but I can't answer for how Al's going to play it. He could play it dirty, Bart. I don't trust the guy when he's upset. Listen, I don't like what's happening in this City, or in this country come to that . . ."

"And that's why I should go to Colorado Springs?" asked Krumnagel very quietly, now that the car had come to rest in front of police headquarters. "I thought that when people didn't like what was going on in the City, or in the country, it was up to them to put it right. I was always taught that that was what democracy's all about. I was taught the City belongs to us . . . the country too, come to that. That's what made it wonderful . . . and meaningful . . ."

"Oh, Christ," sighed Marv, "it's not all high-flown words and fine sentiments, Bart. You could have done something when you were in power. Did you? Did you?"

So it was going to be like this. Krumnagel snarled a little, guilty and aggressive at one and the same time.

"Sure I could have done something. I could have committed suicide. I could have committed Harry Carey, or whatever they call the goddam thing. Every police chief's caught between what he thought before he made it, and what he found on his desk when he did make it. And every goddam time he's caught right there between the lousy focking world as it is, and the cries from his corner — 'cause make no mistake about it, it's the chief of police what's in the ring, not his assistant. His assistant? He's sitting right there fingering the towel, hoping he's going to have to throw it in . . . I had to put up with Al Carbide . . . Every time I looked at my corner, I knew that someone out there hates me, wants me to fail, hopes I'm going to give up, see . . . Like I said, I had to put up with Al Carbide. He got his wish, the lucky bastard. And now Al Carbide has to put up with Marv Armstrong. It's not easy Marv. It's not easy."

Marv shut his eyes. He was in a kind of moral pain.

"I know it's not easy, Bart. That's why I suggested Colorado Springs. Christ, it doesn't have to be Colorado Springs."

"It don't have to be no place," said Bart briefly, opening the door. "Let's get this shit over with."

In spite of his bravado, the business of having to enter his police headquarters as anything but its director was very painful for Krumnagel. There was no fancy dress. The atmosphere was dull, functional, embarrassed.

"There's no more Rabbi Patrol?" Krumnagel asked. Marv shook his head.

"So what happens now?"

"The rabbis get their skulls cracked."

"Business as usual?"

"Too true."

"Figures."

Krumnagel declared that he was living in the Valley Forge Transient's Hotel. Room 1140. And he gave the undertaking not to leave town without informing the police. Not even to go to Colorado Springs. And he was fingerprinted. They already had his fingerprints, of course, but in the wrong section of the police department. And they photographed him. He maintained a miraculous dignity, and shook Marv's hand before leaving, managing to avoid a total breakdown. As he strode out into the unfriendly night, the tears of outrage began to blind him. God, let something happen, to take my mind off this nightmare! He looked around, and imagined he was being followed. That was enough. He walked. The other guy walked. He stopped. The other guy stopped. So Al was going to play it dirty? Great. It was something to occupy his mind.

17

It was the longest night of Krumnagel's life, longer even than the first night in prison. Here he felt strangely vulnerable, because the fire escape ran right past the window, and the device which locked the window in place was caked with white paint, and had obviously never served. The old air conditioner was covered with dust, and responded to none of its rusty dials, only managing to exude a vague smell of burned rubber from its one-time exertions. The television, an ancient portable on a tubular trestle table, gave triple vision on a couple of channels, and nothing but disturbance on the others, while when certain timbres sounded, the carcass would vibrate as though a pin had fallen into the works. Krumnagel sat and stared at it hoping that it would serve to take his mind off his predicament. Instead he failed to take in a single clouded image.

Restless, he rose and crossed to the window. The neon signs were playing havoc with his imagination, sending their red and white reflections against the lace curtains and the Venetian blinds stuck halfway open. He imagined he saw shadows on the fire escape, and anyhow, he couldn't breathe with the window shut and no air conditioning. He touched the window, and it seemed to fly up of its own accord. He looked down into the street, and saw two men standing on the opposite sidewalk, like in gangster pictures. It was not terribly late, they were outside an all-night supermarket, why shouldn't they be there? It's a free country, isn't it, as everybody never tired of saying? They had every right to be there, and a cop would have every right to ask them what they were doing there, and they would have every right to get annoyed at the cop's question, and the cop would have every right to tell them to cool it, and they'd have every right to resent being told to cool it, and the cop would have every right to tell them if they didn't cool it, he'd run them in, and they'd have every right to believe they were being threatened and to exercise a citizen's right to self-defense, and the cop'd have every right to be faster on the draw once he was confident they were aiming to draw themselves, and shoot them dead, having first unsuccessfully attempted to wound them of course. That was democracy, and it was a privilege to be back again whatever the conditions. At least a man stood a fighting chance. Oh, brother, you can say that again. And yet, what were those two guys doing there? They weren't even talking to one another. They were just standing there like tailor's dummies. One thing was for sure, they weren't police.

Krumnagel sat on the windowsill, and soon got tired of watching them. He kept imagining movements at the extremity of his vision, and turning his head to find nothing there. Nerves. No doubt about it. He returned to the interior of the room, put out the lights, and tried to rest awhile, but the flickering of the television prevented his dozing. He probably wouldn't have been able to in any case, but he didn't want to be bereft of every source of light, and what the hell, the neons were going to keep him awake anyway, and he felt defenseless with the curtains drawn.

Once he was resigned to thinking, he tried to organize his thoughts, to make of them something constructive, to really "think things out." He couldn't quite make it. The feeling of chaos was too pervasive, the inability to identify his enemies among the shambles of a carefully organized existence. Armstrong was a friend. He felt fairly sure about that. He'd always liked the guy and pushed him for promotion. Remember? There was nobody to remind but himself. But what game was Edie playing — apart from the eternal game of womankind? Did Al really think he had been rough with her, or were these just excuses? Were the two of them in cahoots or at loggerheads? And how come the mayor knew about his arrival? It made it sound as though he were a pretty important figure around these parts. Couldn't be Celebrity Service, could it? Did they run to Galveston, Texas?

Anyway, why this hostility? Wasn't this America, for the love of God, where a man's earnings are sacrosanct, and his dignity his birthright? What kind of a court was it could confiscate a guy's life savings in absentia, because he was in prison in a foreign country, no doubt on a trumped-up charge, being foreign? He had to get himself a good lawyer. And yet, wasn't this the last of the do-it-yourself countries, with a great pioneer background, staking a claim and defending that claim with your lifeblood against all comers, women and children cowering in the covered wagon? Who needs a lawyer when a plain-speaking man has the courage to hold up his head and tell it the way it is in public, man to man, man to men? The Rockefellers never made their fortunes by relegating to lawyers what they could do by themselves. The lawyers came in with the cities and the growth of fear. In a sense they were un-American, although they had now eroded their way into the main-stream of American life. This was the century of the middleman, the century of total employment, when shrewd operators made nonexistent occupations seem essential, and amassed fortunes by coming between people who had, in the past, negotiated very efficiently without intermediaries, and yet who no longer trusted their common sense faced with the growing complexities of business practice.

Krumnagel resolved to surprise them all. Come to think of it, he had recieved a scroll of honor from a grateful City (must remind Edie to return it). He was a pretty important guy who had fallen on evil times. Even in this he was not alone. There was Samuel Insull and Warren Gamaliel Harding, to name only a couple. He couldn't think of any others at the moment. He was going to go straight to the mayor and lay his case on the line. He'd always got on fairly well with Mayor Calogero, he imagined. Not as well as all that. Fairly well. They respected one another, he insisted to himself. And where there's respect . . .

He looked out of the window. Those two guys were still there. One of them transferred his weight from one foot to the other. They were real all right. What in the hell were they doing if they weren't watching him? There wasn't a tin cup or a Seeing Eye dog between the two of them. One thing, Krumnagel said to himself, whatever happens from here on in, there's got to be no more changes of mind. Changes of mind look like weaknesses. The good guys is good guys, and the bad guys is bad guys and never the twain . . . know what I mean? He came away from the window to give those introspections more of a chance of a hearing by the inner ear.

He had often tried to analyze the nature of bravery. It was a quality which had always intrigued him, perhaps because he had selected a profession which, more than most, had recourse to sheer guts when arguments came to a sudden stop. There was something thoughtless and yet self-effacing about heroism, the way he looked at it. "If heroes had the time to think, there'd be no heroism," he liked to say, and he compared heroic actions astutely with the lightning reactions of sport. "The greatest home runs was hit when the ball was coming so fast the guy didn't have time to think."

By the same token, cowardice is the logical consequence of hope. "If a man knows there's no way out, he's going to be brave, I don't care who he is — but if there's a chance of reprieve, why he's not going to commit himself to courage till he knows the outcome," he had once written to Mayor Calogero when a convicted raper and murderer who had just had his fifteenth appeal turned down after eight years in prison showed the greatest fortitude after his lawyers had run out of legal maneuvers, whereas he had spent a multitude of sleepless nights before. For some unaccountable reason Krumnagel became conscious during his endless night that he himself was being put to some kind of test. And not unnaturally he searched into the deep well of experience to find precedents, guidelines in the dark, any detail, any seemingly innocuous triviality which might be of some use to him. Once he knew what he was doing, he was no longer afraid. He was suddenly on better terms with himself than he had been for a long time — perhaps because he was alone. He had no need to show off for the alter ego's benefit. The two Krumnagels were in agreement, identical twins. He looked out of the window. The two men had gone. It was symbolic. The air became easier to breathe. He settled in a chair to sleep, but he left the television on. There was nothing on but a pulse of light, like a heartbeat. He closed his eyes and fell into a dreamless slumber. Every now and then he opened his eyes because the silence had become too deep to be reassuring. He slept better after the sky had lightened. The day holds no terror for the lonely sleeper.

He woke earlier than he had hoped, and prepared to go and see the mayor. He ate breakfast in a drugstore, and then took a taxi around half-past nine to City Hall. He still looked around, and imagined he was being followed, but it no longer really worried him, because now his immediate future was in focus.

In City Hall, he went up to the sixth floor and found a new girl at the desk.

"Hi," he said, "where's Miss Shopenhower?"

"She got married, and left City Hall. I'm Myrtle Kollyris."

"Greek?"

"Originally. From Corinth, Greece. Mom's from Sparta. Are you from the old country?"

"No. Is the Big Man in?"

"Is that what you call him? I'll ask. Who shall I say wants to see him?"

"Chief . . . that is, Mr. Krumnagel."

"Would you spell that, please?"

Grudgingly Krumnagel spelled out his name. Things had certainly changed in his absence. The Greek girl was evidently of such competence that, having got him to repeat the spelling three times over, she then couldn't read her own writing. He had to bellow his name into the intercom. The mayor told him to come right in with what sounded like a kind of relish. Krumnagel was heartened as he knocked on the door. When he went in, however, he was surprised and a little embarrassed to find he was not going to be alone with the mayor. Also present were Milt Rotterdam, Joe Tortoni, and Judge Weyerback. They all smiled agreeably.

"And how's our jailbird?" asked the mayor. The others chuckled. Was that supposed to be funny or something?

"You're acting as though I'm interrupting something, folks," Krumnagel said, looking from one to the other.

"Don't overestimate your importance, Bart," the Mayor replied. There was something indescribably ugly in his manner. "Whether you're in the room or out of it is strictly immaterial. I want you to know that."

Before Krumnagel had time to react, the phone rang. The mayor picked it up.

"It's Mr. Shilliger," Miss Kollyris said.

"Put him on." The mayor smiled in friendly anticipation.

[301]

When Boots Shilliger came on the line, the mayor's conversation was so full of obscenities that the actual dialogue resembled a code. Krumnagel frowned. What's the idea, dressed nice, well-groomed, manicured, and talking dirty like that? Dirty? That's the understatement of the century.

"Sure, sure, sure, just walked in," said the mayor, looking at Krumnagel, and neglecting to swear, perhaps out of deference to his distinguished guest. "Yeah I'll tell him . . . are you crazy, who is he anyway, nothing . . . it's a waste of good breath . . ." Then the swearing began again till the end of a substantial conversation. As the mayor replaced the receiver, Krumnagel spoke.

"I never heard you talk dirty like that, mayor. What came over you?"

"Did I shock you?" the mayor asked, adjusting his tie, which had his initials on it in Gothic letters. It was personalized.

"Didn't shock me exactly, I don't shock that easy, but as the State Father of the Year two years running, you —"

"Turn on the hi-fi, Milt," the mayor interrupted. As the canned violins thawed out of their deep freeze, the mayor switched on his tiny Japanese transistor, and some cartoon animals began chasing each other on a miniature screen.

"You're not gathered here to watch television, are you?" Krumnagel asked, now entirely baffled.

"Lean forward," instructed the mayor.

Krumnagel did so.

"You wanted to know why I talked dirty? You must know that I am being arraigned on charges of extortion. I have a pretty good notion my wire is being tapped by the F.B.I. — and I'm just making damn sure that if this room or the wires are bugged, none of the tapes ever get on national television during a senate investigation, see. All they hear is a series of bleeps. That's why I talk dirty. It's not on account I think dirty. I don't talk that way in front of my kids."

"I understand," said Krumnagel. "That's pretty shrewd thinking."

Tortoni and Rotterdam leaned into the conversation, while Judge Wayerback stayed out of it as though emphasizing that he was only part of this sinister group by virtue of some secret force majeure.

"So you think I'm pretty shrewd, do you?" the Mayor asked. "Just whose side are you on, Bart?"

There we go again. Krumnagel frowned. Extraordinary how everybody seemed to ask the same question.

"Why d'you ask, Mayor?"

"It was you warned me that Al Carbide was keen on smashing rackets, remember?" He put up the sound of the television a point, and looked around the room briefly. "You mentioned names."

"I certainly recall something of the sort, yes," Krumnagel said.

"Well, I just want you to know that Al Carbide is the best police chief this city ever had. He's cool, efficient, upstanding, and he minds his own goddam business, and I thank God the day he took over."

Tortoni and Rotterdam nodded briefly, and looked to Wayerback, who was forced into a small acknowledgement. Krumnagel felt the cold fury rise in him, but this time he imagined it was under perfect control.

"I certainly am glad to hear it," he said, "since he learned all he knows from me."

"It's got nothing to do with what a guy learns or don't learn," snarled the mayor. "It's to do with what a guy is or is not. He's not a horse's ass. The rest of the sentence, I leave to your imagination."

Krumnagel rose.

"You called me in to tell me that?" he asked.

"I didn't call you. Why should I call you? Who the hell do you think you are? You came of your own accord, and I showed you courtesy, that's what happened. Courtesy I showed you, but that's all over now. You want a job? Sorry, Bart. There's nothing in this city for an asshole like you."

Tortoni and Rotterdam nodded.

"Don't you want to turn down your television a little? I'd like the F.B.I. to hear what I've got to say to you, Calogero," Krumnagel said loud and clear.

Tortoni and Rotterdam glowed with a kind of admiration, and even Weyerback turned his head to look.

"Sure you get on good with Carbide, and the extortion charges will make him look like he's on the side of the angels, and by the time Judge Weyerback's through whitewashing you, the rackets are going to look like the greatest charity organization after the International Red Cross."

"Have you any idea how much the boys and I give to charity every year?" Calogero roared, while Tortoni increased the volume of the canned violins urgently.

"It's a fraction of what you should be paying in taxes. That's the American way of evasion. Give to conceal how much you're taking," Krumnagel roared back. "And what's your rakeoff on the ball park, or is that a trade secret?"

"For your information, it's a nonprofit-making organization," shouted Calogero.

"That figures. That's what first made me suspicious," Krumnagel howled back.

"Get out of here! No, wait," Calogero dropped his voice, and signaled with his hand. Tortoni lowered the volume.

"I advise you strongly to get out of town," Calogero said, reasonably.

"There's nothing to say I have to," Krumnagel replied.

"Common sense, perhaps?"

"Oh? How come?"

"Why don't you go back to Europe, Bart? It seems to suit you there."

"Are you being funny, or something?"

[304]

"Only next time, if I were you, I'd travel by a regular ocean line. It's more comfortable than a cargo ship even if it is more expensive. And there's got to be fewer temptations . . ." said Calogero, pursuing his thought.

Krumnagel smiled slightly. He was impressed. Don't sell the Greeks short.

"Oh, I get it."

"Finally?"

"I'll say that for you. The rackets work quicker than Celebrity Service."

"Neither of the two organizations you mentioned are interested in you as a person, Bart. Speaking for myself, I got no time for interfering fools. Nor do I care for petty thieves. Ingratitude either. When I find all these elements gathered in one and the same man, I tend to find he stinks. I have scruples, see, and I set myself pretty goddam high standards. My kids are proud of me. Can you say the same?"

"I don't have none, but I'll tell you this —"

"You're free to go now, Bart."

"I'm going, don't give yourself further aggravation. I just want you to know I'm not scared of you, of any of you."

"It could be your loss," said Calogero with a shrug.

"You was wrong to call me an asshole."

"My pleasure."

"I love this City . . . and I remember the words you used about me at my testimonial, and they was beautiful words and they came from the heart and they was true," Krumnagel felt his eyes become moist in spite of his determination, "and let me tell you, I hate what you're doing to this City . . . I hate what you're doing to it."

Calogero pulled at his tie, tugged his neck free, and spoke with sterling dignity.

"What I'm doing to this City? Do you know that we come third in these United States in pro capita contributions to the war in the Far East? In weight of books and magazines, we're running second. I got to hang my head in shame because you hate what I'm doing to the City?"

"Who's talking about the goddam war? I'm talking about the City!"

"This country is at war," said Calogero. "That means this City's at war."

A great commotion began in the street. The movement of thousands of people.

"There's your war," said Krumnagel. "Right on cue. I'll leave you to fight it. Kind personal regards."

The mayor was at the window.

"Shut that music off. And the TV. Those long-haired cock-suckers from State and Crown of Thorns U. Shit! There was no demonstration authorized for today. They got it coming to them, I tell you. One false move, and I'm going to ask Dar-wood for state troopers."

"Great. I'll leave you to play soldiers against school kids. I don't want to spoil your pleasure," Krumnagel said, near the door.

"When my country is involved in a foreign war, it's not my duty to ask who my enemy is, and why he's my enemy, but merely to help crush that enemy," Calogero said, his voice trembling with self-righteous richness.

Rotterdam nodded, and Tortoni stood automatically. Only Weyerback shifted uneasily.

"That's a beautiful thought," said Krumnagel savagely, "and it's convenient you can find your enemies in a foreign war so close at hand."

He left and went down to the ground floor by the stairs.

He knew where he stood, and it was a relief. The crowds of protesters were milling around in swirling eddies, while some of Al Carbide's riot police, shining under plastic domes, tried to forestall the elemental movements of the mass of students without being carried off their feet. A policeman or two on horses made their appearance, the horses frisking and stomping under the influence of the gathering nervousness.

Some of the students were shouting slogans with a jungle insistence, while others seemed to be there by accident, smiling good-humoredly amid the tumult. One girl — as so often happens, the least suitable — stripped off her blouse and bra and appeared topless, lending herself with abandon to a mime expressing the destruction of a Vietnamese village by the Green Berets. Before long she was entirely naked, and lay inanimate in a pool of red paint, a vision of horror for those easily horrified. Gradually the communal gaze was carried upwards, both the police and students shading their eyes as they followed the progress of a college athlete who was scaling the flagpole of City Hall. To Krumnagel's delight, Mayor Calogero appeared at his window to a great surge of catcalls and whistles. He turned his head, looked upward, and shouted to the student to get the hell out of it. An ironic wail of derision rose from the crowd, and a huge cry of encouragement, and then of victory, as the flag of North Vietnam gathered the wind and fluttered from the flagpole. To Krumnagel, who wasn't too hot at distinguishing any flag but that of the United States, and who thought the flag of subversion now flying from City Hall must be that of Crown of Thorns U., it seemed that the mayor wasn't having much success in crushing his enemies in the foreign war, and it made him happy.

He had no desire to become caught up in the action, and he clung to the side of City Hall, and made his way away from the center of the turmoil, being content to watch the demonstration from fairly far away, the other side of the square. Suddenly, above the hubbub, he heard once again the celestial tinkle of temple bells, and turning, saw a group of Buddhists walking slowly and reflectively towards him, measuring every step as though each one took them nearer eternal truth. He thought back to Arnie Brugger's curious phrase which had somehow lingered in his consciousness — "their possible glimpse of heaven."

They were led in their measured chanting progress by an absolute giant of a man, whose small head still carried the traces of hair-roots, and who had daubs of paint on the bridge of his nose. His expression was one of a distant gentleness tinged with humor and self-deprecation, in contrast to his features, which had been designed for less thoughtful, more violent contingencies.

"Won't you buy a joss stick, and support our temple?" he asked Krumnagel.

"Buy a what?"

"A stick of incense," explained the Buddhist, with a voice and articulation of quiet splashing in clear water. "We have jasmine, sandalwood, and essence of oleander, but frankly, they all smell the same."

"I don't even have a home," said Krumnagel allowing himself a certain degree of bitterness. "What should smell so good?"

A surge of girls closed around Krumnagel, smiling and atinkle with bells.

"Why don't you come to our temple and worship? That is our only home," explained the giant, his eyes monstrously kind.

"You people Boodists?" asked Krumnagel.

"We belong to the sect of the Well of Infinite Reflection," said a girl.

"Yeah, I used to have to clear you out of parking lots and places. I used to be police chief of this crazy city."

"We never ask what people were, only what they wish to be," intoned the giant, and then chanted a quick canticle, joined by the others. Krumnagel briefly adopted a vague position of reverence. He had a great respect for other denominations. In a free country you had to have.

"You look like a Marine or something yourself," he said to the giant.

"All that's past," smiled the giant. "I have found a meaning to

[308]

my life, and what happened before is washed away like a sickness."

"For the sake of the record, were you in the Marine Corps?"

"There is no record, there is only the truth."

They sang a few more words, and tinkled their bells.

"I was in Vietnam," said the giant to put Krumnagel out of his misery. "We were told we were going in there with napalm and rockets to teach, but I came back with nothing but love and penury, having learned."

"It's a crazy world," reflected Krumnagel, trying to be helpful with a little homespun philosophy of his own. "You know something," he went on, "it sounds like a Bible story. Remember Samson. He got rid of his hair also, and he was a big guy by all reports."

The giant grinned absolutely without malice.

"Samson was blind if I remember rightly. I can see."

"Well, I didn't mean to say —"

"I mean I can see with the inner eye," the giant explained. "Christianity was fine as far as it went, but it's been sold out, it's cheapened and corrupted and a weapon for hate."

"Sold out?"

"There was always a preacher to bury the dead and to bless the living on their way to a new killing. It was always the same preacher to do both, with the same words, and the same lip service to the powers that be, pulling rank on behalf of the Almighty and preparing us for the Last Judgment, the Greatest Court-Martial of them all. Don't remind me of it." He tinkled urgently, and a song of peace broke from the hushed throats of those courting life like lovers.

To this murmured madrigal there was joined a truncated discordant percussive sound of voices, unmusical and strident and ruthless. Across the square there burst a tidal wave of construction workers, roughnecks in working clothes, wearing hollow metal helmets and waving American flags. They broke into a run when they saw the students, a slow sinister run like an

[309]

infantry attack in a long-forgotten war. Their faces brooked no argument, and they had about them all the dignity of laboratory rats, trained to enter the little door with the Stars and Stripes painted on without question or hesitation, their minds uncomplicated by doubt, and therefore by humanity. The last bastion of reaction is never the officers, always the sergeants. Long after the officers have recognized the inevitability of change owing to the solidarity of the men, the sergeants are still there upholding a dead world, paying homage to witch doctors and painted images, prey to the militant servility of their calling, yelling and shouting without respect for words or meaning. And here they were, on the double, flushed with the joy of activity, and drunk on hatred for all the infinity of human endeavor which lay beyond their comprehension.

Krumnagel and the Buddhists found themselves in the direct course of the attack. There was a group of police not far away, but apart from that no other obstacle on the way to the students.

"I am not afraid," chanted the giant, and the song was taken up by the others. The first wave of the construction workers rushed past them, their attention entirely absorbed by the students, and the offending flag fluttering over City Hall, and for a moment it looked as though the Buddhists might escape the attention of the intruders. Towards the tail end of the attack, however, there was a solid wedge of slower-moving belligerents, including some militant veterans wearing forage caps and business suits. This final wave carried Krumnagel and the Buddhists forward towards the students, gathering the group of police on the way. As the rush slowed down owing to the proximity of the enemy, the attackers looked around like fishermen to see what they had caught in their nets.

"Why aren't you out in Indochina fighting?" a hateful gentleman in a forage cap with Okinawa written on it yelled at the giant, his nostrils flaring.

The Buddhists sang their gentlest hymn.

[310]

"Come on fellers," shouted Okinawa, unwilling to trust himself to attack alone.

"At least they're honest," cried another. "They're dressed in yellow." A gale of derision greeted this taunt.

Krumnagel frowned as a multitude of Bible stories seemed to overwhelm him. He was suddenly plunged into a host of Sunday school moralities.

Okinawa hit the Buddhist, who smiled.

"Cut that out," cried Krumnagel, on the side of Jesus.

"Who in the hell are you?"

"You heard me. Cut it out. This guy don't want to fight. You got no right to make him."

"Is that a fact?" asked Okinawa in mock wonder, striking the giant again.

Krumnagel seized Okinawa by the throat, gathering shirt, tie and lapels in one huge freckled fist.

"Let me go," shuddered Okinawa.

A construction worker smashed his metal helmet on Krumnagel's skull, and knocked him down. Then they had a go at the giant.

Krumnagel struggled to his feet, blood trickling from his scalp. He called to the police, holding off a few rabid gentlemen in forage caps.

"All right fellers, over here," he called to them.

The police looked at him, but didn't move.

"What's the matter with you bums?"

Krumnagel plunged across to them.

"Have you got orders or something? Is that it?" he screamed into the face of the nearest policeman. Remember me? Chief Krumnagel? If you don't break up that fight I'll knock the shit out of you . . . all of you . . ." The police were impassive, embarrassed.

"Ever heard of a thing called duty?" Krumnagel ranted. "Or don't Carbide mention that no more? I'm embarrassed to be an American today . . . I'm ashamed."

One policeman made a helpless gesture.

"What's that you say?" Krumnagel yelled, placing his ear to the plastic dome.

"Please . . ."

"Please," echoed Krumnagel in disgust, and turned in the direction of the giant. The giant was no longer there, but a group of hostile men in helmets and caps were looking down at something on the ground and seemed to be engaged in kicking. Blind with fury, Krumnagel pressed through the crowd. On the ground lay the giant, trampled and inanimate. One of the girls had sought to protect him by lying across him. The crowd was like a barbaric hunt, trumpeting their triumph and blinded by the smattering of blood, a primeval scent in their nostrils, and every sense, oral, tactile, and sexual bent towards an ecstasy of destruction. There was slaughter in the air, carnival laughter, strident and searing, the laughter of relief, laughter as an alternative to tears. Faces were hideous, they registered nothing, only reflecting the cacophony of the absurd, the obscene, the loathsome. Sense was carried away in the great belch of the subconscious. Krumnagel seized Okinawa again with a tenacity born of rage. He hated that face, the cap was an insult. He stared into those hysterical, unfulfilled, unhappy eyes, as though trying to understand how man can ossify into miserable, lonelyheart, peephole moralizers who go spreading their ugliness around them as a public service. First of all, Krumnagel took the cap and threw it miles into the sea of humanity.

"That's my cap!" yelled Okinawa, as though he had been castrated.

"And this," said Krumnagel reasonably, "is your face," and punched him cruelly and viciously till he dropped from sight into the jungle of stamping feet and derelict possessions. It was too late to be of much help to the giant, but Krumnagel fought as he had never fought before; not even in prison had he found such delight in battle. There he was merely protecting himself against misinterpretation, here he was the only representative of uprightness, of honesty and light. He knew what he was doing, and so joy and judgment reappeared in his every action. Nevertheless, he was outnumbered by the forces of darkness. Suddenly the police began moving in. It was about time. Krumnagel was collapsing. He was hanging on to a construction worker who couldn't get him far enough away to hit him.

"Stand up and fight," the construction worker kept shouting in a muddy unresonant voice. Krumnagel laughed as he held the worker to him like a dancer. He laughed at his shrewdness and at the other guy's perplexity. All the same the fires were flickering, were dying. He laughed while he could.

A tremendous roar rose from the crowd, and peace fell over them like a mantle.

"Oh, say can you see . . . in the dawn's early light . . ." The hymn rose from thousands of lungs in ragged unison.

Through one half-closed eye (the other was closed entirely) Krumnagel managed to see that the offending flag of North Vietnam had been removed, and the Stars and Stripes was fluttering in its rightful place once again, a small committee of workers standing on the roof with their yellow hats over their hearts.

One after another, the police, their uniforms unstained by battle, pulled their plastic domes off their heads, placed them over their hearts, and joined in the fervent singing.

Krumnagel closed his available eye, and muttered a short phrase to himself before passing out cold. "Now I seen everything . . ."

18

When Krumnagel opened his eyes, all was white. A smell of
medicine made him suspect that he was not about to face his
Maker. A pity. He felt he had an awful good case at the moment — cases that good don't come every day. He was proud
of his resilience in having such a thought at such a time. He
tried to move. That was less amusing. It was worse than the
day after his beating in the prison. He looked around without
moving his head, which was all wrapped in bandages. He saw
a man looking down at him, a man in civilian clothes. It took
him a moment of concentration to focus. It was Armstrong,
brandishing an envelope.

"Marv," he said, a little pained. He was sore with the police.
"Hi, Bart."

"What you got there in your hand, feller? Warrant?"

"Tickets."

"Tickets? I don't get it."

"Tickets for Colorado Springs . . . airplane tickets."

Sentimental son of a bitch. Heart of gold, though, and in the right place too.

"Why Colorado Springs, for Christ's sake? What's so desirable about Colorado Springs?"

"I know it, that's why Bart. And I happen to like it. And I think you'll like it too — for a while.

Krumnagel tried to pull a wry face, but it was too painful, and then, the nerves which controlled his expression wouldn't respond to wry.

"What is it then — retirement area for senior citizens . . . clock golf, card tables, TV room?"

"No!" Marv cried. "It's a wonderful place with a wonderful climate. I went there, Bart. I didn't send my dad."

"And who do I have to thank? The mayor?"

"Compliments of the entire police department."

"Including Al."

"Excluding Mr. Carbide."

Krumnagel sighed.

"It's awful good of the boys, Marv — but you know. Only time I ever got given a gift by the entire Police Department you remember what happened, don't you?"

"Are you figuring on shooting a guy down in Colorado Springs?"

"No," said Krumnagel reasonably. "I admit I'll be more liable to do that if I stay here."

"That's what I figured."

"Still —"

"It don't have to be Colorado Springs, Bart. Just anywhere takes your fancy for a while. You can trade in your tickets for any of equal value. Just for a while, Bart. Please."

Krumnagel thought for a moment. Whatever else he had to complain about, there was no lack of friends. And yet, there was something disturbing about the haste of the offer. Was his life in danger, or was Armstrong worried about his reactions to the way things were going? He frowned slightly. He had instincts, and sometimes they had led him in the direction of utter clairvoyance, when he was fresh, that is, and untroubled. Not when he was tired or overtense.

"Marv," he said suddenly, "what happened to the Boodists?"

Armstrong shifted nervously, and glanced inadvertently to one side. Krumnagel, open to every nuance, turned his eyes sideways, and noticed that the bed next to his was surrounded with screens.

"The big fellow," he insisted. "Jesus."

"Jesus?"

"The big guy with all them other cheeks."

Armstrong hesitated.

"Well, there's an awful uproar about it, Bart."

"An uproar, huh?"

"Well, I might as well tell you, he's dead."

There was a long pause while Krumnagel fixed Armstrong mercilessly with a look as terrifying as it was solemn.

"You know who killed him, don't you Marv. The police department."

Armstrong would have none of it.

"Now you're going too far, Bart."

"Listen, I was there!"

"I know. That's where we picked you up."

"You could have picked me up sooner. Prevented me from getting beaten. And prevented the big guy from dying."

"Well, maybe that's why the boys were so eager to cough up financial contributions to your tickets when I suggested it. They're very embarrassed about what happened."

"Embarrassed? They didn't even recognize me!"

"Of course they did."

"But they got orders — I was right, wasn't I?"

Armstrong looked unhappy.

"We all got orders, Bart, you know that, don't you? You remember. The state troopers. The mayor asked for them. They winged a couple of students this afternoon. Thank Christ they didn't kill no one here. The big guy's enough for one riot, but all the press is down here, the networks, the big papers with a national following. Every second guy in the streets seems to have a microphone. And the administration had already accused them of biased reporting before a single story's out."

"You trade in the tickets, Marv — buy your wife a new hat. I'm not going no place."

"Now, Bart, don't get bitter for Christ's sake —"

"Bitter? I get a jail sentence of seven years because I shoot a man in self-defense and here a bunch of guys with comic hats kick a defenseless guy to death and they're going to get off scot-free because they're veterans and they know the words of all four verses of the Star Spangled Banner. What kind of lousy justice is that?" Krumnagel roared, kicking off the bedclothes and giving the moribund in other beds a new lease on life.

"We got to bide our time," soothed Armstrong, fighting with the bedclothes, "till we're big enough to do something."

"I heard that before. We all say that on our way to the top, but once we're up there on the tightrope, all we think about is that falling from grace is kind of personally painful. Al Carbide was full of fine words before he made it. Now he's one hundred percent the mayor's man. And you know who told me? Calogero himself. Come on, Marv, if there's got to be killing, for God's sake let it be the right people. Don't waste your bullets on the innocent while there's the guilty still walking free, their pockets full of percentages and credit cards —"

"I got news for you," Armstrong said, trying to change the subject. "You asked me to find out how Red Leifson lost his legs, remember? It was an accident with a farm tractor, at age ten."

[317]

"I should concern myself with a pair of buried legs now?"

"You did ask me, that's all."

"I remember, I remember every damn thing. Who was on traffic control duty the day I left to go to Europe? Fourteenth of May. It was you, wasn't it Marv?"

"I don't rightly recall."

"Well, I do. There was the mother of all snarlups on the Cross State Turnpike with no sign of no chopper."

"Oh, sure," Armstrong confirmed, "that was the day the chopper blew a gasket, and there was a six car pileup on Beauregard at Bluefields. Two dead."

"Pretty good recall you got also," said Krumnagel. "Yet who gives a shit now — except perhaps the relatives of the two dead, and even they got to be thinking of other things by now. People forget, Marv. They forget. That's the trouble with them. They forget, and they pretend not to see. A guy can lie bleeding, they prefer to leave the aggravation to the competent authority — police, ambulance men, the next passerby. Why get involved? It could be as time-consuming as jury duty. Who needs it? Well . . ." He spoke slowly and with a deadly precision, "We got to arrange things so that people don't forget."

"How you going to do that?" Armstrong asked lightly.

Krumnagel looked at him with uncanny eyes, uncanny because they seemed so mysteriously happy.

"That Boodist had no business dying on us, Marv. But now he's gone, it's up to us to give him a fine memorial."

Armstrong stared at Krumnagel, who nodded slightly as though he spoke with the authority of destiny itself.

"Only one more question, Marv. Where them construction workers come from? What's constructing around here on that scale? There must have been four, five hundred of the sons of bitches . . ."

"They put double crews on to finish the ball park in time —"

"For tomorrow night's inaugural game?"

"That's right."

"You see," said Krumnagel. "It all fits, like it was written. I couldn't have imagined it better. So they came out of the fockin' ball park . . ."

Armstrong hadn't the faintest idea what Krumnagel was talking about, and rather than ask for an elucidation, he felt he would leave it that way, for the sake of his peace of mind, just as the prophet Krumnagel had said. He replaced the tickets in his pocket, and walked off with a "See you, Chief" of deceptive casualness. Within himself, he tried hard to find replacements for his thoughts.

Krumnagel demanded noisily to see the doctor once he was certain that Armstrong had gone his way.

"I want to get out of here," he declared.

"In my estimation, you're in no fit state to leave," said the doctor.

The doctor pointed out that in his present condition, Krumnagel could well be a liability to society, since his left hand was so bandaged as to be temporarily immobile, while the swathes round his head protruded like a canopy over his left eye, causing him to hold his head in a position of haughtiness which was utterly out of keeping with his character.

"How much longer do you expect me to wear these goddam bandages?" he asked.

"We'll take a look at the damage in a couple of days."

"Yeah?"

Krumnagel began to undo the bandage around his hand.

"Don't do that!" ordered the doctor.

"You want me to start hollering?"

He had known prisoners bang their plates with their spoons in order to lend emphasis to their complaints by assaulting the nerves of the authorities.

"No, I do not want you to start hollering," replied the doctor

[319]

rather stiffly. He was unused to these methods, and felt bound, in the interests of his own equilibrium, to revert to childishness himself.

"I hope you get run over by a truck," he said, as he left the ward. "An eight-wheeler."

Krumnagel felt much weaker than he thought he would, and the blinding white sunlight both dazzled and dazed him. He leaned against the railings for support. A glance upward while breathing deeply, and his eyes met those of the doctor, watching his progress vindictively from a window. That was enough. Krumnagel's life seemed to have been a series of provocations or incentives (he thought of them as challenges, naturally), which drove him forward from one foolhardiness to the next. Those who think of existence as a battle enjoy the exhilaration of the action too fully to consider the consequences of their actions. It often appears to them that those who bother with foresight are not living life to the full. Those who drink to slake their thirst are not concerned with vintages.

While the doctor was at the window, Krumnagel had to walk with a sure and measured step. It was accepted by his particular code of honor that he could, if it were inevitable, collapse when out of sight. He hailed a taxi. The driver slowed down, then accelerated away although empty and on duty. There is something about men in bandages which scares away taxis. Affluent society might well be, but for that very reason it is litigious. It is easier to love your neighbor in his absence, and it is easier to send flowers to a hospital than to go yourself. And indifference may be reprehensible without a show of involvement, but rather than stand up and be counted, most people prefer to send a financial contribution and squat in a low place out of sight.

Krumnagel staggered to the corner of the street, when necessary bouncing himself off the shop-fronts to rediscover his balance. At length a compassionate motorist drew up to the curb. There are Samaritans hidden in every crowd, and their virtue is that they are never afraid to reveal themselves, albeit with a kind of jocular bitterness about the lack of compassion which surrounds them.

"Can I help you?" asked the motorist, a farmer by the look of him and the state of his car.

"You're not going my way," said Krumnagel.

"How can you tell, feller? Jump in. Your way is my way. Can't let you walk — not in that condition. Fresh out of hospital, are you?"

"That's right."

Krumnagel eased himself into the front seat with a mixture of relief and regret. It would be too bad if this man succeeded in reestablishing his belief in human nature now that his mind had found a certain peace in its haven of vengeance.

"Where d'you want me to go?"

Krumnagel named the address, which was that of Arnie Brugger. They drove in silence.

"What happened?" the farmer asked eventually.

"You wouldn't understand."

The farmer was puzzled. He smiled slightly.

"How come?"

"I got involved."

"Oh."

The farmer kept his emotional distance.

"Can happen to anyone," he said at length.

"You never said a truer word," Krumnagel replied.

They arrived.

"Don't get involved again," said the farmer pleasantly.

"Why not?" asked Krumnagel, almost belligerently.

"Well, if you must, hurt the other guy more than you get hurt yourself."

"Sure will," Krumnagel smiled. "Thanks."

Arnie's bell took a long time to answer. A Negro girl opened the door.

"Dr. Brugger's residence."

"Is he in?"

"You a patient?"

"Not yet, I'm not."

"Well, he's at the hospital, don't get back till late."

"Late? What's late?"

"Couple hours."

"I'll wait."

"Not inside you won't. I got orders."

"I'll wait here."

She shut the door, and he heard the chain rattle.

He woke up a while later to find Arnie Brugger trying to open his own door surreptitiously.

"Hi, Arnie."

Arnie looked around in fright.

"Who's that?"

"Bart Krumnagel."

"Jesus Christ, Bart, what happened?"

"I got hurt."

"Hurt? Accident?"

"Deliberate."

"Deliberate?"

"I got hurt deliberate. I got to see you, Arnie."

"Not now, Bart."

"Now Arnie. I need to see you now."

"I got a dinner."

"Cancel it."

"I can't, Bart. Honest."

"Say you'll come later."

"Bart believe me —"

Krumnagel seized Arnie by the lapel with his better hand. He must have looked terrifying, because Arnie cringed, the dead embryo of a smile lying limp on his lips.

"Remember what you once said to me, Arnie?" Krumnagel asked. "Funny thing, I remember the precise words you used." His face took on a look of tender and lunatic reminiscence, and

Arnie felt he was being sucked into a world of fantasies as relentlessly as a drowned fly swirling at the gate of its underworld as the bath runs out.

". . . if you ever drop out, then I'll help you," Krumnagel murmured like a part of the most sacred litany, and then he redirected his gaze at Arnie, smiling savagely and possessively. "Them was the very words you used."

"I don't remember, Bart, I mean it."

The grip on the lapels tightened.

"Tell me again you don't remember. Just tell me that once more, you dishonest son of a bitch . . ."

"I remember your coming up here . . ."

"Sure you do. The Boodists in Leverett's parking lot."

"Yes, yes. And Mervyn Spindelman was up for a drink."

"That's correct. That's precisely right."

"Hey — you know something, we don't want to talk out here, Bart. Why don't we sit down where it's comfortable . . . in the parlor?"

"You mean that? Because I'm warning you, Arnie — if you try to take advantage of me because I can't move too good, I'll kill you."

"You'll do what?" laughed Arnie, unable to conceive that this could be anything else but a joke.

"I'll kill you," Krumnagel replied, very simply. "Didn't you hear? I been out in England practicing, and now . . . well you know, it's like everything else, it gets to be a habit."

Arnie looked deep into those erratic eyes.

"Come in," he said, opening the door and beckoning Krumnagel forward with the cautious gesture of one who is determined to prove to a crackpot that there is no risk of a trap.

They entered the hallway and then the parlor. Arnie closed the front door behind him, but left it off the latch. You never know.

"Well now, tell me all about it, Bart, but make it quick if you don't mind. Tonight is the Annual Dinner of the Holders of

[323]

Research Fellowships in the Psychiatric Field — it's a pretty darned important occasion and I am making a speech which will be carried on nationwide educational networks —"

"Take me along as a test case. The largest focking guinea pig in captivity. I mean it."

"Please, Bart."

"O.K.," Krumnagel said, suddenly conciliatory. "I'll let you go to your dinner. It won't take me that long to spoil your evening anyhow."

"What's on your mind, Bart?" Arnie sat on the edge of an armchair, his arms folded on his chest, attempting to look relaxed.

"On my mind?" Krumnagel sat heavily, to Arnie's ill-disguised dismay. "You know something, that's a good question? On my mind. I never thought what those words meant before — just said them without thinking — but if you think, they're real meaningful."

"Yes . . . yes, they are." Arnie seemed to be adding his seal of approval to them.

Krumnagel looked at Arnie kindly.

"If ever you drop out, I'll help you . . . remember now?"

"Sure. Yes. It all comes back now," Arnie replied curtly.

"I figured it would."

"But, you know, Bart — I'd always help a guy in trouble, even if I hadn't remembered, that's the way I'm made."

"Oh sure, I know that. Your son fixed it that way for you." Krumnagel twisted his knife while Arnie flinched, looking at his watch.

"Well, it's happened," Krumnagel went on slowly. "I dropped out. Not voluntarily, you understand. I was pushed over the edge, kind of. Now I need your help, Arnie."

"Why don't you come to the clinic —"

"There's no time, Arnie, that's why." Krumnagel applied a little vocal pressure. "You know I killed a guy."

"I read about it, yes," Arnie sighed.

[324]

"Well, that was a foolish thing to do now, wasn't it?"

"Yes. Yes, if you say so yourself — the way it turned out."

Krumnagel leaned in to make himself seem more conspiratorial.

"Yeah, it was foolish. But you know what was foolish about it, don't you?"

"Of course."

"Tell me."

"It's . . . it's always foolish to kill a person." Arnie disliked this kind of conversation.

"Oh, no," replied Krumnagel, as though disappointed in his best pupil. "It's not the killing that's foolish. It's killing for no reason. See, the construction workers and them lousy veterans, they had a reason to kill that Boodist. Hate. Sheer hate. I didn't have no such reason. I really deserved my sentence on account of I was a bum, a cretin. I killed a guy I didn't even know. Now there's another thing I found out. No one's ever going to get arrested for killing the Boodist, that's one, and there was too many murderers, that's two. That's what I call smart killing, Arnie. Now, I don't have that kind of advantage. I got to figure on help. All I got is hate. That I learned right here, in my own City."

Arnie had grown pale and no longer looked at his watch.

"Bart," he said, "the man has not been born who doesn't need help at some time or other, and slowly psychiatry is pushing forward into the darkness of man's mind —"

"You gave me all the crap before," Krumnagel interrupted brutally, "and you even told me I was sick because I didn't care to fly on the thirteenth. Listen, I ain't concerned with the darkness of man's mind — I'm concerned with action, always have been, and that's the way I'll go I guess — not in the gas chamber though, out there in the open with a gun. Only —" (He became quiet again.) "— I don't reckon on going just yet. I got a little killing to do first. And after that, a little living."

"Killing?" Arnie asked tonelessly.

"Killing. Tomorrow evening. The ball game. They're all going to be there, aren't they? Edie and Al."

"You want to kill Edie?"

"Who said I want to kill Edie? Poor stupid bitch. I don't kill to put people out of their misery. If they're that miserable they probably deserve it, and who am I to put an end to it? As for Al Carbide, I don't settle small accounts that way, Arnie. Embarrassment's good enough for him, the breakdown of his security regulations. No sir, when Krumnagel kills he goes right to the top from now on."

"Right to the top?"

"That's right. I don't waste bullets on creeps like Red Leifson. He'll drown in his poison one of these days. I don't even go for a crook like Mayor Calogero — sooner or later Shilliger or Rotterdam or Tortoni's going to do the job anyway, or one of the syndicates. Eight o'clock the game starts, am I right? The governor of the state, Darwood H. McAlpin, shakes hands with both teams, and unveils a plaque. I got news for you. He's never going to get back to his seat. He's never going to see no ball game. He's going to be dead."

"But for God's sake!" Arnie cried in horror. "What's he ever done to you? Al Carbide I could understand —"

Krumnagel interrupted with a fearful intensity.

"That son of a bitch gave me the tickets for 'round the world, didn't he?"

Arnie had abruptly gained access to a thought process as an explorer might burst on an undiscovered world, and now it lay before him, brightly lit, with too many details to take in at one and the same time, and yet its broad outline plainly visible, and the rest correctly guessed.

"You blame him —"

"Where is he? In his office, or by his pool most likely, drinking highballs. Meanwhile the wrong people's getting killed in the City, and the wrong people's taking the rap. I'm going to

shoot that bastard, and then Arnie, I'm going to plead temporary insanity. That's where you come in."

Arnie felt he was going to be sick.

"I can't recommend it, Bart. Honestly."

"I didn't come here for no advice. You was ready enough to
get the child rapers and the homicidal homos and the other
weirdos off, now it's my turn. I dropped out Arnie, remember?
You get me off the murder rap, that's all I ask. You and Spindelman."

"Spindelman? He'd never —"

"Are you kidding? Defending a police chief on a charge of
murdering the governor? That's one of them cases he don't
look for the money. That's a strict case of helping his reputation. Can you think of a better one? A guy served the City
loyally for close on thirty years, good enough to rate a civic
luncheon, and to be awarded a testimonial, and tickets around
the fockin' world, first class yet, not tourist or charter flight —
and this same guy gets unfair treatment someplace overseas —
comes back to find the city he loves a cesspit of violence, corruption, graft, you name it — and what does he do? Why, he
does the clean thing, the American thing, his thing — on account of he's against violence and graft and corruption, get it
— and since no one will listen to him, he shoots the goddam
governor to draw attention to these things."

"Bart, listen to me —"

"Put that into high-class English, and you got yourself a hell
of a case."

"You're taking the law into your own hands."

"Did Jesus Christ get a permit from city hall before he
cleared them money lenders out of the temple? No sir, he did
not. He was just lucky in one respect, they didn't have guns in
those days."

"Bart!" Arnie said urgently. "Go away for a few days."

"Colorado Springs? I know. No dice."

[327]

"I'll take you in the clinic for a while."

"Sure, starting the day after tomorrow, I'll take treatment. It'll be a pleasure."

Arnie tried another tack.

"I know you're not serious, Bart. I don't know why you want to take a revenge on me. It's a little cold-blooded, I'd say. My heart is not all that strong." He covered it with his hands. "I had trouble while you're away. They gave me a few years more."

Before Arnie could foresee it, Krumnagel was up and shaking him like a rag.

"You're going to get me off, Arnie. You and Spindelman. The two of you between you. And you just tell your heart to hold out that long. You made me a promise, and you're going to live up to it, see? You're going to say I was crazy enough to kill the governor and then I'm going to recover, see, owing to the medicine you give me. It's going to be a miraculous recovery. One of the most miraculous on record. And you're going to get a lot of credit for it. You and Spindelman. Think of it. Sacco and Vanzetti, Loeb and Leopold, and now Krumnagel. If you need a corrupt judge, find one . . . you know every one. I don't have to tell you. Just do it. I'll pay you later."

"You'll pay me?" Arnie asked. "How?"

"I'll write a book. My life. Just consider this whole incident as the start of the publicity campaign for the book. I don't even have to write it — I found that out in England. I just lend my name to it. They do the rest. I didn't even read the goddam thing — all I got to do is live it. Then later, they'll make a movie of it, and there I'll be, shaking hands with the actor playing the part of Big Bart, all over the magazines."

Arnie felt like pouring ridicule on Krumnagel, but his virulence just wouldn't flow. It had been done too often, too successfully in the past. Caryl Chessman had held out long enough for literati to protest the gratuitous execution of a considerable literary figure. The so-called sweet smell of success had already

[328]

grazed Krumnagel's nostril, in fact; if it hadn't been for that two-timing Delilah Edie, he'd be spending royalties already.

Arnie made one last effort to speak on behalf of human dignity and all those other virtues a man feels it incumbent upon himself to represent when there's no one else around.

"Bart," he said, "I see the same rottenness about as you do . . ."

"Only you've learned to live with it —"

"That's not what I was going to say, Bart. I let you talk. Now let me. Fair's fair."

"Sure. I only got to remind you you got a dinner tonight, Arnie. I gather it's kind of important."

"Who cares about the dinner when there's a human being in trouble?" lied Arnie.

"You're coming to see my point of view —"

"That always was my point of view, always will be. It's more than a point of view, Bart. It's medical ethics, no less."

"Great stuff, Arnie. Only don't waste it on me. Save it for the jury."

"There's not going to be a jury, Bart, for the simple reason there's going to be no crime. What you're trying to tell me is that you are bitter, unhappy and disappointed. I understand why — and believe me there is a cure for it. But why take it out on the country that gave you the opportunity to be the man you have become, and drag its name in the mud with derogatory publicity? In this great country of ours, every man, woman and child has the choice of rectitude or felony, the straight road or the crooked, the right way or the wrong. That is the price and peril of the freedom we enjoy, and at every crossroad we have to make and reconsider our choice. You are at such a crossroad. For God's sake, Bart, and for all our sakes, make the right choice!"

Krumnagel looked at him with a mixture of affection and pity.

"Bullshit," he said.

"Aren't you even going to gratify my argument with a rebuttal? Don't you think you owe me a reply?"

"Bullshit," Krumnagel repeated. "That's my reply. You're trying to divide up society into the good guys and the bad guys again . . . you all do it, and I know why. I've worked it out, and it took me a long time. You know something? The good guys *are* the bad guys. Think about it. Put it on your mind, as you like to say. That's what's wrong. There is no choice. There is no democracy. The law's in the hands of the people all right — the wrong people — but that don't mean we're free. Carry an American flag in your hand, you can get away with any damn thing, even murder, I seen it. Dress up as a Boodist, and you don't stand a dog's chance. It just needs Jesus Christ to come back and get himself a fair trial to show the whole charade up for what it is — hey, maybe he's been back, often — maybe he makes it a practice, like a beach bum testing the water every now and then. I'll tell you something Arnie, it hasn't got no warmer in two thousand years. Now go to your dinner. I don't want you to be late. Remember, you're a good guy, and good guys are punctual. I don't want there to be no confusion."

Now it was Arnie trying to restrain him, to keep him from going.

"Don't be a fool, Bart!"

"I seen it like it is, Arnie. I'm no fool. I'm going to do the dirty work, and you're going to get me off, you and Spindelman."

"What if we don't?"

Krumnagel shrugged.

"Ever since I got back, everybody's been trying to shut me up. The mayor, the police department, everybody. Now if you kill a guy, the one thing you get is a trial, and the one thing you can do at a trial is talk. I can talk plenty, on account I got plenty to say. I can say you encouraged me to kill the governor

— told me you could get me off, as you got all the other off in the past, remember?"

"But Bart, it wouldn't be true —"

"It don't have to be true to stick. Haven't you got wise to the system yet? After a time people don't remember whether it was true or not, they just remember it was said. And I don't have to be selective in what I say either. I can throw as much mud as I like. Some of it is bound to splash onto you. I can say I got you on a homosexual rap while I was police chief, but I let you off at the request of a highly placed accomplice."

Arnie was red with anger.

"I'm not a homosexual, Bart, and you know it!"

"Like I said, you don't have to tell the truth no more, don't you understand what I been telling you?" Krumnagel shouted.

"You couldn't bring yourself to do a thing like that!"

"You don't know me. The good guys *is* the bad guys, like I said. I got on the wavelength. I give you the facts. Now start working on the case."

"I'll call the police, tell them you're going to shoot the governor!" Arnie cried, in a last desperate effort to stem the tide.

"They get calls every ten minutes around the clock with tip-offs of that kind. If you want to join the crackpots, that's your privilege, Arnie. Like you said, you got the choice between the straight road and the crooked. Go ahead, exercise your constitutional rights as a nut case." He put his thumb in his ear, waggled his fingers painfully, stuck his tongue out, squinted, and left.

This time Arnie locked the door behind him, and walked about desperately for a moment, trying to collect his thoughts. He was alone in his part of the apartment, and wanted to keep it that way. Communication with anyone at the moment would be more than he could stand. He shut the door. Then he poured himself a stiff bourbon. Sitting at his desk, he looked up Mervyn Spindelman's number at his hotel in Cincinnati, where he was busy defending a gigolo who had killed a sixty-year-old toilet-tissue heiress. He dialed the number. They took quite a time finding Spindelman. Arnie betrayed his agitation by talking to himself. At length the great advocate came on the line, a note of irritation in his voice, as though elevated thoughts were being disturbed by this workaday intrusion.

Agitatedly Arnie blurted out what had happened, having to start all over again once or twice, owing to his incoherence. Spindelman was inclined to be olympian and infuriating.

"Arnie," he said, "I'm surprised you calling me with a story of such small caliber . . . it's not a criticism of you at all . . . it's rather a paean of praise of your golden heart . . . and since golden hearts are simple hearts, it stands to reason it affects your head. First of all, I think it is true to say in your profession that those who cry out suicide are rarely those who take their lives . . . it is the silent ones who resort to action . . . What? . . . Well of course there are exceptions . . . there are exceptions to every rule, otherwise this business of being alive would be an even more intolerable bore than it is . . . Will I accept the case? . . . There's no case, Arnie . . . But if it should by some chance become one, I can imagine few which sound more eminently defensible . . . I should certainly deplore one of those brilliant boys in California or Washington being offered the brief . . . That's what Krumnagel said? . . . That's most impressive, Arnie . . . He must have learned a great deal in captivity . . . I think one always does . . . Some of the greatest works of mankind have been conceived in monasteries and some of its most poignant thoughts came out of prison . . . Lenin conceived his revolutionary plans in the silence of the reading room of the British Museum . . . Men don't leave each other alone, I think that's what it all boils down to . . . It's when they do that daylight appears."

"What in the hell has Lenin to do with this?" Arnie permitted himself to bark.

Spindelman laughed good-naturedly.

"Was the experience as terrible as that?"

"It sure was. I'm not exaggerating one iota. The man is desperate. Christ, Mervyn, I've got some experience in these matters. Do you think I ought to warn the governor?"

"Arnie, there are some people who are gifted at stopping runaway horses; others are not. When someone who's not tries to do it, there's always a disaster. The governor won't believe you, but someone's going to overhear your warning, and if the worst happens, you're going to be on the mat for not having been more persuasive."

"But for crying out loud, Mervyn. I'm alone to have this thing on my conscience!"

"No, you're not, Arnie. You're far too clever for that. You got me to share it with you."

"Doesn't it worry you?"

"Not in the least. I don't happen to believe the governor deserves to stay alive any more than most people. He's an incoherent, inbred ass, and he'd have as much impact on my conscience as a mosquito would have on an elephant."

There was a pause.

"All right, Mervyn. You win. If the worst happens, what do I do?"

"When is this confounded ball game?"

"Tomorrow at eight o'clock in the evening."

"In the evening?"

"It's a night game."

"You're going, of course."

"Wild horses wouldn't drag me there. As a psychiatrist, I loathe the sight of people in the mass. It makes me lose my faith in the individual, without which . . . if you follow."

"Very well. Did Mr. Krumnagel intimate when he wished to perform the dastardly deed?"

"He said the governor was going to shake the hands of both

teams and then unveil a plaque, which I presume is on the edge of the field. Then he said the governor wouldn't get back to his seat, since he'd be dead."

"Right. The handshakes are going to take ten minutes, I suppose. He'll probably know a few facts about ball players and be interested in their answers — it's about as far as his knowledge of public affairs will stretch — give him twelve minutes, what do you say?"

"O.K., that's 8:12."

"Then his speech will last five minutes — no more. His saving grace is that he's short-winded. That takes us to 8:17, by which time he will begin climbing back towards his seat. Tragedy could overtake him around 8:18. There'll be a scuffle. Have you a dinner date tomorrow, Arnie?"

"No."

"I'd just pass by police headquarters around nine o'clock."

"On what pretext?"

"Oh, you just happened to be passing."

"Where will you be?"

"I'll come along on my way back from the airport. I get in at a quarter of ten."

"Do you think it's going to happen then?"

"I hope and pray not," said Spindelman earnestly. "But in any case, police headquarters is on my way home."

19

The lights beat down on the ball park like those of a gigantic operating room, isolating the observers in the wings of darkness, concentrating on the center of interest. The two teams were lined up, one or two of the players shifting nervously, nearly all of them chewing. Monsignor Francis Xavier O'Hanrahanty beamed goodwill and a sense of occasion from his Dutch cheese face, and presented his players to the smiling governor, whose network of wrinkles made him seem almost Oriental. True to form he spoke to each player as though their every destiny had a pressing interest for him, but he was too far out of earshot for the words to be distinguished. Occasionally the graticule of the telescopic lens crossed over his face, his neck, his body. He shook the hands of the other team. The monsignor smiled a little less, but the governor's cheeks were gathered like a canopy around the corners of his eyes. He was all pleasure and the public expression of decent humanity. Eventually he was guided to the inner wall of the ball park, where a piece of the concrete bastion was covered with the state flag. The governor spoke briefly with considerable intensity and that hesitant eloquence which had made him many friends, seeming to mark him as a creature of lucidity coupled with more than one man's ration of charming fallibility. The words were inaudible because a severe whistling in the loudspeaker system prevented them from carrying. A ribbon was pulled and the state flag collapsed, revealing a plaque with the profiles of a man and a woman on it, the donors of the ball park. The cheerleaders began hopping around, waving their fluffy wands, and agitating their slightly obscene knees. The governor started to climb the steps to his seat. He turned sideways as he walked, talking with evident interest to the monsignor. The graticule covered his head, his neck, his back. He was obscured by smoke.

The huge face of the monsignor turned aghast, deformed in a great silent howl. The wheelchair began cascading down the steps, Red Leifson petrified in terror. Al Carbide whistling, but with no noise coming out of the whistle. Edie grabbed him. "It's Bart! Bart!" Al Carbide shaking himself free like a villain of the silent screen, and she fell to the ground with a resentful look swimming in mascara. Flashback. Improvements. The governor was shaking the teams' hands again. Close up of Leifson speaking his spiteful thoughts into a tape recorder, his legless stumps covered with rugs. The monsignor smiling, endlessly smiling, so sure of celestial support in all his goings in and comings out and hoverings on the brink. God, how those teams could chew! Half close your eyes and you're in a factory. More words from the governor, his jaw rippling with intensity and interest under suntanned leather skin, each pore as pure as a dewdrop with aftershave and masculine scents, woods, leaves, grass. The halt before the state flag again. More well-chosen words, perhaps the same well-chosen words, with the public address system screaming fit to break eardrums. The flag sagging, the profiles, the girls with the knees like Soviet field marshals in a huddle hopping and beating the air with their paper flyswats, their faces glistening with healthy asexual effort. The graticule moving with the heartbeat. Hold your breath this time. That's better. The governor and the monsignor climbing the steps, their smiles tempered with gravity, speculating on the quality of the contemporary youth no doubt. The graticule centers just above their heads. The heads move into the target area. The governor takes up all the room. Neck. Back. Once again a wrench, and he's covered in smoke. The same agonized look on the monsignor's face, blood streaming down it this time. Don't overdo it. Cancel the blood. Blood canceled. Acknowledgement from the monsignor. Blood on anyone but Christ is a blasphemy, my son. O.K., I'm easy, reverend. Al and the silent whistle, Edie dressed as Clara Bow, Red Leifson suddenly at the wheel of a racing car, cornering too fast. A stutter of tires, he covers his face with his arm. The car's a total wreck. Just a couple of legs tripping lightly from the wreckage and walking away. Correction. Back to square one. Monopoly. Lose two turns. The governor smiling at the teams. Chew, chew, chew. Questions. The teams are growing a little tired of answering. They're not intellectuals. They're men of few words and many home runs. The governor understands this. His grin is fiercely masculine as before. The turn of the state flag. A few well-chosen words, a few thousand, a few million, let's get on with the game. Saved by the bell. A relentless ringing. Is it an air raid? Is it "them"? The Russians, the Chinese, the Bad Guys from the Other Planet, who want to control us, and have no time for democracy? The governor looked skyward, shielding his eyes. Suddenly he is surrounded by generals, all chewing like the players. Time for a few well-chosen bombs? Christ, he'll never go up them steps if the ringing don't stop, and then he won't ever get killed. Is there no way to stop

[337]

the ringing? There was. Krumnagel woke up and switched the alarm off.

Apart from his recurrent dream, he had had a peaceful night. Although most of the dream was a phantasmagoria, it was based on the thoughts he had formulated before dropping off, and had a curious lucidity. He knew his plan by heart, and the dream constituted a series of recognized variations on the theme, which had hardened in his subconscious like cement. He was very calm, because he knew precisely what he was doing. It was now eight. He got up, shaved, brushed his teeth, showered, taking care to keep the bandage around his head dry. Then he dressed and had breakfast at the drugstore on the corner. Orange juice, wheat cakes, Danish and coffee. Three cups. His wounds still hurt him, but he had come to terms with them. He knew how to move so that the pain would be bearable.

After breakfast he took a taxi to the bank and withdrew all his money except ten dollars. Hodnick was intrigued by the extent of the withdrawal, but Krumnagel avoided all questions and in answer to an inquiry about his injury, replied that he'd been run over by a cab. When he left the bank, he walked over to the Friendly Frank Ferruccio Ford car lot, and bought an inconspicuous car of popular make. If you're going to take the initiative, you got to do it thoroughly. And you got to have a sense of psychology.

He drove his car off to a neighborhood shopping center, and bought himself a pair of rough overalls and a yellow tin hat. He changed into these in the toilet of O'Reardon's Four-Leaf Clover Bar, where he stopped for a beer. Then he bought some light cigars, and at Leaman's Stationery Store he managed to buy the last American flag going. Yes, there'd been quite a run on them. There were none to be had in the entire City. Yes, sir, we were living in patriotic times. The reaction was sure setting in.

Krumnagel drove over to another part of town, and parked

[338]

his car in a parking lot. From here he walked to the Honeyburg Brothers Sports Shop, which had a catamaran in the window, and bought himself a set of golf clubs. To the salesman, he seemed curiously indiscriminate in his selection of clubs, which was fairly natural since Krumnagel had never played the game in his life. With the golf clubs on his back, he walked over to a disreputable store which specialized in Nazi insignia for youthful perverts to play Mensch and Ubermensch in, sets of coffee spoons with eagles and swastikas on them purporting to come from Eva Braun's scullery, and other bits of macabre memorabilia. The owner was a sallow man with sorry teeth and a shock of white hair, who stood around dressed in some of his own better relics. He had also a selection of service revolvers, rifles, and even an antitank gun with, so he said, shells. He was accompanied everywhere by a police dog which did clever things like biting people by numbers.

"I want a rifle with a telescopic sight," said Krumnagel.

"Why don't you go to a mail order house?" asked the owner.

"I only want to scare the bastards," growled Krumnagel, "and since Kennedy and all them other assassinations, I don't trust the mail order houses no more. I don't know how reliable they are."

"Goddam right. Ask me, you want to do more than scare the bastards. Kill a few. Kill 'em. I'm sick of all this crappy sentimentality just because they're kids. The national guard's kids too. Cleancut kids, not greasy pinko kikes that want all the advantages of America without any of the responsibilities. Kill 'em, and compel their parents to watch. We'd soon clean up this country, I'm telling you. Ain't that right, Wotan?"

The dog showed two rows of yellow fangs, and looked up winningly for further instructions.

"Wonderful dog you got there," said Krumnagel.

"Sure is. Late property of General Hans Von Krempel — I don't know if you've heard of him — they called him the Red Angel of Minsk."

[339]

"Oh, sure," said Krumnagel, who hadn't, and who thought it an odd name for a general.

" 'Course, he's not for sale."

"I should hope not."

"I'll show you what I got," said the man, pleased with Krumnagel's general attitude. He brought out three or four sniper's rifles.

Krumnagel bought one with a lot of filigree work on it, Belgian. He liked the feel of it, and it was compact enough to slide down into the golf bag and nestle unseen among the clubs. And then, it was the only one for which the shopkeeper had live ammunition in stock.

"A hell of a lot of crackpots around," Krumnagel thought as he made his way back towards his car. "Jesus, if that stinking dog was really the property of a Nazi general, he'd have to be twenty-seven or twenty-eight years old by now, and yet that crazy storekeeper really believes his own story . . . He's never done that simple bit of arithmetic."

There were only two further purchases which Krumnagel had to make. He bought two freshly made sandwiches, cream cheese and jelly, and chicken salad. It would be a long vigil, a long time without food. Then he went to Boone's bookshop, and browsed for a long while among the shady paperbacks. Luckily the garrulous proprietor was away, and with his bandages and construction worker's costume, nobody recognized him, although some of the noisier members of the so-called silent majority had called out militant encouragement to him in the street.

After much meditation, Krumnagel came away with two books, *The Thoughts and Teachings of Buddha,* and *Hot Lips,* by an authoress writing under the name of Veronica Vulva. He made his way back to the parking lot, and drove his car up to the ball park. There was no one on duty yet. It was too early in the day. He lit a cigar. As he walked in, he passed one or two construction workers.

"Hey, what happened to you?"

"Oh, got beat up I guess," Krumnagel replied, unhurried.

"Hey, you know something those kids didn't put up much of a fight, but some of them had a lot more spunk than we're in the habit of giving them credit for."

"Yep. I guess I was just unlucky. The guy I picked out knew karate," said Krumnagel.

There was laughter at this.

"You one of Donovan's fellers?" one of them asked.

"That's right," said Krumnagel.

"Local 1908?"

"1908 it is."

"They're forming up on the other side, the east side."

"Is that right?"

"This is a ball park you know, buster, not a golf course," another of them shouted.

"I figure on playing tomorrow," Krumnagel called back, "and I had my car broken into and a lot of stuff stole. I ain't riskin' it no more."

"That's the trouble with popular makes."

"Yeah, but with the others you got the problem of spares and resale values," someone else said.

"Sure thing. Nothing's perfect I guess."

"We're marching on the university buildings in five minutes, Mac," the original interlocutor informed Krumnagel.

"Thanks for telling me as though I didn't know. I'll just take me a piss."

"Don't waste it here, buddy. Use it on the students!" a voice called, but Krumnagel was already out of sight down the high concrete corridors. He found the toilet, and entered a cubicle, locking the door. The cubicle he chose was the central one of several. By standing on the seat, he could reach the circular ventilator quite easily, and by adjusting the Venetian-blind arrangement of the slats, he could, from a certain angle, see the governor's box opposite, and squeeze the rifle butt through the aperture. The accommodation for the telescopic sight was not quite so happy, but he had several hours before him, and at a pinch, he could even prize the entire ventilator out of its socket and give himself a clear field of vision. Before getting down to work, he ate a sandwich, and read a couple of pages of Buddha's thoughts, which seemed so out of tune with his present mood that he quickly switched to *Hot Lips*, which gave him a glimpse of those genital satisfactions he had never known with Edie. Between them the two books made him feel sad. This was perhaps not a time for thought at all, but rather a time for thoughtless application, and so he set to work doggedly removing the ventilator from its housing. Around four o'clock he was ready. The lie of the land looked surprisingly like his dream. He loaded his gun, and he waited as a big game hunter waits for the rarest of captures, vigilant and immobile and utterly sure of himself.

Four hours later it was dark, and the teams were lined up on the field, shifting like racehorses in the night air, eager to go, chewing to a man, while the governor and Monsignor Francis Xavier O'Hanrahanty passed them in review. Perhaps out of a sense of occasion, the monsignor was hardly smiling at all, and perhaps out of a sense of premonition, nor was the governor. The plaque was unveiled almost demurely, and the governor's speech could hardly be called a speech, just a few hesitant words spoken in honor of those so mysteriously rich that they could give their native city the gift of a ball park. The governor began his ascent to his box, and the graticule appeared on his back like a crusader's cross.

The next morning in London, Sir Neville came down to breakfast in a moderately good mood. He had slept well, but had woken up once or twice for no particular reason.

"It's old age, Mrs. Shakespeare," he confided. "Before sleep becomes eternal, it gets lighter and lighter."

"I daresay," said Mrs. Shakespeare, going into the kitchen.

Sir Neville took his paper and began reading the front page. By the time Mrs. Shakespeare returned with the toast, he was staring before him, motionless except for his lips, which seemed to be moving vaguely. He was drained of color.

Without bothering to ask him how he was, Mrs. Shakespeare ran into the kitchen and began looking down the list of essential telephone numbers, which always hung there by the phone. Just then the doorbell rang. Mrs. Shakespeare hesitated, then ran to open the door. It was Bill Stockard.

"How is he?" he asked urgently.

"Oh, sir . . ."

Mrs. Shakespeare's expression was enough. He walked quickly into the dining room.

"What's happened?" he heard Mrs. Shakespeare ask behind him, but he had no time or inclination to satisfy her curiosity.

Sir Neville looked at Bill, and seemed to recognize him. There appeared to be a trembling desire to speak. Bill lowered his head so that Sir Neville need make the minimum effort.

There was a murmur of sorts.

"I beg your pardon, sir."

It happened once more, with what almost looked like a perverse and childish effort not to be understood.

"I'm sorry, I can't make out what you're saying, Sir Neville," Bill said with brutal frankness.

This time Sir Neville made the effort to communicate. He did it with difficulty and pain, and water oozed out of his left eye, which flickered as he sought to formulate the words.

"Let's call the doctor, shall we, Sir Neville? We'll have you better in no time," Bill said briskly, sounding to himself transparently insincere. "What's the number, Mrs Shakespeare?"

While Mrs. Shakespeare found the number, he reflected that the doctor was just an excuse, a form of cowardice, a relegation of authority. In the old days, disease was contagious, but in this innoculated new world, it is chaos of the human spirit which is contagious, and as a symbol of this, heroes and villains are interchangeable. Perhaps they always had been, but for the first time in evolution, a growing number of people are apparently able to accept such sophistication, and they are further able to look at the spiritual confusion without needing the signposts of morality and without an acceptance of judgment, mortal or divine. And perhaps, under this onslaught of compassless navigation, the weak had become violent merely in a panic at seeing the world of recognizable values slipping away from them as inexorably as a sunset. The possibilities of this uncharted spiritual landscape made Bill shudder, and he seized at the warm sounds of convention as a child seizes its mother's skirt.

"Hullo, Dr. Thwaites? . . . I'm speaking on behalf of Sir Neville Nym . . . Not too well, I'm afraid."